For Bob Royce.
8-8-88, a day of new beginnings.

LENKK PRESS
Copyright © 2013 by Julie Royce
Second Printing Copyright © 2019 by Julie Royce
Graphic Designer: Jay Horne
Artistic Designer: Julie Rosas
Editors: Margaret Lucke and Violet Moore
ISBN 978-0-9988004-4-8

PILZ

A Novel

J.K. ROYCE

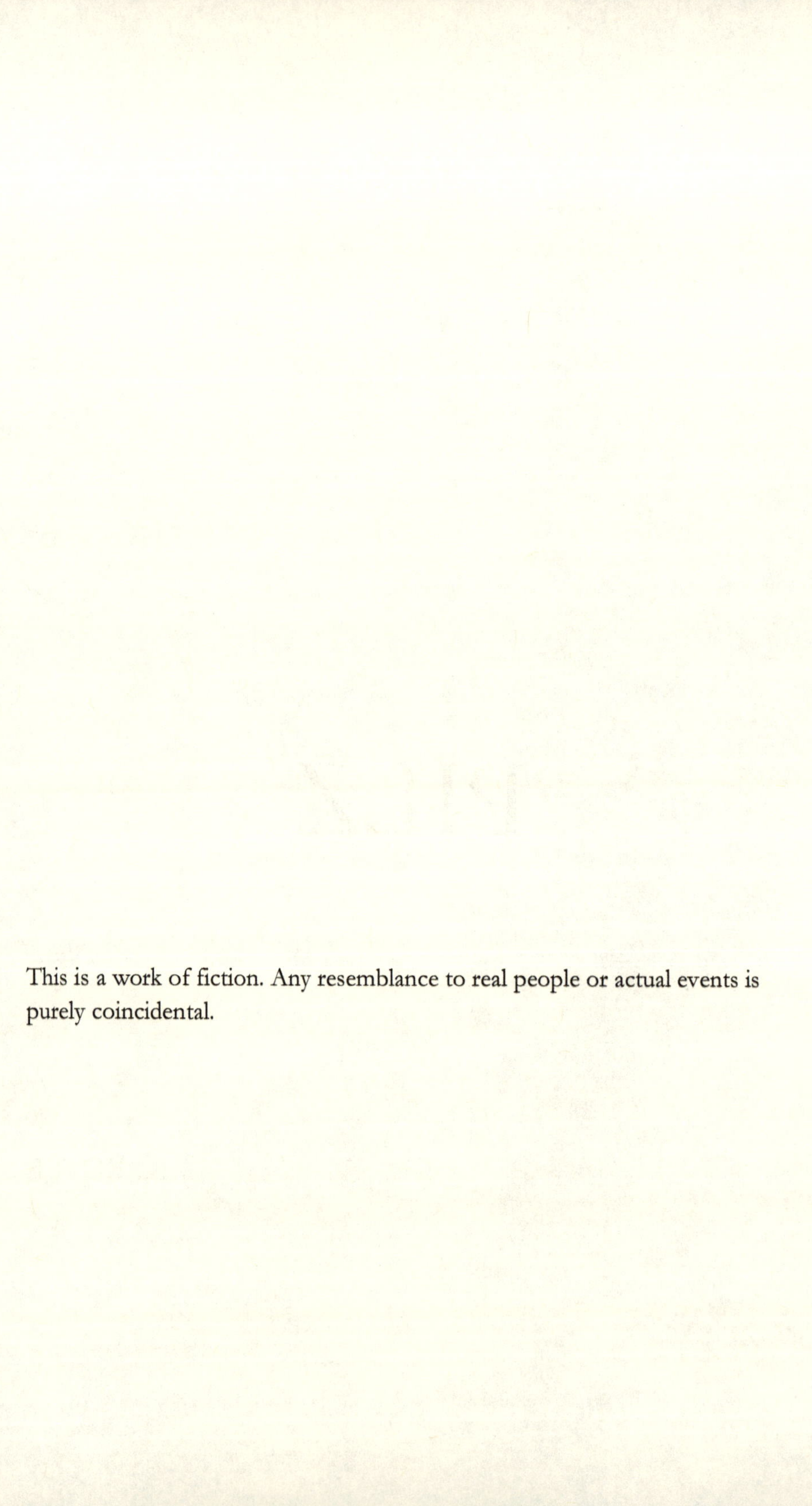

This is a work of fiction. Any resemblance to real people or actual events is purely coincidental.

PILZ

"Doctors are the same as lawyers, the sole difference being that lawyers only rob you, but doctors rob you and kill you too." Anton Chekhov (from the play Ivanov)

1

Blood. That was how it started. The rest—doctors selling drugs and blackmail and murder— came later. The puzzle took a month to piece together. Most of what happened, I had no power to prevent. Or so I told myself.

Monday, September 26

Fresh tire tracks gouged the manicured lawn bordering my driveway. The damage caught my attention as I waited for my garage door to inch open. From inside, the taillights of Derek's Porsche reflected back at me. They flashed a sadistic, slanty eyed, mocking wink. Another miserable night with your ex-husband camped in your guestroom, they taunted. I maneuvered my Corolla alongside the fancy sports car.

"Damn it, Derek, you're staying in my house. Could you please not let my cat out?" Jussy snaked between my legs before I unlatched the connecting door from the garage to the kitchen and stepped inside. I dropped my briefcase on the floor.

Silence hinted that my unwelcome guest might be napping. I thought it better not to disturb a sleeping dog. I kicked off heels that put me a smidgen under six feet. I twisted my head side-to-side until I heard a crack. I had spent two grueling, fourteen-hour days in trial against a doctor charged with peddling illegal prescriptions for OxyContin and Fentanyl. His motive, greed. The result, two dead teenagers at a pharm party. Criminal charges were pending, but until the sleazebag had his day in circuit court, it was up to my division of the Michigan Department of the Attorney General to prevent him from practicing medicine.

Unwinding after the gut-wrenching testimony would be difficult enough without Derek slinking about. Pleasant conversation with my ex would be impossible.

I collapsed onto a counter stool and mindlessly flipped through the day's assortment of bills and advertisements spread across the granite countertop. A ripped envelope exposed my bank statement. My freeloading, former spouse presumed it was okay to rifle through my correspondence. Next to the mail sat an open Coke can and a plate with a half-eaten turkey sandwich. Crushed corn chips littered the tile floor.

"You can clean up after yourself. I'm not your mother, I'm not your maid, and I'm sure as hell no longer your wife." I shouted so my voice would carry upstairs.

Dead air ignored my rant.

I hoisted Jussy and eyed a dull red stain on her white paw. I splayed her claws but found no sign of a cut. I climbed the winding staircase to the second-floor landing with her pressed to my chest. The hair on her neck stood up. Her snarl punctuated the quiet. Something viler than Derek's cloying, musky cologne hung in the air. His presence sullied my home more than his scent. I wanted him gone.

I peered through the guestroom's open door at the unmade bed. Both the overhead and nightstand lights blazed, wasting electricity.

"Derek?"

Across the hall, I spied a legal document lying in front of the closed double doors to my study. I bent down and picked up the deed to my house. Underneath it was a folder labeled, *Casey-Medical.*

"You're a dead man." I yelled loud enough that Derek would hear me even if he were in the basement family room. "Where do you get off going through my files?" I reached for a doorknob but paused my hand mid-air. If he had been snooping, would my ex have been so obvious? I replayed the morning trying to recall if I had pulled the doors shut before I left for work. I hadn't. I never closed them.

My house whispered danger. I ignored its warning and pushed the doors open.

Derek's orange and patchouli scent couldn't mask the smell of rusty metal. I flipped the light switch and inched into the room. "What in God's name . . ?"

I half-tossed, half-dropped Jussy. She hissed, then bolted.

A smashed picture frame lay close to the threshold. I knelt, reached for the ripped snapshot of my daughter Natalee and me windsurfing Lake Michigan last summer. I stuffed the ruined image into my jacket pocket.

My brain stalled, unable to process the disorder—drawers emptied, documents blanketing the floor like a snowdrift after a Michigan blizzard. My ransacked file cabinet contents added to the jumble.

I slumped to my knees, touched the papers cresting the mound. A transcript of my law school grades. Newspaper clippings about the state takeover of Employers Mutual. Scraps of my life since I was old enough to vote. Two decades of meticulous filing reduced to a mishmash. Cold sweat crept down my back. "Damn it to hell." I cursed under my breath.

I spotted the telephone and laptop under the desk, the computer's hard plastic shell smashed, the phone fractured. Splashes of crimson clung to splinters. They created the bizarre image that the machines had battled and then bled to death.

I stood again, righted a bookshelf from the massive mahogany Partners desk, and spotted a deep ragged gouge that left my locked drawer gaping open. Inside laid a stack of loose poems. Poems riddled with sentiments about failed love . . . rape . . . murder. Desperate, I picked my way through the debris, collected the verses into a neat stack, then clenched them against my body.

The pictures were gone.

The dozen eight-by-ten glossies of a naked Derek and his lover were conspicuously absent from the clutter. *Crazy.* Who broke into a house, bashed open a locked desk drawer, and only stole X-rated photos? The pictures carried an enormous emotional price tag. I kept them to remind me that divorce had been the right decision.

Red-brown splotches streaked the far wall like a Jackson Pollock painting. My head spun with dizzying thoughts. None of them good.

I touched a droplet about to fall from the arm of the overturned desk chair, rubbed it between my fingers, brought it to my nose, and smelled its raw meat stench.

Blood.

Derek was exasperating. I despised him at times, but I was years past wishing him hurt or dead. A fetid taste rose in my throat. I swallowed hard, and it retreated. Something primal, more palpable than dread, raised goosebumps on my forearms and replaced anger and confusion with terror. An intruder had violated my home, had stood where I was standing. I shrank from the study, imagined a psychopath crouched behind the closet door. With a rush that was the backlash of horror, I sprinted to the living room taking two stairs at a time. What had I been thinking? Any sane person would have fled when the first hinky sensation suggested trouble.

I struggled to jab buttons on the cell phone that I withdrew from my blazer pocket.

A woman's voice answered after two rings. "This is the 911 operator. What is your emergency?"

"My den's trashed . . . a break-in. My ex-husband's car is here. He might be hurt." I gasped for air. My heart threatened to launch from my chest.

"Your name and address?"

I swooped up my shoes from the living room floor and stammered out the information, adding, "The wall. It's splattered with blood."

I looked for Jussy. My fearsome watch cat had fled the scene, hiding until she was good and ready to be found.

"Get out of the house. Now." The voice was calm but the order unequivocal. "I'm sending the police."

I edged sideways through the kitchen into the garage so an intruder couldn't sneak up on me. I slid into my car, pushed down the button locks, and stashed the poems under the seat before I backed into the driveway, clutching the steering wheel in a white-knuckled death-grip.

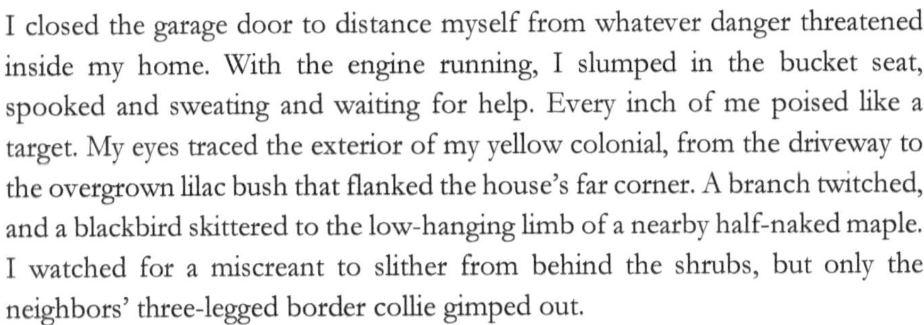

2

I closed the garage door to distance myself from whatever danger threatened inside my home. With the engine running, I slumped in the bucket seat, spooked and sweating and waiting for help. Every inch of me poised like a target. My eyes traced the exterior of my yellow colonial, from the driveway to the overgrown lilac bush that flanked the house's far corner. A branch twitched, and a blackbird skittered to the low-hanging limb of a nearby half-naked maple. I watched for a miscreant to slither from behind the shrubs, but only the neighbors' three-legged border collie gimped out.

Measured by my rampaging mind, an eternity had elapsed since my 911 call. My watch disputed my conclusion. Less than three minutes had passed. I rocked back and forth, tightened my arms around myself to control the shivers but got little comfort from the gesture. It takes fewer than ten minutes to travel between any two points in Okemos, a bedroom community to Michigan State University and the state capital. I willed a patrol car rocket speed.

I tried Natalee's cell. No answer. Lights flashed onto Hatch Road a block away. Within seconds, two squad cars from the Meridian Township Police Department, sirens blaring, skidded to a halt and blocked my driveway. A silver Dodge Charger squealed in behind them. Seconds later an ambulance screeched to a stop at the end of the caravan.

Mr. Anderson raced, sock-footed, from next door. At eight on a Monday night, the excitement trumped an *NCIS* rerun. "What's happening?" I heard him ask the first officer to jump from a cruiser.

"That's what we're here to find out. Step back, please." The cop's bark carried clout and the sting of impatience.

Porch lights blinked on down both sides of the street. Curiosity painted the faces of neighbors streaming my way. I relaxed a degree as the uniformed officer from the Dodge started toward my car. I eased out to greet him.

"I'm Sergeant Peter Lockhart," he said. "Can you identify yourself and tell me what is going on here, ma'am?"

"I'm Casey Lawrence. Someone trashed my study."

In the brief moment before either of us spoke again, I studied the cop as closely as he scrutinized me. He had short-cropped, curly, carrot-colored hair. A neat row of yellow-domed pimples dotted the dead center of his forehead. He either suffered adult acne or was younger than my first impression.

When my brain again found its voice, I asked. "Why did they send an ambulance?"

"You told the operator someone was hurt."

"I didn't say someone was hurt. The blood. It looked like someone might—"

"Be hurt." He finished my sentence, and then, expressionless, waited for me to explain.

"It did . . . it does. . . look like that, but I don't think there's anyone inside." I sank against my driver's side door. Tension knotted the muscles of my face. How did a guy who looked like he hadn't celebrated his thirtieth birthday get to be a police sergeant?

The sergeant released me from his probing eye lock and looked toward my house. "When you got home, how did you get inside?"

I pointed to the garage door.

"Can you open it, please?"

I looked down at the remote device in my hand, pressed the button for the garage.

Lockhart gestured toward a mustached man with rosy cheeks and an extra twenty pounds bulging over his belt. "Krueger, over here."

The man, who boasted more salt than pepper hair, joined us.

"This is Ms. Lawrence," Lockhart said.

"Ma'am," Krueger said. "Nice to meet you." I put him in his mid-fifties and pictured him playing Santa during the holiday season. If age or distinguished looks were a prerequisite for the job, he should be the one in charge.

"Grab one of the other guys and check every inch of the house," his boss ordered. "Make sure no one's skulking about before we take Ms. Lawrence inside."

Despite the earlier rebuke, Mr. Anderson had again pressed closer to the action. His eyes widened, but he smiled as the two cops unholstered their weapons and entered the garage. To him, it might have made good entertainment, but the guns triggered my hands to shake again.

Lockhart walked to my front door. I followed as he studied the sidewalk and entry. Autumn winds had blown a tangle of yellow, red, and orange leaves into one corner of my porch. Yesterday I had ignored them. Now I wished I had swept them away rather than let them create the impression of a sloppy homeowner.

The sergeant fiddled with a tape recorder the size of a cigarette pack, clicked it on, slipped the device in his right breast pocket, and attached a tiny microphone to his lapel. He angled his head toward his chest and began talking.

"Report notes for suspected burglary at 1561 Cherry Hill, Okemos, Michigan. Preliminary visual inspection of the front door shows no sign of a break-in." After he poked about the porch to his satisfaction, he walked the perimeter of my house, peered around Boxwood branches, pushing and pulling them to see if they trapped evidence. He eyed windowsills and squinted through every pane of glass. I stumbled after him wishing I wore flat-heeled shoes. He continued his inspection until we returned to the front of the house, and the older cop rejoined us.

"We cleared every room." Krueger's breath came in gasps. I didn't imagine him running a ten-minute mile anytime soon. "Everything neat and orderly. Nothing I can tell is out of place except the upstairs study. Looks like a tornado blew through there."

Derek wasn't inside. I knew that was a good sign, but the news raised more questions than answers. Where the hell was he? His car was in my garage so how had he gotten to wherever he went?

"You two." Lockhart motioned to the lanky officer who had checked out the house with Krueger, and a stockier one keeping neighbors at bay. "See if anyone witnessed anything suspicious. And throw yellow tape around the place.

I want no one messing up my crime scene until we check for prints and evidence." He walked over to the nearest squad car, grabbed flimsy blue shoe covers and disposable gloves, and pointed. "We'll go in through the garage. Ms. Lawrence, we've checked the house for intruders. It appears safe. You lead the way. You can give us details, but don't, I repeat, don't touch a thing."

We marched single file past the lawnmower, stepladder, and hanging bicycles.

The sergeant handed Krueger paper booties, and both men covered their black work shoes before they commented on the Porsche. "A 911 Carrera Cabriolet. Great set of wheels. Must have set you back as much as I paid for my house."

Before I disabused him of any notion that I owned a Porsche, he leaned close to the recorder and added another comment: "The door to the house from the attached garage shows no sign of forced entry." He opened it, stepped back, and let me enter ahead of them.

I couldn't tell which of the two men wore Old Spice, but I recognized the aftershave my grandfather used to wear. The smell was strangely comforting, although I would have preferred a lighter touch. The sergeant had me retrace every step I had taken. After we finished the first floor, we traipsed upstairs, past the bedrooms, to the study.

Lockhart peered into the ransacked room. "Someone left you quite the mess."

If I wanted reassurance, that wasn't the vibe I caught from the young sergeant. It was no easier seeing the room for the second time. A shroud of absurdity hovered. The blood, or what looked suspiciously like it, hadn't disappeared.

Lockhart's eyes targeted the crime scene like a Blackhawk helicopter zeroing in on a war zone. He held his right hand like a crossing guard. "You stay out here." He motioned me to wait where I stood, braced against the room's doorframe for support. I remained where he pointed, as rigid as a department store's display mannequin but less animated.

After a quick survey, he said, "Krueger, call the state boys. We're gonna need their crime lab and some assistance. Unless I miss my guess, that ain't paint decorating this room. And grab the camera."

"Sure thing, boss." The Santa lookalike fished out his cell and walked away from us.

Lockhart slipped on thin gloves.

"Ms. Lawrence, have you disturbed anything?"

My brain faltered. I nodded. My mouth refused to spit out words.

"What have you touched?" Buried in his reasonable question, I heard exasperation.

"I set the bookshelf and desk chair upright. Picked up pieces of glass. Moved papers. Crumpled a torn photograph." I avoided looking him in the eye as I withdrew the wadded photo from my pocket and handed it over.

"Anything else?" His eyebrows puckered to match his downward-sloping mouth.

"Not that I remember. I wasn't thinking of preserving evidence."

After several long seconds, he dictated more notes. He described the mayhem and added, "Crime scene looks staged. The placement of the chairs intentional, not like a struggle. Stains on the wall and carpet near the closet might not be blood. State Police lab will confirm." He turned off the recorder.

"We've called the State Police," he said, as though I hadn't been standing there and heard every word. To Krueger, who had returned with a camera, he added, "Shoot the room while you wait for the state boys. I'll take Ms. Lawrence to my car—it's quieter than the living room with people parading in and out. I want to question her while everything is fresh in her mind."

As we trudged back through the kitchen, he declined the Coke I offered. I craved a scotch and water spiked with Alka-Seltzer but opted for discretion and grabbed a bottle of Dasani.

Lockhart opened the driver's side rear door of his Charger. I pushed aside a sweatshirt and a bunch of fast food wrappers before I climbed in. A whiff of men's locker room overlaid with stale grease accosted me. He took the front passenger seat. I wondered if he considered it a psychological advantage to have me sit behind him. More like a suspect than the victim.

Bright street lights denied me the anonymity of darkness. Gaping neighbors magnified the spectacle. Their eyes accused me of violating their peaceful suburb with my unrepented sins.

3

I heard a click and saw the small red light on the recorder Lockhart had removed from his pocket. He placed the device on the armrest between the front seats. With a second click, he turned on the dome light. He shifted his torso so he could watch me as we talked. "Ms. Lawrence, let's cover a few background details. Anyone other than you live here?"

"My daughter and our cat." Before I mentioned Derek, he cut me off by his next question.

"Your daughter's name?"

I hesitated, grappled for a way to keep her out of it but came up with nothing. "Natalee Lawrence."

"How old is she?"

"Sixteen."

"Where is she right now?"

"Play rehearsal at Okemos High School."

"Does she have a key to the house?"

"Of course."

"Do you know if she's ever lent it to anyone?" His questions came as fast as bullets from a semi-automatic Glock.

I fired back answers with equal rapidity. "No, sir, I don't think she would do that."

"Who else has keys?"

"Mr. Anderson, next door. He's a retired widower, always home. I leave a key with him in case we lock ourselves out . . . and my friend, Tom Wright."

"A boyfriend?"

I nodded. I hated the word, its lack of specificity. At this moment I couldn't think of a better way to describe our relationship, so I moved on. "Ginny and Jon Beckman, my neighbors two doors south. They water and feed Jussy—the cat—when we're gone. That's everyone I can think of."

"Where are you employed?"

"I work for Attorney General Joseph Sawicki."

"Good man. Are you one of his secretaries?"

My secretary was smarter and harder working than most attorneys I knew, yet his assumption sounded disparaging. I steadied my voice before I answered. "No. I'm the first assistant attorney general in the Medical Professionals Division." Maybe he registered a glint of approval, but it disappeared before I could be sure. In my peripheral vision, I watched the last of my neighbors straggle back to their intact homes.

Lockhart tried to scrawl a note on a six-by-nine pad, but his pen refused to cooperate. He scrawled circles, laid the recalcitrant Bic aside and without missing a beat asked, "What do you do there?"

I refocused. "I take licenses away from doctors and other health professionals who violate the Public Health Code. Mostly Vice. I see a lot of drugs, sex, guns. Same stuff cops see."

"Anyone you've pissed off?"

"I don't make friends with the doctors I prosecute, if that's what you mean. Their licenses are valuable. But these are white-collar crooks. Get rid of me and another Assistant AG takes my place. They know that."

"Any angry calls or threats in the past few days?"

"No."

"Walk me through what happened when you got home tonight."

I had provided a live reenactment as I led him through the house, and now he wanted everything repeated. I sighed and marshaled my thoughts. "It had rained all day, and as I waited for the garage door to open, I noticed tire marks in the soggy ground by the driveway. I was irritated with my ex-husband. The ruts looked like they would require—"

"Your ex-husband?"

"Yes. That's Derek's Porsche hogging two-thirds of my cramped garage."

"You said only you and your daughter lived here?"

I tried not to fidget, but the backseat of a cruiser encouraged squirming. I struggled to keep my voice even. The last thing I needed was to add to what already raised his antenna. "Only Natalee and I live here. Derek is visiting from California."

The cop's unruly eyebrows shot upward as if he expected divine guidance. He rubbed his forehead with the fingers of his right hand.

"How long has your ex-husband been living with you?"

"He arrived a week ago today. And he's not living with me."

"Why is he here?"

"My daughter invited him to use our guestroom. I preferred not to make a scene." This wasn't about me, I thought. It was about my missing—presumably injured or dead—ex-husband. If Lockhart craved the complete exposé of my life, he could buy me a drink some night, and I would be all talk. Right now, I needed this man's focus on that damned blood in my study. He needed to find Derek.

"Does he stay with you often?"

Arguing with the cop served no useful purpose. Short, to the point answers, I told myself. "I hadn't seen him for eight years."

"Have you reconciled since his return?"

I did a couple of seconds of square breathing. Deep breath. Hold. Exhale. Hold. "If you're asking if we're sexually involved, absolutely not. He sleeps in the spare bedroom. I spend as little time around him as possible."

Lockhart's face turned to granite. Gave no clue to his thoughts. "What happened after you entered the house?"

"It was getting dark. I thought it was odd that no lights were on downstairs."

"Why did that seem strange?"

"Derek would have turned them on, but he never turns them off."

The cop tracked my every twitch and blink. "Sounds like you weren't happy with your ex-husband."

I felt like a paramecium in a Petri dish. "Would you turn flips if your ex showed up on your doorstep?"

He let my question slide. Probably too young to have an ex. I described the kitchen and the crushed Fritos.

"Did it look like there had been a scuffle?"

"No." *It looked like my sloppy ex-husband didn't care if he made a mess.* "I considered paying bills, but something seemed off."

"In what way?"

"The Porsche in the garage, but no sign of Derek. My cat's paw looked bloody, I thought she had a cut. A half-eaten sandwich on the snack bar. I went upstairs to find him."

"Did you inspect every room?"

"No." My patience threatened revolt with my stomach in hot pursuit. "But by that time, I had been in the kitchen, could see the dining and living rooms. I didn't check the bathrooms or basement, but Krueger did, and I'm sure if he had found Derek chopped up in a bathtub, he would have mentioned it." Good thing I had worked all day and had an airtight alibi because the cop gave me a fierce you-didn't-really-say-that-did-you scowl. I added 'no sense of humor' to the list of character flaws I compiled for him.

I recapped to the point I entered the study without him asking another question, so I continued. "It was dim inside the room, but the hallway light was enough to let me see it was trashed."

"You went in rather than call the police?"

"I wasn't sure what had happened. Guess I wasn't thinking clearly."

"What next?"

"I noticed the locked desk drawer had been bashed open."

"What do you keep in a secret drawer?"

"It's not secret. Just locked."

"What was in it?" I gave him high scores for persistence.

"Deed to my house, an atomizer of Divine Folie perfume—"

"You stash perfume in a secret drawer?"

"At $400 for a one-ounce bottle, it keeps Natalee from using it. I didn't see it in the drawer, which made no sense. Thieves don't steal perfume."

He closed his eyes, gave a slight shake of the head but didn't pursue it. Instead, he asked, "Anything else in that drawer?"

"Birth certificates, a folder of poems." I hadn't meant to tell him about the poems, but the words slipped out. I clamped my mouth tight and avoided looking at him as I swallowed the part about stashing the verses under the front seat of my car. If his Bic weren't dead, he might have jotted a note that I appeared flustered. The urge to grab a Scotch and my need for the Alka-Seltzer had grown stronger in the last ten minutes.

"What kind of poems?"

"Nothing a burglar would be interested in."

"Why do you keep them in a secret drawer?"

"It wasn't a secret drawer, just a drawer with a lock."

"That's not an answer." I added another twenty points to his personality profile for sheer doggedness.

"Haven't you ever written private things?"

"Private in what way?"

"Private like Nat already thinks her mother is a dinosaur. She doesn't need to read poems to confirm her opinion."

He blinked. Still no comprehension. I might be from Venus, but he attended a police academy on Pluto.

"Sometimes I write little poems about my feelings." *The hatred and fear that follows a brutal rape. How it feels to kill a man.* "Everything the mother of a teenager does embarrasses them. I didn't want her reading that stuff."

"Were they pornographic?"

"No, Sergeant Lockhart, they weren't dirty little limericks if that's what you're insinuating."

"Did the burglar take the poems?"

"You saw my study. I can't tell what's missing." I skipped mentioning that I was pretty sure the nude photographs of Derek had waltzed out with the burglar, although part of me itched to see the cop's eyebrows dance another couple inches upwards and meld into that mop of curls.

"Anything else in that drawer?"

I have cultivated many vices in my life, practiced some of them to a fine art, but lying wasn't among them. Especially to the police. My mouth felt full of peanut butter. My tongue stuck to my palate, and garbled words tripped out from behind gritted teeth. After another swallow of water, I shifted in the seat and then answered.

"Not, um, that I can, um, remember." He might understand why I didn't want Natalee to see nude pictures of her father and hid them in a locked drawer. But he would never get why I kept them in the first place. I decided they were not germane to the investigation. I stifled a black-humored smirk. If Derek found the pictures, they had probably boosted his ego to a full-fledged erection.

"You're sure? Nothing else in that secret drawer?"

"Reasonably." I understood why innocent people confessed to crimes they didn't commit. Whatever it took to end the questions.

Before he asked anything else, a car door slammed. We heard the panic in Natalee's voice as she screamed, "Mom, what's happened?"

4

I met Natalee midway up the driveway. Her wide emerald eyes flashed from an oval face that mirrored a younger me. "Are you okay?" she asked. "What's going on? Why are the police here?" Her breathless voice squeaked several decibels higher than usual.

"I'm fine, honey. Looks like a burglary, but it's over. No real damage and not much missing." I was grateful the gawkers had dispersed, and the ambulance had returned to its life-and-death duties. I put my arm around her thin shoulders, guided her through the garage into the kitchen. Lockhart tagged behind us but headed upstairs. I eased my daughter into a chair at the table and changed the subject. "How was rehearsal? You must be starved."

"Mom, I don't give a damn—darn—about the play right now. Since when does it take two police cars to investigate a simple burglary?"

"Sit, and we'll talk. It's not as bad as it appears." I may not lie well, but I exaggerate with the best of mothers. "How about I warm some leftover lasagna? I have chocolate chip cookies from Great Harvest." I poured low-fat milk into a Sesame Street cup that Natalee had drunk from since she was two.

"Sure, but what's this about?" Her hand caught mine as I released the drink. She tightened her grip as though pressure would force me to spill details.

I pulled away, fiddled with the microwave, bought myself a few seconds. "Well—?"

I handed her a fork and napkin, steadied my voice. "When I got home the study was vandalized."

"I want to see." She bolted from her chair, but I blocked her path, guided her back to the table.

"Honey, the police don't want us upstairs. Not much to see and they're trying to process evidence. The burglars threw stuff around."

"Where's Dad? His car's in the garage." She had my slender build and high cheekbones, but she shot me an expression that was pure Derek. It demanded that I stop stonewalling.

"He's not here. He must have gone off with a buddy." I spun the story as I went.

Nat sniffed a forkful of the lasagna I had placed in front of her as though the basil and garlic might offer more truthful answers. "What would burglars want with anything in our study?"

"I'm guessing they believed we keep jewelry or money in the locked desk drawer." *What if she'd been home when it happened?* Unnerved by conjecture, I leaned against the counter and clamped my fingers around the edge for support.

"Just that room?"

I nodded my head to answer her question and tried to dispel disconcerting thoughts.

"Maybe Dad interrupted them?"

Lockhart and Krueger tramped back into the kitchen before my daughter obligated me to fabricate more fiction.

"We'll be here a while gathering evidence. Fibers, hair. Anything that can help us figure this out." He didn't bring up blood samples. "Can you and your daughter stay someplace else, at least tonight?"

When this registered, I asked, "Can I get some of our things from upstairs?"

He looked over to the man holding the camera. "Krueger, escort Ms. Lawrence upstairs."

"I'm coming too." Natalee jumped up.

"Let your mother get your things," Lockhart said. "The fewer people shuffling around up there the better. You want us to find the culprit who stole your mother's perfume, don't you?" I could have kissed the sergeant for his intervention and feeble attempt at humor. My opinion of him jumped a notch.

Natalee's grim face refused the officer the satisfaction of a smile. She looked at me. "What about tonight?"

"It's Ginny's or Tom's." I offered her a choice between our neighbor and the man she dubbed "Mom's beau friend."

"Tom's," she said. "I have a math assignment, and he's the whiz with numbers."

"I'll call him while I'm getting our clothes. What do you need besides pajamas, underwear, and a toothbrush?"

"My Hollister jeans and purple Cotton Express shirt."

"Okay, you've got 'em." I resisted the urge to hug her, unwilling to risk my calm appearance sabotaged by jitters she could feel.

I grabbed my daughter's clothes and remembered the tiny calla lily tattoo I had spotted yesterday. She bent over to pick up Jussy, and it peered from an inch below her waistline near the center of her back. She hadn't asked for my permission, not that I would have given it. It had surprised me, but I decided to take a day to formulate an appropriate punishment rather than ground her for the rest of her natural life. Today was an even worse day to bring it up.

I dialed Tom as I walked to my room and rummaged through drawers for a long, high-necked, flannel nightgown. "We've got a problem here." I summarized the burglary in less than a minute. Krueger stood in the doorway, eyes fixed on his watch. "Can Nat and I stay with you tonight?" I knew the answer.

I grabbed the next outfit in my work rotation, a navy pinstripe Alfani suit bought at an end-of-season-clearance and a fire-engine-red cashmere mock turtleneck sweater.

"Leave a number," Lockhart said when Krueger and I returned to the kitchen.

I wrote both my cell and Tom's landline on the back of a business card and handed it to him. "When Derek shows up, tell him to call me. And please make sure you don't let the cat out." I looked back to Natalee. "Okay, Sunshine, let me give Jussy some extra dry food, then we're out of here. I have to stop at Ginny's for a second though."

I backed the Toyota the short distance to the Beckman's house. "Wait here. Keep the windows up and the doors locked."

"You called it a simple burglary," she said as I climbed out of the car.

"I'm a mom. Moms get paid to drive their kids crazy with caution. Just do it."

Nat rolled her eyes but didn't argue.

Jon and Ginny Beckman had been my neighbors for ten years. They moved into the subdivision after me. Clean-cut, bright, each balancing a high-powered career, he a doctor, she an interior designer. They hosted barbeques, headed the neighborhood watch, and removed flyers when homeowners were away.

They oozed perfection. Despite this major flaw, I loved them.

Jon answered the door with the first peal of the bell, "I figured you would eventually get around to telling us what the hell's going on," he said.

"It's good to see you too." I stepped into the comfort of his waiting hug.

"We've been worried crazy, but the cops wouldn't give us a thing." Ginny walked from the kitchen into the foyer and stood next to her husband. He let me go and put his arm around her waist.

"Sorry. I didn't mean to rain bedlam on the 'burbs. It's just a burglary."

"Right. Like an Aston Martin Rapide is just a car." Ginny scrutinized me the way she would examine a house ripe for renovation. "You had two squad cars, an ambulance, and a throng of neighbors larger than any block party we've ever thrown."

"I love a good show."

"Come in. Have a drink and tell us about your latest production," Jon said.

"Do you and Nat want to stay here tonight?" Ginny asked.

"I appreciate the offer, but no. We'll stay at Tom's. And a rain check for that drink, Natalee's waiting." I looked at Jon. "Any chance you could give me a prescription for Ambien? It won't be easy to sleep tonight, and tomorrow's a bitch of a day at Med Pro. More scumbag doctors, you know the drill."

Jon ignored the slur to his profession. "I think I can do that. How about a sample to get you through the night and a script you can fill tomorrow?" He rummaged through a black leather satchel that stood in the foyer beside a bronze sculpture of a mother with two small children. It looked like the artwork had packed the bag and planned to head out on vacation. A burglar targeting the Beckmans would, with little effort, find a script pad and any samples Jon stashed in that bag. Both should have been left under lock and key in his office. Everyone fudges, I thought, it's just how much and where they draw the line.

He grabbed a pen from his right shirt pocket, signed the script, and handed that and the sample to me.

"Not so easy." I touched my right fingers to the underside of my left wrist and pretended to check my pulse. "Don't forget to make a note." Working in the Medical Professionals Division of the Attorney General's office, I knew doctors were accountable for every dose of controlled substance they prescribed, gave away, or dispensed. Jon's license could be yanked for violations.

"Not a big deal," he had told me many months ago when I trudged next door and sought his medical help. It was a Friday night, a few weeks after my transfer to Med Pro. A sore throat had derailed me, and I spiked a fever of a hundred and one. Exhausted from a long day of trial, thoughts of waiting in an emergency room had been as appealing as a New Year's Day Polar Bear Plunge in any of Michigan's great lakes. Dr. Jon gave me a prescription for amoxicillin along with five or six samples to get me on the way to recovery. Since he wasn't my regular doctor and was doing me a favor, I later made a chart with my name on it and typed an abbreviated medical history which I stapled on the left side. There were volumes that a neighbor didn't need to know about my personal background, but I included enough to justify the drugs.

On the right side of the file, I attached a sheet for him to record brief notes. I told him to jot down a line or two about my visit.

"You may think it isn't a big deal, but trust me, it depends on the investigator's motivation. The last thing I need is to get my friend in trouble. Just keep a record."

Tonight, as he wrote me a script, I rattled off a hypothetical entry to cover the Ambien: "Patient distraught after home burglarized. Trouble sleeping. No other symptoms. Vitals normal. Given one Ambien sample and an Rx for thirty to be used at night as needed. No refills. Something short like that will do. Can't forget to cover our sexy butts."

I grabbed the pill and the prescription. My friends hugged me good-bye.

I studied my house as I walked back to the car. *Damn you, Derek. I knew you'd bring trouble.*

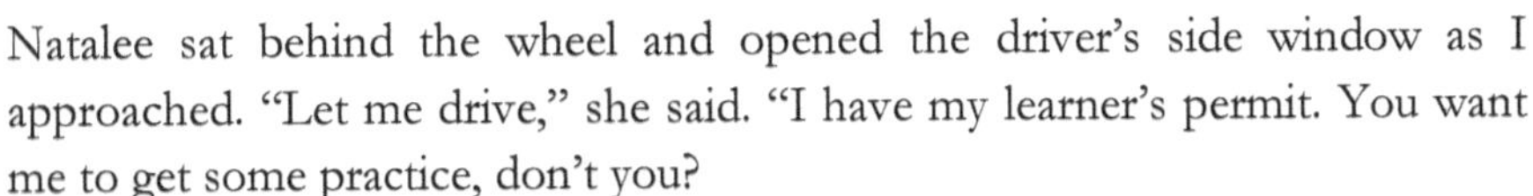

5

Natalee sat behind the wheel and opened the driver's side window as I approached. "Let me drive," she said. "I have my learner's permit. You want me to get some practice, don't you?

I looked toward Hatch Road, thankful no State Police cars had yet responded to Lockhart's call and entered the neighborhood.

I handed her the keys and turned my thoughts to Derek. Eight days ago, I had opened my front door to find my ex slouching against the porch railing. The smirk I had considered charming when I had first met him so many years earlier, failed to move me.

"Aren't you happy to see me?" He held his palms up and boosted the mouth action to a full chuckle.

I couldn't tell if he was serious. "Surprised is more like it," I said.

"It's been too long."

"I don't know if I would say that." I stopped, determined not to provoke an argument.

Years had passed since we battered our marriage with infidelity, accusations, alcohol, and even the depravity of a pervert named Jimmy Scroggins. It no longer mattered. I liked things fine when my ex was two thousand miles away.

"Can I come in?"

"Why?" I crossed my arms, made no attempt to look hospitable. With my question hanging between us, Natalee had bounded down the stairs.

"Is it for me?" she asked before she saw her father.

"I'm not sure," I said.

"Hi, baby, it's me," Derek said.

I shut my eyes and abandoned all hope he would disappear. Natalee's "Dad?" answered my question of whether she remembered him. When my daughter added, "You are staying for a while aren't you?" followed by, "We've got a spare room," I knew I had lost control.

She led her father into our house. I lagged a dozen steps behind, my mind contemplating uncharitable questions. *Down on your luck? Need a place to crash and finagle a few bucks for a new scam?*

During the divorce proceedings, I would have been happy if Derek had stepped in front of a bus. Sixteen years had passed since our split. Our daughter had been in second grade the last time he dropped by to see her. He had ceased to be relevant, but I didn't need him to rain havoc on our lives. Be rich and happy, I thought. Be sloppy-fat and content. Grow old on Mars. And do it with someone I've never met.

I let him stay because it was what Natalee wanted. The nights he spent in our guestroom I kept my bedroom door locked.

"Do you think Daddy's okay?"

Natalee's question brought me back. I pictured Derek's battered, bloody body dumped on some isolated country road in Williamston or Bath. That would be a bitch to explain to my daughter. Only slightly easier to concoct a story for her if the study was his handiwork, and he had found a new way to screw me.

"I'm not sure, sweetie." I reached over and patted her leg as she clicked the right blinker and pulled into the Grove's parking lot. "Hopefully we'll know soon."

The ride to Tom's took five minutes. Because of Natalee, neither Tom nor I were on board with living together unmarried, and neither of us was ready for "I do." I worried more about what the parents of my daughter's church-going friends thought than I did about sin and eternal damnation. Shouting distance was the compromise.

Natalee followed me up the walkway. I knocked. When Tom didn't answer, I twisted the doorknob. It was unlocked. "Company," I called out.

Tom came from his bedroom, towel drying his wavy blond hair, wearing only a pair of cut-off jeans. He hugged me and took our garment and duffle bags. The sight of his pecs, toned by a hundred push-ups each morning, was almost enough to turn my mind to something other than my missing ex-husband and blood. I crumpled onto the sagging couch.

Tom had adjusted well to a modest two-bedroom apartment furnished with cast-offs his ex-wife had planned to donate to the Salvation Army after their divorce. I picked up the TV remote, punched in Channel Six, WLNS, and checked my watch. It was nine-fifty p.m.

"Have you guys eaten?" Tom shot me a knowing glance.

Natalee nodded.

"I'm not hungry," I said. "But I could use a drink."

"It comes with a bowl of Tom's mouth-blistering chili, straight from Johnny Rockets."

Before I could argue, Natalee said, "I need you to help me with a math assignment. It's chain rule for derivatives. I'm lost."

"Two minutes to heat your mom's chili, then I'm all yours."

As the microwave nuked the chili, Tom grabbed a highball glass and poured me a double Glenlivet and water.

I withdrew two Alka-Seltzer from my purse, removed the foil and plopped them in the glass he handed me. I saved the Ambien to take with my second drink.

"You've got no respect for good booze," he said.

"Sure I do. It's like scotch and soda, but it settles my stomach while it eases my mind."

I chugged two strong sips and began to relax. Not enough to tempt me to retrieve any of the work files I had left in the car, but enough to let me shower and watch the last of a made-for-TV movie while he and Natalee tackled a subject that was part of the reason I became a lawyer—to avoid math.

My attention wandered from the lame flick parading as entertainment. I thought back to the first time I had described Tom to Ginny. "I've met someone who might be the one," I had told her.

"Details." Her eyes had twinkled. My best friend gave me a bear hug, then shook me by the shoulders to loosen the flow of information.

"Delicious looking. Eye candy. Distinguished and sexy."

"Good for starters, but don't get hung up in the tinsel, girlfriend. Is he rich?"

"Relatively, at least until his divorce two years ago. First wife got the fifty-five-hundred-square-foot house in Whitehills and three-thousand-a-month spousal support for five years. The attorneys who fought their battle got the rest. His name's Tom and he's regrouping, as he calls it."

Ginny persisted. "What's this hunk do?"

"He's a janitor at our building. Met him in the ladies' room when I entered despite the yellow sandwich board warning it was closed. He cleans toilets."

Ginny's hearty laughter pandered to my silly side. "Seriously, doctor, lawyer, what?"

"He's head of the accounting firm Wright and Jacobs. He's well read, he loves theatre, and his dance moves make Michael Jackson's old moonwalk look clumsy."

"Now we're getting somewhere."

Together with Jon and Ginny, Tom and I formed a two-couple mutual admiration society.

Forty-five minutes later, Natalee and Tom closed her books. She kissed me goodnight, and he made me a second cocktail.

"Easy on the scotch. I've exceeded my limit." I swallowed the Ambien with my scotch chaser.

"How about a foot massage?" he asked as we waited for the local news.

"Does that require an answer?"

He manipulated my arches and the balls of my aching feet, easing muscles stretched like taut rubber bands. "It'll be okay. It's just your den. I'll help you put it back together when the police get out."

The half-assed smile I mustered was not for the comfort I took in his promise.

At eleven the TV squawked the lead news story. "We are following breaking developments tonight." News anchor Alex Pressman's voice brought me back from my near-catatonic Ambien-and-alcohol-induced haze. "Few details are available, but Assistant Attorney General Casey Lawrence called 911 at eight o'clock this evening to report a burglary at her Okemos home."

I jerked up, desperate, but with no means to stop the onslaught.

"Sources inside the police department confirmed the appearance of blood at the scene. Ms. Lawrence and her daughter were not home at the time of the break-in. Police are trying to locate the ex-husband, Derek Lawrence, who was staying with her and is now missing.

"You may recall Ms. Lawrence was an outspoken critic of Michigan's Attorney General Joseph Sawicki during his litigation to take over Employers Mutual where she worked. The police ask that you contact them at the number on your screen if you have any information concerning the whereabouts of Derek Lawrence, or the person or persons involved in this burglary. We'll continue to bring you details as the story unfolds."

"Damn. Damn. Double damn." I kept my voice low to avoid waking Natalee. "It had to happen on a slow news night. Bastard Pressman. He makes it sound like Derek is living with me."

Tom opened his mouth. Nothing but air escaped before he closed it.

"And no way that asshole could resist a jab at the comments I made about Sawicki. They're ancient history." I picked up a brown corduroy pillow and heaved it at the TV. "Now I've got to tell Natalee about the blood before she hears it from her classmates."

"Maybe her friends missed—"

"If they did, their parents will serve up details along with Cheerios for breakfast. Screw Pressman. Screw his hundred-dollar haircut and screw his friggin' fancy pinkie ring. Smug bastard."

Alex Pressman was a bad reminder of a serious lapse in my judgment. The morning after the only one-night-stand of my life, he left with more than a smile on his face. What I shared with him in confidence glared back at me from the front page of the *Lansing State Sentinel* where he quoted me as calling

Attorney General Sawicki "a dirt ball who got his law school diploma from a box of Fruit Loops."

When Sawicki's intended takeover of my company succeeded, I figured I had dumped my career in the crapper as surely as if I had sent the AG a gold-plated resignation. He wasn't likely to find a spot in one of the twenty-five divisions for an attorney he considered a deluded malcontent.

I had underestimated Civil Service rules that thwarted any attempt by Sawicki to rid himself of me. The basis for his lawsuit was that Employers Mutual was created as a state agency and should never have been operating as an independent company. He argued he was litigating to get back what rightly belonged to the state. The corollary that followed his theory was that if Employers Mutual was a state agency, then its employees were protected by Civil Service regulations. He couldn't fire me without cause.

I had only one meeting with the man nicknamed the Persistent General for his tenacity. "You have medical expertise," he said. "We can use you in Med Pro. Report to Shirley Rathburn tomorrow. You'll be her first assistant." With that, he banished me to the sixth level of hell.

6

Too much scotch had not been enough. The morning after the burglary, I awoke in Tom's king-sized bed, tangled in his brown suede bedspread. My head throbbed and Natalee curled up without covers a few feet away. Tom had insisted he would be comfortable on the futon in the smaller bedroom. Before saying goodnight, he kissed me on the forehead, and whispered, "Things will look better tomorrow." Then he left me to the company of disturbing memories. Memories that flitted through my mind like birds in the Alfred Hitchcock film classic, frightening and thick, and everywhere. If Derek turned up as a corpse, I would have a new ghost to haunt me.

The gray drizzle of daylight argued with Tom's optimism. Nothing looked cheerier. My hope that a good night's sleep would chase away the lingering cobwebs of my nightmares faded when I checked my cell. No missed calls. We still didn't know if Derek was alive or dead.

I was nursing a cup of tea when Natalee bounded into the living room, dressed and ready for school.

"Honey, I have to tell you something." She flinched, knowing those words didn't preface something she wanted to hear. "The police found red splotches in the den. Could be anything, including paint or ketchup. We won't know until the lab results come back." I kept my voice even and my expression void of emotion.

Her face paled. She didn't respond. I couldn't tell if she was angry that I had withheld critical information or if she was just scared.

My daughter squinted at Tom, who had marched into the kitchen and was pouring himself a to-go cup of coffee. Her jaw clenched, her words chilled, she said, "Mom's not ready. I need to get to school. Can you drop me on your way?" She endured my goodbye hug with her arms plastered tight to her sides, her head twisted at an exaggerated angle away from me.

"Leave your cell on vibrate and tell your teachers I may need to contact you. I'll check with the police and call if they have any news about your father."

She didn't even nod.

It takes twenty-five minutes to reach my office. Twenty in route and another five to walk the three blocks to the G. Mennen Williams Building from the mud lot. Reserved parking is not a perk of my state job. After the recent rains, I could have used boots to navigate the rivulets. Instead, I relied on Nikes and picked my way through the mire. Heels waited, stashed in my bottom desk drawer.

Each morning I greeted my boss, Shirley Rathburn, and she pretended not to hear me, distracted by whatever file she nosed into. It was our morning Abbott and Costello routine. Shirl's the straight man. I'm Costello anticipating what she thinks I screwed up. Sometimes I went the extra step and asked for trouble. I would plop myself on a chair in front of her and lob questions like, "Are you going to the AG fundraiser?" or "Do you want to carpool?" or "Did you catch those Lugnuts last night?" Anything to see how long she ignored me.

I am Rathburn's tough break. As a spoil of the war between the Attorney General and Employers Mutual she got me, a lawyer who knew nothing about licensing law. And yet, thanks to the bang of a judicial gavel and Civil Service rules for state agencies, I was the first assistant and second highest-ranking attorney in the division. Add that my pay grade was higher than any of the regular staff attorneys, and it didn't bode well for us becoming one big happy family.

Toying with Shirley usually buoyed my spirits, but this morning I wasn't up to clever repartee. I had lost my starch.

My secretary, Louise Eunice Atwater, the bright spot of my work life, wasn't at her desk, but a large iced tea waited next to my telephone. To Louise, I was never the malcontent who fought state take-over, but just another dumbass attorney she needed to train. In my year and a half in the division, she had helped me evolve from the new kid who had never drafted a complaint, or even read the Public Health Code, to a lawyer who reveled in cross-examination—the chance to draw blood, all the while smiling.

I turned on my computer, studied a display of my case list and wracked my brain for a connection between work and the red streaks in my study. From those I had prosecuted, I considered the top prospects.

Dr. Donald Johnson traded Fentanyl prescriptions for an AK-47 and a Walther P99. When a subpoena was served on his house, investigators found one hundred and nine guns, a half dozen sabers, and several tactical knives. Enough to arm a small third-world army. Little doubt he could frighten one lone assistant attorney general. But he had lost his license two years ago. Another year and he could seek reinstatement. The timing was wrong.

Dr. Julian Westover had answered my subpoena by asking investigators, "Do you want to see the files of my real patients or my cash drug patients?" He was more likely to take the money he had squirreled away in the Caymans and spin himself a happy retirement than worry his wealthy bald head over a little sparrow like me.

Dr. Brandon Bartholomew admitted, "Sure, I gave several patients scripts for Ritalin on the condition they brought half the pills back to me. I needed those pills." When I had asked if he was addicted, he said, "I don't think so. You might disagree." Whatever brainpower got him through med school was eroded by drugs. If he had hatched a plan to burglarize my study, he probably would have left a business card.

My vote for scum doc of the year went to Dr. Austin Kemp, the fertility doctor, who at last count had, unbeknownst to his patients, fathered over a hundred children using his sperm. He should pay child support for every one of them, but after I took his license, he had no income. He wasn't a prime candidate for my burglary. He clung to a naïve hope he would beat the charges with an argument that he merely gave the women the children they wanted.

I considered each of my other files and settled on Dr. Ahmed Khoury as the most likely candidate for any connection between my work and trashing my study. Khoury's trial loomed two days away, and he faced revocation of his license. Targeting me wouldn't stop prosecution, but maybe it was too early for him to understand that I was replaceable.

I needed to talk to the police. I heard every sound from adjacent offices and understood that thin walls forced Rathburn to eavesdrop on me. Still, I shut my door for the illusion of privacy.

"This is Casey Lawrence." I identified myself for the police receptionist. "I would like to speak to Sergeant Lockhart if he's available." She put me through.

"Good morning, Ms. Lawrence," Lockhart said.

"I'm just checking in. Have you heard anything from my ex-husband?"

"Afraid not. We've issued a missing persons alert and sent his California driver's license photo to all local law enforcement. Nothing's come back."

His pause made me uneasy, as though he expected a response. I stood to relieve nervous energy, looked out my window for a pleasant distraction, and found none. "Can Natalee and I go home?"

"We've finished processing the scene, so I don't see why not. Leave the study doors closed for now. And until you get the green light from us, don't go in there. We would prefer you didn't clean up just yet."

"Sure. It gives me an excuse to keep Natalee out. She's already scared. I don't want her to see things that make it worse. How about the guestroom?"

"That's not a problem. You expecting company?"

He got paid to pry, but there was as much reason to ask me that as there was for me to answer. Still, I did. "No, but I'm uneasy being in the house alone until we know what's going on. I may ask a friend to stay with us."

To his credit, he didn't ask if it was my boyfriend. Instead, he said, "Probably not a bad idea."

"Have you determined if it's Derek's blood on the walls?"

"We're hoping to get a blood analysis back in a day or two. For now, we're running down leads."

"Like what?"

"We'll bring you up to speed when we get something. In the meantime, we need you to come in. A couple of loose ends," he said. "What does the day after tomorrow look like for you?"

"Thursday? I'll make it work. I have a trial starting at nine so the earlier the better. Is seven-thirty okay?"

"It's good for me. And we'll take your prints for elimination when you get here."

A Rorschach of doodles covered my notepad. Some scribbles had ripped through the page. "You'll call if my ex-husband shows up?"

"Of course."

He already had my business card, but I said, "Let me give you my secretary's direct line. She can track me down if I'm not at my desk."

"That's a lot of concern for an ex-husband—"

"He's my daughter's father. I'm guessing that was blood in my study." Edgy crept into my voice, and I fought to remain civil.

"Do you think Mr. Lawrence might have gone back to California?" he asked.

"You can answer that better than I can," I said. "Airlines give you passenger lists. You searched my guestroom. Was his suitcase in the closet?"

"It was. Along with a few papers we'll talk about on Thursday."

I had enough worries without wondering if the photos of Derek had reappeared. Or whether Lockhart had stumbled on something even more damning.

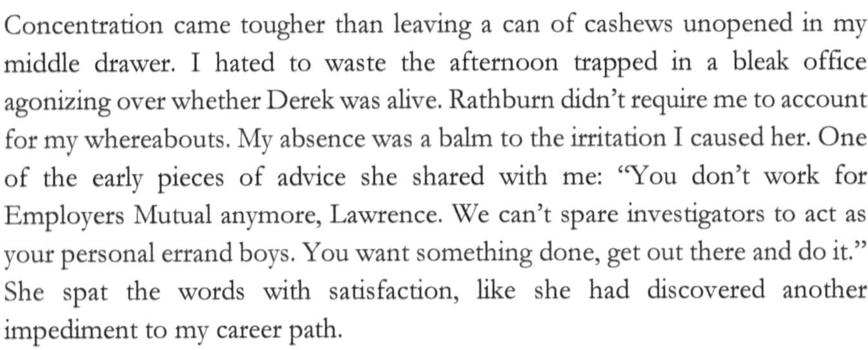

7

Concentration came tougher than leaving a can of cashews unopened in my middle drawer. I hated to waste the afternoon trapped in a bleak office agonizing over whether Derek was alive. Rathburn didn't require me to account for my whereabouts. My absence was a balm to the irritation I caused her. One of the early pieces of advice she shared with me: "You don't work for Employers Mutual anymore, Lawrence. We can't spare investigators to act as your personal errand boys. You want something done, get out there and do it." She spat the words with satisfaction, like she had discovered another impediment to my career path.

I headed home to double-check that the sergeant had closed the study door. I locked it for good measure and then changed into clothes I saved for dirty jobs. Mossy gray paint splotches added colorful touches to navy corduroys paired with an oversized sweatshirt warning, THE POLICE NEVER THINK IT'S AS FUNNY AS YOU DO—a gift from my ex-cop friend, Rad.

I removed my contacts and washed off all traces of makeup. The mirror reflected a few strands of silver dappling my strawberry-blonde hair. My best feature threatened to knuckle under to the ravages of time, but my skin continued to thank me for the religious use of Neutrogena sunscreen with an SPF of 70. It shaved five years from my forty-one. I tied a smiley-face bandana around my head and grabbed dorky, unfashionable glasses.

Our house, decorated with an eye to cheerful since no defined style suited me, seemed eerie and quiet, unready to confess its secrets. I had no desire to stay a minute longer.

I headed toward Dr. Ahmed Khoury's office. At the first stoplight, I called Nat and hoped she had remembered to leave her cell on vibrate.

"Have the police found Dad?" she asked after the fifth ring. I assumed she stepped out of her classroom. At least she was speaking to me again.

"Not yet. It's possible he had an emergency back in California."

"No way Dad would fly off without telling me." If her face matched her frosty voice, it was just as well I didn't have to see her right now.

"I'm sure you're right, but I can't explain it." My creative side was out of reasonable explanations. "I want you to go home with Ethan after school. I'll pick you up at six."

"Ethan has football practice." Her tone suggested I should know her boyfriend's schedule.

"Then go home with Trish."

Natalee jumped on the exasperation in my voice. "Mom, I have things to do after school." It was a whine. I hate whining but pretended not to notice.

"Natalee, this isn't negotiable. Until we figure out what's going on, I need to know you're safe."

She disconnected before "I love you" was out of my mouth.

Next, I called Tom, cut short the pleasantries and admitted, "I don't want to spend the night with a pillow over my head, hiding from the bogeyman. You willing to stay in the guestroom until my courage shows up?"

I was uncertain what I hoped to find at Khoury's office, but at least it was a distraction. I would experience his waiting room; feel his practice crawl over my skin. When Ahmed Khoury lost his medical license, I would indulge myself in a flood of righteous indignation. I had read the reports from Chace Gannon, the licensing investigator assigned to the case. Khoury's practice smelled like the after-game uniforms of the Detroit Lions. But things aren't always what they seem. I couldn't afford to blow this case. If I didn't prove my allegations, if I screwed up any little thing, I would find myself in an unemployment line. Rathburn would serve Sawicki my carcass along with just-cause for termination.

Then they would break out the champagne and pat themselves on the back for accomplishing something Civil Service had restrained them from doing earlier.

Dr. Khoury operated out of a once-gracious Victorian, now repurposed as his drop-in clinic, on a section of Martin Luther King Boulevard that didn't flatter its namesake. Only six blocks from my office in the G. Mennen Williams Building, the neighborhood sported skeletal structures with cracked windows for eyes and ripped-off front doors that imitated mouths, open wide, screaming.

My mud-spattered Corolla blended with the handful of other cars parked in Khoury's lot. My caved-in right rear fender, from Natalee's underestimation of the distance between our driveway and the mailbox, was a nice touch. Better theft deterrence than a burglar alarm. A government attorney's salary. and the student loans that still took a chunk of every paycheck, meant I didn't expect to drive a Mercedes anytime soon.

The clinic's white clapboard sides bore scars and lacerations inflicted by angry assailants who owned the neighborhood after dark. To the north, a vacant lot sprouted weeds around the charred remains of a building that had stood there weeks earlier. The air carried the scent of cannabis that could have come from any direction.

To the south was an old house in worse repair than the clinic. Its blue exterior was tagged with the ornate *313* graffiti of a Detroit gang that sold cocaine and controlled substances on a nearby corner. Two men, seated in webbed lawn chairs on their paint-chipped front stoop, guarded this crumbling castle. One was so obese his butt stretched the woven plastic strips until they sagged to within an inch of the warped porch planks. The deep ebony of his shaved head glistened with sweat.

The second man had a golden-colored complexion that, prior to the fear of melanoma, whites had lain in the sun for hours hoping to replicate. He flaunted a powerful build and a face handsome enough that a film director might risk whiplash for a double-take. He whistled when I closed my car door. "Mm, Mama. Bring that sweet thing over here. Let me put a permanent smile on your pretty face." Glazed eyes offered favorable odds his boast was idle bravado.

From the parking lot there appeared to be a side entrance to the clinic. I stood for a moment and debated whether to try its heavy metal door. It bore no markings that identified it as a patient entrance. I opted to go around to the front and brave a sidewalk buckled from harsh Michigan winters. Large chunks of concrete jutted up at dangerous angles. My flat-soled, dirty tennies let me navigate without a problem. The wooden porch creaked beneath my weight. I stepped inside and held the door open for a woman close on my heels. An entry hall separated Khoury to the left from doctors Day and Kessler to the right. The wall outside Khoury's office displayed a small engraved placard: WALK-IN PATIENTS WELCOME. NO APPOINTMENT NECESSARY.

Patients lounged and lolled and squatted in the crowded waiting room. Most appeared between the ages of fifteen and thirty-five. Some looked older, but hard living sculpts haggard faces. About half of the patients sat in orange plastic chairs. Khoury needed to invest in more of the flimsy K-Mart blue light specials to accommodate his burgeoning practice. The trifling number of cars outside meant patients lived within walking distance, were dropped off, or took public transportation.

The room smelled of dirty clothes retrieved from laundry hampers. Traces of rubbing alcohol and cleaning agents suggested an attempt to disinfect the place. They couldn't camouflage sweat that had proven too much for overtaxed deodorant.

A hand-printed notice on the cheap paneled wall next to the reception window advised: PAYMENT DUE WHEN SERVICES PROVIDED. Next to it, another read: PLEASE SIGN IN.

I wouldn't stay long enough to see the doctor, but rather than draw unwanted attention, I walked over to the counter and scratched *Jenny Smith* on the log. On the other side of the opening, a receptionist filed inch-long, black-polished fingernails that could double as weapons. I pegged her about the same age as Natalee and wondered why she wasn't in school. She eyed me: up, down, then up again, before asking, "Ever been here before?" From the description in investigator Gannon's witness report, I guessed she was Tammy Truxall.

"No. It's my first time." I accepted the clipboard she handed me.

"What's the problem?"

"I would rather discuss it with the doctor."

"Fill out the form and bring it back. The doctor is running behind today. It'll be close to half an hour." I took the board with a pencil attached by a grayish-white, fraying string, and moved from her line of vision.

A half hour to see everyone ahead of me? I counted twenty-six patients and did the math. A minute each and maybe enough time left for a quick bathroom break or a cup of coffee. Gannon designated the sleazy operation an *Ah-Stick Clinic.* When I asked him what that meant, he said, "The doctor uses a tongue depressor and gives instructions, 'Open your mouth. Say, "Ah." And follows that with, 'What do you want today?' Then he writes a prescription for whatever the patient requests."

"Mr. Jones." The nurse who called the next patient wore a wrinkled white uniform blouse and baggy matching pants. Gannon had described Hilda Fagan as an older, bleached-blond, black woman who wore the look of a tough life.

When Jones vacated his seat, I slid into it, next to a young woman whose belly stretched, ready to pop out a kid any minute. She had stringy, mud-colored hair and vacant gray eyes.

I wondered if she was old enough to vote. "When are you due?" I asked.

"Not for a couple of months." A faint smile crossed her chapped and cracked lips.

"Do you know if it's a boy or a girl?"

"Not for sure, but I think it'll be a boy. I'm gonna name him James after my brother who died in Afghanistan. My boyfriend, Mickey, wants the kid named after him, but unless he marries me, it ain't gonna happen."

"It's my first time here. I've been feeling a bit down lately," I said. "I asked my doctor for Valium. He told me to see a shrink and work my problems out." I rolled my eyes and shook my head. If the gesture was overdone, I didn't think she noticed. "Problems? I haven't got problems. I just feel better when I take Valium. You would think doctors would understand, wouldn't ya?"

"Doctor Khoury ain't like that," she said. "You'll like him. He tries to help. He only gives me stuff that shouldn't hurt my baby. Whatever you need, you jes tell him. He'll see that you get it."

"What's he charge?" I tapped my scuffed black purse with its broken shoulder strap. "I borrowed fifty bucks from my old man to get here today. I can't be doing that often."

"It's a hundred bucks a pop," she said. "It's your first time. He'll probably take the fifty and let the rest ride 'til your next visit."

She shifted in the hard chair and then leaned forward and massaged her low back with fingers unadorned with anything other than ragged cuticles. When she sat up straight again, she said, "When you get in to see the doctor, tell him you need the Blue Vs if that's what you want. But tell him you got some mighty awful pain in your back. Tell him you tried everything including T3s and Percs. Who knows? Might be your lucky day. If he gives you Red Dids, you can get maybe a hundred a tab on the street. That'll pay for your Vs and your visit, and you'll have a chunk left over for next time."

"I don't wanna sell the stuff," I said. "My old man would beat me if I got caught."

"Jeez, if that's what you're worried about, and you get any good stuff, let me know. I'll give you thirty a tab for the Red Dids, less, of course, for Percs, but even ten for them or T3s. I'll sell 'em myself."

"How do I reach you?" I asked.

"Shit, I don't usually do this, but you look harmless. You ain't Vice or anything, are ya?" She squinted her eyes and assessed me for the first time since she had started babbling.

"Do I look like Vice?" If I lost my day job, there was always acting.

"No, ya look too dumb. No offense or nothin'."

She hadn't pegged me as an attorney or a cop, and her opinion proved that four years as a Poly Sci major at the University of Michigan followed by Georgetown Law hadn't stamped a red "I" for intelligent on my forehead.

She ripped a sliver of paper from the pages of a two-year-old *Popular Mechanics* lying on a chipped walnut Formica coffee table. "You have a pen?" she asked.

I dug through my purse and handed her one.

She scribbled the word *PILZ*, her name and telephone number on the scrap and handed it to me. "My name is Sherri. That's with an i, not an ie or y. You got a number where I can reach you?"

I rattled off my cell number as the nurse called, "Sherri Smith, the doctor is ready for you."

"Nice meetin' ya," Sherri said before she walked through a doorway into the dingy hallway beyond.

I ripped the intake form from the pad, folded it into quarters and stuffed it in my pocket. I tucked Sherri's phone number into my billfold behind Nat's picture. As soon as the nurse turned toward a file cabinet on the other side of her chair, I slipped out. Ten people arrived during the fifteen minutes I had been in the office. About the same number was called by the nurse to see Dr. Khoury. Three, besides Sherri and me, were named Smith.

8

Wednesday, September 28th

Making love in a waning Ambien fog was more erotic than I would have imagined. Relaxed, uninhibited, a symmetry of sensations unfettered by annoying thought processes. Tom slept in my guestroom. Between the sleeping pill and his crawling into bed beside me for an hour near morning, my mood improved.

I walked into the kitchen as he poured himself a cup of coffee and carried it to the table. "I could fix you an Eggo or a Pop Tart to go with that . . . maybe a couple of slices of toast." I draped my suit jacket over the back of the chair and hugged him before I sat down.

"No time. A shot of caffeine and I'm good." He arched his eyebrows, gave me an appraising look and a long, low whistle. "You look way hot. Too bad I can't miss my morning meeting."

I flushed. "I think they call it afterglow. And careful. Talk like that can get you in trouble."

"Bring it on." He winked. "Well, maybe bring it on later tonight."

I liked the comfortable, sexy feel of Tom in my kitchen. Maybe the fortune I had spent on therapy paid off. I reached across the table and took his hand. "Thank you for staying."

He swallowed a final gulp, then stood and pulled me up, rested his forehead against mine, and held me close for several seconds. "I love you," he said.

I was at my desk by seven-fifteen. WKAR softened the bleak office atmosphere with Tchaikovsky's Piano Concerto Number One. I dumped the dregs of yesterday's tea onto a mite-ridden spider plant. A gift from Natalee when I was transferred to Med Pro, it languished on the window ledge. I lacked the heart to throw it away. I felt a kinship with its struggle and liked the way it blended with the bargain-basement desk and dented, rusty wastepaper basket that had welcomed me my first day in the division.

Next to my morning Earl Grey, five thick files stood at attention. I had blocked my morning calendar to prepare for the Khoury trial. Chace Gannon would stop by after lunch and help me debate strategy.

Gannon held a pharmacy license, a background that made him a hell of an investigator for cases involving drug abuse or over-prescribing. During my year and a half at Med Pro, Chace Gannon had been my friend, my confidant, my teacher. Six months of that time, he was also my lover.

Between a deviant named Jimmy Scroggins and my divorce from Derek, sex rarely surfaced on my radar. I chalked off the Alex Pressman incident to an erratic blip, but it motivated me to see Dr. Conrad for therapy. The doctor had helped me work through intimacy issues as layered and complex as a Dostoevsky novel. Chace Gannon, separated but married, wasn't the ideal candidate with whom to begin an affair. Then again, maybe because he was safe, he was.

The working relationship between Chace and me had abetted our subterfuge. We could grab a Pepsi for him and a mint tea for me, claim a cafeteria table, and spread papers about us for an air of legitimacy. Much of the time, I learned the ropes of Med Pro. Some of the time, I used his shoulder to cry on. The remaining time we tantalized each other with suggestive talk that didn't raise a single eyebrow because we whispered it from unflinching, straight faces.

I first met Chace after he sent me an investigative report on one of my files. It described a twenty-two-year-old nurse who took eighteen Percocet a day. I had been at Med Pro less than a week and wanted to ensure the complaint

I drafted was accurate, so I called him. "There must be a mistake in the Jensen investigation report," I said.

"What makes you say that?"

"Anyone taking that many Percocet would be dead."

"You're new to the division, aren't you?" he asked.

"It's that obvious?"

"Tell you what, bring your file and meet me in the cafeteria next door—Ottawa building, lower level."

"How will I know you?" I welcomed a chance to escape and closed my file before he answered.

"I'll be the tall, sexy, good-looking guy who, against all odds, is sitting alone."

"A more objective description would help." I said it over a giggle that refused containment.

"You won't need it. The place is empty this time of day . . . okay, I'm wearing a yellow shirt with a Mickey Mouse tie."

Ten minutes later, I headed toward a guy who looked like he and a personal exercise coach were on a first-name basis. I guessed our birthdays fell within five years of each other. He crowded forty, which side I couldn't tell. His wavy black hair tickled the top of his collar. He looked Latino except for cobalt blue eyes that danced in a face two degrees the quirky side of handsome.

I offered my right hand. "You must be Chace."

He didn't so much shake my hand as fondle it. "Was it the good-looking or the sexy that did it?"

"Neither." I snickered and pointed at his chest. "The tie."

"Gift from my daughters when their mom took them to Disney World."

His unassuming confidence quickened my pulse. I tried to slow it and get back to business. "I was a workers' compensation attorney at Employers Mutual," I said. "I have some medical background. I've taken hundreds of doctors' depositions. I know the knee bone's connected to the shin bone."

"What you don't know is a damn thing about drugs and addicts," he said.

"So?"

"At Med Pro, you aren't looking to prove a guy's malingering. Or was hurt while enjoying three-way sex, rather than when he lifted a hundred-pound drum of crude oil at work. Here, we don't give a rat's ass about workers who claim to be psychologically injured because their feelings got hurt. And we care even less about low back pain, unless it's the excuse for getting drugs."

"You have a low opinion of workers' comp."

"No. But I did a six-months stint for one of their defense firms before coming to the state to fight vice. Bored me to death."

"Your current work is more fun?"

"Investigating sleazy doctors suits my temperament better than a regular pharmacist's job counting pills all day. No late shifts make family life easier. And it's safer. No dispensing drugs to addicts high on Red Dids or Purple Peelers, or wondering if some punk will shoot me for the shitload of drugs behind the counter."

"Sawicki sent me to Med Pro because of my medical—"

"The AG's the east end of a horse galloping into the sunset. He sent you to Med Pro because he couldn't leave you at Employers Mutual to ferment trouble. Civil Service wouldn't let him fire you. Here, he expects to bury you like a piece of bad evidence. He hasn't a clue about what we do. Doesn't care to know unless it brings accolades, the more the better, preferably with a flattering picture and his name spelled right." Gannon winked with a brand of cocky that was more endearing than offensive.

We sat for a minute, sipped our drinks and sized-up each other. A flight of steamy imagination soared my brain corridors. When he looked into my eyes, I wondered if we indulged the same fantasy. I willed my mind back to the case. "So, tell me about our nurse who manages to down all those Percocet without keeling over dead," I said.

"Easy. Percocet is addictive. It's a Schedule II drug. You know drugs are classified according to their addictive properties from Schedule I to V?"

"Vaguely."

"Percs are a combination of Oxycodone and Tylenol. Drug abusers like the buzz. They crush or chew them to speed up the morphine-like effect. It's a dangerous game, but the human body forgives and builds a tolerance. That's what happened to our nurse." His long, slender fingers tapped the coffee cup in front of him. Sexy hands. I like sexy hands.

"She probably started by sneaking a single tablet a day out of the locked medical cabinet at her nurse's station," he said. "Don't know if she had a key or lifted it from a desk drawer of someone who did. She might've had, or convinced herself she had, a headache every afternoon about three."

Watching Chace's facial expressions was as fascinating as listening to his story. I waited for him to go on.

"Then she increased the dosage. The more she took, the more she needed to maintain the euphoria. She played Russian roulette and bet that she could spread the pills over the course of a day without killing herself."

"How did you catch her?"

He shifted his eyes, maybe to avoid my hungry stare that had little to do with a narcotic dependent RN. "Addicts aren't the wisest birds in the tree."

"And she wasn't counting on someone as clever as you?"

"Exactly." His uninhibited laughter was as irresistible as a hot caramel sundae with toasted pecans to a woman who had deprived herself of dessert for too long. "Nah, seriously, clever has little to do with it. A first grader can outfox a junkie looking for a fix."

"So, she called and said, 'Hey, Mr. Gannon, I'm abusing Percocet,' is that it?"

"Might as well have. She knows we get ARCOS reports."

"Which are?"

"Automated reports that track the flow of controlled substances from their manufacture to final distribution, maybe a pharmacy or sometimes the locked medical cabinet on the hospital floor. It takes us a while, but when a hospital can't account for four thousand dosage units of Percocet, it's just a matter of figuring out whose back the monkey's on."

"And that's easy?"

"Pretty much. You get yourself a short list of people with access and one always stands out. Start asking questions, more often than not a co-worker pipes up, 'Oh, yeah, Sally misses a lot of work, and I see her in the medical cabinet when she has no patients on the ward.' Something like that."

"You aren't giving Sherlock Holmes a run for his money?"

"Afraid not. Sometimes it's even easier," he said. "Sally's reported by her supervisor before I have to waste my energy reading the ARCOS. I use it to confirm what I've already been told. Although if you think it's hot to consider me brilliant, carry on the delusion." He winked at me again, and I tingled in a way that had no place at work.

My fling with Gannon was as much an accident as it could be, with me anxiety-ridden from the past, full of self-pity over my job situation, and him eager to charge in and play Sir Lancelot to a woman who appreciated him. All of that was before he reconciled with his wife, Katya. I have told myself there was no reason for guilt. Useless emotion—guilt—worthless as shaving your legs to sleep alone.

After we ended the sex, knowing he was off limits made the flashbacks more delicious. Until Tom Wright arrived in my life.

Six months after Chace and I broke off the affair, in a twist of irony that continues to amuse me, Chace Gannon introduced me to Tom. Gannon needed a primo numbers person to help him with a file. Tom's creds were impeccable. He had sorted out an earlier financial puzzle for Licensing Regulations and became their go-to man for money trails. My path might never have crossed his, but for the fact that Gannon invited me to their meeting. I settled myself across from the hunky accountant who wore a suit like a promise and smelled as inviting as an ocean breeze. I was less captivated by the convoluted scheme of insurance fraud my former and soon-to-be lovers wrestled to unravel than I was by extraneous details, such as the accountant's dimples when he smiled, his clean manicured fingernails, close shave, leather-strapped sports watch, silver and onyx stud in the left ear. As Tom stood to leave, I offered him my card. He called the next day.

Chace Gannon remains unaware of the forces he set in motion. Maybe it wasn't irony so much as cosmic design. The world needs harmony. Chace returned to his wife but introduced me to Tom and kept everything in balance. Until some bastard waltzed into my study and disrupted the equilibrium.

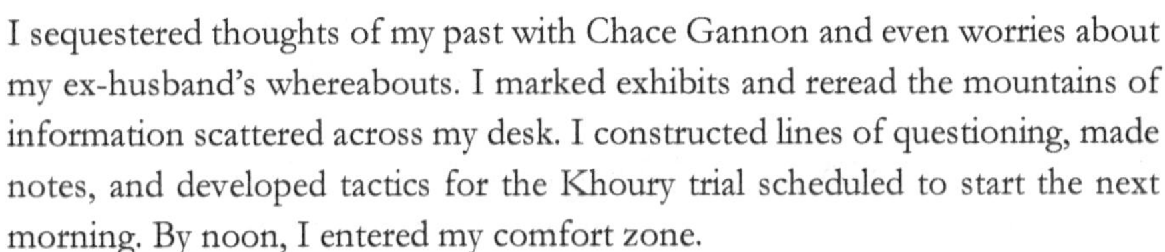

9

I sequestered thoughts of my past with Chace Gannon and even worries about my ex-husband's whereabouts. I marked exhibits and reread the mountains of information scattered across my desk. I constructed lines of questioning, made notes, and developed tactics for the Khoury trial scheduled to start the next morning. By noon, I entered my comfort zone.

I had blocked the afternoon for Gannon to help me troubleshoot weaknesses in my case. Our affair had ended, leaving friendship scuffed but intact. Now our most impassioned activity was debating case strategy. He had interviewed Dr. Ahmed Khoury on two occasions in the past five months. Chace would be my star witness. Today I would dry-run my direct examination of the information I hoped to get into evidence through him and consider his responses. Surprise is a bitch. Commandment Number One in an attorney's bible: don't ask your witness a question if you don't know the answer.

I didn't stand when Gannon knocked on the frame of my open office door. He closed it after he entered and then eased his body into a chair across from my desk. "How's life treating you, Lawrence?" After we quit sleeping together, we stopped addressing each other by first names.

"You're not here to listen to me gripe. We've got work to do."

That knowing grin and the playful twinkle in his eyes reminded me how comfortable we had been together.

"I can do both," he said.

I put my finger to my lips and spoke in a hushed voice. "We'll be here late into the night if you get me started."

"That could be arranged." His left hand held a super-sized drink that he placed on my desk. His wedding ring loomed larger than the Pepsi.

I shook my head and gave him a tight grimace. "A night with you wouldn't help. In fact, I'm quite sure it would confound matters."

His whisper matched mine. He understood both office politics and thin walls. "That bad? Poor baby. I'm a willing listener."

I ignored him and got down to business. "Let's go over this case from the beginning." Even though the conversation was now case directed, I kept my voice soft, hoping Rathburn couldn't hear. "I filed the formal complaint four months ago, while the boss enjoyed a two-week vacation in Tahiti."

"I remember. It was her thirtieth wedding anniversary, right?"

"Good memory." My fingers tapped a march on my desk as I toyed with the import of a complaint filed without Rathburn's approval. "As the first assistant, it was my job to make sure nothing slipped through the cracks while she was gone. I found a skeleton file on her desk, mixed in with new cases awaiting review. It contained a single letter that, if the date was correct, had been sent to our division a year and a half earlier."

"Right. Maxine Sheppard. She wrote that Khoury prescribed drugs that killed a couple of guys. I did a priority investigation. Had the report in your hands three days later."

"Right on all counts," I said.

"I suspected Maxine Sheppard was a fake name but turned out she was real. Real enough to die in her house, three blocks from Khoury's clinic, before I could interview her." Chace leaned back, crossed his feet at the ankles and locked his fingers behind his head. "Death listed as natural causes. Cardiac arrest. Her ticker gave out at forty-three. No autopsy."

"We had run into a dead end, pun intended." For a second I wondered if I would have been better off if I had left it alone. Maybe Shirley Rathburn wanted this file closed.

"Yeah, but Sheppard's death didn't foil super-sleuth. I nosed around, identified one of the guys, who she mentioned in her letter had croaked, got his medical records, sat on the clinic for two days, and found enough circumstantial evidence, that added to the ARCOS numbers, let you file a complaint."

"Four counts to be precise: Incompetence. Lack of good moral character. Practice outside the scope of a license. And selling or giving away controlled substances for other than lawful medical purposes."

"All of this rehashing, you seem distracted. Is there something about this case I don't know?" He cocked his head to the side and squeezed his eyes to narrow slits, encouraging my answer.

"I'm just talking it out, hoping something clicks. Maybe a connection between how this case began and the trouble I'm in. You've read about that?" Raising the subject unleashed a slow burn in my stomach. I gulped a slug of tea to quench the heat.

"I've wanted to ask if there was anything I could do, but it seemed wrong to intrude."

"Because we're not sleeping together, you mean?"

The last trace of good humor vanished, and serious washed over his face. "No, because if you wanted my input or help, you only had to ask. And to answer your other question, I don't detect any obvious connection. Khoury's an ass-wipe, but I don't picture him burglarizing your house. There's no way he's messed up in anything violent enough to draw blood."

I considered his assessment.

In the pause before I spoke again, I heard Rathburn in the next office: "Yeah, well, that's the deal. Best I can do. Take it or leave it."

"Forget my situation, we've got a case to prepare," I said.

"Let's get to it."

"I spent yesterday afternoon in Khoury's office. Can you explain why a dirtbag like Khoury risked his medical license for a few bucks?"

"Whoa, partner." He sucked in air and whistled. "Khoury isn't interested in a few bucks, you know that."

"Yeah, yeah. I read your report. But it's his profession . . . his reputation."

"Our doctor-friend decided it was worth the gamble for a shitload of money. Was willing to hurt a lot of people in the process. My report will make that dignified judge itch to climb over his bench and bash his gavel against Khoury's pea brain." Gannon's face grew animated. He was on a roll, and to broadcast outrage he didn't speak in hushed tones.

"I'll be satisfied if the medical board yanks his license, and our criminal division gets him thrown in prison for a chunk of years," I said.

"Think about it, Lawrence, Khoury sees up to two hundred patients a day. I drive by his operation at seven forty-five when you're still getting your beauty sleep."

"I'm up before you every day of the week."

"Whatever. The point I make is that a line halfway around the block waits for his doors to open. Folks in bad need of a fix. The rest of the patients, those with a pill or two left, show up later."

Gannon ignored the low buzz of conversation coming from adjacent offices and continued. "Khoury sees maybe a dozen legitimate patients in a day. For those, he keeps meticulous records. The rest crave their OxyContin, their Fentanyl, their Percocet. He bills the dopers' insurance just like he bills insurance for the regular patients. If they are uninsured but have managed to snag someone else's card, that's fine by the doctor. Gets a double dip either way."

He stood and paced the short distance between my office walls. My eyes followed him, appreciating the lithe way he moved that body.

"The addicts slip him a hundred in cash. That's hidden money. Not on the books. As near as I figure, in a year he could have about three million tax-free dollars in an off-shore account," he said.

I flipped through my exhibits and scanned the evidence that supported Gannon's conclusion. "You're the one who told me ARCOS reports would rat him out sooner or later."

"Heavy emphasis on later," he said. "Khoury probably planned to take off for some sunny beach before we caught up with him. A tropical paradise where he wouldn't give a tinker's damn about his medical license. Drink piña coladas and thumb his nose at us working stiffs for the rest of his cushy life. He got greedy. Waited too long."

"Why hasn't he skipped, now that I've filed a complaint?"

"Lots of reasons." He held up his right fist and began opening his thumb and fingers as he ticked off each. "The cops got him in their crosshairs. His passport's been yanked. None of Khoury's patients will testify against him. The money that changed hands was cash. He may believe he can beat the rap."

Gannon lowered his voice again. "Big contributor to Sawicki's and Governor Kilpatrick's campaigns. Helps to have friends in high places." He tilted his eyes toward the ceiling. High places in our vernacular meant the seventh floor.

"How do you know that?" I whispered back.

"C'mon, Lawrence. I'm a curious son of a bitch."

"Yes, but—"

"Campaign contributions are public record. I couldn't resist getting the info for the AG and Gov, then running a search that cross-referenced them to doctors we've sanctioned, or who are subjects of a current investigation."

"Interesting little list?" That voice inside my head again asked how this might be related to my missing ex-husband.

"Interesting, yes, but not as short of a list as you might think." Gannon refueled with a couple of swigs of his soda. "I found that twenty doctors we suspected of being dirty had maxed contributions to Sawicki and Kilpatrick. More interesting, since five hundred's the cap and that's not enough to bribe a file clerk, lots of welfare patients who see these doctors also make donations."

I nodded at the implication that doctors funded contributions by indigent patients. "What did you do with the information?"

"Not a frickin' thing other than tuck it away in my that's-damned-interesting file. Doesn't mean Sawicki knows about their dirty practices. Then again—"

"He may."

"Exactly."

None of this was in the reports. My mind kicked into overdrive. I considered what a conspiracy of these doctors might gain by trashing my study. But the answer remained *nothing*.

After Gannon paused to let me digest what he had shared, I asked, "Anything else about Khoury and Sawicki?"

"You mean like Sawicki's a sport-fishing enthusiast and loves to test Lake Michigan waters for Coho and Chinook salmon? He does this with his friend Ahmed Khoury from the decks of the doc's 53-foot Carver 530 Voyager."

"You are kidding."

"Nope."

"How'd you find out about this?"

"Ah, Lawrence, have a bit of faith." He sported a smug grin as he lobbed a surprise or two into the equation. "I followed Khoury on his day off. That's Monday, by the way. A young preppy-type in Dockers and deck shoes boarded with Sawicki. The unidentified guy had blond hair, layered in some sissy cut he didn't get from any regular barber. A perfect inch above his collar. It had damned streaks. Probably came from a bottle. I won't even venture a guess whether his tan was sprayed or natural."

"More stuff for your that's-damned-interesting file?"

"You've got it."

"You're scaring me. Do you think we can lose this case because of those friends in high places? Or worse, that those influential friends are pissed at me for coming after the doctor?"

He helped himself to a handful of peanut M&Ms from a bowl on my desk. "We won't lose the licensing case. No evidence the medical board is dirty. Khoury never expected your complaint. Rathburn went on vacation, and you and I spoiled things. Evidence is trickier in the criminal matter. You know that better than I do."

A flurry of thoughts silenced me. A dirty doctor, millions stashed away, and the strong possibility of jail in his future. That was more than enough for him to want me scared. But there they were again, those glitches in the logic: Khoury knew the kind of people who could forge him a new passport. And scaring me wouldn't make the case go away now that the medical board had its hooks into him.

Gannon broke my reverie. "Take a look at these." He pawed through his briefcase and brought out a sandwich baggie with what looked like a half dozen four-by-six photos inside. "These aren't official evidence. They just illustrate my that's-damned-interesting file."

I flipped through pictures of three females who appeared to be edging out of their teens. They all wore bikinis that required careful Brazilian waxing. In one photo, Sawicki touched champagne glasses with a redhead. In another picture, the other two sat on Khoury's lap, one on each knee. The doctor had his arms around the women, fingers resting on their ample breasts.

I scrutinized the image. "I know this girl."

"How?"

"In the picture, she's cleaned up, her hair has highlights, and it's before she was pregnant, but I'm sure this is Sherri Smith. I met her yesterday at Khoury's office."

"No surprise. Khoury brought the babes."

I pulled the slip of paper Sherri had given me from my billfold. "She can't even spell pills."

Gannon chuckled as he scanned the note. "She can spell okay. *PILZ* is how dopers write pills to describe prescription drugs used for recreational purposes."

"This friggin' job is an education in dirt I never wanted to know about." I replaced Sherri's phone number behind Natalee's picture and then studied the last photo. "Your young preppy is Mark Rodgers. Sawicki's right-hand man. Arrow-straight as they make 'em. It would be easy to mistake him for an FBI agent. All professional. All business. The boy next door grown up and responsible." I sealed the baggie before tossing the snapshots back to him. "Looks like Dr. Khoury may have lost respect for the Hippocratic oath."

"Hey, girlie girl, your naivety is refreshing. Didn't law school teach you that profit trumps oaths every day of the week?"

"I missed that class." I scowled to underscore my contempt for Khoury, then shrugged and shook my head. "None of this does me any good tomorrow. Irrelevant as how many games the Luggies won their first season."

"Not to mention the trouble an assistant AG could get her skinny self into if she suggested Sawicki is involved."

I nodded. "Right, I may not love my job, but it pays the bills, and I'm never bored." Then I raised my voice. "Hell, I'm even growing fond of Shirley Rathburn."

Gannon packed up his papers.

Thinking aloud, but back to hushed tones, I said, "There isn't a scintilla of hard evidence that Sawicki acted outside the law. Even his financial support from Khoury stopped short of statutory limits. Bad choice of friends is not a crime."

"Not last time I checked." Gannon latched his briefcase and waited for more questions.

"One last matter. I've subpoenaed Hilda Fagan and Tammy Truxall. What's your take on them?"

"Are you asking what I think they'll say if you put them on the stand?"

"Yes."

"They'll protect their boss."

"Why? He's rotten."

"Only to you. Tammy Truxall thinks he's the next coming of Christ. He bought her a car, bailed her no-account brother-in-law out of jail, gave her extra money to buy groceries for her ailing mother."

"A regular second son of God. I get it."

"She's a high school dropout. I would guess a marginal receptionist. As she puts it, 'he never yells at me, and he's nicer to me than my daddy ever was,' which probably means he isn't diddling her. She would do anything for him.

Getting straight facts about the number of patients Khoury has was harder than a pervert at a peep show. She only gave me what I already knew."

I jotted a note on the Truxall statement, *nix as a witness*. "And Fagan?"

"Same song, different verse. The heavy makeup she uses to caulk that saggy wrinkled face doesn't fool anyone. She's beyond her prime. Lost her nursing license several years back because of a drug problem. When she got it reinstated, no one would touch her. If Khoury hadn't hired her, she would be waiting tables in a two-bit coffee shop."

Miserable witness, I scribbled across her statement before asking, "Is she clean?"

"She says she is. I can't say for sure. But she credits Khoury with helping her give up drugs and insists he's only aiding folks who would kill or steal if he wasn't there."

My scowl must have been more obvious than I intended.

"You disagree?" he asked. "Her story is that people who come to her boss are abandoned by everyone else. Her words to me were, 'Without Dr. Khoury, desperate folks would turn to counterfeit stuff. Look what the fake Fentanyl did to Prince.' She might even believe her spin."

I pushed aside the possibility there was a scintilla of truth in Fagan's viewpoint. "So, don't call either of them?"

"Let 'em sit in the back of the courtroom to keep Khoury honest. Put them on the stand, and I promise perjury. They'll paint him as the male Mother Theresa."

At six, Gannon and I quit for the day. I entertained doubts about whether I was ready, but my case was as prepared as it was going to get. Tomorrow would be show time.

10

Thursday, September 29

I live for September, Michigan's most perfect month. Thirty days of paradise that separate summer's sweaty, scorching heat and ninety-percent humidity from brutal, bone-chilling winter winds. On my way to Sergeant Peter Lockhart's office, I welcomed the sunshine streaming through my car window as a favorable omen. I upped the volume of WMMQ Classic Rock, strummed my fingers on the steering wheel to the rhythm, and with a voice someone had warned me could cause babies to cry, sang along with Bobby McFerrin, "Don't Worry, Be Happy."

I had a premonition, or maybe baseless optimism, that everything was okay. Lockhart would share encouraging news: Derek was alive, and there was a less apocalyptic explanation for my burglary than someone sending me a warning or wishing me harm.

After our meeting, I would return to work and kick Khoury's rich ass.

The sergeant didn't stand when his receptionist ushered me into his office. He returned my be-happy smile with a thin, tight scowl. "Have a seat, Ms.

Lawrence. Thanks for coming in." He set a small recorder close to me, pushed the button, gave the date, time, and case number. "We'll record this so I don't make any mistakes in my report."

I searched his face for signs of good news; his unflinching eyes offered none. I dropped into an office chair that lacked enough cushion to soften sitting. If the cop had a fuzzy warm side, his workspace didn't reflect it.

"When we talked the other night," he said without further preliminaries, "I didn't get a list of people who've been in your study."

"You mean ever?"

"At least as long as you've lived there. We need to fingerprint them for elimination. Prints can last thirty, forty years."

I considered for a moment and then gave him full names and phone numbers for Jon and Ginny, Tom, my former housekeeper, and two of Natalee's friends. I paused, thought about it more and added, "My moving company was Two Fellas with a Dolly, but I don't remember the names of the men they sent."

"Thanks. On your way out, we'll print you. Schedule an appointment for Natalee. We'll contact the others."

"The school has a fingerprint identification card for Natalee. I'll authorize them to release it to you. If that isn't good enough, let me know."

All business, he plowed down a new line of inquiry. "What did you keep on your laptop?"

"Personal emails, not much else. My casework and important files are on my office computer. It's backed up by the State of Michigan every night."

"It wouldn't do a thief any good to destroy your personal computer?"

"Not a bit." I shifted in the uncomfortable chair and crossed my legs. Tired of waiting for him to tell me something that mattered, I asked, "Have you found Derek?"

"No, but we've run a check on him." Lockhart's stare shifted to a stack of documents in front of him. He fondled sheets of paper, flaunting what he knew and I didn't.

He's getting serious, I warned myself. My body braced for the onslaught.

"Came up with a few items of interest. NCIC shows no outstanding warrants, two prior arrests, two convictions, one for carrying a concealed weapon and the other for security fraud. Your ex served time for the second."

"I know about the gun. You had to go back seventeen years to dredge that up. We had an intruder. Derek bought it for protection. I heard about the prison stint secondhand and have no details." I had never told Natalee that her father served time in Susanville Prison. California is a long way from Okemos, I hoped she never found out. "Even that was years ago, right after our divorce. A bad time."

He licked his lips like my answer left a vinegary aftertaste. "About six months ago, Mr. Lawrence's former employer, Harbor Springs Investments out of Palo Alto, let him go for suspected embezzlement. They found themselves short two million over the three-year period he worked there. They couldn't prove it was him. He threatened a lawsuit if they pursued it. Beats me how they hired an ex-con."

I began to think Bobby McFerrin should stick his be-happy bullshit where other misguided optimists would never find it. "Is there any positive news?"

"Not exactly, but we found some curious things in your ex-husband's suitcase."

I averted my eyes, then worried that I appeared evasive, raised them again to meet his stare. "Like what?"

"For one, the Delta tickets from Detroit to San Francisco," he said.

"Why would that surprise you? He has to go home. Sooner's better than later."

"He was scheduled to depart yesterday afternoon at four-thirty. He wasn't on that flight." He let the words hang in the air as though he had no intention of going on until he sized up my reaction.

"So, he changed his mind?" It came out sounding like a question, but I didn't expect him to share an answer, if he had one.

"Right, but he didn't notify the airlines." He shuffled the papers he had sprawled across his desk back into a squared stack. "Can I get you a cup of coffee or a donut, Ms. Lawrence?"

Good technique, I thought. Drop loaded information and let me stew for a few seconds. "No, I'm good."

"If he planned to fly to California, do you know what he intended to do with the Porsche? That's a mighty fine car." The cop hesitated. His smirk warned me there was more coming. "Did you know it's paid for?"

"No. How would I know that? And if you find out why it's still in my garage, maybe you could share that information."

"That's the point. We can't ask Mr. Lawrence. His credit cards haven't been used since the burglary. Your ex-husband is, as they say, off the grid."

I didn't like where my mind went. The cop thought I knew something about Derek's disappearance. Or believed I was responsible for it. His glare was as transparent as if he had accused me outright. I might be a victim, but the faint blond hairs on my arms stood up.

He flipped through additional papers, seemed to scrutinize one. "Among other things in his suitcase, was the title to that fine car—signed over to Natalee."

It was so like Derek to try for a grand gesture without thinking of the consequences. A grimmer explanation replaced my irritation: Derek was scared. Maybe afraid he might be killed.

Lockhart picked up another sheet from the stack. His frown deepened. "Have you seen this before?"

I examined what he handed me, skimming for pertinent information. It was a life insurance policy issued by Cardinal Insurance of Palo Alto. Derek was the named insured. The policy limit was $1.5 million, double in the case of accidental death. I was the beneficiary. I would have sworn Lockhart was yanking my chain if the evidence wasn't burning my hand.

"Absolutely not." I glowered, daring him to call me a liar.

"Derek didn't mention it?"

"Never."

"His company paid premiums while he was employed, but Mr. Lawrence made the last payment the day before yesterday. The beneficiary will change to Natalee when she turns eighteen."

He stood, walked to the window and opened the blinds. "Might as well let in the sunshine." Before he sat down again, he poked his head outside his office door and asked the receptionist to bring him a cup of coffee and a jelly donut. She delivered both before he uttered another word. "Ms. Lawrence, have you ever gone by any other name?"

"My maiden name was Flowers." It was truthful as far as it went.

"Any others?"

Powdered sugar snowed down on his crisply pressed navy-blue shirt. *Should I volunteer more or see if he pursued it?*

"Is there a problem?" he asked when I didn't offer an instant answer.

"No. The name on my birth certificate is Angel Rosebud Flowers." I had skipped breakfast, my stomach growled, and I wished I had taken him up on the donut offer.

"Then why aren't you Angel Rosebud Lawrence?"

"Think about it, Sergeant. Angel Rosebud Flowers? It's no small burden to live with a name like that. Sounds like someone who works at Velvet Fingers Massage Parlor."

I detected the faintest glimmer of a smile, but it disappeared in a millisecond. "Did you legally change your name?"

"No, sir. But from my first day at Bad Axe High School, I refused to answer to anything other than Casey. No law against calling yourself anything you want, so long as there's no intent to defraud."

"But your legal name remains Angel Rosebud Lawrence?"

"Only to my deceased grandmother." I reached for my purse and extracted my driver's license to prove I was Casey R. Lawrence.

He looked toward my ID and shook his head. "I know what your driver's license says."

"You didn't find one for Angel Rosebud Flowers or Angel Rosebud Lawrence, did you?"

He didn't answer that but forged on. "In my experience, government agencies require legal support for a name change. How did you get a social security card and driver's license without legally changing it?"

Did he think any of this mattered, or did he enjoy the game? I ground my teeth, chewed the inside of my cheeks, nervous habits that foreshadowed a ferocious headache. I gave him a pared-down version. "Teachers and doctors began writing Casey on my files. I stopped using a middle name, opting for the initial R. I figured the last name would take care of itself when I married." I checked my watch. I had no time for this. My trial started in an hour. "For God's sake, what is this about?"

"Just being thorough."

"Go ahead, run any name you want through CAD, NCIC, DMV, or any other fancy legal computer system. You won't find a thing."

"No need to get huffy, I'm just doing my job. You want me to do my job, don't you?"

"Of course." I did my thirty seconds of square breathing. "No stone unturned. That's how we get justice, isn't it?"

He paid no attention to my attempt to put us on the same side and picked up another sheet of paper. It was a verse I wrote after Jimmy Scroggins' death. It must have been separated from the pile of poems I removed from the burglary scene. He laid it aside. But not before I read from upside-down the dark, bold title and wished I had called it something other than *Assassination*.

The sergeant was toying with me. The cops would misconstrue the meaning of the poem, think it referred to Derek, and any attempt to clarify would make the situation worse. A wave of revulsion engulfed me. I clutched the arms of the chair to still my shaking hands.

"Have you ever owned a gun?" Lockhart treaded farther into dangerous territory.

"Derek owned a couple, the one stolen and the one that got him arrested, but no, sir, I've never owned a gun." I warned myself not to panic, try to appear relaxed. He couldn't know what I had done with the gun that Derek reported stolen. "Am I a suspect? Do I need an attorney?"

He didn't answer with the speed or in the tenor I wanted. I felt trapped in a chess game with my opponent poised to topple my queen.

After what seemed eons, he said, "That's up to you. A wife is always a person of interest when a husband goes missing. This case is no different. If you think you need an attorney, we stop now."

I knew that trick. I wondered where he got his information. I had been a model citizen, broken no laws in the seventeen years since my closet became home to Scroggins' skeleton.

Derek may have suspected what I had done, but only a dead man and I knew for sure. If the police ever asked, I banked that a guilty conscience would keep my ex from sharing his hunch. He had dropped the bread crumbs that brought the bastard to our door.

I decided Lockhart couldn't have anything damning. "You think I killed Derek? That's outrageous." Even deep breathing couldn't soothe the tsunami rolling in my stomach.

The sergeant ignored my question and asked, "Do you have any reason to believe your daughter uses drugs?"

"Absolutely not." Finally, something easy to answer.

"Derek?"

"Your guess is as good as mine. He had a habit many years ago, but he got clean. He didn't have glassy eyes or seem impaired last time I saw him."

"And you?"

"I'll be happy to pee in a cup."

"That won't be necessary at the moment."

It was a fishing expedition, and I was the worm skewered to the hook. "If you change your mind, be sure to let me know."

He ignored my sarcasm. With his interrogation technique, I guessed he got that a lot.

"We're just gathering evidence," he said.

"If you have much more evidence to gather from me, we can schedule a return date. I have a trial at nine."

"That's fine. I think we're about done for now."

"Any chance I can get a copy of the inventory you made of my study contents and Derek's stuff in the guestroom? Maybe your write-up of the incident?"

His smile didn't pair well with the cold glint in his eyes. "I wish I could," he said, "but I can't give out evidence that could find a trail into the wrong hands and compromise an ongoing investigation."

Now I was the *wrong hands*. So much for the premonition that started my day. "Can you at least tell me if it was Derek's blood in the study?"

"We don't have a sample of his for comparison. It was O positive and Derek's records from the prison infirmary in California indicate he's O positive."

"Him and about forty percent of the population." I closed my eyes for a moment. When I opened them, I still sat in front of Lockhart.

"Maybe Natalee could give us a sample," he said. "They'd have some of the same markers."

"Not without a court order." Let him think what he damn well pleased about me. He couldn't prove a thing, and so long as I was on this side of my grave, there was no chance I would offer up my daughter for a blood sample to confirm her father had been injured or killed. They could find some other means to obtain the information. I stood to leave.

"I'll walk you out. We'll scan your fingerprints on the way." He clicked off the recorder and marched me to the booking room counter where a large monitor and official-looking equipment waited.

"Turn your head away and relax," he said. "It's easier if you don't try to help."

He took my right hand and placed the fingers, one at a time and then the four fingers as a unit, on the scanning plate next to the computer screen. He repeated the process with my left hand. After that, he printed each thumb. When he let my hands go, I turned back and watched him check the images before he hit the SAVE button.

"I appreciate your cooperation, Ms. Lawrence," he said when we reached the building's exit. "You have a nice day."

"I wish I could say it's been a pleasure," I said as he turned toward his office. "But, I'm an optimist. Maybe you'll find something useful when you stop chasing dead ends."

Lockhart suspects you, I warned myself as I walked to my car. Murder victims are always killed by a spouse, ex-spouse, or lover. Never before today had I been the prime suspect for anything more serious than filching an occasional candy bar from the Bad Axe grocery store. And that was before I turned ten. I parted ways with crime early, fearing it would block a legal career.

Now I worried that the cops had stumbled onto evidence of something far more damning than petty theft.

For as long as we had known each other, William Radowski's square head boasted a crew cut that obscured where bald began. My former investigator didn't sport the cut of your cool young exec or NBA star who shaved his head when his hair thinned, but rather a prune job like a marine drill sergeant. Right now, it was a most beautiful image.

The traffic on the freeway caught my sideways glances as I fumbled through the contents of my Coach bag until my fingers traced the shape of my cell. I punched Rad's number from my contact list. A pang of guilt reminded me that we had lost touch since he retired six months earlier.

He answered "I'm listening" on the second ring.

Those words soothed the fears of a woman knee deep in a dung pile. "I really, really needed to hear your gruff voice," I said.

"Hey, CJ, is that you?"

"If by CJ, you mean Casey, it's me."

"To what do I owe the pleasure of this call?" he asked.

"I need to see you."

"Music to my ears."

I breathed easier. "They think I did it."

"Did what?"

"Don't you read the paper?"

"Oh, yeah. First assistant attorney general's house burglarized. Husband missing. Blood at the scene. That the 'what' you mean?"

"That's it."

"How can I help?"

"I just left the office of Sergeant Lockhart of the Meridian Township Police. He's got an initial report and an inventory of what they found in my study and guestroom. Won't let me see a thing."

"Can't jeopardize the investigation, huh?"

"So he says."

"Party line when they deal with a suspect."

"I want to see what they have."

Traffic was sparse. I gunned the accelerator and watched the odometer climb to eighty-five before regaining control of my emotions and my speed.

"I've got a few friends with the state boys," he said. "They assisted in the investigation, didn't they?"

"Uh-huh."

"I'll see what I can find out."

"How about I buy you breakfast at the Daybreak tomorrow at seven?"

"Best offer I've had in months." He paused for a mere second before adding, "Hey, wear that sexy burgundy number that used to drive the men crazy. Maybe black nylons and shoes with really high heels?"

As I pulled into the mud lot, I thought about the first time Rad had called me CJ. I was the newly promoted Chief Claims Counsel at Employers Mutual. In the course of Rad's investigation on one of my cases, he had convinced a back-injury claimant that he possessed a videotape of the guy "in every position except missionary" with the wife of the fellow's best friend. He advised the poor sap that the fictitious film was recorded through a tiny opening in the closed curtains. It proved the man's back was in dandy shape. Rad threatened the "malingering son of a bitch" with "drop your case or expect to watch the unedited version at the hearing. There's no way in hell my insurance company's gonna pay this trumped-up claim voluntarily." He promised the claimant that Mrs. Claimant would be on the witness list so she could enjoy the show.

When I heard the story, I called Rad into my office, closed the door, and castigated him for twenty minutes.

When I finished, it was his turn. "Ah, Casey the Judgmental. My lovely, law-abiding Casey the Just. My politically-correct, boss Casey." He paused, unwrapped a piece of gum he took from his pocket without offering me a stick, put it in his mouth, and looked me square in the eye. "Listen up. This is the first rule of engagement according to Rad. Sometimes you gotta do what you gotta do. It's all about the greater good."

"Not in my office. And not as long as my name is above yours on the Org Chart."

Rad promised no more skirting the law to get evidence. We both knew he wouldn't keep that promise.

The morning after that meeting, I ran into Rad at the coffee machine. He held out the pot and offered to pour mine. He smiled and whispered, "How's my Casey the Judgmental this morning?"

The dirty look I gave him had ferocity sufficient to freeze Lake Superior in mid-July. He never called me his Casey the Judgmental again. Mostly he kowtowed and called me Casey. Sometimes, he couldn't resist, and CJ slipped out. As far as I knew, neither of us ever disclosed to another soul how the nickname came about.

When he had worked at Employer's Mutual, Rad was a sexual harassment complaint scouting a victim. Thinking back to that story reminded me that somewhere tangled with his sexism, political incorrectness, and questionable ethics was loyalty, which he practiced to a fault. If my life were on the line, and I could choose one person to save me, I would call Rad. I needed to believe he was my knight in slightly tarnished armor.

11

I hustled to my office, grabbed a two-wheel dolly for the Khoury files, and then steered them across the footbridge connecting the Williams Building to Ottawa Tower North where our administrative courtrooms were located. These were not the rich mahogany chambers of circuit courts, but tiny cramped rooms that, like my office, lacked ornamentation. Not so much as an imposing oil painting of some over-the-hill judge. I doubt any administrative law judge ever sat for a portrait. ALJs, like the attorneys who practiced before them, retired into comfortable obscurity. The walls weren't even used to promote government propaganda: DURING FLU SEASON WASH YOUR HANDS FREQUENTLY or THEFT OF GOVERNMENT PROPERTY IS A CRIME AND WILL BE DEALT WITH HARSHLY.

What distinguished this from any other faded government space was the raised judicial platform, where the black-robed judge sat when court was in session, and the dual flags, Michigan and U.S., flanking it. About mid-room, between the folding chairs lining the back wall and the judge's bench, stood two rectangular tables with four chairs at each. Walking in from the judge's entrance at the back of the room, the prosecution sat at the left table and the defense at the right. Sometimes the latter used the full allotment of chairs. The accused came with a cadre of attorneys equal to their ability to pay. A medical license was a more valuable commodity than the venue suggested. For the prosecution, there was always one attorney. We were spread too thin for more.

This morning I asked Chace Gannon to take one of the three empty chairs at my table. I inhaled the smell of his spicy cologne. It offered a breath of vitality to the otherwise nondescript setting. I welcomed the heat of his body. An investigator sitting next to me gave the appearance of strength. It also provided quicker access to him if I had questions, or if he scribbled me a note on his legal pad.

Everyone in the room stopped fidgeting or organizing their documents into neat piles in front of them when a fiftyish-looking man with thick bifocals and an eagle-beaked nose entered. He took his seat behind the bench. After a few seconds to give the players time to grasp the gravity of the proceedings, he began.

"Good morning, I am Administrative Law Judge Gerald Kennally. We are here today in the matter of *The State of Michigan vs. Ahmed Khoury*. Would the parties introduce themselves for the record, starting with the attorney for the state?"

My brain flipped a switch and turned on attorney mode. No longer Mom, friend, lover, or even scared-shitless, suburban housewife, I stepped into the role and shut out everything else.

"Casey R. Lawrence on behalf of the Attorney General and the People of the State of Michigan, your honor." Even now, I preferred feeding Lockhart's suspicions to identifying myself as Angel Rosebud Flowers and blowing the illusion of a dignified professional.

"Ron Marshall of Marshall Donovan Hovey and Saks for Dr. Khoury," said Khoury's lead attorney.

"Conrad Donovan of Marshall Donovan Hovey and Saks, also for Dr. Khoury."

"Jamison Saks of Marshall Donovan Hovey and Saks for Dr. Khoury."

As opposing counsel identified themselves, I wanted to ask what had happened to Hovey. Instead, I glanced over and locked eyes with the doctor who was looking in my direction. I studied his coal-black eyes. Neither medical school nor age had extinguished the intensity they reflected. I wanted Ahmed Khoury to feel my zeal. He was the scum of the earth. He turned his head away. I didn't need a trial consultant to tell me he acted guilty.

The accused wore a slate gray, custom-made suit with darker charcoal pinstripes. His bold, silk-flowered tie cost more than my entire outfit, blouse and shoes included. I felt like J. C. Penney off the rack compared to an ad for *GQ*. Khoury's physique, aided by the meticulous snip of a tailor's shears, looked firm, no middle-age spread. When he wasn't at his office raking in the bucks, he probably jogged barefoot on a private beach in Tobago and built rock-solid calves while the Caribbean licked his feet. His thick hair retained some dark brown from younger days. If you asked ten average Joes on the street to describe him, I would guess nine would include the word distinguished in their top three adjectives. I might have experienced a moment of admiration for his style if his crimes hadn't poisoned my mind.

When he turned back toward me, I maintained my glare. I wasn't afraid of him or his high-priced legal entourage. Khoury's three attorneys each charged four hundred fifty dollars an hour for trials, where they huddled at counsel's table and plotted strategy. They charged three hundred fifty an hour for prep. The doctor was lucky this was Michigan and not New York or California where lawyers billed two or three times that rate.

I was helpless to suppress a sneer directed at Khoury's expensive mouthpieces. I did rein in the wink twitching in my right eye. Before Kennally had entered the courtroom, the starting lineup for Marshall Donovan Hovey and Saks taunted, "You can't seriously hope to win this case," and, "If you don't come to your senses, we'll have you tied up in court for the rest of your short-lived legal career."

Their tactics annoyed me, but confirmed that Khoury's brilliant advocates handled few administrative licensing cases. They missed the broader picture. I'm an average attorney, although I work hard to do a good job. Any lawyer who squeaks through a third-rate night school, and avoids washing out only because Daddy doubled the tuition fee as an incentive for his sweet girl's admission, would win most of these cases. I am grateful for the two deadliest weapons in my arsenal. They increase my odds of winning to about ninety-eight percent.

The first is that the accused's final judge is his professional board. An administrative law judge, like Kennally, agonizes over rulings, objections, and evidence, but he or she only drafts a Proposal for Decision. That proposal, along with whatever responses the parties wish to make, is forwarded to the Board of Medicine. When the board gets wind that a doctor traded Fentanyl to a young female patient for fellatio in his office, exchanged Dilaudid for guns, or as Khoury did, sold prescriptions for profit, the board is less concerned about legal niceties than landing a devastating punch to the practice of the dirtbag who defiled their professional reputation. The board doesn't cut the pervert a millimeter of slack. It has no patience for technicalities.

My second secret weapon: our tiny staff of five attorneys handled all licensing misdeeds for every health professional in the state of Michigan. Inadequate staffing carried the imprimatur that the accused did something pretty damned egregious to get our attention.

We got through a handful of preliminary matters before Kennally directed his standard warning to the defense table. "While I'm flattered to have all your big-league attorneys in my humble courtroom, you get one chance to ask questions or object. I won't tolerate three attorneys stumbling over one another and dragging out this process, so choose your spokesperson. Are we clear?"

Marshall, Donovan, and Saks nodded and said in unison, "Yes, your honor."

"Ms. Lawrence, do you have an opening statement?"

Just once I wanted to wax poetic and say, "Respondent is a first-rate, snotty-nosed, ass-scratching, dog-fucking, son of a bitch who should be run over by a big rig and left squished like carrion for a crow in the middle of I-96 as an example to others like him." Fun to consider how many seconds it would take opposing counsel to object. Equally amusing for me to wonder if they could restrain themselves to one spokesperson to express their collective outrage.

Instead, I summarized my case. I had to prove the allegations in my complaint by a preponderance of the evidence. When placed on the scale of justice, it had to tip, ever so slightly at least, toward my version of events. I expected satisfying that burden would be as easy as overindulging in too many chocolates from my bottom desk drawer on a stressful morning.

When I finished, Kennally asked, "Mr. Marshall, do you have an opening statement?"

"May it please the court, your honor, we'll reserve." That meant I wouldn't hear the angel choir sing Dr. Khoury's praises until the completion of my case. I could write the defendant's opening statement as easily as my own. It wouldn't deviate by more than a word or two from all the other insipid openings I had endured in this courtroom.

"Ms. Lawrence, call your first witness," Kennally said.

"The People call Chace Gannon to the stand."

For the next hour, I walked Gannon through his reports and his visits to Khoury's clinic. I was almost finished with my direct examination and looked over my notes to catch anything I had missed.

During my pause, Kennally pounced. "Ladies and Gentlemen, it is now eleven fifty. I have a prior engagement at twelve. I suggest we stop and pick up at one thirty." The judge had an inviolate commitment to play euchre in the cafeteria with three of his cronies during the noon break.

As Gannon and I walked into the corridor I said, "Since my direct isn't closed, care to do a bit of Monday morning quarterbacking during lunch?"

"With your company as the incentive? Of course."

"My office okay?" I asked.

"Not unless you've got a George Forman Grill hidden in your file cabinet. I'm starved."

"The cafeteria it is." We had a five-minute head start on the crowd. Gannon lined up to order while I found us a table near the windows. I had eaten the first cupcake from the pack I extracted from my briefcase by the time he joined me. I was ready to devour the second. For dessert, I had a Heath bar.

"That poison will kill you," he said.

"Your grease is better?" I pointed to his cheeseburger, fries, and apple pie. "Mine's high octane fuel for the afternoon."

As we ate, we dissected every question I had asked and every answer he had given. If we missed anything, it didn't announce itself during lunch. At exactly one twenty-three, Chace and I were back at the prosecution's table. Seven minutes later Donovan and crew walked in.

"Didn't see them slumming lunch in the cafeteria," Gannon whispered. "Probably had sushi catered to their law offices. Compliments of Dr. Khoury."

Kennally followed close on their footsteps. Between the hem of his black robe and his Reeboks, khaki pants peeked out. He smiled, which meant the card gods had been good to him.

Marshall rose the moment the judge took the bench. "Your honor, there's been a slight complication. At least we hope it's slight. During the lunch hour, Dr. Khoury called his office. There was a message from his daughter's school. His little girl became violently ill this morning and is at Lansing General. We ask that the court grant us a short postponement so my client can be with his sick child."

"Do the People have any objections?"

Willing to risk being dubbed the new Queen of Mean, I said, "Yes, your honor, we do. It has taken nearly six months to get this matter to hearing. I strongly oppose additional delays. This doctor is a menace to the public's safety."

"I would remind you, Ms. Lawrence, that if Dr, Khoury were such a risk, you should have sought a Summary Suspension—a remedy of which I see the People did not avail themselves," Kennally said.

He was correct, but that didn't stop me from trying. "Your honor, the People believe Dr. Khoury represents an enormous danger, but the situation didn't come to our attention soon enough to satisfy the legal definition of imminent danger—"

"Counsel for the People is right about that." Donovan jumped on Kennally's bandwagon. "Imminent danger requires getting the case to the board close to the time the alleged conduct occurred. The People, if they want to suggest the doctor is a hazard to the community's health, have been woefully remiss in pursuing the matter." He was right. My argument lacked persuasiveness. The file had languished for weeks on Rathburn's desk.

"I agree," Kennally said. "A few more weeks shouldn't be critical."

I packed up my files, trying to keep everything in order so I wouldn't have to sort it again for the next hearing date. Kennally's eyes danced. He had heard enough. He pulled out his calendar. He still did it the old-fashioned hardcopy way.

"He'll be on the links in half an hour," Gannon wrote on my legal pad.

"And three other state employees will ditch work and join him," I scrawled back.

"November first and second look good to me," Kennally said. "Can the parties be here?"

"Yes, your honor," I said.

"I have another matter those days," Marshall said.

"Then you should be happy Dr. Khoury has more than one attorney," Kennally said. "I'll see anyone from your office who cares to join us on those dates. We stand adjourned."

Khoury and his attorneys left the courtroom as a pack. Gannon and I lagged a few steps behind. I overheard the doctor whisper to Jamison Saks something that sounded awfully like, "We need to warn her," but Saks shook his head and picked up his pace.

12

Friday, September 30

The phone's jangle woke me. "Casey Lawrence," I mumbled.

"Change of plan," Rad said.

"What's up?" I struggled to sound alert and glanced at the clock radio: a minute to six.

"I think it's better if you meet me at my place," he said. "I'll have a cup of tea waiting for you."

"Why?"

"No chance of anyone eavesdropping."

I was now wide awake and wary. "What are you afraid someone might hear?"

"We'll talk when you get here."

"Rad?" He hung up before I got more.

The shower's soothing spray didn't calm my worry. Did the change of plan somehow involve Jimmy Scroggins? Unable to keep the nightmare at bay, my mind rolled the seventeen-year-old horror like an ancient thirty-five-millimeter movie reel on slow speed. Every ugly detail remained crystal clear.

The bastard had slithered that day from the shadows near the stacked washer and dryer. Even from a distance of ten feet, I smelled him, the fetid body odor of someone who hadn't bathed in days, the reek of stale sweat so strong it mimicked a dead animal. I pivoted, and the chilling image of a man I had never seen before seared itself into my brain. His greasy straw-colored hair pulled into a tight ponytail left his hard-featured face exposed. Beneath days' worth of stubble, his skin had a raw reddish cast.

I zeroed in on the lethal-looking hunting knife he brandished. I yelped a high-pitched screech, tripped backwards. The tiny apartment kitchen boxed me in with no escape route. He used his body to shove me against the cabinets as he pressed the flat of the blade against my right temple so it didn't break the skin.

"A shame to mess up a pretty face," he said. "You're gonna enjoy this. Don't fight, and I won't hurt you." Fleshy lids hooded bloodshot eyes. The smirk plastered across the pinched tight line of his mouth did nothing to camouflage his rage.

"Please—" I begged.

"Don't snivel." He interrupted before I could offer him the $500 in my jewelry case to leave. I pulled back to deflect the powerful clenched left fist that swung toward my face. It caught me with enough muscle that I crashed to the floor, my cheek throbbing.

He knelt beside me; secured the knife between his knees while he ripped off a piece of duct tape from a roll he had roped to his pants. An adrenaline surge got me to my hands and knees, then to a crouched position from which I lunged toward scissors that rested on the countertop. I made it halfway, but he was too quick. His hands flew to my throat. I fought to breathe. Then darkness.

I regained consciousness lying on the hardwood floor of the living room, naked and balled into a fetal position with my hands trussed in front of me, my feet bound, and my mouth taped shut. I opened my eyes a slit so he wouldn't know I had come to. My ripped skirt and blouse, along with my bra and panties, were strewn on the floor around me. The absence of pain in my genital area told me that all he had done was look, maybe touch.

He slouched on the black leather couch, a Michelob balanced on his knee. With his free hand he fumbled with a plastic baggie and razor blade he withdrew from the pocket of his loose low-rider jeans. He dumped white powder onto the glass coffee table, cut it into fine particles and divided it into neat lines. He scooped a portion onto the long nail of his pinkie finger, carried it close to his spidery blood-vessel-lined nose, and inhaled. He dropped back. Waited. Sniffed two more lines.

The mantel clock showed two p.m. I lay motionless. Maybe he would stay away from me, absorbed in his drugs, until Derek arrived home.

He snorted another line and stood. I closed my eyes as he strutted toward me. He knelt, turned my face toward him, and slapped one cheek, then the other. Gentle at first, then harder when I didn't respond. "Wake up." He placed his fingers on my pulse. "Quit fucking with me, bitch."

When I didn't open my eyes, he delivered a blow with the back of his hand. It cracked my nose. With my mouth taped, I fought to breathe through the blood filling my nostrils.

"I said wake up," he snarled.

I opened my eyes wide but twisted my head to avoid looking at him. He made no attempt to disguise or hide his face. He intended to kill me.

"That's more like it." He kicked off dirty sneakers leaving his feet bare. He unfastened his blue jeans, dropped them to the ground, kicked them aside. He wore no underwear. He didn't bother to take off his orange flowered shirt. He ripped the tape from my ankles and flipped me onto my back. I fought to keep my legs closed. He drove his fists between my tightened thighs, pushed them apart, and climbed on top of me. With my arms still bound, the pain of his weight was excruciating. I screamed, but duct tape imprisoned the sound in my throat. Tears mingled with blood dampened my cheeks.

He reached down and fumbled with his penis, worked up an erection that defied the amount of cocaine in his system. He rammed himself inside me, tearing my flesh with such violence that blood lubricated my unyielding body. Grunts of satisfaction accompanied his final thrust. When he rolled off, I turned onto my side and hoped he would dress and leave. Without retrieving his pants, he turned on the TV and fiddled with the channels until Oprah's face filled the screen. He padded to the kitchen, and I heard the refrigerator door open. I wriggled my wrists to loosen the tape, but it held tight.

He returned to the living room and with a half-open mouth chewed cold pizza. He dropped the crust and eyed the remaining two furrows of white dust. He leaned close to the table and breathed the first row. He sank back, rested his head against the sofa, took his time before inhaling the second. He then shuffled toward me, forced me face down. In my peripheral vision, I watched him fondle his penis again, but when it didn't respond, he raped me from behind with the knife handle.

He crawled off and lay spread-eagle on the area rug. I followed his dilated eyes to the clock: Three thirty. Oprah upbraided a man for wearing a disgusting toupee, and the guy yanked it off and agreed to go bald. I had two hours to survive before Derek found me.

When the monster moved toward me a third time, I expected to die and hoped it would be fast. He stood for several seconds, then said, "I gotta take a whiz. Don't remember where your bathroom is. Little golden rain's good for ya." For the first time, I was grateful duct tape covered my mouth.

The memory of that warm stream of his putrid-smelling urine caused me to jerk back from the shower stream. I turned the water off, stepped out, and grabbed a towel. I had a half hour to dress and make it to Rad's.

13

I knocked, and from inside the small Cape Cod, Rad's gruff voice boomed. "It's open."

A giant of a man hunched over the retro Formica kitchen table. His hairy-knuckled hands gripped a coffee mug. "Sit down. Help yourself to a cup of tea." He pointed to a yellow-and green-flowered teapot and one matching bone china cup and saucer. A cloth napkin, wrinkled but neatly folded, sat next to a plate of Pepperidge Farm Chessman cookies. A manila folder and a box of Kleenex signaled I wasn't just the honored guest at an ex-cop's idea of a tea party.

"Mind telling me why we're here instead of the Daybreak where you could get a hearty breakfast?" I asked.

"I told you," he said. "Privacy."

Our silence danced around where to begin.

The house had that stagnant smell of bars before smoking bans went into effect. "Seems odd," I said, "you sitting in your own home without a Camel dangling from your fingers while you puff little O's in the air."

"Only because I love you, CJ. Figure I don't need to blow secondhand smoke in your face."

Rad hadn't given up the habit even when his wife, Bertie, lost her battle with lung cancer five years earlier. Her disease metastasized to the brain, pancreas, and liver. He cleaned her when she messed herself and watched pain rob her of the last remnants of joy. He witnessed her body shrink until she weighed eighty-nine pounds and couldn't stand alone. She often didn't recognize him. After her death, loneliness didn't render Rad a gentler, more sensitive man. It just made him appear uncomfortable in his own skin and forced him to eat more Big Macs. He insisted he preferred a heart attack to lung cancer.

"Hey, you wore the burgundy." A broad grin animated his craggy face.

"I'm not above using any means at my disposal." I winked and returned his grin.

"That's the spirit. And mighty fine means they are."

I hadn't talked to Rad in several months and was sorry I had let a busy life and work get in the way of spending time with a friend. I knew he was lonely, and I hadn't been there for him. It seemed callous to expect him to dash to my aid now, but I needed help.

I reached across the table, touched the manila envelope in front of him. "Looks like you got something. Anything good?" I asked.

"Not for you." His eyes held mine for a long second before he stood, walked to the counter, poured himself more coffee, and asked, "Is the tea okay?"

I guessed it was left from when Bertie was alive, but I nodded and lifted the cup by its fragile handle for another sip, waiting for him to muster the courage to continue.

"Where were we?" he asked after he sat back down.

"You were about to show me the bad news."

Rad opened the file and handed me six sheets stapled into one report. Across the top was written, "Evidence Inventory. Case Number 4669." Beneath that, my name, address, and date of the incident.

Using my index finger to keep my place, I scrolled down the pages: "Broken phone. Dell desktop computer. Thirty-three files (including Bar Association, Car Title, Medical Records-Casey, Medical records-Natalee, Receipts, Deed to the House). I paused at the entry "poem," then went on reading. Two framed pictures, glass broken. Green halogen desk lamp, smashed. Three orange Tic Tacs." Lines and more lines detailed the scraps of my life.

Halfway through and overwhelmed, I said, "I'm surprised they didn't log dust bunnies."

"Probably would have if you weren't such a damned fussy housekeeper."

I inhaled a deep breath and kept going. "What the hell?" Item ninety-five on page three stopped me cold. The police logged a packet of pills identified as OxyContin and another containing Fentanyl. I hadn't recovered from the jolt when my eyes carried me to the next bombshell. Item ninety-six was two ounces of marijuana.

"I was waiting for you to get to those." Rad nodded toward the remaining stack of papers. "The investigation summary indicates they found the dope and pills behind your bottom desk drawer. Could they be Natalee's?"

It took a few seconds to wrap my mind around the question. "Can I swear she's never smoked dope? No, I'm her mother. I hope she doesn't do drugs—"

"Let me help you out. If Natalee used drugs, would she hide them in your desk?"

"No way!"

"How about your ex? Any chance they're Derek's?"

"Same logic. If they were his, he would have buried them in his suitcase. Probably would've locked it."

"I'm afraid that leaves us limited explanations."

"Other than someone trying to set me up, what's your best guess?"

"I exaggerated. That is the only alternative I see."

"So, the question is who and why?" I asked.

"Pretty much."

"The police?"

"You've been watching too much TV. How about Derek?"

"Talk about not making sense. I go to jail, and he becomes the custodial parent. He didn't volunteer for the job when Natalee was born, and I doubt he's grown into it. Plus, he would have college to pay for. It's not Derek."

"Just asking. You wearing this burgundy outfit around him?"

I ignored his comment. "I can't explain it." I continued scanning the inventory. Page six detailed the contents of Derek's suitcase from the guestroom. Besides the airline tickets, I got a description of the underwear he brought with him. He was now a boxer guy.

"Shit." I came to an entry for eighty-six-hundred in twenties in a plain white business envelope.

"Yep," Rad said. "That's the second thing I guessed would grab your attention."

"Tell me there are no more surprises."

"Not surprises, exactly, but look at the investigative report." He handed me two stapled sheets. I zeroed in on a notation *Assassination: murder and revenge!!?* scribbled next to the word *poem*. My verse might not win prizes, but I understood how it planted suspicions. I cursed myself for not making sure I had all the poems before I called the police.

As I digested the import, Rad said, "Sounds like you either have a vivid imagination or a shady past. Care to tell me which?"

"A bit of each, maybe." I recalled every damning word of the poem:

> *Death, not easy,*
> *brutal, barbarous, bloody,*
> *better than he deserved.*
>
> *His life ebbed.*
> *Shrouding me*
> *with the burden*
> *of survival.*

I set the report aside and clenched my teeth. I had no desire to rehash the past.

"Why don't you tell me about the Casey who wrote that poem?" Rad gave me several seconds. When words failed me, he rested his hand on my forearm and prodded. "I think you need to tell me about it. You can't keep your private investigator in the dark. You have to trust me."

"It isn't important. It's longer than a stretch as a motive for Derek's disappearance."

"Apparently Lockhart thinks it's a short hop, skip, and a jump from there to guilty. So, talk."

14

Sweat dampened my underarms. My gut burned. "Could I have a glass of ice water?" I asked. The lace-embroidered napkin slid from my lap to the floor. I grabbed a kleenex and blew my nose, but words defied me.

"It's okay, Casey. There's no hurry." Rad fumbled with a glass, plunked in ice cubes, turned on the faucet. Never took his eyes off me.

Where should I start? I thought about the months after Scroggins's attack. I had quit my job, spent way too many hours in bed with covers pulled over my head to seal out the light. I let the phone ring without answering it. In a good week, I showered or brushed my teeth more than once. External bruises healed. I turned my back to my husband, unable to tolerate his touch.

When my survival instinct kicked in, I immersed myself in self-defense classes. A poster in the gym quoted Susan B. Anthony: I DECLARE TO YOU THAT WOMAN MUST NOT DEPEND UPON THE PROTECTION OF MAN BUT MUST BE TAUGHT TO PROTECT HERSELF. The words offered hope. I was on my way to an orange belt in six months. Each time I punched, kicked, kneed, or elbowed a vital point, I aimed the blow at *him*. Jimmy Scroggins. Derek bought a gun. A .38 special. He taught me to shoot. Even with a gun, I wasn't safe. *He* was still out there.

I gave Rad a bare bones summary of the attack, whispering so his kitchen walls couldn't overhear and judge me. I dabbed my wet cheeks with wadded tissues and stared at my teacup, avoiding his eyes. "In spite of Derek's halfhearted insistence that I go to the authorities, I figured he was relieved that I refused to bring the police into it. I had no proof but believed my attacker was his cocaine source, and the creep had been in my house before. I believed his connection to Derek was the reason he hadn't killed me. He figured we didn't dare go to the police.

Derek took the couch and rugs to the dump. We moved the next weekend in case the bastard came back. I think it scared my husband clean. If that didn't, the fact that Derek was about to become a father did."

Rad pinched the bridge of his nose between his thumb and forefinger and squinted hard at me, body language that forced me to answer his unspoken question.

"Yes, Natalee is Derek's daughter." I stared out the kitchen window. The sun was coming up in the east like this was a normal day. I paused, shoring up courage before my confession. "It isn't the rape that complicates my current problem," I said. "It's what came after. That's the story I need to tell you. I'm pretty sure it doesn't have a thing to do with my study or what Lockhart has learned, but you asked, and you deserve to know."

"I'm listening." Two words, but Rad spoke them softly, slowly, in a way that conveyed the concern his tough-guy veneer didn't make easy for him to express.

"Several months after the assault I noticed an ad posted at a local supermarket for a chest of drawers. I wanted to refinish a small dresser for a nursery. I ripped off a phone number tag and called. A woman answered. She gave me an address and said she would be home that afternoon.

"I pulled in front of a faded bungalow a few blocks beyond Ann Arbor's student ghetto. I was skittish going to an unknown location, even to meet a woman, and considered aborting the errand. I dealt with my reservations by transferring Derek's gun from my purse to my coat pocket."

My voice told the story, but it sounded emotionless and far away.

"A man answered the door. He stood in shadows, all the shades drawn. Before he said anything, I told him, 'I talked to your wife about a chest of drawers she has for sale.' I moved my right hand into my pocket and gripped the gun. It was the reaction of a rape victim.

"He stepped aside to let me in and pointed to a small room beyond where we stood. He said, 'She ain't here but told me someone might stop by.' My eyes adjusted from the bright sunlight to the darkened room. He was clean-shaven, his hair short. He had added a few pounds, but when he spoke, I had no doubt. I recognized *his* voice."

I looked at Rad. He had emptied his coffee cup but made no move to get more. I sipped water, chewed on an ice cube before continuing.

"By then the bastard blocked my exit. He eyeballed me like he knew me from somewhere but couldn't quite place where. 'How much she say she wanted for it?' he asked. I managed to stammer, 'Twenty dollars.'

"After a few seconds, he urged, 'Go on in,' and pointed through the open bedroom door, 'I kin show it to you, if you got cash.'"

Rad rubbed his forearm across his forehead to remove the sweat beaded there. I clenched my mouth tight, wanting to hold back the story, but I knew I had to finish.

"I thought maybe I could take a look at the chest, give him an excuse of why it was too small, too big, too something, and get the hell out of there.

"He followed a step behind me into the room. 'Nice perfume,' he said. He touched my shoulder and let his fingers linger there.

"I spun around, swerved to one side, desperate to cut and run. He seemed to sense my movement and stepped the same way. It surprised me that I didn't slump, quivering, to the floor. Instead, I grasped my swollen belly. It was about more than me. My baby had a right to live. I withdrew the revolver. Shot him before I lost my nerve."

Rad's sagging face turned ashen. He reached over and clasped my trembling hands as though he could will me his strength.

"The bullet got the guy in the side of his neck and blood spurted on the walls and on the little dresser. He didn't exactly drop. More like he fell, knocking me to the floor. A beer bottle he had been holding struck the chest of drawers and shattered before he landed on me. He swiped the jagged chunk of glass that remained in his hand across my arm. Then he dropped it and grabbed me by the hair. With his other hand, he held his neck to stop the bleeding. It was pointless."

I rolled up my sleeve and showed Rad the ragged scar on my left arm. "The gash was deep, and the sting surprised me. Jimmy Scroggins—I learned his name from the newspaper account of cops finding a drug pusher's body—was losing a lot of blood. I squirmed away and stood up. He strained, tried to rise, but fell back. Blood half-gurgled, half-gushed like a tired drinking fountain.

"Rad, self-defense wouldn't fly. I hadn't reported the sexual assault, and I was in his house. But I feared being raped again. Shooting the bastard has never troubled my conscience. I hoped the cops would label it a feud between drug dealers and clients. The irony isn't lost on me. To this day, I've never even tried cocaine. Yet I suspected then, and believe to this day, that Scroggins was Derek's supplier."

Rad's closed eyes, said he had heard enough, but I added, "I'm certain Lockhart is dangling a line for clues. He can't possibly know about Jimmy Scroggins."

15

Neither Rad nor I spoke for several minutes. I needed time to regulate my erratic breathing and regain my composure. With the hardest part over, Rad got the lesser details. "After the rape and before I shot Scroggins, I had struggled to put the pieces of my life back together. Derek was a part of the puzzle that no longer fit. He tired of waiting for me to get over it. I tired of him looking at me like I was damaged goods. Maybe we just tired of each other."

Telling the story exhausted me, but Rad had asked for everything.

"Monogamy wasn't a word in Derek's vocabulary," I said, "either before or after Jimmy Scroggins. Besides other women, alcohol became his constant companion. We attended one counseling session together. He crowded one end of Dr. Weiner's overstuffed sofa. I scooched as far to the other side as possible without severing the armrest.

"When we got home, Derek said, 'I don't have a problem. And you need to move on. Forget it. Be grateful you're alive. It's over.'

"We had an ugly fight. During the next several hours, he medicated himself into a stupor with Jack Daniel's. By the time I went to bed he was stumbling, and his words tripped over one another. Later, when he slid in next to me, the stench of booze revolted me as much as his clumsy attempt to make up. At first, I pushed him away, but his whiskey was stronger than my energy to resist. I lay there, not speaking, not resisting, like I was dead. I'm sure if you asked him, he would say it was the last time we made love. For me, it was another violation. That was two months after the rape, and I'd had a period in between. There was no doubt I conceived Natalee that night."

Rad balled his hands into fists the size of ham-hocks. The dangerous look in his eyes unnerved me. "For your sake and Natalee's, I hope Derek's alive. But promise me that if we find him, I get one good punch at the bastard before we turn him over to the cops."

I shook my head. I wouldn't wish those lethal weapons on anyone, not even Derek. "Natalee was born nine months later. By then my marriage was as dead as Jimmy Scroggins. My life needed new direction. I was accepted to Georgetown Law and moved my daughter and me to Washington, D.C."

I blew my nose again, wiped my eyes, and sat up straight. "Other than a day here or there, when my obstinate mind demands a detailed rehash, that ugliness is behind me."

Rad puffed his cheeks full of air and blew it out slowly. "Maybe."

"I didn't hurt Derek, although there were times in the past that I would have relished the opportunity. He isn't dead. I feel it."

"But you can see how it looks? A cheating ex-husband back in town. The cops' theory may be that he forced himself on you. I assume you'll admit you didn't want him here."

"I already told the police that much. That's the thing. I didn't want him here, but he isn't important enough anymore to make an issue of it. I work all day. I spend a few evenings with Tom while Derek gets time with his daughter before he heads back to California. Not a huge deal. Uncomfortable. Aggravating. Nothing more."

"*More* is exactly what a good prosecutor will make a jury think."

"Rad, there's no body. Without a body, it would be a hell of a stretch."

"Men have fried on nothing more than circumstantial evidence. In a few of those cases, the corpse was never found."

"If there's no body, there's no cause of death, there's no time of death, there's no way crime scene geeks can probe for trace. This is insanity. I don't know why we're talking about it. Maybe Derek is off on a blowout bender and hasn't listened to the news."

Rad shuffled through the papers, then asked, "Is there anything else about you or your recent burglary I should know?"

I was grateful to change subjects. "What? After my darkest secrets, you think I'm holding out?"

"I'm just asking."

Compared to telling him I had killed a man; the glossies were a summer picnic in Petoskey. I uncrossed my arms, took a deep breath. After a minute of working up my nerve, I said, "There are some eight-by-ten glossies of Derek missing . . . and a bottle of expensive perfume that was in the drawer with them."

He ignored the comment about the perfume. "What kind of glossies?"

"He was naked." I tried to say it with a straight face and without blushing.

Rad's mouth dropped open. "My sweet little CJ has a kinky side?" Even after he spoke, his lips didn't fully close, and his eyes remained open wide.

I shook my head. "It's not like that."

"Enlighten me."

"The pictures were of Derek and his lover-of-the-week, an acquaintance of mine. A private detective with a telescopic lens and no concern for privacy laws delivered them to me."

"Didn't you once read me the riot act for doing something similar?"

If he expected me to look sheepish, I'm sure he was gratified. "I never said I was perfect. I had been raped, my marriage fell apart, and I was pregnant. You can understand why I considered it a bleak period in my life. I believed Derek slept around. He denied it. I had to know."

"Keep going," Rad said.

"I never had to use them. By the time we filed for divorce we were broke. There was no property to slice up. Pretty straightforward stuff. But I had paid for those pictures, in more ways than one. A few showed a frontal view, fully aroused. I haven't seen the real thing since before those photos were taken. Derek doesn't know they exist."

Rad bit his upper lip with his teeth and scrunched his eyes as though trying to bring the situation into clearer focus. "Unless he's your burglar. Any ideas why someone else would want those glossies?"

"Certainly not for blackmail. I don't give a damn if they're posted on the internet."

"The cops didn't itemize any photos on the inventory," he said. "And they would have if they found them in the study or Derek's suitcase. From the way you describe the son of a bitch, I think he would find them flattering. I don't think he would destroy them." He paused but was apparently ready to let it go. "Besides the pictures, anything else missing?"

"Not unless the thief took my rosewood-handled, boar-bristle hairbrush. It's missing from my bathroom." His expression didn't budge from serious, so

I added, "Only kidding, I'm sure my cat traipsed off with it clutched in her mouth because it smelled like me."

He ignored the cat comment and pushed on. "I know the cops asked, but this is me, Casey. I need the short list of people who might hate you, need something from you, or know anything about the Jimmy Scroggins incident."

"It might not be a short list of people who have a grudge—comes with my work territory. But no one I can think of would do this. As for blackmail, Scroggins is a secret between you and me. Derek might have suspicions because the same afternoon Scroggins died, I drove myself to the hospital and got sixteen stitches in my arm. I concocted a story that I had been rollerblading, lost control and skidded under the edge of a parked-car bumper. Not the most believable explanation, but no one pushed it.

"I told Derek someone stole the gun from my locker at the gym. I never offered details. He reported it missing to the Ann Arbor police. To save me from going through their questions, he told them it was stolen from his car, and he couldn't be sure when."

"Where is that gun now?" Rad asked.

"Deep in the middle of the Huron River. Before I pitched it, I tried to render it untraceable. To make a rifling match harder, I mixed a couple of tablespoons each of bleach and white vinegar, added a small amount of steel wool, spooned it down the barrel, and swished it around with the end of a straightened coat hanger covered with cheesecloth. I filed off the serial number, but I was convinced the cops could perform some magic trick to retrieve it, so I dismantled the gun with a screwdriver and scattered pieces over a twenty-mile stretch of mucky river bottom."

"Not bad. I like the part about the bleach. Doubt it worked but pretty creative. Maybe you and I aren't so different after all." That thought seemed to amuse him, and he beamed the first smile I had seen since we sat down an hour earlier. "Any jealous lovers or wives of lovers, anything like that?"

"No one." Even though it was Rad, or maybe because it was Rad, I didn't mention Katya Gannon. Chace and I ended it before Katya caught on. A couple of hang-up phone calls proved nothing. I would bet my next three paychecks those were wrong numbers. *If Katya had a clue, wouldn't she have done something before now?*

16

I would have traded a hundred bucks for a good excuse to duck out of work. With neither the hundred bucks nor the excuse, I preferred poring over new cases at my desk to surmising how the evidence stacked up against me or wondering whether Derek's bloodied and battered body lay sprawled in a dumpster.

In the four days since my study was rampaged, I had postponed shopping with Natalee for her homecoming dress, shelved the decision of whether she could stay out all night at a chaperoned after-party, and avoided mentioning the tattoo. I longed to be a regular mother again and worry about everyday problems.

"Hi, Shirley," I called as I strode past my boss's open door. Some things hadn't changed. She ignored me, and I needed an Alka-Seltzer. Serious under-medication for what was coming.

While I waited for my computer to download email, I grabbed a bottle of water. Poured half of its contents into my teacup, dropped in two fizzy tablets, waited for them to dissolve. Then swallowed a couple of swigs before I read:

Why are you ignoring me? Mistake. Your past isn't buried as deep as you think. If you're smart, like your Georgetown Law degree suggests you should be, you'll get back to me. Before you share this email with Sergeant Lockhart, you need to know that could be hazardous to Natalee's health. Don't waste time trying to track this. It's a temporary email account, and I'm using a Wi-Fi hot spot. I'll use a different one next time.

My chest thumped the erratic pattern of an out-of-control jackhammer as I considered Natalee in danger. If this was a legitimate threat, how could I protect her? I chewed the insides of my cheeks and bit my lips. I recognized the sender's tag, Advice4U@yahoo.com. I had received earlier emails from that address. I clicked on the DELETED ITEMS in my mail and retrieved the prior messages. The first had arrived the day after the burglary:

Good morning, Ms. Lawrence. We're going to be business partners. I've got a proposition that will prove advantageous to you. Email me a response, and I'll provide details.

It sounded like a Central Bank of Nigeria hoax. I had deleted it. The second email had come yesterday.

I haven't gotten your reply. You're missing a one-time-only opportunity.

Again, no alarms. My mind had been on bigger obstacles than a pathetic Internet scam.

Rereading the most recent email, I concluded that whoever sent it had access to more than a state bar directory. I was a chosen target. For what? Were they bluffing, or did they know about Jimmy Scroggins? I clenched my teeth, trapping a lump that rose from my heart to my throat.

I was afraid to ignore the email, nearly as afraid to learn more. I touched REPLY . . . typed *I'm listening.*

I suffered through the day alternately handling mindless paperwork and checking for an email response. Imploding panic killed my concentration. I decided to leave an hour early.

"Hey, Shirl. Hold down the fort. I'm out of here." My boss, nose buried in case law for a brief she was writing, ignored me. I programmed my voice to bubbly. "Have a great weekend . . . and thank you, I'll have one too." I lied.

Under other circumstances, a night with Tom was right up there with inheriting a million bucks. But Natalee was staying with Trish and that unleashed a landslide of emotions. A twinge of jealousy started the avalanche. It reminded me that my daughter preferred Trish's mom to help them with their science project due on Monday. Next, useless guilt cried for attention. If we were in danger, Nat should be with me. Finally, inadequacy trumped both jealousy and guilt. When I hesitated before giving my approval for the girls' weekend plan, Trish's mom said, "If the burglar returns, isn't Natalee safer here? My husband's an ex-marine, I'm sure he can protect us from a thief." I hated that she was right.

I unlocked Tom's front door at five-thirty. I had an hour before he arrived home. I had promised dinner, and although I had no appetite, cooking passed the time. I set groceries on the counter and rubbed my forearm where the loops of plastic bags had dug into my flesh. I tossed my jacket over a chair and stepped into the galley kitchen. I deposited the heavy cream, feta, and freshly grated Parmesan in the refrigerator, thankful I hadn't relied on Tom for any ingredients. A carton of Diet Coke and a take-home bag from El Azteco added little to my menu. A Teflon-coated frying pan rested in the sink. I squeezed a drop of liquid detergent onto the cooking surface, ran some hot water over it, called it good. I sautéed scallops and shrimp before turning the burner to warm, cooked linguini, and then diced apples and pears for a fruit salad.

With dinner under control, I filled a tall glass with ice, moved to the living room, and reached for the scotch. Tom had suggested a movie. My eyes wandered over the titles that stood on the shelf next to the booze: *Fargo, Inglourious Basterds, The Big Lebowski, Raising Arizona.* He had a copy of every Quentin Tarantino or Coen brother DVD ever released. Wedged between the efforts of his favorite directors were *Nights in Rodanthe*, and the oldie, *Fried Green Tomatoes.* Hours of great entertainment, but tonight I wasn't looking to be entertained. I poured myself a stiff drink.

I still had a half hour before Tom waltzed in. I drew myself a hot bath, eased into the water and closed my eyes. The conversation with Lockhart roared back, chortling something about "how does it feel to be a murder suspect?" I replayed every question and my answers from yesterday's meeting. I reconsidered the information Rad had shared: the inventory, the investigative report, the drugs, the poem. How much did the cops know? And who the hell was Advice4U? There had to be answers and connections, but I couldn't piece them together. I was grateful when the front door slammed. A second later, from the kitchen, I heard the tinny bang of a pan lid.

"Something smells amazing," Tom yelled.

I guessed that he referred to the garlic, not a lingering trace of my Chanel Chance. "I'll be right out," I called back. I toweled off, grabbed his terrycloth bathrobe from the hook on the back of the door, and slipped it around me. As I padded into the kitchen, I caught him popping a whole scallop into his mouth.

"Sorry, I couldn't resist." He kissed me, then pulled a bottle of chardonnay from a skinny brown bag and reached for the corkscrew. "You look like a little girl in that bathrobe, hair pinned up, and not a trace of makeup."

"That's me. Wholesome, young, and clean. Except it's a two-scotch night." I handed him my empty glass, and he freshened the ice.

"I assume this means you don't want this overpriced chard?" He poured himself the wine and followed me into the living room where he added a generous splash of Chivas to my drink and handed it to me. "Bad news?" he asked.

I nodded. He watched me sip the scotch. Waited for me to explain.

Sex serves many purposes. At that moment, I craved an antidote to fear. Alcohol provided courage to ignore the small inner voice that insisted it wouldn't work. I swallowed and appreciated the burn in my throat. Stone-cold sober was overrated. I kept my eyes fixed on Tom's and whispered, "I need you."

"You've got me." His smirk said he knew where this was going and liked it.

I undid his belt buckle, unsnapped and unzipped his pants, and gave them a slight tug so they dropped to his ankles. His black dress socks stood dignified above sagging trousers. His eyes shifted from confused to surprised to hungry, all in a flash. His mouth touched mine and covered it with enthusiastic kisses.

I pushed my tongue between his lips and tasted the fruity wine mingled with the fire of my scotch. I pressed tightly against him, backed us toward the white alpaca rug in front of the couch. I untied the robe and let it fall to the floor.

Tom hobbled out of his pants. He kissed my breasts, but I ended his foreplay by dropping to my knees. I grabbed his buttocks, letting my fingers dig into his warm flesh, and pulled him to my mouth. Nothing hesitant, tentative, or demure in my grasp. My passion, unhampered by convention or reserve, was functional, forthright. At the same time impoverished. Love-making was an avenue to somewhere other than where I was.

I lay back on the stringy, matted fur rug and closed my eyes. No searching his sweet, sympathetic, understanding face.

"You're beautiful," he whispered in my ear and followed it with, "I love you."

I put my fingers to his lips to quiet the words. "Now."

He entered gently.

"Harder . . . harder . . . harder. Oh, god. Oh, god." My blasphemy sounded raspy. My breath came in gasps. With each push, my fear took a baby-step backwards. I sucked in air and tried to exhale the feelings of the past several days. I hoped climax would also expel the dread and the anger. For a single moment, my mind was blessedly empty.

Unlike other times we made love, there was no joy, no fun, no humor. No one-degree-cooler-than-the-center-of-the-sun sexual heat that usually consumed us. None of the enthusiasm that worried us that the apartment walls, papier-mâchéed together and as soundproof as mosquito netting, were too thin to contain our lusty moans. This time it had been an act not so much enjoyed as needed and completed.

I buried my face against his chest. Sex didn't alter the circumstances or make me feel less alone. Nothing had changed except that I needed a shower and felt awkward in front of my lover.

I started to rise. Tom reached out and drew me back. He held me. We lay in silence for several minutes. With one finger he traced the outline of my mouth, then kissed me so softly I didn't feel his lips as much as the warmth of them on mine.

Again, he asked, "So, tell me. What happened?"

I took a deep breath and collected my thoughts. I described my meeting with Will Radowski, the insurance policy, the police reports—including the pills and the dope they had found in my desk—and the emails minus the part about knowing something from my past. I would never tell Tom about the poems or Jimmy Scroggins.

"What's Radowski's take?"

"He thinks I'm being set up. Logical conclusion if you add it all together."

"Do you think it's Derek?" He punctuated his words with light kisses on the top of my head.

"I doubt it. He has no reason."

"That's good, isn't it?"

Unless he's dead. I fought to kill the thought, mouthed the words before I voiced them. "Unless he's dead." I took a small sip of the chardonnay from Tom's glass, but the weight of my utterance turned the wine bitter. *Unless he's dead.*

"I have this uneasy feeling," I said. "Maybe it's guilt."

"Not what I would expect from the woman who preaches guilt is a useless emotion."

"I've fantasized less than charitable scenarios about Derek since he arrived."

"That sounds so Catholic. As an ex-altar boy, I promise that whatever you thought, it didn't hurt Derek. It had nothing to do with what he's done or what's been done to him."

I let Tom hold me, but I couldn't quiet the thought: *Then where the hell is he?*

17

Saturday, October 1

I woke early and tiptoed into the living room to watch the sun breech the horizon. Flame-colored streaks splashed across the eastern sky. I opened a window to eliminate the fishy smells from last night's dinner. The air that wafted in promised another unseasonably warm day. Two weeks ago, I might have taken advantage of such a flawless morning and headed to South Haven Beach with Natalee. Today, more urgent matters pressed for attention.

I curled up on the couch and waited for Tom to emerge from the bedroom, half-asleep and tousled. To crowd out less pleasant images vying for space, I filled my mind with memories from our first date. I pictured him sitting in the booth at Bennigan's and the grin that exploded when he looked up and saw me approach. I pictured his long, ringless fingers wrapped around his drink. I pictured the silver and onyx earring in his left ear. I had asked him if it meant he had a rebellious streak. His face turned serious. He told me his younger brother died at thirty-one of AIDS.

"I have worn his earring in my right ear ever since," he said. "My way of holding on to a piece of him."

When Tom joined me, he was barefoot but already dressed in blue jeans and a black t-shirt.

He leaned over and kissed me on the forehead before he dropped onto the couch beside me. "You look like you could use California Eggs Benedict," he said. "Your share of the linguini ended up in Tupperware. You didn't eat more than a bite or two last night. I'll spring for breakfast at Beggar's."

I laid my head on his shoulder. "Thanks for the offer, but I'm not hungry."

"I was afraid you might say that. Casey, you've got to—"

"Eat. I know. But I woke up with a strange appetite to do laundry, vacuum, scrub toilets . . . the fun stuff. I'll grab an Egg McMuffin on my way home."

"Seriously? I lose out to a vacuum cleaner and McDonald's?" His dejected expression said my intended housekeeping jag befuddled him.

I worked up a smile that defied my state of mind. "Nothing personal. I need to make peace with my house. Scour away the taint that covers it."

"I don't like the idea of you going home alone. Who knows what this emailing lunatic might do."

"I've considered that, but whoever Advice4U is, he wants something from me. He won't hurt me until he sees if he can get it. I've told him I'll listen. I may not be brave enough to stay alone at night but broad daylight? I'll be fine."

Tom ran his fingers through my hair, gently twisting the curls. "How about lunch then? You don't want to overindulge this cleaning compulsion."

"Better pass on that too. I need a couple of hours at the office." I sat up straight, drew my feet out from under me, and planted them on the floor, pondering how to put my thoughts into words. "I didn't want to leave before you got up. About last night—"

"What about last night?" he asked.

"I shouldn't have drunk so much, and I didn't mean for it to be so—"

He shook his head and pressed a finger against my lips. "Don't analyze it. We're adults. We care about each other. It was good."

I relaxed. He was right. Better to leave it alone.

He stood, pulled me up. "I'll walk you to your car. The sooner you finish, the quicker I see you. In the meantime, keep your house doors locked and your cell phone in your pocket."

"No argument."

"I could grab paperwork and tackle it at your house while you humor this neatenizing streak."

"Tempting, but neither of us would get much done." I rolled my eyes, patted his butt. "I'll call if I change my mind and to let you know about tonight, your place or mine." I could handle the house's creaks and groans with the sun shining, but I still needed someone to help me keep the darkness company.

An extravagance of purple asters and white mums brightened the front yard of my house. Natalee and I had spent a weekend in late spring creating the flower garden. We alternately dug in dirt and read paragraphs from *Perennials for Dummies*, a used book I had found at the Okemos Library sale. She giggled when I rubbed my hand across my forehead and left a streak of rich black potting soil. I cupped some water from the hose and splashed it over my face, then doused her for laughing at me. She tried to back away from the spray, tripped over the handle of the shovel, and landed on her back in the middle of our lawn as Rich Spaulding, the co-captain of the Okemos football team, drove down our street.

"There will be payback," she said.

The flowers didn't seem to mind our irreverent approach to gardening and showed splashy blooms, defying an early September frost that had killed our neighbor's plants.

From outside, the place looked like nothing had changed except there was a Meridian Township police car parked next door in Mr. Anderson's driveway. I assumed they were pumping him for information about me.

I pressed the garage door opener and fought the panic that Derek's Porsche rekindled. I stepped into the kitchen and bolted the door behind me. A thud sounded from the basement family room. *A maniac lying in wait, ready to attack.*

Before I fainted or fled, Jussy appeared at the top of the open stairway between the kitchen and lower level.

"You trying to kill me?" I had heard that same dull thunk more nights than I could count. Jussy crash-landing from the back of her favorite chair before she flew up the steps. This morning I imagined villains lurking in every shadow, and Jussy's noise sounded different. I bent and stroked my purring cat. "Happy to see I'm alive, huh, or thinking about a can of Fancy Feast?" I opened the cat food and turned my face to avoid the liver smell. "Sorry, Tom's apartment doesn't allow pets. Scary being here alone, right? You're safe. No one's out to get the family cat."

The house swallowed me into its mirthless presence. I put on some old Buddy Holly to change its mood, cranked up the volume, and danced a first load of laundry downstairs to the beat of "Brown Eyed Handsome Man." I glanced around, in case the noise had been Advice4U and not the cat. In spite of my skittishness, no one jumped out at me, and neither the camelback couch nor the pink flowered wingback chairs had moved an inch. Not even the library books Nat had left on the counter had been disturbed.

By eleven, I had folded the first two loads of clothes, scrubbed floors that hadn't been swept or mopped since the police tracked in five days ago, changed the CD to Madonna's "Hard Candy," and listened to her promise to supply me any flavor I wanted. The kitchen smelled clean again, thanks to Pine-Sol. But whiffs of fresh air and Jack Pine couldn't make me forget what had happened upstairs where the taint lingered.

Closed doors and a police warning kept me from the study, but the guestroom wasn't off limits. I schlepped the vacuum and dust spray up the steps. The bedding that Derek slept on had been collected and bagged as evidence. The police could check it for semen but wouldn't find any, at least not mixed with my body fluids. When Tom stayed over earlier in the week, I had remade the bed with clean linens.

A set of never used Ralph Lauren Edgefield Plaid sheets remained in their original package on a closet shelf collecting dust. *Use the good stuff*, a voice reminded me, *or your heirs will.*

I pulled the crisp linens from a clear-plastic, zippered case, shook them out, and rubbed my hand over their cool, smooth finish. I stripped the faded, worn set from the bed and put on the new ones. As I tucked the sheets between the mattress and box springs, my fingers grazed a piece of paper. I pulled out a slip, no bigger than the strip from a fortune cookie. On it was written: *K* and a phone number I didn't recognize. Anyone could have put it there. Nat often invited more friends to spend the night than she could comfortably cram in her room. They spilled over into the guestroom.

I shoved the scrap into my jeans pocket and continued making the bed. Maybe I would stop at Macy's on my way to the office and buy the matching bed skirt and duvet. I vowed to reform my hoarder instincts. I threw the old sheets down the laundry chute. I would wash them and start a box for Goodwill.

While I waited for the last load of laundry to finish the wash cycle, I poured myself a glass of iced tea, sat at the counter, and dialed Tom.

"I'm thinking of inviting Jon and Ginny to play euchre or Scrabble tonight. You up for that . . . and spending the night here?"

"Yes to both," he said.

"I'll pick you up. Otherwise, you have to leave your car in the driveway. The Porsche has appropriated the extra space in my garage. Better to not broadcast you're staying over. I don't need neighbors fretting that I set a bad example."

I dialed Ginny. While I waited for her to answer, I thought about the day the Beckmans moved in. Ginny had rung my doorbell after the last piece of their furniture was off-loaded from the moving van.

"I'm Ginny Beckman, your new neighbor." She had thrust her hand toward me as we took stock of each other. At thirty-nine, she had wrinkle-free, porcelain skin and the figure of a Barbie doll, including the oversized breasts.

She said, "Jon, my handsome, usually organized husband, made a slight miscalculation. He packed our first-night necessities in a wooden crate, neatly labeled it, and nailed it shut, but he forgot to leave out something to open it." Her smile lit up a face that belonged on the cover of *Vogue*. "You don't happen to have a crowbar?"

"I do," I said. "Come in." She stood in the entry while I retrieved the tool from the garage. I handed it to her. "If you need a break, I could order a Spag's four-cheese pizza and stop by in forty-five minutes with a great Pinot Noir I've saved to share with new neighbors . . . if you drink wine. Otherwise, I've got a well-aged Coke Classic."

"Absolutely. We would love to try the neighborhood pizza, and a bottle of wine sounds like a perfect wind-down to an exhausting day." The friendship had been comfortable from those first moments.

Ginny answered on the fourth ring.

"It's Casey. Hope I'm not interrupting anything."

"Not at all. I just walked in from running errands. I knocked last night with a hot apple pie straight from the oven but no answer. We wondered where you were."

"I stayed at Tom's. I don't feel safe alone here at night. Still got the pie?" I had skipped the Egg McMuffin, and warm sweet apples that smelled of cinnamon sounded pretty damn good.

"Sure," she said. "Want me to bring it over?"

"Tempting. But let me practice some delayed gratification. Do you have plans for this evening?"

"Nope. Not unless you count doing mock-ups for a job I've got."

"How about a game night with Tom and me? The house feels weird. It needs an infusion of friends to change the karma. Bring the pie."

"And if it's awful, I blame it on being a day old."

Ginny's laugh reminded me of how much I missed her. "Let's say seven, and I'll make a pot of hearty homemade soup." I wanted to see the Beckmans and play-act ordinary. I didn't know if it would be my last chance to mimic normal.

18

It was a few minutes before noon, but I'd had enough alone time in the house. I headed for the G. Mennen Williams Law Building. On the way, I made my quick stop at the Meridian Mall. Macy's didn't have the duvet and bed skirt in queen-size, so I put them on order. I entered my office at twelve forty-five. The plan was to spend a couple of hours reviewing new complaints and then take care of as many piles of correspondence as I could before I picked up Tom.

Whoever said "The road to hell is paved with good intentions" must have had a premonition of what headed my way.

I picked up a new file that stared at me from the stack and read a letter addressed to Shirley Rathburn from the chair of the Board of Veterinary Medicine.

> *It has come to our attention by posted advertisements (see attached) and a phone call from the dissatisfied owner of a St. Bernard that Chiropractor Kenton Dallywell holds himself out as qualified to manipulate dogs. Treatment of animals is clearly beyond the scope of Dallywell's chiropractic license. The Board of Veterinary Medicine would appreciate an investigation and subsequent complaint filed against Dallywell. We look forward to a response at your earliest convenience.*

This was a turf war—the veterinarians didn't want chiropractors treating animals. I didn't go a hundred-fifty-thousand dollars in debt to Georgetown Law to protect dogs from chiropractors.

I set the dog file aside, picked up the next case, and skimmed the medical and investigative reports.

Patient D, the three-hundred-and-ten-pound complaining witness against psychiatrist Andrea Schultz, M.D., had written, *Dr. Schultz makes me get naked and then jump rope for twenty minutes before we start each session. After that, she screws me.*

I was flabbergasted. But even in my current state of mind, I couldn't suppress a politically incorrect grin. This was way more serious than manipulating dogs. I realized it would take skilled direct examination of the witness to convince an administrative law judge and the Board of Psychiatry that Dr. Schultz became aroused watching Patient D's rolls of flab, along with his flaccid penis, bobbing up and down. It would be an even tougher sell to persuade them that after this titillating foreplay, she wanted to get down and dirty with her sweaty patient. Both problems were superimposed on a system that often had a hard time believing a woman could take sexual advantage of a man. I would interview Patient D. He might be credible. And an interesting distraction.

I flipped to the pages below Patient D's statement. By charging his doctor with misconduct, Patient D waived confidentiality to his medical records. As I read the presenting history more closely, a sentence jumped from the page and stopped me short: *Patient admits he rubbed bacon grease on his penis to entice his German Sheppard to lick him to climax.*

If people didn't believe Bill Clinton when he told the grand jury he did not have sex with that woman, no judge would take the word of a patient who admitted to sex with his dog over that of an upstanding professional woman. I was sure Shirley Rathburn laughed her ass off thinking of me arguing this case. The good news was that I, too, could bury files.

I had enough of new files. I switched on my computer. While waiting for the screen to light up, I dug out the phone number from my jeans pocket and dialed the Lansing exchange. A recorded message announced, *"You have reached the office of Dr. Ahmed Khoury. We aren't available to take your call right now. If this is an emergency, go to your nearest emergency room. If it isn't an emergency, please leave us a message, and we will get back to you as soon as we can."* A logical explanation for why someone had written down that phone number escaped me. I credited Derek with the deed. He seemed the most logical candidate.

While I considered the import of my conclusion, I punched the SEND/RECEIVE on my Dell. The first message that came up promised to turn me into a modern-day Clarence Darrow. Below that tempting offer loomed an email from Advice4U@yahoo.com.

My right brain urged me to read it, while my left brain's ambivalent fear center insisted I crawl under my desk and hide. The message had been sent at six-fifteen last night. I stared at the address for a few seconds before opening it, steeling my courage. Goosebumps the size of marbles rose on my arms.

Good, Casey. I knew you'd be reasonable. Withdraw your complaint against Dr. Khoury. I have friends to make sure no one questions you. Dr. Khoury is a tiny fish. You are going to help me in many ways. I'll make it worth your effort. I don't expect something for nothing. Keep our arrangement between us, and the police will never hear my story about Jimmy Scroggins.

The silence mocked me, my mouth went dry, panic rampaged wild. There it was. *Someone knew.* The only person I had told was Rad. My blood turned to ice. My fingertips numbed. *How? Why had they waited seventeen years?*

Rad was in Grand Haven helping his older sister move into a retirement complex. He wouldn't be home until after midnight. I cursed myself for not buying that man a cell phone and showing him how to use it. Did the email require an immediate response, an agreement I would withdraw my complaint? Was it safe to wait to reply until Monday? Advice4U couldn't know I received the email on Saturday. I would call Rad tomorrow, seek his input.

Through sheer force of will, I overrode my lungs' reluctance to take in air. I gasped several deep breaths. I hit PRINT, retrieved a copy of the message, folded, and put it in my purse. I made copies of the three earlier emails and created a growing bundle.

After thirty minutes of staring into space, the best plan I came up with was to grab Natalee and disappear. It seemed more reasonable by the second. We could fill a suitcase, list the house with a Realtor who could only reach me on an untraceable cell, and vanish. Natalee would be safe. I wouldn't spend the next twenty years in prison. And Advice4U would be just another bad memory.

As I planned an absurd escape, my cell phone rang.

"Casey?" At first, I didn't recognize the voice. I had expected Tom or Nat, or even Advice4U, whose voice I wouldn't recognize. This voice was familiar.

"Derek?" I asked when it hit me.

"Yes."

"Where are you? What the hell is going on? The cops think you're dead." My brain needed a jumpstart. I tried to hold my voice steady, but fear, anger, and worry made me sound like a mewling infant.

"I know." His words echoed as though coming through a tunnel, and he didn't sound so good.

I had a million questions, but a jumble of words spilled out. "The study . . . blood . . . yours? The life insurance . . . I don't get—"

"Casey, stop. Listen. I don't know how much time I have."

"What's that supposed to—"

"Please." His voice cracked, and I heard deep choking sounds.

I stopped mumbling and let him talk.

"I'm fine for now . . ." Muffled gasps filled the pause. "I am so, so sorry for everything. You deserve better."

"Derek, where are you? I need to let the police know you're okay. Your daughter is worried sick about you." I couldn't manage, "so am I."

"You have raised her well. She's incredible. No matter what happens, she's the one good thing that came from my life. I'm proud of her. Promise me you'll make her understand that."

"You're scaring me. What the hell is this about?" I reached for a pad of paper to write down anything important, a phone number, an address, a name. My hands trembled with such force that I tipped over the dregs of yesterday's tea and soaked a pile of notes for an upcoming trial.

"The blood in the study was mine. They paid me for it. I got sucked in by nasty people. They threatened to kill me and hurt Natalee if I didn't cooperate. They want it to look like I'm dead. They knew about the life insurance and considered it a convincing touch. You have to back off some cases. They can destroy you. They believe you killed Jimmy Scroggins."

I remained quiet. Better to neither confirm nor deny.

He continued without waiting for a response. "I was supposed to disappear. But I couldn't leave and let the bastards ruin everything for you and Natalee. Casey, these men are no amateurs. They won't hesitate to do whatever it takes to get what they want.

"Be careful. Don't—" I heard a door slam before the phone went dead.

19

No! Derek! I pleaded with silence. "Damn it, I need to know where you are." I dropped the phone and lost my battle to hold back tears. The combined weight of old grief, new fears, and mistakes of a lifetime crushed me.

I don't recall how long I collapsed in a near catatonic state, but it was four-thirty when I drove to the Meridian Township Municipal Complex. A glance in the rearview mirror showed swollen bloodshot eyes staring back from a blotchy face. I appeared to have aged a decade since Monday. For the second time in as many days, I entered the squat brown building that housed the police department.

"I'm Casey Lawrence. I need to talk to Sergeant Lockhart about my missing ex-husband."

A quick look must have convinced the duty cop this was important. He made a call, and then said, "Sarge is on his way."

By the time Lockhart tromped into the reception area, my waterworks were in check. "Ms. Lawrence," he said as he studied me, "what's happened?" With a hand on my shoulder, he guided me into his office. I took the same chair I had occupied Thursday morning. I didn't have the same good feelings about this meeting I'd had then.

"Derek called. He's alive," I said. My body felt twitchy, like my nervous system was fueled by a dozen shots of straight caffeine. I willed Lockhart to leap tall buildings and locate Derek in the next five minutes.

"Where is he?" he asked.

Reality crashed with a thud. There was no magic elixir. "I don't know. But he's alive. The blood is his. Someone planted it to make it look like I hurt him."

The sergeant took out a notepad and picked up a pen, but instead of writing, he turned squinty, razor-sharp eyes toward me. "Why would someone do that?"

I couldn't share details about Scroggins and blackmail without prompting questions I was unprepared to answer. "I don't know. But my ex-husband *is* alive. He sounded anxious, worried, maybe even scared. Before he could give me details, he was cut off." I repeated the words of my conversation with Derek as close to exact as I remembered them, up to the part about Scroggins and fixing cases. Then I took a deep breath and slumped farther down in the chair. I waited for Lockhart to comment. His pursed lips and hesitation foreshadowed conclusions that I preferred he not draw.

He started with the easy stuff. "We're going to need your cell phone to trace the call."

"Of course." I pulled the cell and the emails that rested on top of it from my purse, handed over the phone, but held onto the messages. "You have to believe me. I talked to Derek."

"Let me make sure I've got this straight. Derek called and said someone was trying to set you up, but he didn't say who it was. He's alive, but you have no idea where he is. He's frightened, but you aren't sure why. It was his blood in the study, and he gave you a story about being paid for it. Is that pretty much the sum of it?" he asked.

"You make it sound—"

"I'm just repeating what you've told me. Maybe the phone trace will give us answers."

There was nothing I could add.

"Is that something important?" He pointed to the folded sheets of paper in my hand.

"No, sir. It's my to-do list for the day." I shoved the emails into my jacket pocket. I would have begged for help if I thought it would do any good, but distrust etched lines in the cop's baby face. If I gave him the messages from Advice4U, he would add, you've gotten emails that can't be traced; they could've come from anyone. You're the beneficiary of a hefty life insurance policy on which your ex pays the premiums. And we need to find out who this Jimmy Scroggins character is. Like I planned the whole thing.

I rose to leave. Even from where I sat, it sounded like an implausible story concocted by a guilty woman who knew the police would find her ex-husband's blood in her study. It could have been worse. He could have added, we know all about the fella you killed. That was still my secret. I planned to keep it that way.

My brain raced like a hamster on a wheel, and like the hamster, it spun circles that got me nowhere. Next to guilt, worry is the second most useless human emotion. Imagining horrors that might never materialize. If worry weren't enough, its close cousin, dread, polluted brain synapses already clogged by all that useless guilt and worry. I was a mess.

My life was complicated to an unbearable degree. I had told Lockhart about Derek, but not about Scroggins or Advice4U. I would tell Advice4U whatever he wanted to hear to keep Natalee safe and me out of jail. I would tell Natalee that her father called, but we got disconnected—damn cell phones and dropped calls. Luck surfaced in pitiful supply these days, but I hoped Derek would reappear before my daughter learned the police considered her mother the prime suspect in her father's disappearance. I wasn't sure how much to tell Tom. I trusted him, but he would disapprove any plan that cut Lockhart out of the loop. I would tell Rad everything when he returned. He was the one person I believed could help.

I considered calling Ginny and canceling our dinner plans but decided a temporary diversion beat obsessing over the skulking shadows surrounding me. It was too late for grocery shopping or making homemade chicken soup. I called McAlister's Deli on Marsh Road and asked if they could have a sandwich tray and large Greek salad ready in half an hour.

With sunglasses covering my puffy eyes, I picked up Tom. We stopped for the food and arrived home in time for me to grab an ice pack that I pressed against my face while I called Natalee to see how she was and tell her I would be home if she needed me.

I had ten minutes left to take a quick shower before Jon and Ginny were scheduled to arrive. I don't understand the chemical dance that fear enjoys with the sweat glands, but I smelled ripe. A double swipe of deodorant, a hasty comb through my hair, my favorite Susan Bristol sweater, and I looked more hospitable than I felt.

"What's the game?" Jon asked as he reached for the glass of whiskey and soda Tom held out to him.

"You're the guests," I said. "You name it."

"Scrabble," Jon said.

"Fine by me," I replied. "Tom? Ginny?" Both nodded. "Partners or everyone for themselves?"

"Each on our own. What do you say we make it a dollar a point?" Jon asked. He rose and stepped to the side table where he grabbed an inch-thick sandwich and added enough extra mustard to half-empty the small Dijon jar.

Ginny laughed and chimed in. "It will give me a chance to win some spending money. Jon's got us on a tight budget, saving for our cushy retirement."

"No way I'm playing for money when Jon's in his lucky mood." I wasn't ready for food. I laid a warm hand on my queasy stomach to quiet the squall raging there. While Tom and Ginny fixed their plates, I unboxed the game board, tile racks, and bag of letters.

We drew to see who started. Jon got an A and played 'sanding,' using all seven of his letters for a score of sixty-eight.

"I see why you wanted to play for money," Tom said. "Maybe we should reconsider partners. Jon and me against the women."

"Beginner's luck," Jon said.

Over the next four hours, we played three games. Jon won one, I won one, and Tom won one. The words I played—death, funeral, extort, threat, and squeeze—reflected my mood, but no one seemed to notice.

"Hey, if we went with total scores and had bet, Casey would be fifty bucks richer," Jon said.

"Only because I got both the Q and Z in the middle game and managed to unload them on a triple word using all my letters for a hundred twenty-five points," I said.

"How about one game of Euchre before we call it a night?" Ginny asked. "Or are you guys too tired?"

I looked at Tom. "Shuffle the cards," he said.

"This time let's give ourselves an incentive. Losing couple owes the winners dinner at Ukai Steakhouse," Jon said.

Tom and I nodded agreement. "Deal," I said.

The score stood eight to eight when a blunder I attributed to my distraction cost us the game. If he noticed my mistake, Tom overlooked it. He turned to Jon and said, "Looks like I take out a bank loan. We're buying."

Jon grinned like a kid whose dad pulled into the driveway with a shiny new Schwinn. It would cost us a few bucks, but it was worth it to make him that happy. For me, it was enough I had bluffed my way through the evening. But it wasn't over yet.

20

Sunday, October 2

I awoke at three and couldn't stop tossing. I slipped from bed and padded down the stairs, Tom's soft snores fading behind me. The full moon shone through open living room drapes and cast rivers of yellow across the oak flooring. Jussy sat on the windowsill surveilling the front yard for the slightest movement.

With the streetlights, I saw well enough to grab a mint tea bag and fill a mug with water from the bar hot shot before settling down on the sofa. My cat bounded to the floor, climbed on me, butted her head against my chin, and twisted around twice before settling down on my lap. Stroking her thick fur was better than the trifecta of serenity: a bubble bath, a glass of wine, and square breathing all at once.

My tea was half gone when I noticed car lights creep onto Cherry Street. I heard the soft hum of a finely tuned engine. The vehicle wormed its way to the end of the street, turned, and wended back to a halt in front of my house. I dropped Jussy and moved to the window for a better look.

The driver opened the car door. The interior light came on, but his face was angled away from me. He reached across to the passenger's seat and grabbed something before stepping out. He appeared tall, maybe six-three, but my frame of reference was the car against which he stood. In dark pants and hooded sweatshirt, he towered like the villain in a John Carpenter film.

I tiptoed to the front door, grateful it was steel rather than cheap wood. I fingered the deadbolt to make sure it was latched. I listened as the intruder clomped up the sidewalk and then the steps of my front porch. Eyeing him through the peephole, I saw only the hood covering his bowed head. I heard the doorknob twist. My knees wobbled. I crouched to the floor and leaned against the entry hall table that held a heavy diamond-cut crystal bowl Grandma Rosebud brought with her from England. If my body shook any harder, I risked sending the heirloom crashing to the tile floor.

The sound of footsteps retreated. I tested my shaky legs for strength, then inched back to the window and watched the shadowy figure return to his car. The interior light blinked on again, but the door shut so fast I saw no more than I had the first time. I tracked the vehicle as it moved halfway down the block before headlights came on.

I struggled to make out the license plate, but the attempt was futile. At first, my view was limited to the car's side, and when it was far enough away to see the back end, the numbers were indistinguishable by moonlight. It was a dark car—black, navy, maybe burgundy. It looked like a tank. My estimation of size was colored by fright. I guessed a Buick Park Avenue or BMW. Something big like that. I'm no whiz with cars. It was a four-door sedan with a rear passenger-side bumper sticker. Like the numbers on the plates, the sticker's message was blurred.

I slumped on the floor for several minutes after the car retreated from the neighborhood, afraid to breathe too loud. Afraid to move. Afraid to open the front door. My heart pounded with such vigor that I grabbed my chest to settle it down. The nervous sweat was back. A sick feeling of helplessness consumed the calm Jussy had imbued me with moments earlier. Terror was not a useless emotion.

Convinced that the uninvited guest was gone, I unfastened the deadbolt and opened the door about six inches. A rolled manila envelope dropped from where it had been propped between the doorknob and doorframe. I scooped it up, secured the deadbolt, and carried the delivery into my windowless first floor half-bath, where I shut the door before flipping on the light.

I undid the metal clasp and opened the envelope wide enough that I could peer inside. I imagined nothing deadly fitting in that skinny space. Still, my guts churned. My chilled hands trembled like trees in a twister. More than keen intellect told me that nothing good was left by a hooded thug in the dead of night. I extracted a thin stack of photos. A half page of paper stapled to the top picture obscured the subject, but I would have gambled my full account of vacation leave that I had recovered my missing pictures of Derek. I read the computer-generated note that smelled of Divine Folie.

I'm disappointed. Your choice of company this afternoon was reckless. Lockhart isn't going to help his chief suspect. Maybe you need more encouragement. You have until Tuesday noon to withdraw the complaint against Dr. Khoury. Give my best to Natalee. I hope she enjoyed the weekend with her friend.

In my tiny fortress, I collapsed against the door, a trapped animal trying to figure its next move. Lockhart had my cell. I crept to the kitchen and used the landline to dial Rad's number. He had told me he was driving home late, so I had planned to call him in the morning. It was now technically morning and this couldn't wait. Rad lived alone, so at least I wasn't bothering anyone else when I woke him. "It's Casey. Sorry about the ungodly hour. I need to see you."

21

Sunday morning, I dropped Tom at his place and pulled back into my driveway with enough time to shower and start the coffee before Rad arrived. He appeared on my doorstep gripping a bag of Krispy Kremes in one hand and a small black plastic case in the other. I answered the door barefoot, dressed in baggy blue jeans and a navy and gold sweatshirt that proclaimed: FRIENDS DON'T LET FRIENDS BE UNIVERSITY OF MICHIGAN FANS. He was a staunch supporter of the Wolverines. My hair was wet and gathered into a pony tail.

"Why in hell would you open the door without knowing who it was?" He frowned back at my freshly scrubbed face.

"I checked the peephole."

"Not so, CJ. My finger covered it."

I wanted to scream, *my life is bad enough without you testing me*, but I skipped the first part and just said, "Testing me?"

"Something like that. You failed and—"

"I knew it was you." I stepped back from the door to let him enter.

He wasn't through lecturing. "Lame. At best, you *thought* it was me."

"You're right. It was careless. Anxious to see you, I guess."

"I'm flattered. But, seriously, kid, until we know you're safe, you gotta be careful."

"I promise." I grabbed the donuts from his outstretched hands and smirked. "For me?"

"The breakfast of champions," he said.

"Coffee?"

"Do geese fly south for the winter?" Rad moved three flowered pillows to the side and plopped down on my couch. It looked too fragile to hold a man whose weight probably doubled mine. Laugh lines radiated like sun rays from the corners of his gray eyes, but with dark bags under those eyes, he only looked old, not happy. "Black, and the stronger the better," he said.

I savored the aroma of the fresh coffee as it finished brewing. I put the dozen donuts on a plate, poured Rad's coffee into an MSU mug, and carried both to the table in front of him. He bit off half a donut, swallowed before he said, "Okay, what the hell happened that made you call me from the throes of a wet dream?"

I described receiving the emails, pulled hardcopies from my purse and handed all but the last one to him. As he read, Rad did the cop cliché proud and reached for his third donut. He responded to my stare with, "What? They're Krispy Kremes. Nothing but air. Takes six of 'em to equal one regular donut." Then, without missing a beat, he turned the conversation back to business. "Did they reply to your 'I'm listening'?"

"That's the strange thing. I was sure I would get a response before I left Friday night."

"You didn't?"

"I left earlier than usual, but at four-thirty there was nothing. Yesterday afternoon I swung by the office to catch up, and that's when I got this." I handed him the last email from Advice4U. "It was sent Friday night at six-fifteen. Our suite clears out at five sharp—even the attorneys leave early on Fridays. It's a morgue after that, well, except for me. I usually stay late and catch up rather than drag work home." The sick thought that someone was watching me and could unbury my past caused me to pass on the donuts.

"Your new pal hoped to catch you alone," Rad said.

"I'm glad you said that. From me, it sounds paranoid."

"Remember the old saying, CJ: Just because you're paranoid doesn't mean they aren't out to get you."

I squeezed my eyes shut tight for a moment and shook my head. "The point is, I didn't get that last email until yesterday."

I waited for him to read it. I reconsidered a Krispy Kreme. Maybe starch would soak up the acid in my empty stomach.

"Did you respond?"

"No. I wanted to talk to you first."

"Still doesn't explain the middle-of-the-night call."

His coffee cup was empty, but I didn't interrupt the story to get him a refill. The bite of donut I had chewed to a doughy glob didn't want to go down. I swallowed twice to move it along. "It gets worse. I was agonizing over that last email when Derek called on my cell. He's alive. Or was yesterday afternoon. He sounded anxious. Panicky, like he was in trouble. I could be reading my feelings into it."

"Where is he?" Rad asked.

"I don't know." I described what happened at my meeting with Lockhart.

Before I got to the part where I didn't think the cop bought my story, Rad interrupted. "Not hard to see where this is going. The sergeant figured the most recent events make you look even guiltier. Suggested you made it all up? Right?"

"Guess it was naive to think he would believe me." I plunked the remainder of my half-eaten donut back on the plate.

"Get to the part about why you called me in the pitch black of night when normal folks are either fucking or sawing logs," he said.

"I'm getting to that. Middle of last night I couldn't sleep. I sat exactly where I am now when a car pulled up in front and brought me a present." I had reinserted the pictures and note in the envelope, redone the clasp and slid it under the couch so Tom wouldn't see it. I felt around and extracted it, handed it to Rad and waited for him to peruse the contents.

Before I offered more, his eyes widened and he said, "Your ex looks buff, I'll give him that. And damned athletic. I see why you kept the pictures."

His humor fell flat. Lacking a proper retort, I ignored it.

"Look, you and Jesus Christ are the only two people I've ever believed could walk on water," he said. "And Christ wasn't a personal friend. But, Casey, you've got a serious problem."

"I didn't call you to hear what I already know. I'm scared. The bad guys have my attention."

"It's good you're scared. Fear inspires caution." He appeared lost in thought for a few seconds before he said, "Show me your study."

"Lockhart said to stay out."

Rad peered over bifocals and gave me his are-you-fucking-kidding-me look as he set his cup on the pink marble coffee table. "I came prepared." He struggled to pull a pair of thin plastic gloves over his rough fists. "Don't want 'em to find my prints in there. Show me the damage."

As we walked through the kitchen, I picked up a key to the study from under a pot of fresh parsley. I clutched it tight, fingernails biting hard against the palms of my hands. "I locked the room in case Natalee got curious."

Upstairs, I opened the door and inspected the shambles from outside peering in. "Lockhart's guys took the papers and the phone and computer," I said. Chalk marks outlined the bloodstains, punctuating the room like evidence of a dead body even though there wasn't one. Charcoal-colored fingerprint dust covered nearly every surface. "Not much to look at, is it?"

"I thought you were a better housekeeper than this." Rad put his arm around my shoulders. Even with him standing next to me, I felt vulnerable.

"What are we searching for?" I asked. If there were clues, they escaped my detection.

Rad moved into the room and navigated overturned furniture with surprising agility for a man his size.

"I'll know it when I see it," he said. "You sure nothing was missing besides the perfume and glossies?"

"If there was anything else, I didn't catch it. And now if I see something is missing, I have to assume the cops carted it off."

"Okay, let's take a different approach," he said. "Was there anything strange about what you saw that night, anything that shouldn't have been here?"

"Rad, everything was wrong. Really, really wrong. Look at this mess." Tears threatened, but I quelled them and sucked up a dose of stoicism.

"At least from the emails and the note, we can assume this is related to your work. Advice4U expects you to fix cases. And he knows about Scroggins. That's more than we had Friday morning. We just have to figure out who he is and how much he wants, besides dismissing the complaint against Khoury."

"*Besides* is the operative word. Ask me if I would let that asshole off the hook to get out of this. A month ago, I'd have said, no frigging way. But the rules have changed." I clenched my hands so tightly together that the knuckles turned white, and my fingers felt gripped in a vise."

"A little fudging my principles for a greater good? I'm no martyr. I want Natalee unharmed. I want her mother at home with her, not locked away in Jackson doing twenty-to-life. I could compromise—at least enough to bury Khoury's misdeeds."

To his credit, he didn't remind me of a lecture I'd given him on this exact subject. Instead, he said, "Nobody goes to this trouble or risk for one doctor."

"Except the doctor himself, if he's trying to save his practice?"

"Nah. He might call you, meet you, corner you somewhere. It wouldn't be all this cloak and dagger shit. This is bigger than Khoury. The email told you that. They're going to demand more. Plus, we know Derek is involved." Rad's eyes continued to roam the room as he spoke.

"You're not making me feel better." I stood motionless and out of his way so he could figure out what had happened.

"What's going on at work these days besides Dr. Khoury?" he asked.

"Same old drugs and money and sex."

"Most powerful motivators known to man." Rad shuffled toward the window and squatted to examine the stains. "Derek already told you it's his blood. No reason to doubt that part of his story. Even if he hadn't copped to it, we could guess the blood wasn't the result of any kind of scuffle. Look at that wall. Big splashes with drizzles running to the floor."

"So?"

"There ain't no way I know that a struggle ends up looking like that. Someone took Derek's blood and did a bit of fancy artwork with it. Even the township police have figured it didn't look right."

"They suggested the possibility, but it doesn't make sense that the cops think I was involved."

"I can think of a million and a half reasons they would assume you were. Pay someone to eliminate your ex-husband, and you're a rich woman. Wait much longer and if anything happens to Derek, Nat gets the money. That's if he keeps paying the premiums, but there's no guarantee he will. You had motive to do it, and do it now. That's how they see it."

He stood and paced the room, eyeing it with three decades of crime scene experience. I clung to great expectations. "You said you would know what you were looking for when you saw it," I said. "So, have you found it?"

"I wish. Nothing sticks out."

"Then can we be done here?"

"Yeah, this room ain't gonna give it up." Rad started toward me, bent, and used his hands to smooth his footprints in the frieze shag carpet. "Can't have the police come back and wonder whose size fourteens these are." He stopped talking and picked up something from between the twisted fibers.

"What is it?" I asked.

"Nothing. Just a paper clip with one prong bent open and an orange Tic Tac to match the three the police inventoried."

"Is it possible our intruder tried to open the locked desk drawer with a paperclip?"

Rad closed the door behind us, and I relocked it. He removed his gloves, stuffed them in his shirt pocket. "I suppose, but if he did, it doesn't help us. Can't get a print off a paperclip."

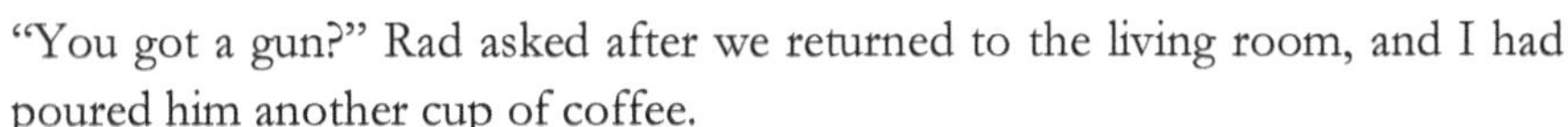

22

"You got a gun?" Rad asked after we returned to the living room, and I had poured him another cup of coffee.

The question surprised me. "Not any more. Like I told you the other day, I dumped the evidence connecting me to Jimmy Scroggins."

"It's time for my little Casey to pack a pistol again." Inside the box he had brought with him rested a menacing hunk of black steel. It was a Smith and Wesson .38 Special, the twin of the revolver I had used on Scroggins.

"I'm not sure I remember how to shoot," I said.

"Like the first time you get laid. You never forget." He brought out a handful of bullets from the front pocket of his khakis. "These are great equalizers for piss-poor shots. JHPs. Jacketed hollow points. The important thing is you can count on 'em to give you the most damage for the pop. They expand and cut an ever-wider path traveling through a body. Found a fella once who had a tiny hole—smaller than a dime—just below his right nipple. Turned the poor bastard over, and the exit wound was the size of a cantaloupe."

"I haven't held a gun, much less shot one, in seventeen years." I reached over and touched the cold metal, let my fingers caress the sleek barrel.

"This is the release." Rad clicked open the cylinder and reminded me how to load, unload, and sight. "Mostly, if someone comes at you close range, don't worry about sighting. Point the damn thing. It'll do the rest." He handed the gun to me.

It was heavy and awkward, but I liked its strong feel.

"Keep it loaded and near you at all times. I'm serious. You go to the basement, take it with you. You watch TV, you park it on the couch next to you. You take a shit, it lays on the bathroom counter. You go to work, carry it in your handbag. Clear?"

"Aye-aye, sir." I ran my fingers along the barrel. "Don't I need a concealed weapon permit to carry it in my handbag?"

"Don't go getting technical on me. The chances of you getting caught with the gun are considerably less than the chances of some piece of crap drug dealer doing you bodily harm. I got friends and can fix the former. The latter is unfixable." He scowled as though he knew the next part of his lecture would upset me. "Tell Natalee what's going on. She deserves to know for her own safety."

I strained to imagine a story that protected my daughter from more ugly news and at the same time kept her safe. It was a losing exercise. "I will," I mumbled. "You don't happen to know anyone I could pay to watch out for her, do you? I drop her at school, but I don't want her going anywhere during the day or after she comes home unless someone's keeping an eye on her. It would have to be someone who's licensed and could tell the school superintendent what he's doing. Wouldn't want him busted as a perv for loitering in the school driveway ogling young girls."

"As a matter of fact, I do know someone. I'll call him this afternoon, get back to you tonight," he said.

"Tell him from seven, when I drop her at school, until six, when I pick her up at a friend's. Later if she stays for play rehearsal. It's not foolproof, but anything that helps is good."

"It'll cost you a few bucks."

"Whatever it takes. I can come by more money but not another daughter."

He nodded. "Now, if you see an old silver Merc lurking, it's just me. Any other strange cars, call. I don't care what time it is. And I want an update every day. You got that?" He headed toward the front door as he gave the last of his instructions.

"Thanks, Rad. I don't know what I would do without you."

"I don't want thanks. I want careful. And don't forget the calls. If I don't hear from you, I'll show up at your office. Make an awful ruckus."

I walked out with him to the driveway.

"Are those the tire tracks you told me Derek made the other night?" he asked.

"Same ones."

"I thought you said Derek drove a Porsche?"

"He does. It's in my garage."

"That ain't the tread from any tire that comes standard on a Porsche. Show me Derek's car."

We traipsed back inside and through the door connecting the kitchen to the garage. Rad stepped over to the Porsche. It was locked. He towered so high above the tiny car that I pictured him picking it up and shaking it like a cheap snow globe to get a better look at the contents as they floated back to the seats and floor. He knelt and ran his fingers over the tire tread before he returned to where I stood.

"Those tracks out front ain't from this Porsche. I'll have McAvoy hustle his butt out here to make an impression before the rain they're predicting washes away the detail."

"Who's McAvoy?"

"Another friend from the old days. Where's your phone?"

I pointed him to the kitchen wall. Rad's bag of tricks contained many friends and a few gadgets, but nothing as new-fangled as a cell phone. It reminded me I still needed to buy him one and beg him to carry it since my safety was at stake.

When he hung up, he added, "I didn't spot anything interesting inside the car, other than maybe that bag from Kositchek's. Your husband's a high-end shopper."

"All I know about his finances is that I don't get child support and never thought it was worth pursuing. At least not until Lockhart told me that damned car is paid for."

"You might reconsider the child support thing. That's a hundred-thousand-dollar babe magnet he's parked in your garage. If he ever wants to sell it cheap, let me know." Rad gave me a bear hug. "I've gotta get goin'. McAvoy will be here for the impressions within the hour. I doubt he'll knock or anything. Ignore him. You can assume it isn't a bad guy when he starts pouring dental stone in the tread marks."

"I thought you said to call you if I saw any strange cars." I winked to let him know I was kidding.

"You're right. Glad the lesson took. McAvoy drives a beat-up white Taurus. He's about five-foot, six inches tall and almost as wide. Dresses in sweats and covers his bald head with a Spartan baseball cap. No accounting for taste. And, Casey, maybe you oughta marry that Tom fella," Rad called behind him as he walked away. "Your house is too damned fussy. You need someone who'll leave newspapers lying around once in a while. And make you get rid of that girlie couch and pillows."

The sky clouded over and rain threatened. Rad's buddy made it before the storm. I dialed my daughter's cell to tell her I would pick her up in ten minutes. Her phone was turned off, so I called Nora Thornton, Trish's mom. I tried to sound matter-of-fact. "I've got some time this afternoon and decided to pick up Nat early and go shopping. May I speak to her please?"

"Sure," she said. "We're done with their science projects anyway. I'll get her."

When Nora came back to the phone, she sounded winded. Her news buckled my knees. "Casey, Natalee's gone."

❦

23

I squatted, dizzy, hyperventilating.

"Nat told Trish she needed to study at the library," Nora said. "She must have snuck out. I'm so sorry. Do you want me to help you look for her?"

"No." Horror slipped a quiver into my voice. "Let me talk to Trish."

There wasn't a full moment's pause before Trish came on the line. "Hi, Mrs. Lawrence. I know Natalee wasn't supposed to go anywhere alone, but she wanted some books from the library." She reiterated her mother's "so sorry."

"The Okemos Library?" I rushed my words; every second counted. The nervous energy surging through my system threatened to knock me on my ass.

"Yeah. The school library isn't open on Sunday."

I hung up, scrambled for the Toyota, headed for Okemos Road. I braked to a stop in the library's handicap parking and rushed inside as the rain began. I scanned the aisles, looked behind every shelf, dashed into the ladies' room. No sign of Natalee. I interrupted a librarian pointing an elderly woman to the genealogy tomes. "Have you seen Natalee Lawrence?" My breathless question begged forgiveness for my lack of manners.

"Yes. She left, maybe fifteen minutes ago. Is something wrong?"

"I hope not." Wasting no time with details, I raced back to my car.

A blaze of lightning, followed seconds later by a boom of thunder, prefaced a deluge that made it tough to see even with the wipers flying. I crawled the street, eyes peeled for my daughter. I turned right on Hamilton, and there glimpsed a solitary figure with a familiar red jacket shrouded about its head. I pulled alongside.

"Natalee?" I lowered the passenger-side window, and rain drenched the seat.

I stopped, and she bounded into the car, her face as crimson as the jacket. From the trapped-animal look in her eyes, I suspected that more than rain dampened her cheeks, and that her body shivered from more than the cold.

I put a hand on her arm. "Honey, tell me what happened?"

Through sobs, her words heaved and fell. "I know I'm supposed to be at Trish's, but I wanted a head start on my history paper. I figured the library wouldn't be busy when it opened at one. I wouldn't have to fight anyone for the books I needed."

"Why didn't you have your cell phone on?" I asked.

"I was in a library, Mom. I tried to call you when I left, but you didn't answer your cell. Our landline beeped busy."

"Lockhart has my cell, and Rad must have been on the kitchen phone when you called." She had disobeyed my strict instructions, but I felt culpable. "What happened?"

She lowered her eyes and stared at the backpack on her lap avoiding my question. After several seconds she said, "A man walked into the library a few minutes after me. He sat across the table with *The Wall Street Journal* spread in front of him. When I looked up, he gawked at me. It creeped me out. Even when he smiled and dropped his eyes back to his paper, something wasn't right. He was still there when I left. I got as far as the corner at Hamilton when it started to rain, and the wind turned my umbrella inside out. As I struggled with it . . ." She gasped a breath, closed her eyes. "A black car pulled up at the light. The man inside—the one from the library—opened the window and asked if I wanted a ride. I said, 'No.'"

Maybe it was coincidence. I don't believe in coincidences.

"He drove off," she said. "But a couple of minutes later the same car inched behind me. I walked backwards watching it approach. I considered taking off between buildings to lose it, but a cop car passed going the other way, and the driver hit the gas and disappeared."

"Do you know what kind of car?" I asked.

"The trunk had a Lincoln logo."

"And the man? What did he look like?"

"He was a white dude, dark hair combed straight back but too curly to stay in place, maybe your age. About as tall as Dad. Lots of muscle. Scar on his left cheek. I didn't want to stare. That's all I remember."

We arrived home by the time she finished her story. I hugged her tight. "Take a warm shower and get into dry clothes. I'll fix hot chocolate. We need to talk." While I heated the milk and added cocoa, I dialed Rad, told him of Natalee's misadventure, described the man.

"Good thing I spoke to a couple of guys who can help you," he said. "I think you want someone there around the clock. For the money, I'm sure they'll be happy to each pull twelve-hour shifts, seven to seven for a few days. They'll set it up with the school. It'll cost you fifty an hour. Explain what's going on to Natalee so she doesn't freak."

"It's next on my agenda. In fact, can one of your guys come tonight?" Even if Tom stayed, I knew I would get no sleep if there wasn't someone standing guard.

"Give him an hour."

By the time I sprinkled the steaming chocolate with a handful of miniature marshmallows, Natalee sat on the couch. I handed her a cup, plopped next to her and started relating bad news. I explained the threatening emails and the message delivered in the middle of the night. I told her Rad had given me a gun, and we had arranged for some guys who used to be cops to protect us. I insisted she be aware of her surroundings. She would keep her cell phone in her pocket at all times. Even when we were home together, she was never, never, *never* to answer the door without checking who it was. Never.

I neglected to mention the nude photos, I downplayed my concern about her father. Jimmy Scroggins's name never came up. Even with those omissions, I would have endured a root canal without Novocain rather than watch her digest my latest update. Her wide-eyed grimace and lack of words told me she might be out of argument but was disappointed with me for getting us into this predicament.

When Tom offered to spend Sunday night, I said, "We're not alone," and explained our hired bodyguards.

There was a long silence. "Casey, I don't like this at all."

"Which part? The only thing I have any control over is the rent-a-cops, and I assume you agree they are a good idea?" I bit my tongue. I had no sweet left in me.

"If you change your mind—"

"I won't. I've shut, secured, and deadbolted everything. We're locked up tighter than Jackson State Prison and guarded by a guy with a nine-millimeter. I've got my fearsome watch cat. And Rad gave me a loaded gun . . . just in case."

Fred arrived at six-thirty and introduced himself. He would alternate shifts with Ernie, another retired cop doing private security gigs. We discussed how it would work. I offered my living room couch. He said, "Better deterrence to any douche bag inclined to break in if I sit in my car in the driveway. Let 'em know they gotta get through me. If anything happens, it's nipped in the bud and we keep the commotion away from your daughter." We agreed it was best to preserve as much normalcy as possible.

Natalee slept with me. Jussy bedded down between us. The .38, loaded with hollow tips, stood sentry from the nightstand nearest me. I skipped the Ambien to remain hyper-vigilant. Rad, Tom, and 911 were on speed dial. At least we wouldn't make it easy for the son of a bitch.

24

Monday, October 3

To my twitchy mental state, the howling wind portended danger. Loud claps of thunder, my ragged nerves, and the lack of an Ambien played together to create a restless night. Twice I eased from bed and tiptoed into the guest room and peered out a window from which I could see Fred's car. I sought assurance that he was still there.

By morning the storm had killed our electricity. The clock radio didn't go off, but years of habit and my troubled slumber woke me without the music. I remained under the covers watching Natalee sleep. I twisted the two-band unity ring on my right ring finger and looked over at its twin that she wore on a chain around her neck. She had saved her allowance and bought them, mine as a Christmas present, five years ago.

"One band represents you, the other is me. We'll always be together," she said when she presented me with the gift.

I chuckled remembering an eleven-year-old's passion that allowed no room for growing up or changing the center of her existence. I never took the ring off, cherishing the constant reminder that for now Mom remained the most important person in her universe.

"What are you staring at?" Nat asked when she opened her eyes and caught my gaze fixed on her.

"You. I'm thinking how much I love you."

She ignored my professed affection. "You snore."

"That's a lie."

"Isn't."

"That's a horrible thing to say to your mother." I reached over and brushed her hair out of her eyes.

"Fine, they were soft, dainty snores."

"I do not snore."

"Okay. Whatever. You don't snore."

"Tell me the truth."

"Mom, we're sleeping in the same bed, there's a gun on the nightstand, an armed security guard in a car in our driveway, and you're worried about snoring?" She propped herself on one elbow and gave me her smug I'm-more-grown-up-than-you-sometimes look. She was no longer eleven years old.

"You're right. Just proves that even with our world shaking like San Francisco during the big one, I can be as shallow as the next woman. So please tell me I don't snore."

"Maybe I dreamt it." She sat up, twisted left and right to stretch awake, and then said, "Or maybe you had the covers over your face and gulped for air."

"That explains it. You tried to smother me. I gasped for oxygen. That's a lot different than snoring." I tossed my pillow at her.

Natalee bounded from bed and serenaded me with the sound of her laughter. Yesterday afternoon I believed I might never hear that sweet sound again. Testament to the human spirit, I thought. She had inherited my glass-half-full personality. She bent over the bed and pulled the covers up on her side, and I did the same on mine.

I picked up Jussy and hoisted her above my head. I lowered her to face level and rubbed my nose against her cool damp one. "I had better get my lazy butt in gear, or we won't be able to afford your kitty kibbles."

Having no hot water sped up my shower. I grabbed my clothes, assisted only by the morning light filtering through the window and spreading dimly into the closet. My suits hung, organized by color, next to matching blouses. I could dress in less than three minutes. In the past, I had timed it to prove the efficiency of my system.

While I waited for Natalee, I retrieved the *Sentinel*, cocooned in a sloshy plastic bag on my doorstep. I waved at the man sitting in the navy-blue Camry in the driveway, and he waved back. The paper was damp around the edges but readable. News of the storms and torrential rains that left fifty thousand without electricity had pushed *Blood Splotches Confirmed in AAG's Study* off the front page. The article had landed on page ten and ended with:

The Sentinel has learned that Casey Lawrence told police her ex-husband, Derek Lawrence, called her on her cell phone Saturday afternoon. Police attempted to track the call that bounced off a tower in Okemos, but it came from an untraceable phone.

"I'm out of here in one minute," I yelled up the stairs. It would have been nice if Lockhart had shared this news with me. I would pick up my cell on the way home since it did him no good.

Nat met me at the car, carrying one of my cashmere cardigans, her backpack, and a granola bar. The Toyota tailed us to school, where I dropped my daughter. I dabbed on makeup at stoplights between there and the highway.

At nine-thirty I had a hearing scheduled against Dr. Jackson Wainwright. The previous Thursday, the chair of the Board of Medicine signed a summary suspension that forced Wainwright to close his doors. The unilateral action entitled the doctor to an immediate abbreviated proceeding. I had to produce enough evidence to support continuation of the suspension until a full trial was scheduled.

There were two entrances to Med Pro. If I passed the first and entered through the second, I walked directly into my office. I generally favored the first door because I'm gregarious by nature. I loved my morning dose of Shirl's cheerfulness. Today there was no time for social niceties. I nodded to Louise but skipped office small talk. I didn't need a blow-by-blow of everyone's weekend, and they sure as hell weren't about to get the scoop on mine. I closed my office door.

I peered out my sixth-floor window. The rain had dwindled to a light drizzle that wrapped the huge elm and maple in gossamer moisture webs. I watched the traffic below, waiting for someone to turn the wrong direction on one-way Pine Street. My view didn't get more amusing than that.

The hearing started in an hour. I needed to sort and mark exhibits. Before I finished, Louise knocked and peeked at me through the narrow glass panel of my door. I motioned her in.

"I thought you might want to know that a policeman named Lockhart called me, and he's coming here this morning. I'm guessing I'm not the only one he'll talk to. Anything I need to know before he arrives?"

"Don't worry about it. Just answer his questions the best you can."

She handed me two new files. "You might like these moved along as fast as possible. One is Dr. Cameron Day, who practices out of the same building as your Dr. Khoury, and the other is the Buy-Smart Pharmacy on South Logan. Gannon's investigative reports make both the doctor and the pharmacy sound pretty bad." Louise read every file assigned to me, probably knew the details of many of them better than I did.

"I'll give them a look after my summary suspension," I said.

Louise was part ghost, whispery voice, and able to move without a sound. If she entered when my back was to her, I turned around, and she would just be there. According to her rendition of history, she had been with Med Pro since God was born. From others, I had learned that she was the workhorse of the division, and that greasy fast food was her weakness. Someone said she was divorced and had a grown son. If she wanted me to know about her personal life, she would tell me. I gave her plenty of opportunity.

Louise eyed the empty 32-ounce neon green plastic container on my desk. "Want an iced tea?"

I would have endured a Lockhart grilling for a glass of strong caffeine since the storm had messed with my morning fix at home. "You don't have to do that."

"That's why I don't mind."

When Louise returned, I was on the phone confirming with Chace Gannon that he would be my first witness. I nodded and smiled my appreciation as she placed the tea on a folded paper towel next to my notepad.

I gulped several large swigs, left the rest for later. I gathered my files and charged off to another skirmish, this one to inflict a mortal wound on Wainwright's practice.

25

I hustled into court with seconds to spare. I thanked Judge O'Rourke and launched my opening statement. Doctor Percival Gibbs, chairperson of the Board of Medicine, huddled next to the judge. Only during summary suspension hearings did the Medical Board chair sit behind the bench. After the evidence was presented, Gibbs, not O'Rourke, would decide if Wainwright retained his license until the full hearing.

I called Gannon to the stand to provide a description of Wainwright's practice. He identified himself as an investigator for Licensing Regulations and established his credentials.

"Mr. Gannon, have you met Dr. Jackson Wainwright before today?" I asked. A trial isn't unlike a play. I had my lines; they were called questions. My witnesses had their lines. I knew what they would say because I had already asked them the same questions in my office when we prepped the case. I never put words in their mouths and for the most part, avoided obvious hints, but I knew the gist of their testimony. If I didn't like their truthful answers, I would skip the question. Maybe ask it a different way.

"Yes, ma'am," Gannon said.

"Can you describe how that came about?"

"I looked over the ARCOS reports for his office purchases and found them ten times what I expected for an office his size."

"What do you do when the ARCOS report identifies a potential problem?" I asked.

"Depends upon how serious the numbers are. Sometimes I monitor the situation for the next couple months. In this case, I had also received a complaint about Dr. Wainwright."

"From whom?"

"Steven Braybant. Mr. Braybant called Licensing Regulations and got transferred to me. He told me his wife, Arlene, was killed by Dr. Wainwright."

"Killed? How?" I asked.

"Not like murdered or anything, but Braybant said the doctor gave her too many drugs. She died of an overdose."

"Did you undertake a full investigation?"

"Yes," he said. "I decided to do an undercover of Wainwright's office."

"Can you tell the court what that means?"

"I dressed down . . . you know, wore faded blue jeans frayed at the bottoms, a yellowed t-shirt . . . work boots . . . tried to blend with the patients of the doctor's practice. Went in and asked to see the doctor."

"You waltzed in without an appointment?"

"Yes, ma'am."

"And he was willing to see you?" I was the straight man asking questions to let Gannon tell the story. At appropriate openings, to add impact, I raised my voice in feigned shock.

"Yeah. I just signed my name. Actually, I signed John Smith on an intake roster and was called in the order of my arrival time."

"You first met Dr. Wainwright in the examining room?"

"That's right."

"Is the man you met sitting in this courtroom?"

"Yes. There." Gannon pointed to the doctor, who was busy studying his manicure.

"What did you tell Doctor Wainwright, once you were alone with him?"

"I told him I was a good buddy of Evan Capshaw. From my investigation I knew Capshaw was a patient at the clinic, so I said, 'Evan knows I gotta little need for drugs and told me you're a good doctor and can help me out.'"

"How did Wainwright respond to that?"

"He asked me what I wanted."

"You mean asked what was wrong with you?" I said.

"No, asked what I wanted."

I furrowed my brow, blinked a couple of times, shook my head for emphasis. "How did you answer that?"

"I told the doc I wanted Librium, Empirim 3—that's with codeine—and Methadone."

"Did the doctor ask you why you wanted those drugs?"

"Didn't have to; I told him I wanted them to build up my stash for a party. I added that what I didn't use I would sell to a friend so I could buy blow . . . you know, cocaine."

Dr. Gibbs rolled his eyes, his sigh audible to everyone in the room. Wainwright's attorney, Marvin Crystal, removed his glasses and rubbed the bridge of his nose.

"Was Dr. Wainwright upset by your audacity?" I struggled to keep a straight face. This was more fun than I'd had in a week.

"Objection, calls for speculation." Crystal rose to his feet and threw up his hands like he had to stop a charging locomotive. It was dramatic overkill.

I didn't wait for the judge to rule. "Let me rephrase," I said. "What did Dr. Wainwright say after you told him why you wanted the drugs?"

"He didn't say anything. He wrote out three prescriptions and gave them to me. Then he said, 'I assume Capshaw told you the fee?' and I handed him three hundred dollars, a hundred for each script. I later learned, after I got the doctor's office billing records, that he also billed Medicaid for my visit. I had offered him a Medicaid card with the name Joseph Jackilani on it."

I handed Gannon copies of the three prescriptions made out for John Smith. "I'm showing you what the People have marked as exhibits one through three. Have you seen these before?" Attorney Crystal looked at copies of the exhibits I had provided him before the hearing began.

"Yes, ma'am. Those are the prescriptions Dr. Wainwright wrote me," Gannon said.

"Thank you. Your honor, the People offer exhibits one through three."

Judge O'Rourke asked Crystal if there were any objections, and when he offered none, said, "Exhibits one, two, and three are accepted into evidence."

"Did you ever tell Dr. Wainwright you were Joseph Jackilani?" I asked

"No. I told him I was John Smith, and that the card belonged to a friend who said I could use it."

Chairperson Gibbs scribbled furiously. Then he looked up and glared chilling accusations at Wainwright who shifted his position and turned away.

Gannon laid the foundation for the medical records of ten patients who received large numbers of controlled substances—Dilaudid, Percocet, Doriden, OxyContin, Fentanyl, Methadone—with insufficient medical reasons in the files to justify prescribing them. I entered the ARCOS reports and the Medicaid billing documents into evidence.

During Gannon's testimony, Judge O'Rourke yawned and looked like he might fall asleep. The outcome was in the hands of Dr. Gibbs, and it didn't appear the judge wasted energy following along. Gibbs, on the other hand, couldn't mask his outrage. A tide of red rose from his neck to the spot in front of where his comb-over covered the crown of his head.

By the time Crystal started cross examination, I knew Gibbs had tuned him out. Nothing would change the doctor's mind. A couple of inconsequential questions so his client would believe he earned his fee and Crystal folded. "No more questions of this witness."

I called my next witness to add emotional impact and demonstrate the real-world tragedy caused by Wainwright's overprescribing. "Can you give us your full name and spell it for the record, sir."

"Steven Kenneth Braybant." Then he spoke the letters, clearly and slowly. S T E V E N K E N N E T H B R A Y B A N T.

"Thank you. Mr. Braybant, are you married?"

"I was until a month ago."

"What happened at that time to end the marriage?" I asked.

"My wife died." Braybant pulled a handkerchief from his pocket and blew his nose. I couldn't have staged the pause better; it gave his words time to settle on Dr. Gibbs.

"Do you know what caused her death?" I asked.

"Yes and—"

"Objection, your honor. Speculation," Crystal argued. "This witness isn't a doctor."

"Sustained."

I figured it might be Crystal's last victory and an easy one to get around. "Mr. Braybant, when your wife died, were you given a death certificate?"

"Yes."

I pulled my next exhibits from a stack of papers. "Are these copies of the death certificate and autopsy report you received?"

"Objection. If Attorney Lawrence wants the cause of death before this court, let her bring the medical examiner." Crystal tested the waters to see how far to push.

"Overruled. This is a summary suspension, and we want the hearing completed this morning. Mr. Crystal, I will allow the copy of the death certificate and autopsy report, unless you tell this court you believe they are bogus. I warn that before you impugn the integrity of our assistant attorney general, you better have solid evidence to back up your suspicions."

"No, your honor." Crystal back-peddled with admirable smoothness. "We don't suggest they are forgeries, and I have nothing but respect for Ms. Lawrence. However, my client doesn't agree with the listed cause of death. This is a summary suspension, and we haven't had time to secure an expert witness, but we plan to argue Arlene Braybant suffered a heart attack unaffected by drugs."

"You can argue anything you like. But save it for the hearing in full. The death certificate and autopsy report are in," Judge O'Rourke ruled. "Mr. Braybant, you may answer the question."

"Yes, those are the documents I was given," he said.

"What is listed as the cause of your wife's death?"

"A drug overdose. A propoxyphene overdose. That's Darvons."

"You've sat in this courtroom and heard Mr. Gannon testify that you called him and accused Dr. Wainwright of killing your wife. Did you do that?" I asked.

"Yes, ma'am."

"How did he kill her?"

"My wife had what her psychologist called an addictive personality."

"Objection." Crystal was on his feet again.

Before O'Rourke could respond, I said, "Your honor, the People aren't offering this testimony to prove Arlene Braybant had an addictive personality, nor even that it's what her psychologist told her, we offer it to establish what Mr. Braybant told Dr. Wainwright."

"I'll allow it with those limitations," O'Rourke ruled.

"Mr. Braybant, is that what you told Dr. Wainwright? That your wife had an addictive personality?"

"Yes. I told him she was addicted to prescription drugs."

Crystal looked up, started to rise, but must have reconsidered. He plunked back down. The judge shot him a smile as if to say thanks for not wasting any more of our time.

"From personal knowledge, are you aware your wife took prescription drugs?" I asked.

"Yes," Braybant said.

"Can you tell the court what medications you actually witnessed her taking?"

"Valium. T-3s. Dilaudid, and Oxycodone when she could get them. She died from Darvons."

"Did she ever take illegal drugs?"

"I know she used cocaine. Sometimes marijuana, but with Dr. Wainwright's prescriptions, she didn't have to go out and look for drugs. He gave her what she wanted. She could leave her legal pills in plain sight."

"Didn't you feel that made it safer? I asked. "She didn't have to turn to crime or buy street drugs?"

"If your question is whether I wanted her buying drugs on the street, of course not. But I expected Dr. Wainwright to help me get her into treatment. Arlene needed help."

"Why did you expect him to do that?"

"He's a doctor. It's his job to spot addicts and treat them. I begged him to stop the drugs. I told him I had rushed Arlene to the ER for an overdose. That was the week before her death. She got hold of some Oxy, took it with Valium and some other stuff."

"Why didn't the ER doctor have her committed, if you know?"

"I asked him to do that. But he believed Arlene when she swore it was an accident, and since the drugs were prescribed, he told me I needed to talk to Dr. Wainwright."

"Objection. Hearsay," Crystal said. He hadn't given up.

Even though Crystal's objection was legally sound, Judge O'Rourke said, "Overruled. Continue, Ms. Lawrence."

"Mr. Braybant, was Arlene suicidal?"

"Absolutely not. She became a grandmother six months ago, and she loved that little grandson of ours more than anything else in the world. No. She wanted to live."

"Then why did she take drugs?" I asked.

"She ruptured a disc four years ago and had surgery. It didn't help. She developed scar tissue. Had constant pain."

"She needed the drugs?" To deflect the impact, I asked the questions Crystal might ask.

"She needed pain management," Braybant said.

'You aren't a doctor are you, Mr. Braybant?"

"No, ma'am, but I could see what happened when she took drugs. She needed higher doses to get the relief she wanted. She liked what the drugs did for her. At some point, it was unclear to me whether what she wanted was pain relief or the high."

"Tell us about the night she died."

There was another pause. Steven Braybant again blew his nose on the handkerchief that remained clutched in his hand, and then used the cuff of his shirt to wipe tears from his cheeks. Several more seconds passed. He appeared to wrestle with his grief before answering. Attorneys can't prep witnesses' emotions, but sometimes we get lucky.

"About a week after I pleaded with Dr. Wainwright to help her, I had to work late. Arlene called me and said she felt real bad. I warned her not to take more than one Darvon and to make sure she didn't take anything else with it. When I got home at eight-thirty, she was sitting on the couch, slumped to one side. I tried to talk to her, but she wasn't making sense. I dialed 911. She stopped breathing. I tried mouth-to-mouth. By the time the paramedics arrived, she was dead."

I had intended to ask Braybant what Dr. Wainwright charged for meeting with him. I weighed the shamelessness of the doctor charging a worried husband a hundred dollars against the tears now dampening the courtroom. I said, "No further questions."

"The defense has no questions for this witness." Crystal's smartest move.

The People rested. Without time to prepare a defense, Crystal called no witnesses. Gibbs' pencil rapped the desk in rhythm to his foot's tap on the floor. It was almost noon and he had heard enough. My closing argument took less than two minutes. Crystal talked for twenty. In the end, he wasn't good enough to spin bullshit into a believable fairy tale.

Gibbs needed no time to reflect. "The summary is continued until a full hearing can be held in this matter," he said.

It would be a long time before Jackson Wainwright reopened his office doors, but I wondered if he had been brazen enough to close the ones to my study.

❦

26

Got a damned cell. Hope you're happy. Louise handed me the message when I returned to the office. She had highlighted in pink the word damned and drew a smiley face next to it. I dialed the number Rad had left. His input seemed a wise prerequisite to any plan I hatched.

"Hey, old buddy," I said when he picked up. "Glad you learned how to activate the little gizmo."

"Little gizmo? Shit. Thing's a fuckin' mind-blowin' piece of crap. I press *end* when I want it turned on? Tell me how that makes sense? If it's in my pocket, the caller hangs up before I can fish out the vicious thing. If I put it anyplace else, it's a trick to see how bad my memory is. Flashes a message that I missed a call. Like I'm dimwitted and didn't know that. Give me a real phone any day."

"Yeah, but I wouldn't be able to reach you at all times." I imagined Rad's fingers fumbling on a gadget sized for elves and smiled. "Be happy you don't have to use it to track appointments and plan your life."

"Okay, I proved I can answer this cussed contraption. What's up?"

"You know how to take the fun out of lighthearted," I said. "But I've got a response for Advice4U."

"This better be good."

Someone needed to tell Rad to keep his mouth close to the phone, but I realized the distance between his ear and mouth wasn't exactly standard-sized, so I strained to hear and forged on. "I don't know. That's why I called you."

"You're learning. Shoot."

"The Khoury hearing is continued to November. I don't like that charlatan practicing until then, but we need the time. Not to mention it wasn't my choice."

"No arguments so far," Rad agreed.

"What if I promise the thug who writes these emails that I plan to cooperate? Explain to my middle-of-the-night visitor that I have no loyalty to the attorney general."

"Hell, he knows that."

"Yes, but I'll caution him, or them, that if I withdraw my complaint against Khoury, someone on the Board of Medicine will get suspicious."

"A reasonable concern," Rad said.

"Advice4U claims to have friends in our office. I wouldn't be surprised if he does. My short list includes Sawicki, Shirley Rathburn, and Mark Rodgers." My right hand held the phone while the fingers of my left worked to release tension by massaging my tight trapezius muscles. "But not everyone can be in the goon's back pocket, or he wouldn't need me."

"True. And crooks like him never know how far to trust their kind of friends."

I heard a toilet flush but didn't ask. "Exactly. So, I play to his insecurity. Try to make him think I have a better way."

Over the sound of running water, he asked, "Which is?"

"I'll suggest that the last thing he needs is questions from the board. Instead, he should let the matter rest until the continued hearing, and then I'll lose the case. Looks more natural. His doctor gets off either way."

"Can you do that? Lose it, I mean?"

"Tough to do, but the scumbag may not know that. It gains us a few more weeks." Maybe my voice sounded more convincing than I felt.

"I think you need to add a safety clause. If he doesn't like your proposal, or if he suspects it's bullshit, it puts you and Natalee in danger."

I expected Rad to give my idea the green light. It was the best I came up with. "I don't hear a better plan." I tasted blood as I chewed the inside of my cheeks, that nasty habit my scared-self indulged.

"Not a better plan. Maybe an addendum to your message. Stroke his ego. Add a line that encourages further contact if he gets the notion to escalate . . . if he's pissed you didn't do it his way."

"Like what?"

"Something like, 'I believe this is the best way to accomplish your goal, but you call the shots. If you disagree, I'll follow your instructions to the letter. I'll withdraw the complaint by tomorrow noon.' Never question his power. And send that email as soon as we get off the phone so he has plenty of time to digest it and respond before the deadline."

"And if he doesn't buy my suggestion? Do I give in? If I withdraw my complaint, shit will fly. I'm just not sure from where. I have no idea what I would tell Shirl to justify it."

"Then we hope your email works. If it's rejected, call me. We'll talk back-up plan."

"What's that?"

"I've got until tomorrow noon to figure it out."

I considered every word, changing *wills* and *mights* until satisfied that nothing I wrote would set off Advice4U. The finished product lacked poetry but served the purpose:

> *I got your note Saturday night. I only stopped to see Lockhart to let him know Derek is alive. I thought it might get the cop off our backs. You have my attention. I'll help you. But if I withdraw the petition without good cause, the Board of Medicine will ask questions. My boss might go ballistic. It could get tricky. We can play it another way to get what you want: The case is scheduled for continuation on November 1 and 2. If I finish the trial, but lose deliberately—and subtly so no one gets wise—, it's more believable. If you disagree, let me know. I will withdraw the petition tomorrow as you instructed. You run the show.*

I printed a hard copy, as I had with each of our earlier emails, and then hit SEND. I opened sent mail and hit DELETE, opened my deleted mail file and again hit DELETE to make sure the email was gone. I knew enough about computers to worry nothing was ever final, but I hoped the computer hack in our department wouldn't trip over this or any of the earlier correspondence between Advice4U and me. In a full audit, I might be in real trouble.

I sent the message at 1:11 p.m. and considered it a good omen for no reason other than I was due a bit of luck. At least it gave the prick plenty of time to answer if he didn't like my counterproposal.

With crucial business finished, I picked up the Day file that Louise had delivered earlier in the morning. The complainant, Beverly Comstock, alleged that Dr. Cameron Day over-prescribed to her nineteen-year-old daughter, Kimberly. On the first visit, Dr. Day wrote Kimberly a script for Tylenol 3 to treat chronic pain syndrome associated with a two-year-old healed shoulder fracture. Two months later, Kimberly graduated to Percodan. By the time Beverly Comstock found her way to Licensing Regulations, the worried mother had watched her daughter ingest a hundred Dilaudid a month. In her complaining letter, Mrs. Comstock wrote:

> *Kimberly seems incoherent most of the time. I discussed the problem with Dr. Day, but he told me it's not my concern, she's an adult. I don't know what I can do other than ask you people to investigate this.*

I opened my briefcase and took out the Wainwright file. I thought Steven Braybant, my witness from the morning's hearing, referenced Dr. Day. I flipped through the pages to the third investigative report:

> *Mr. Braybant describes his wife as out of control at the time of her death. He admits she probably begged Dr. Wainwright for the Tylenol 3. She also saw Drs. Richard Jones and Cameron Day. Braybant wasn't sure if his wife obtained prescriptions from them.*

I ran a computer search for Cameron Day MD and found that Shirl had a closed case on him. I pulled the old file and skimmed it. The complainant charged Dr. Day of fondling her breasts when she sought treatment for asthma. In response to the allegation, the doctor said that the young woman was angry when he refused her drugs. Shirley closed the file with a note: *Talked to M.R. He recommends no action. Unwinnable case of he-said, she-said.*

I got to the good stuff when my phone beeped and Louise said, "It's Mark Rodgers from Executive."

As I waited for the click that indicated my secretary had hung up, I pictured Mark Rodgers. I guessed he was a decade younger than me. His small neat mustache made him look distinguished and older. He was a man for whom I envisioned a well-chiseled chest under those navy suits and pale blue shirts. He alternated two power ties: one with red and navy stripes, the other, almost identical, with green and navy stripes. A good-looking man, maybe, but too pretty for my taste.

"Hi, Mark, this is Casey. What can I do for you?"

"Attorney General Sawicki wanted me to check the status of the Day case." His voice was rich like the worsted wool Italian jackets he wore.

"Just got it this morning. I'm reading it as we speak. Pretty sure from what I've seen so far that I'll be filing a complaint. I'll try to draft it today."

"I'll pass that along to our boss."

"Is there something I should know about this case?" I asked.

"No. Mr. Sawicki has been friends with Dr. Day for many years. They were roommates at Michigan State back in the days when it was still Michigan State College of Agriculture. The AG hopes there's some mistake."

"Does that affect how I handle this?"

"Of course not." He overplayed indignation, carefully enunciating each word. "Mr. Sawicki hopes his friend did nothing wrong, but as attorney general, he wants the truth."

"I understand." I wasn't sure I did.

"Let us know if there's anything we can do to help. Keep me in the loop. And thanks, Casey." Mark Rodgers was a climber. Being groomed to be God's right-hand man, but for now, God's go-fer. Screw him. I was sure many women would welcome the chance.

Every five minutes or so, as I reviewed the Day file, I hit the SEND-RECEIVE on my email. By three, I hadn't gotten a reply from Advice4U. My concentration fell in proportion to the increasing fear that zigzagged through my brain. I set aside the case and skimmed the Buy-Smart complaint. It, too, failed to engross me. The investigative report was a month old. I called Gannon for an update.

"Can't get enough of me, can you?" he said.

"That and I wondered if there was anything new with the Buy-Smart Pharmacy at Ottawa and Martin Luther King?"

"Funny you should mention them. I dictated an addendum to my initial report. It languishes in the secretarial swampland as we speak. You'll get it in a day or two."

"What's the gist?"

"The last ARCOS report shows Buy-Smart dispenses more Dilaudid, Tylenol 3, and Percodan than the big Detroit operations. Puts Buy-Smart number one in the state for those drugs. Must be they have an awful lot of cancer patients."

"Right. Who's the pharmacist there?" I asked.

"Guy by the name of Allen."

"First or last?"

"Last," he said. "I think it's Jim Allen."

It was five-thirty, and the office was empty. The afternoon had vanished. I was tired, but at least Wainwright was out of business, and I was ready to draft the complaint against Dr. Cameron Day. After several false starts, I gave up. What the hell, I thought, that can wait for another day. I smiled at my pun and closed the file.

Before shutting down my computer I did a last SEND-RECEIVE. This one brought me a reply from Advice4U.

You're a smart woman. Your idea makes sense. Don't disappoint us. By the way, we have another small problem. Thanks to you, Dr. Wainwright lost his license. He was hospitalized with chest pain after your hearing this morning. They did an emergency procedure to see what the problem was and tomorrow they do a bypass. He'll be on medical leave, recuperating for six weeks. We need you to get his license back by then so he can return to practice.

I aimed for REPLY, but my shaky index finger snagged FORWARD-ALL. It was a mistake that would send my message to every computer in the Department of Attorney General. I cancelled and tried again. *I'll work on it*, was all I could think to type. I printed off a copy of Advice4U's email and my response, extracted the envelope from my purse, and added the current exchange to the growing collection.

I reread Advice4U's emails and noticed something that hadn't caught my attention earlier. The grammar was excellent, spelling perfect, no slang. The writing suggested someone with a decent education, someone who didn't try to hide his intelligence, maybe even flaunted it. Advice4U intended his emails to convince me it would be a mistake to underestimate him. Message received.

I shut off the lights and locked the office door behind me. Advice4U bought my suggestion and that let me maintain my integrity and maybe stay alive for a few weeks, but I couldn't deliver. My thoughts jumped confounding hurdles at record speed. If Rad didn't get me out of this mess, I had dug a deeper hole for my grave.

27

I had been at work an hour when I decided I could use a bottle of aspirin. For Jim Allen's headache, not mine. As I left, I told Louise, "I should be back by ten if Shirley asks."

The walk to the mud lot took longer than the drive to the drugstore. A weathered sign perched on the flat roof of a one-story, cube-like structure. It identified Buy-Smart as YOUR NEIGHBORHOOD PHARMACY SERVING LANSING SINCE 1943. I entered a drab-orange, brick building that hadn't seen improvements since it first opened. At night, heavy steel security gates closed tighter than the lock on a hospital's medication cabinet.

Inside, at the register, a skinny clerk explained the harsh facts of life to a kid about six. The urchin wore ragged jeans, and holes aerated his Harry Potter t-shirt; neither looked as though it had seen the inside of a washing machine this year. The boy handed the clerk a package of pretzels and a dollar bill. "It's a dollar eight," she said.

"It's all I got."

"Guess you don't want pretzels."

My fingers searched through the lint, receipts, and grunge at the bottom of my purse, where enough change collected to finance Natalee's first semester of college. I pulled out something thin and small. It was a dime. I handed it to the youngster. His smile showed a gap in his front teeth. Yep, six or seven years old seemed about right. And it was a safe guess that no tooth fairy left change under his pillow.

"I'm here to see Jim Allen," I said when the clerk finished the transaction and shifted her attention to me. With the kid gone, I was the only person in the place other than her and maybe Jim Allen, who was nowhere to be seen.

"Jim's eatin' his breakfast and don't like to be disturbed before nine. That's when he starts his shift."

I returned her scrutiny. Carelessly applied black lipstick gave her mouth the jagged, uneven look of mismatched lips. Her plain features guaranteed she would never be a raving beauty, but a steadier hand with makeup could boost her appearance to average. "Well, he might want to start a bit earlier today."

"I doubt it. You kin come back in fifteen minutes."

Her attitude was an irritating itch that demanded a scratch. "I can't do that. I'm expected back in my office before ten. I don't know how long this will take. Tell Mr. Allen that Assistant Attorney General Casey Lawrence is here to see him." I pulled out my ID.

The woman couldn't have acted less impressed if I had told her I was there to count mouse turds under the candy display. In spite of her lack of enthusiasm, she buzzed the boss.

About two minutes later a short, birdlike man with thinning hair came out of the back room. He wiped his fingers on his white jacket. "I'm Jim Allen. What's all the fuss about?" He didn't offer his hand, but neither did I offer mine.

"Your pharmacy area is open," I said as I looked to the side of the store where a sign indicated PRESCRIPTIONS. "Door's not even shut, let alone locked. And you're in the backroom eating donuts." I paused as he gave me a what's-it-to-you-look, then introduced myself. "I'm Assistant Attorney General Lawrence."

"Is that supposed to mean something to me?"

"I'm with the Medical Professionals Division of the Attorney General. I think you have a problem here."

"Why you hassling me?" Allen's sullen expression said he hoped I would disappear.

"I'm not. But I am here to check a few things. You don't mind, do you?" For the briefest moment, I reminded myself of Lockhart.

"What is it you want?"

"Your prescriptions since January of this year."

"Why?" He shot me a confrontational sneer.

"I'll let you know after I review them."

"Maybe I should call my attorney."

"Feel free. Remind him the Public Health Code requires your records be available for inspection whenever requested."

"It's always the pharmacy inspectors who come by. What's to make me think you can order me to do anything?" Tough words, but his voice had developed a stutter.

"Why don't you call that attorney of yours and see." With a poker-straight face, I flashed him the ID I still held in my hand. He seemed as unimpressed as his clerk had been.

He muttered something as he did an about-face and disappeared behind the pharmacy counter. The only word I caught was "bitch." He returned with a cardboard box the size of a piece of carry-on luggage. He dropped it on the floor at my feet. I estimated it held maybe ten thousand scripts. I never won the guess-the-number-of-jellybeans-in-a-jar contests, but there were plenty of slips in that box.

I knelt and skimmed them. In the first hundred or so, the name Jackson Wainwright came up ten times. The name Cameron Day came up at least as often. There were generous numbers written by Khoury and Khoury's other neighbor across the hall, Kessler. The names Cho, Martinez, and Jones popped up in every handful. The prescriptions were all for addictive substances, not an amoxicillin or Flonase in the batch. This would take time.

"You find what you want?" Allen huddled over me like a street musician protecting his tip jar.

"I might have," I said. "I'll take this box with me."

"You can't, I need that."

"You don't need copies of scripts you've already filled. You've got a record in your computer system. Call your attorney if you want. Otherwise, I'll leave you a receipt, and I'm out of here. The box comes with me." It was a bluff. Without a subpoena, his attorney would likely tell him to refuse my request.

Allen straightened up and shot laser rays at me with Brad Pitt baby blues that were his only enviable feature. He seemed to ponder his options. If it came to it, and he became violent, I could take him. At a buck-twenty-five, I weighed more and was in better shape. Until a week ago, I did fifty push-ups and ran four miles most days. I had a brown belt in Karate. He didn't scare me.

I used Allen's indecision to make my exit. I figured it might stretch my luck if I asked him to carry the carton to my car.

28

No reason to risk back strain lugging the awkward box from the parking lot. I pulled under the G. Mennen Williams Building, engaged my flashers, and left the Toyota in a no-parking zone next to the elevators. I struggled the carton upstairs, where I dropped it inside our offices, and then ran back down and moved my car to the mud lot—all in time to avoid overzealous parking police.

"Where have you been?" Shirl called when I strolled past her door. The first time in my tenure with the office that she had greeted me. A bad sign.

"Sorry. I stopped at Licensing Regs this morning. I needed to pick up a report from Chace Gannon." I hoped Shirley would forgo further questions about my absence.

"What's happening on Day?" Her eyes caught me at about shoulder level. I didn't flatter myself that she envied my bustline, she aimed there to avoid direct eye contact.

"I plan to make a few calls this afternoon," I said. "I should have a complaint ready before I leave. Tomorrow at the latest."

"You think it's one we need to file a complaint on?"

"From the looks of it, I would say little doubt. Why the fuck—sorry, I mean heck— is everyone so interested in the Day case?"

I assumed her frown was for the gratuitous fuck that spiced my answer. Shirl brought out the worst in me. "No special reason," she said.

"Why don't I believe that? Oh, yes, maybe it's because I got a call yesterday from Mark Rodgers. Even I know Day's a friend of Sawicki's. Everyone says it doesn't make any difference. For a case that's no different than any other, this one's getting a lot of attention."

"I don't like your insinuation." Shirley's eyes finally locked on mine, but it was a challenge, not camaraderie, I read in them.

"Then how about the straight dope? Am I supposed to give Day the kid-glove treatment? Ignore stuff that would make my blood boil if he weren't buds with the boss?"

"Obviously not. No one expects that." Like Rodgers, she overplayed indignant, but she didn't need me to second-guess Sawicki. If Shirley had seen the political ramifications of the file when it landed on her desk for assignment, it was a damned sure bet it wouldn't be part of my caseload.

"What's our evidence?" she asked. The *our* was a nice touch. Made it sound like we were on the same team. I summarized the information provided by Beverly Comstock.

"Any chance Dr. Day was trying to wean Comstock's daughter off drugs?" she asked.

"Yeah, and elephants have ears that double as wings."

"No need for sarcasm."

"He constantly increased both the number and strength of what he gave her." I hated arguing the obvious.

"According to the hysterical mother," she said. "Not stellar evidence."

"No, not only according to the hysterical mother. According to the patient records. The Board of Medicine will go berserk. I've considered a summary in this one." I studied the humorless woman sitting behind the desk. She might not be my pal, but it was hard to see her mixed up in anything illegal. I doubted she had the gumption for it. She was more the type who would play along but only to a limit.

"It's not like this is the first time someone's complained about Day," I said. Shirley didn't take the bait so I continued. "I saw the case you closed on him."

"Then you also saw that I had no compelling evidence." She hand combed her coarse snarled hair into place, a nervous tell that she disliked the direction of the conversation.

"Right, but when enough people call him a whore, it makes me believe he sells something seductive and unrelated to legitimate medical need."

"Just make sure we can prove what we charge." Poor Shirl. Such an ass-kisser. She couldn't afford a mistake to hamper her upward mobility. It could be a long journey from her office on the sixth floor to the seventh, where our revered leader presided. Some people wanted to make the climb a lot worse than others.

I didn't mention my visit to Khoury's clinic, where I noted the neighbor across the hall was Dr. Day. She would be all over me for branding Day guilty by association. I also kept to myself my visit to the Buy-Smart Pharmacy and the box of scripts I was about to peruse—many, way too many, with Day's autograph on them.

"Let me see the complaint when it's drafted," she said. "And if you need any help, let me know."

I nodded, headed to my office and closed the door behind me.

Jim Allen's filing system left much to be desired. I positioned his cardboard box, imprinted with the words KOTEX MAXI PADS, at the side of my desk away from the door. I opened my bottom right drawer as wide as possible, shoved to one side the bag of Fritos and six-pack of Hershey bars with almonds, and began sorting the scripts into it. Three hours later when I finished, I had piles for Wainwright, Kessler, Khoury, and Day. I also had stacks for doctors Cho, Martinez, and Jones, who had avoided our radar.

Dr. Day's mound contained nearly two thousand scripts. Looking at the size of the other piles, I estimated Khoury might be a lightweight in the group. Dr. Wainwright's number appeared marginally less than Day's, and Dr. Kessler appeared to write more scripts than any of his colleagues. A whole fuckin' herd of worthless scumbags, I thought.

Finished with my initial sort, I placed each doctor's scripts in a separate folder and paperclipped them by patient. The remaining miscellaneous scripts I returned to the box. I would give them a closer look later.

With the information from Dr. Day's scripts, I started a chart on a sheet of legal paper. Across the top, I wrote DR. CAMERON DAY and under his name I made columns for Dilaudid, Percodan, Tylenol 3, Empirim 3, Talwin, OxyContin, Fentanyl, Valium, and Methadone. Down the side of the page, I wrote the names of thirty-four patients for whom the pile seemed excessive. Jean Smith had received scripts for 2,294 dosage units of 2-mg Dilaudid since January 1. Either she took nine tabs a day or sold on the side.

Harry Smith scored enough Ritalin to keep an overcrowded class of hyperactive first graders sedated for the entire school year. His Valium scripts seemed strange mates for the Ritalin. I wondered if Harry was related to Jean, or if either of them were really Smiths. They each filled prescriptions every week for the entire nine-month period covered by the confiscated scripts. It was a good guess that they had a similar pattern the previous year. Even doctors who graduated from no-name medical schools in the Caribbean knew it was ill-advised to prescribe endless quantities of narcotics to non-terminal patients. I guessed the Smiths weren't terminal unless the *Merck Diagnostic Manual* had reclassified drug addiction.

My tabulations for Dr. Day completed, I started a second chart with twenty-seven patients for Wainwright. The afternoon sped by, and I wanted to talk to Gannon. I dialed his extension and caught him at a rare moment when he wasn't swamped. He agreed to stop by to inspect the results of my fact-finding mission.

Ten minutes later he scanned the numbers and said, "You've been a busy woman."

"Yeah, and I haven't gotten to Khoury, Kessler, or the others." I heard the gears in his brain grind.

"I say we subpoena the medical records of Day's patients and take a look at the treatment notes."

"I planned to draft a complaint this afternoon. That would delay it."

"But it should give you thirty-four nails to pound in his coffin."

"Maybe some are legitimate patients."

"I'll make you a side wager there isn't a legitimate patient in the bunch."

"What's the bet?" I asked.

"How about dinner?" Wisps of lust flickered in his eyes, and his smile beamed wicked thoughts my way.

"Not a good idea." I averted eye contact by staring at the summaries on my desk. "How about lunch and only if we work."

"You're no fun anymore, Lawrence."

I let the comment pass. No sense encouraging him. "Maybe you should make a few house calls. Talk to some of these patients."

"That's if I can find them," he said. "And if they'll open the door to me if I do."

"If you want some help, I'll volunteer. We could split the list. Anything to get me out of this frickin' office."

"It may come to that. In the meantime, can I get a copy of these summaries?"

"I'll give you what I've got so far. I'll send the whole report after I finish it, and Louise types it up neat and pretty."

When I returned from the Xerox machine and handed him the stack of charts, I added, "There's something else you should know."

"What's that?"

"Sawicki's hot and bothered about this one. Seems he was Day's college roommate."

"Small world. It wouldn't surprise me a bit if they remained close. I told you my verdict's out on Sawicki. I know our attorney general likes men with big bank accounts and women with big breasts."

After Gannon left, I drafted a complaint against Day, leaving blanks where I could later insert information about specific patients. It was almost six-thirty. I needed to pick up Natalee from Trish's, and I didn't relish a walk to the mud lot in the gray of dusk. I put the afternoon's work in my desk, grateful that for at least a few hours, I had diverted part of my attention from a bloodied study and missing ex-husband.

29

Wednesday, October 5

The next afternoon I sequestered myself in my office, door closed, and hoped that nothing drove Shirley my way. Not that I felt guilty. Besides guilt being a useless emotion, it was my job to put unscrupulous doctors out of business. But I needed to figure out who the players were before I shared my suspicion with Shirl. I hoped my hunch that some of our team pinch-hit for the bad guys was baseless.

I tabulated the numbers for Khoury, Martinez, and Cho and created a chart for each. I was focused on Kessler when my phone buzzed. One ring indicated an inside call. Louise said, "There's a Mrs. Julia Johnson here to see you. Says she's got information about one of your cases. Won't say more than that."

When I opened the door, I saw a fragile-looking woman, shoulders stooped as though she carried a burden too heavy for her slight frame. She squinted to inspect me. "Ms. Johnson?" I said. I believed I fell short of her approval, but she nodded.

"Come in." I held out my hand. She ignored the gesture and clasped her purse like a shield in front of her. "I'm Casey Lawrence. Have a seat." I shut the door behind her.

She sat but said nothing. I studied my guest and considered how to loosen her tongue. I didn't want to spook her. Believable witnesses were as rare as sunshine during a Michigan winter. With a face a judge would trust, this woman was a prosecutor's dream. Her chiseled cheekbones gave her a look of elegance barely diminished by the dark circles under her violet eyes. Specks of black floated in those pools of amethyst and tinged them somber. Her lipstick was a couple of shades too close to cotton candy for her olive coloring, but her mouth was heart-shaped and full. She wasn't Miss America gorgeous, not a ten, but she would hold her own in a room full of eights or nines.

"Louise says you have information about one of my cases?" Still, my visitor said nothing. I noticed a slight tremble in her slender fingers. She fidgeted with a plain wide gold wedding band. "Would you like a glass of water? I might even be able to scrounge a cup of the sludge we pass off as coffee."

"That's not what I need from you." It sounded more bitter than the coffee I offered and confused me. "I'm Katya." She let it hang in the air and awaited my reaction.

"Katya Gannon?" I asked.

"Not what you expected? My mother watched *Dr. Zhivago* when she was pregnant with me and wanted to name me something Russian-sounding."

"I didn't expect anything," I said. "Why did you tell Louise your name was Johnson?"

"I was afraid you wouldn't see me if you knew who I was."

"Why not?" I played innocent and prayed color didn't flush my cheeks in spite of the heat rising in my chest.

"I think you know."

"I'm not sure I do." I labored to hear her. That was good. Maybe her words wouldn't penetrate the thin walls. Shutting the door to my office was a token gesture; privacy was only assured before eight and after five when the office cleared out.

"Ms. Lawrence, I deserve honesty."

"I'll try." Her unrelenting glare made me wish I could skip the disaster barreling toward me.

"I'm not a fancy lawyer or anything, but I love my husband."

"Okay." My mind raced. If she asked me straight out would I tell her the truth? I couldn't decide, and I didn't have much time to reflect on it.

"And he's sleeping with you."

Those eyes seemed to have nailed my thoughts. "Whoa. Back up. I am not sleeping with Chace." As far as it went, it was the truth.

She paused, maybe to process my denial through her internal polygraph, before she said, "Please don't lie to me. You have no idea how hard it was for me to come here."

I wanted to promise her everything was peachy, but I had no way to know that, and she had asked for honesty. I hedged. "I know a thing or two about philandering husbands. If Chace is sleeping with someone it's news to me. He and I are colleagues. He's a damned fine investigator. Helps me win cases. But I would consider it a mistake to sleep with a coworker." Careful wording. I hadn't lied.

"Then you've changed your thinking in the past year," she said, "because you didn't mind sleeping with him then." The voice that spit those words seemed too loud to come from this petite woman.

I remained silent. I couldn't spin an evasive answer to that one. I knew that at least Louise, Shirl, and the attorney whose office was on the other side of mine got an earful. Months of discretion, and I had been outed.

"I hired a private investigator to follow Chace. He told me my husband was involved with someone he worked with. I saw the photos. Are you telling me that wasn't you?"

"I'm telling you I am not sleeping with Chace. And no private eye can tell you different because it would be a lie." My mouth was dry as desert sand and my armpits seemed to be getting all the excess moisture.

"The pictures were taken at quite a distance and were blurred, but even so, I saw that the woman was tall and striking. The online state directory has your picture. My investigator's photos look a lot like you."

"Well, I'm tall. I'll give you that. Striking is a stretch." I hoped self-deprecation would induce Katya to lower her voice.

It worked, she reduced her volume, but the brief smirk that crossed her face disappeared when she again opened her mouth. "When Chace and I separated a year ago, I knew he took up with someone else. I went home one night to get clothes, and I smelled Divine Folie in the house. My sister wears it, and I detest that sweet smell."

Thank you, God, I thought. At least whoever trashed my study had the good sense to carry off the incriminating fragrance of my indiscretion. "I don't own Divine Folie." And I damned sure wouldn't buy another bottle in this lifetime. "But you and Chace worked things out."

"He told you about our problems?"

Great job of sticking my size nine sling backs in my big mouth. "Not much. But we worked together many hours and became friends. He mentioned he could stay late one night because you were gone for a while."

"What else did he say?" She was like a hungry child, frantic for a breast to suckle.

"That he loved you and the girls and was sure it would work out. He wanted the chance to be a better husband." I forgave myself a smidgeon of poetic license. I told her what she craved hearing.

"We did get back together. I was more miserable without him than with him. And the children needed him." She twisted her wedding band. Tears pooled in those haunting eyes. I pushed a box of tissues her direction. Delicate fingers extracted one.

She blew her nose before she continued. "About six weeks ago he came home late. He swore it was work, but I had called his personal line to ask him to pick up a gallon of milk. I tried several times. And there was no answer on his cell. When he walked in the house, he carried the musky odor of sex."

"You know when he works cases, he often has to turn off his cell. And sometimes he's forced to frequent pretty rank-smelling dives." I offered her hope. For both of our sakes.

"I don't think so. A wife knows. Little things. He doesn't want to make love . . . he works longer hours than usual . . . he makes calls from our study keeps his voice low—"

"Have you asked him?"

"I'm a coward. I believed it was you and came here to beg you to leave him alone. I need him. We have three daughters."

"I know. He adores your girls."

"Has he told you that Abbey, our eight-year-old, is autistic? She responds to Chace better than to anyone else."

I imagined her humiliation as she sat across from the woman she believed screwed her husband. If there hadn't been an Abbey, I wondered if she would have done it. It reminded me there was nothing I wouldn't do for Natalee.

"I have a daughter. I understand how you feel, but I promise you don't have to worry about me. I have problems of my own. I will never sleep with your husband." Full disclosure might require me to add *again,* but it was near enough.

"I know," she said. "I've been reading about you in the paper." Maybe the grin she flashed was her way of showing sympathy. Or maybe she pictured me knee deep in shit—getting what she thought I deserved. Maybe she knew all about that.

I didn't mention that I, too, wanted to pummel her husband's handsome, innocent-looking face. I had been misguided if I thought I was special.

"In Chace's defense, I can tell you that we've been swamped. That could account for his late hours and preoccupation." That and a new mistress. So much for a meaningful affair.

"I'm sorry to have bothered you," she said.

"Don't be sorry, it gave us a chance to meet. I hope you're wrong about Chace." I wanted to grasp her hand, hug her as she stood to leave, somehow offer a gesture that said I understood her pain. Instead, I stayed safely in my own space, afraid she might hiss invectives or turn violent. I tiptoed around what I wanted to ask and ratcheted my courage. "If it were my husband, I might hire someone to discourage the other woman."

Her blank stare either answered my question, or said she was the best actress since Audrey Hepburn.

"At the very least I would probably call a few times to unnerve her," I said.

Her eyes widened as she grasped my meaning. She didn't deny phone calls but said, "I know your house got messed up. It wasn't me. My idea of destroying something was to throw a couple of plates against a wall." She smiled, then turned away from me, and opened the door to let herself out. "Thank you for your time."

She was more beautiful when she smiled, I thought. Was she more beautiful when she lied?

30

I wanted to give Katya Gannon plenty of time to clear the building before initiating my own escape. It would be a bonus if the offices were empty when I slithered out.

I shuffled and stacked papers, lined up the stapler, name plaque, even the telephone until everything was parallel. Took a Kleenex and dusted between things. Picked dead leaves off the plant. My concentration had disappeared as surely as the rosy, tear-stained cheeks Katya had displayed to coworkers craning for a peek when she paraded past them

I wondered if I had heard the last of Katya. Her denial aside, I didn't peg her as the type to hatch convoluted schemes to unnerve me. More like a .22 caliber sissy gun aimed mid-forehead if she chose revenge.

Katya Gannon's visit hauled me back to my affair and the last afternoon Chace and I spent together. After his wife left, I couldn't harness thoughts hell-bent on resurrecting the past. Married men, even separated ones like Chace was during our fling, caused more hassle than they were worth.

As lovers Chace and I hoisted discretion to dizzying heights and prided ourselves that no one caught on. We reveled in sex more intoxicating than Beefeaters straight and more addictive than Oxycodone. During the three months we infatuated each other, we understood the romance was as ill-advised as sauntering unarmed into a roomful of gangbangers. We didn't care. Chances for a happy ending decreased exponentially since Chace never planned to divorce Katya. He was passing time until she came back. With hindsight, that was clear.

When Katya moved back home, cold turkey was the only way for Chace and me to end it. A few calls greeted me with eerie silence broken by heavy breathing. I mentioned them to Chace.

He rolled his eyes, shook his head, clutched his heart. His smirk told me that he was trying to be funny, but I wasn't amused then, even less so now. "Pray they were wrong numbers." He paused before adding, "Katya is a woman of many virtues: great cook, loving mother, generous friend, but she's murder in the making when crossed."

I had deluded myself into believing that Chace prepared me to love again. With him I forgot Derek. I forgot lesser annoyances like Sawicki and the glitch in my career path. I almost forgot Jimmy Scroggins and anger and rage. Chace made me forget the reasons, great and small, that I had given up on men.

But for as much physical pleasure as we brought each other, I didn't find happiness. I rationalized that Katya had left Chace, and I was not cheating on anyone. In spite of my justification, there was something missing in love promised to another woman. Even one temporarily absent.

Katya's visit recast that lingering memory. God, I was a sap. And that was the least of my worries.

With sheer willpower, I forced myself to stop thinking about Chace. I immersed myself in more mindless tasks. Organized a file. Reread a medical report that I could have quoted by heart. Proofed a letter Louise had returned to me for signature.

At six-thirty I decided I'd had enough of this day. In the offices of Med Pro, my light was the only one that remained on. It cast eerie shadows over the secretarial desks and emphasized that there was not another warm body in our suite. I took off my Jimmie Choo heels, bought online at eighty percent off retail, and stuck my feet into muddied running shoes. I plunged my hand into the contents of my purse, wiggled my fingers around combs, billfold, pens, lipstick, sunglasses, and assorted change until I felt my car keys. As I retrieved them, my phone rang—two rings—signaling my direct line.

"This is Casey," I said.

"Ms. Lawrence, is this a good time to talk?" It was a voice I had never heard before. It sounded more dangerous than the forbidden sex I had been revisiting and gave me a less pleasurable shiver. Whoever Advice4U was, he had the number to my private line.

31

"Who is this?" I demanded.

"The name's not important. By the way, I liked the pictures. Nice-looking man, your ex-husband."

"That seems to be the consensus." I clenched my teeth, swallowed hard and fought the urge to squeeze the life out of the receiver. If Katya was responsible for any of this, she either didn't believe me or had not had time to call off her dogs. "What do you want?"

"You've got it wrong. What can I do for you? Maybe arrange for a package with, say, ten thousand dollars to be left on your front step for your daughter's homecoming dance. Should buy her a designer dress and pay for a limo and dinner for her and a dozen friends at the classiest restaurant in town. With what's left over, you and Tom can treat yourselves to quite a weekend."

Concern for Natalee's safety restrained my urge to tell the douche bag he could take his ten thousand and stick it up his puckered ass. "That's generous but not necessary. We're fine. There is one thing you can do for me."

"And that would be?" His ingratiating tone threw me. I felt dirty listening to him.

"Tell me where Derek is."

"What makes you think I know?"

All the lying and being lied to gave me a headache. "I'm pretty damn sure his disappearance is connected to your current interest in me." I dismissed as implausible another scenario: Derek *and* Katya conspiring with this joker.

He answered and halted my wild imagination. "That's pure speculation. But let's say I have ways to find out where he is. A sign of good faith from you might convince me to use them."

"What more do you want?" I asked. "I'll see it works out for Khoury when his case resumes. I have several weeks before Wainwright is healthy enough to practice. His situation is more complicated, but I'm working on it."

"Good. But stop pestering Jim Allen."

I felt a cold lump where my heart was supposed to be. "Is there anything you don't know about me?"

"I've got lots of eyes and ears. They pass along information."

Sweat broke out on my forehead and upper lip, and I wiped both with my open palm. "I'm not sure how I can protect Allen. The more I help you, the more I lose credibility. At some point, I'll be of no value to you. I'll get fired for—"

"Let me worry about that."

"I'll see what I can do," I said.

"You better do it fast. This is a tremendous opportunity for you. On the other hand, if you don't make this right, it could be the worst mistake of your life. Do as you're asked, no one has to know your tawdry secrets."

"I don't like threats." I spoke slowly, deliberately. Words, the only weapon in my arsenal, sounded impotent when whispered.

"You shouldn't look at it that way. There are good doctors around here. They care about their patients. A shame if well-intentioned individuals were put out of business by an overzealous assistant attorney general. Even sadder if Ms. Natalee needed a doctor and couldn't find one. Think hard about these doctors and pharmacists before you make any rash decisions. Enjoy your evening, Ms. Lawrence."

When the phone went dead, I cleared my brain, dialed Rad. "Can you pick me up for lunch tomorrow? We need to talk again."

"I could be there in fifteen minutes."

"I can't. I've got to pick up Natalee." I could force my voice steady; I couldn't eliminate the breathlessness triggered by fear.

Rad knew me too well. "Casey, what's happened? How about I stop by your house in half an hour."

"It can wait. Honest. I've got a couple of other things I want to check out tonight. I'll bring you up to speed tomorrow, noon sharp, Pine Street entrance. And don't worry, I have a security guard, remember?"

I hung up, grabbed my coat, and for the first time since my move to the division, locked my desk drawers. As I turned off the light to my office a nagging voice warned that if I put Day and Buy-Smart out of business, the Jean and Harry Smiths of the drug world would find new doctors and other willing pharmacists.

And for my trouble, I might get my daughter killed.

I headed to the mud lot, the sun plummeting as fast as my courage. The chill that caused me to button my jacket had little to do with weather. I pulled my cell from my purse and dialed Ginny. I welcomed a human connection while I walked empty sidewalks to my car.

"It's Casey," I said when my friend answered. "I just left work. Would you let me borrow your husband for a few minutes tonight? I have some questions related to a case."

"Sure, but not until you tell me how you're doing. We haven't heard a peep since Saturday."

Small talk brought me closer to my Toyota. "I'm surviving."

"Why don't you and Natalee stay here until the police figure this out? It has to be spooky sleeping in your house. We've got a guestroom with your name on it."

"I appreciate the offer. I'll keep it in mind, but for now, we're okay."

"If you're sure. Just a sec." I heard Ginny yell, "Jon, it's Casey for you."

While I waited for him to come to the phone, I considered the Aristotle quotation that hung in my den and survived the burglary: THE ANTIDOTE FOR FIFTY ENEMIES IS ONE FRIEND. I was neck deep in bad shit, but I would be in even bigger trouble without Rad, Tom, and the Beckmans. Yesterday Chace would have been on my short list. Now, I put a question mark after his name.

Jon picked up and said, "To what do I owe this pleasure?"

"How about a drink?" I asked. "I'm on my way to get Natalee and wondered if you could stop by our place in about forty-five minutes. I need to pick your brain. Ginny's welcome too, of course, but they're medical questions."

"I'll be there."

I said goodbye as I unlocked the car and quickly scooched inside. When I reached the Okemos exit, I drove a half block north, pulled through the drive-up window of Burger King. "Two Whoppers. I have a buy-one-get-one-free coupon." The attorney general paid me enough that I didn't need to watch pennies, but I would die worried about how much my casket cost.

Natalee bounded down the front steps before I honked. She must have seen me from Trish's bay window. My daughter's denim skirt was six inches shorter than I would prefer, and I still had to talk to her about that tattoo she believed was her secret. Her breasts jiggled beneath a white V-neck sweater as she hurried toward the car. She fastened her seat belt. I leaned over and planted a kiss on her cheek.

At the unctuous smell of grease, Natalee eyed the take-out bag. "I get the onion rings." I didn't argue as she opened the bag and popped one in her mouth.

I examined her face for clues before I pulled away from the curb. Ernie's Camry fell in behind us. "How're you holding up?"

"How do you think?" She glared at me with are-you-trying-to-ruin-my-life daggers that accompanied the grumble in her voice. "I love being banished from my home until you get out of work. I have a bodyguard. And did I mention that looking over my shoulder is a drag?"

"I know. I wish I could fix it. I'm trying."

"Try harder." Her sullenness didn't dampen her appetite. She devoured a handful of the fries, and the onion rings were half gone.

"I've got some good news." I stretched for anything that might cheer her up. "How about a shopping trip tomorrow night? See if we can snag a homecoming dress before all the good ones are gone."

"I'm not in the mood. Homecoming's a month away. Maybe Ethan and I won't go."

"Honey, you can't let this ruin your life. Everything will be okay." Words coated with false conviction.

"Promise?"

"I promise I'll do everything I can. Good enough?"

"If this is multiple choice, I'll take a better option."

"Sorry."

"Then I guess it's gotta be good enough." Natalee hit the garage door opener. "If someone wants to ruin my life, they're doing an awesome job."

My stomach was on fire. With the last onion ring hanging from her mouth, Natalee grabbed the white paper sack and slammed the car door. I felt a twinge of contrition that brought another flicker of heat to my gut. I should give her broiled chicken, a salad, and for dessert a fresh fruit compote. Stress turned me into a dietician's worst nightmare. I hid my Snickers binges from my daughter, then plied her with a thousand calories containing the nutritional value of horse manure.

"I'm sorry, honey. I want answers as much as you do. Jon's coming over tonight. I'll pick his brain for information."

"Why Jon?"

"Because he's a doctor and may have heard something to support a theory I've got. I think this is about the doctors I prosecute."

32

When the doorbell rang, my first thought was the .38 on my nightstand. Rad might be right, but it was impractical to carry a revolver from room to room. Laid on the arm of my comfortable overstuffed couch, it would have a negative impact on ambiance. I expected Jon, and through the peephole, I recognized his contorted face.

"Thanks for coming." I led him into the living room. "Ginny decided not to join us?"

"She's meeting a client." He slouched onto the couch, rested one arm on the sofa back. With his free hand, grabbed a throw pillow and clutched it on his lap. His initial smile faded to serious. "Who's in the Camry parked out front?"

"Part of a long story." I had my back to him as I headed toward the bar. I turned and stopped long enough to give him a brief explanation, ending with, "I don't know what's going on. Except this is serious enough, I've hired a bodyguard. Wave at him when you leave. I'm sure he's lonely." I tightened my mouth. It was as close to a smile as I could muster.

"Casey, this is scary stuff. The cops must think so too. They questioned both Ginny and me about the burglary and your ex-husband. They asked if we knew anything about your life before you went to law school. We told them we had only known you for the last ten years, and you were pretty damned near perfect. But I think you should take Gin up on her offer and stay with us for a while."

"We're safe with my own personal babysitter outside. I'll let you know if I change my mind. For now, my safety isn't why I asked you to stop by."

He opened his mouth as though he were going to say more, and then with the look of a man rejected, he closed it again.

"How about a Wild Turkey and Canada Dry Club Soda?" I reached for an on-the-rocks glass and opened the bottle of soda.

"You speak my language. You never forget what I drink."

"Comes from waitressing when I was an undergrad." I poured the alcohol and mixer and dropped in three ice cubes. I treated myself to a generous glass of Merlot from a recorked bottle in the wine refrigerator. I handed Jon his drink and a coaster before parking myself in one of the wingbacks. "Maybe if I still waited tables I wouldn't be in all this trouble."

"Yeah, and if I still worked on cars my life would be less complicated. Though fixing cars isn't all that different from fixing people. Just a lot less money. Maybe that isn't even true these days. I took the Beemer in because the steering wheel shimmied. I'll need a second job to cover the two thousand dollars they charged me."

Under the bright light from the floor lamp behind the couch, I saw that the man I considered a George Clooney clone—tall, lean, athletic with gray at the temples—had begun to age. The change had been so gradual I hadn't noticed. With little wire-rimmed glasses instead of his contacts, Jon looked more like a college professor than a leading man. His straight hair, cut short, receded slightly at the sides, and for the first time, I noticed a thin spot in the back. Careful combing could cover it, but probably not for long. Crow's feet and laugh lines added character to his face. I didn't often think about whether Jon was good-looking, or even *what* he looked like, but sometime in the last decade, he had slipped from handsome to distinguished.

From the briefcase next to my chair I pulled out the charts I had finished earlier in the afternoon and handed him one. "Take a look at this. I've got a new case, and this is a summary of scripts received by thirty-four patients seeing Dr. Cameron Day." Jon studied the page, and when he looked up, I said, "What do you think?"

"Either Dr. Day is an oncologist, or there's a problem here."

"The latter is the reasonable conclusion. Do you know Dr. Day?"

"The name is familiar, but I don't know him personally."

"How about Wainwright, Kessler or Khoury?" I handed over the additional charts.

"Kessler used to work with Dr. Conrad over on Hagadorn. A personal disagreement caused a split in the partnership. That's all I know. Rumors circulated that they held different philosophies about treatment modalities."

"Anything to do with prescriptions?"

"I can't say." He ran his fingers down the columns of numbers.

"What would justify the prescribing in these charts?" I asked.

He continued scanning the numbers. "You want me to play devil's advocate? You already know the answer."

I nodded. "Humor me."

"You would prescribe these drugs to a patient with a short time to live and excruciating pain to live it in."

"What about someone who's got a long time to live, but is in horrible pain?"

He shrugged his shoulders. "Contraindicated. The problem with pain is that it's subjective. Legitimate doctors know they can't separate the person who wants drugs from the person who is hurting. If a doctor plays loose, he or she is headed for trouble."

I pointed at the charts. "What, besides terminal cases, could account for this?"

"It would be appropriate short-term for someone who's had major surgery. Pain that is expected to subside with healing. But you wouldn't see this for cases of intractable, long-term pain."

"Is that true for all of the drugs listed?" I asked.

"Pretty much. All addictive. Talwin arguably less dangerous than Dilaudid or OxyContin or Fentanyl. Empirim 3 and Tylenol 3 both have codeine. Not dangerous short-term, but they hook you."

"How about Percodan?"

"Same philosophy, but it's not the pariah that either OxyContin or Fentanyl are."

"Methadone?"

"A darling these days. Used to wean addicts off heroin, but I have seen a number of deaths related to it because addicts believe it's safe. It is, if used as prescribed, but drug abusers swallow it like candy."

"Triplicate scripts don't control the problem?"

"They help. They've been around since before I graduated from John Hopkins. Big issue when I was in medical school. Some doctors fought Big Brother monitoring their prescribing patterns. But the abuse of prescription drugs escalated, and anti-crime forces outmuscled a few disgruntled doctors."

He took another swallow of his scotch and raised his eyebrows. "Hey, you're the one who ragged on me about keeping good records, and you know all about trip scripts. So, why twenty questions?"

"Is there a way for controlled substances to become part of the major drug traffic?" I asked. He handed back my summaries. I shuffled the pages, squared the edges into a neat stack, and returned them to my briefcase.

"Sure. Some doctors pad their profits, sell questionable scripts. You see it every day."

"I don't mean one doctor. I mean like a major business where several doctors work for someone who coordinates the whole thing . . . like a drug cartel or something. Anything like that rumored around town?"

"Not that I've heard. Doctors are as greedy as the next guy. I can't imagine they would pay a middleman. They prefer to think they're above dealing with street-level punks."

"What if forced, or blackmailed?" I returned to the bar and poured myself another generous glass of Merlot. I set the empty bottle aside to put in the recycle bin and then freshened his drink.

"Anything's possible. A lot of doctors don't believe Licensing Regulations has the manpower to monitor scripts. So, they take chances." He uncrossed his legs and rubbed his thighs as though he needed to stretch.

"They're right about understaffing. But I would guess the sale of controlled substances could be a lucrative business. If it promises enough money it might get the attention of criminal organizations."

"Your imagination works overtime." The shake of his head added impact to his opinion.

"Maybe—"

"You can bet if a scandal like that floated through the medical pipeline, it would have reached me. We're a pretty tight community."

"The fact that no one expects it in small-town Lansing might make it work," I said.

"Is that what you believe?"

"I'm not sure. I figured it wouldn't hurt to ask what you had heard."

"You didn't have to ask. I've got the doctor police living two doors down, and she's my friend. If I got wind of a scheme like that, you would be the first to know. I want you to find the answers, really, Casey, I do, but I think you're sniffing the wrong dog's ass." His glass was reaching empty again, and he took a big swallow. "Have you mentioned your theory to the police?"

"Not yet. But I will."

He stroked his chin with his fingers and thumb as he seemed to contemplate my options. "I think you should. And, not to change the subject, since we are speaking of prescription drugs and addiction, how are you doing with your sleep issues?"

"Last night I skipped the Ambien. I tossed and turned, my imagination shifted into overdrive. As soon as I think the worst is over, something or someone pushes my buttons again. I was a zombie today."

"Don't take this as a compliment, but you look exhausted," he said.

I touched my face, pinched my cheeks for a bit of color. "Hard to see how you mean that in an unflattering way."

Jon placed his empty glass on the coffee table. "I'm worried about you. I'm the last person to encourage sleeping pills, but you've got circles under those green eyes."

"Thanks."

"Don't mention it. It's my professional assessment, free of charge. My recommendation? Cut the wine for the rest of the night and take an Ambien. In fact, after such a hellish day, it wouldn't hurt if just this once you took an extra half tablet, score it and cut it in two. Your brain could use help to block out everything that's happening long enough to let you get a decent night's sleep. You need your wits about you, and sleep deprivation is the enemy of clear thinking. Make sure you turn in a bit earlier than usual so the drug wears off before you have to haul yourself into work in the morning."

"I suppose—"

"Just watch yourself. If things start to settle down, and you rely on the pills every night, we have to talk. On good days, try to get by with a glass of warm milk before you turn in. Set your MP3 to soothing classical. Get some exercise every day. Best treatment for tension. Besides, it's wonderful for your body and your sex life. I prescribe fifty laps at the Y every night after work.

"I swim like a rock." I sounded like a petulant child.

"You jog in the morning, don't you?"

"Used to."

"Try a good run when you get home from work instead. Loosen up the kinks. It'll get your heart rate up, give you a shot of endorphins. Then chill out before you go to bed."

"How about if I just make love more often?" I expected a chuckle, but Jon was on a roll.

"It'll relax you, or at least divert your attention. But I don't know many people our age, or any age for that matter, who get their heart rate to a sustained hundred and fifty for thirty minutes during sexual intercourse."

"Speak for yourself."

That brought the laugh. "Good to see you still have a sense of humor," he said. "If all else fails, take a vacation. Sometimes the best medicine is to get away for a while." He stood. "I've got to head home. Ginny's bugging me to finish sanding the bookshelves I made for our family room. About time I did it. In a couple weeks we're headed to Florida." He started for the door. "That's what you need. Get away."

"Like I've got time." As tempting as it sounded, I couldn't see a way to run away from this.

"Make time. Hey, I've got an amazing idea. Why not come with us? Do a little fishing. Bring Tom. Get laid. You know, concentrate on the good things in life."

I followed him to the door and gave him a hug.

"Seriously, the place Ginny and I rent in Florida is a dive, an old fishing shack on a little inland lake. But it's got three bedrooms. You, Tom, and Natalee could join us. It would be a blast. Tom and I fish and forage, and the women cook. Natural order of things."

I poked him in the ribs. "You're a closet sexist."

"But you love me." He squeezed my hand.

"Can't help myself."

"If you need anything, you know where to find me. Give some thought to Florida."

"I'll mention it to Tom. And thanks again. It's good to know a doctor who makes house calls."

After Jon left, I clicked the front door deadbolt and reconnoitered to make certain the back door, the connecting door to the garage, and all windows were secure. HBO showed a rerun of *The Spy Next Door*. Under most circumstances, I couldn't abide Jackie Chan fluff, but Natalee joined me, and we passed a couple of hours without crying in our hot chocolate. When my daughter went to her room to tackle homework, I decided to take Jon's advice and turn in early. I needed a good night's sleep. I swallowed one Ambien, considered a second and without cutting it in two, swallowed it whole before I went into Natalee's room. She sat on her ivory eyelet spread and pored over a Latin assignment.

"I'm glad I'm not in school anymore." I sat behind her and rubbed her shoulders.

"Latin's not so bad. It's calculus that kills me," she said.

"Consider law school. That's my advice. Very little math."

"Count on that not happening."

"Probably just as well. The last thing we need in this family is another lawyer." I kissed her cheek. "I'm turning in early, honey. When you get tired, crawl in next to me. Even with Fred parked out front, I prefer having you close."

"I love you, Mom, but I'll sleep better in my own room where your delicate snores won't keep me awake."

"That's against mother's advice," I said. "But before you go to bed, at least open my door and leave yours open too."

I brushed my teeth, washed my face and put on a faded nightshirt. I checked the .38 to make sure it was loaded. Of course, it was. I had already checked it once tonight. Jussy jumped on the bed and snuggled next to me. At least my loyal watch-cat didn't mind that I snored.

Within minutes I was dead asleep.

33

Thursday, October 6

In a drowning nightmare that I've suffered intermittently since childhood, I screamed for help. The garbled words, magnified to deafening volume, rose like bubbles in a fish tank. My lungs burned and my throat was raw. I gulped water and coughed it back into the savage sea. Then I woke up.

The face of the digital clock glowed three-thirty. I had another two and a half hours before my alarm blasted classic rock. I would never go back to sleep. With all of my thrashing to escape water demons, I had worked up a sweat. I kicked the covers off and ran my toes over Jussy's silken fur as she lay curled at the end of the bed. She didn't stir. I heard a noise downstairs. I listened. It was the house making settling sounds. That's what I tell myself about night noises.

Ambien proved me wrong about falling back to sleep. The drug still had a couple of hours of kick. Dreams returned in less time than it takes me to rip the wrapper from my first Carmelo bar on a stressful day.

I awoke the second time only because the alarm shattered the quiet with the Rolling Stones "I Can't Get No Satisfaction." Jussy must have had an even rougher night than I had. She didn't prance over my inert body to remind me it was time to feed her, nor did she crawl close to my face, meow, or nip my ear. Her ceremonial welcome of the new day was off.

I stretched my body to get the blood flowing and spread my arms like a child making snow angels. I extended my legs as far as I could push them. My body and mind rejuvenated by a few hours rest, I anticipated a better day.

My big toe touched Jussy's nose. It was ice cold. I wiggled my foot back and forth to tease my cat awake, then wedged it beneath her. She remained still. I scooted closer, stroked my cat. She was rigid, no warmth slipped through her fur, no shiver of life responded. I looked into her wide unseeing eyes.

I reached over, retrieved the .38, opened the cylinder. Six empty chambers.

I laid the barren gun back on the night stand. Revulsion gripped my insides like cyanide swallowed in a near lethal dose. I grabbed a pillow and muffled screams that came like waves from my nightmare.

～

I raced to Natalee's room. My daughter lay sound asleep. I held my breath, lowered my face to an inch from hers, listened to her soft regular breathing, assured myself she was unharmed before I exhaled. I stumbled downstairs and checked doors and windows. Everything was secured tighter than the Federal Reserve. I pulled a coat over my nightgown and trudged down the porch steps to inform my fifty-bucks-an-hour security guard of our breach. He looked up, saw me coming, and stepped from the car.

"We had an intruder last night." I fought an urge to fire him on the spot. "My cat is dead. My gun is empty. I need to know how this happened. My best guess is they came in the back door while you slept."

He started to say something, but I cut him off. "Get inside and check the place out. Make sure there's no one hiding. Do it quickly and quietly. You've got ten minutes before I have to wake Natalee. Ernie will be here by the time we leave, and he'll follow us. You can do a more thorough check after we're gone."

"Yes, ma'am." He avoided eye contact and handled shame well.

While Fred inspected the house, I sat cross-legged on the hallway floor in front of Natalee's room. When he got upstairs, he ducked into the guestroom and study and came out shaking his head to indicate he had found no one. I mouthed the word "go" and shooed him back to his car with a wave of my hand.

When I trusted my voice, I rose and stepped to Natalee's bedside. "Sweet girl." I kissed her forehead. "You asked me to wake you this morning so you could ride downtown with me. I leave in forty-five minutes." My voice sounded almost calm, almost composed, in spite of the jitters squirming around my insides.

"I'm awake," she groaned. "Give me fifteen minutes. Please. I was up late."

I returned to my room, locked the door so Natalee couldn't walk in, then shuffled to the walk-in closet. I picked up a Macy's shopping bag and grabbed one of the towels from the bathroom. I took both back to my bed, removed tissue paper that remained folded in the bag, and spread the towel atop the rumpled bed sheets. I laid Jussy on one end, wrapped her stiff body, and deposited her in the bottom of the bright red paper bag. I folded tissue around the gun before I planted it next to my cat.

I stripped the sheets, then plodded downstairs and into the garage where I popped the trunk latch and settled the bag inside. I pitched the sheets in the trash can. I wouldn't tell Natalee about Jussy until I had more information.

Back upstairs, I stopped to nudge her, "A half hour sleeping beauty. Then we're out of here."

As I pulled the duvet over clean sheets, my empty stomach mutinied in dry heaves. I staggered for the bathroom. A minute later Natalee knocked on the door. "Mom, are you okay?"

My face perched inches above porcelain, I turned from the commode toward her voice. "Uh, huh. I'll be fine." I wiped my mouth, stood, held tight to the sides of the cold sink, and splashed water on my blotchy face before opening the door.

The concern that etched my daughter's frown sent my stomach into another spasm.

"A little stomach virus," I said.

"Are you staying home today?"

"No."

"I can catch a bus downtown," she said. "Or Ernie should be replacing Fred in a couple minutes. He can drop me off. He might as well earn whatever you're paying him."

I couldn't tell her that today no one was staying in the house without the entire First Infantry Division of the United States Army for protection. Maybe not even then. "I would rather not waste a sick day at home feeling miserable."

"Isn't that what they're for? You wouldn't let me go to school if I were sick."

"Right. But I'm the mom."

She didn't argue. Instead, she exhaled an exasperated sigh and said, "I would hug you, but you smell awful."

I turned away so I wouldn't breathe on her. "Give me ten minutes to shower, brush my teeth, and dress."

"I'll have a cup of mint tea waiting for you. Maybe it'll settle your stomach."

"I love you too."

Natalee was quiet as we drove. She was enrolled in a college-credit English class at Lansing Community College on Thursday mornings and pored over notes for a vocabulary test. I didn't trust myself to initiate conversation.

I recalled the day I brought Jussy home from the animal shelter. Every Christmas and birthday since my daughter turned five, she had given me her wish list, the first a barely legible scrawl that I suspected required assistance from her kindergarten teacher. Subsequent lists chronicled improving penmanship skills, but they all had one thing in common. They began with the word *kitten*.

It was a Tuesday, Valentine's Day, six years ago. I walked into the shelter minutes before it closed. Too many abandoned animals to count. Each searched my face. I couldn't save all the kittens and cats. Choosing one to live was a thankless task. I spotted a black cat with a broad white stripe running down the middle of its back giving it the appearance of a skunk's first cousin. The animal was emaciated and scruffy. Not dirty, but with fur that appeared to have been combed by a weed whacker in spite of the animal's best grooming efforts. She was a pathetic homely cat, but something about her suggested a wise soul.

"I want that one," I said.

That was how Jussy became our cat. Now she was dead. I didn't know how, but someone killed her. And left her in my bed to underscore his power. No subtlety. No one could protect us. I needed to find out who he was and stop him.

34

Compartmentalize, I told myself. I bridled tears that would frighten Natalee and prompt questions. After I dropped her off, I allowed myself a three-minute torrent that lasted from the community college to the mud lot. Then I forced myself to get a grip and hustled to the office.

I detoured to the ladies' room and repaired smeared mascara before showing my face to coworkers. For the next two hours, I photocopied Buy-Smart Pharmacy scripts. When I finished, I piled the originals together and arranged them by date with the most recent on top, like they were when I confiscated them. Or close enough that Jim Allen wouldn't notice the difference.

At eleven forty-five I saw Rad's Mercury turn onto Pine from Seymour. I grabbed the box of original scripts and headed for the elevator. Rad parked facing west, and I crossed the street to meet him. As I stepped off the curb, a blue Saturn splashed through a puddle doing about forty. It sprayed me with coffee-colored water as though the money I had spent on my most extravagant suit meant nothing. Rad's window was open. He smirked as I yelled, "Shit!" then extended his arm and flipped his middle finger at the car's exhaust.

I opened the back-passenger side door and set the box of scripts on the seat. "I'll explain later," I answered his stare. "God, it's good to see you."

"A pleasure to see you too, my pet."

"Pets . . . we need to stop at my car." Pent up hysteria festered toward an emotional explosion. I took a deep breath and sucked in a dose of grit.

"What's in your car?" he asked.

"I'm not sure how to explain it." I stared out the side window. I opened my purse and dug for breath mints to cover the foul taste that gagged me.

"The simplest way is best."

"I have Jussy in a bag." The car slowed as he took his foot off the accelerator. His eyes popped wide. Wrinkles arched up, giving his forehead the look of a Shar-Pei.

"Your cat?" he asked before we moved forward again.

"Yes." I kept my face turned away from him so he wouldn't see pooling tears flood over my lower lids. I swallowed to pave the way for more words, but none broke free.

"That may be too simple . . . why do you have your cat in a bag?" The blinker clicked as we turned into the mud lot. "Don't cry," he said. "Hell, don't tell me anything. I'll take your cat." He pulled parallel to my Corolla. "But what do you want me to do with her?"

"She's dead."

"I assumed she wasn't alive, trapped, and squirming in a bag in your trunk. Why are you giving her to me?" Rad shot me the most convincing look of disbelief I had ever seen and waited for my explanation.

"Rad, she wasn't sick. She slept with me last night. This morning when I woke up, she was dead."

"Honey, cats die. Sad fact of life."

"You hate cats."

"Well, it's a sad fact of life for those who don't hate cats." He shut off the engine and removed the keys from the ignition. He shifted his torso and looked me square in the eyes. "Maybe we skip lunch. I'll take you to get a new cat."

"Great solution. Wrong problem." I interrupted my answer to get out of the Merc. Rad followed me to the back of my Toyota, where I opened the trunk and lifted the bag. Even with the added heft of the revolver, Jussy felt weightless. Before I handed her to Rad, I let my fingers touch the spot where her body propped against the side of the paper bag.

Rad eased the sack between his ice chest and a flat tire and then slammed his trunk shut. We stood looking at each other until it became uncomfortable. The Merc's back bumper was plastered with police stickers, but even GIVE ME THE DONUTS AND NO ONE GETS HURT couldn't make me smile.

Back in Rad's car I took deep breaths, stared at my hands on my lap. "This morning when I realized Jussy was dead, I picked up the gun on my nightstand. I opened the cylinder. There were no bullets."

Rad cocked his head toward me and shook it. "That's not possible. We loaded it Sunday."

"Right. And because I have a touch of OCD, I checked it twice before I went to bed. Somebody was in my house. All the while an armed ex-cop guarded us. That intruder was in my bedroom while I slept. Even worse, they were in my bedroom while my daughter slept in a room down the hall."

The muscles on Rad's massive neck tightened. I watched his Adam's apple bobble as he swallowed. He gripped the steering wheel hard enough that his fingers turned red. He muttered "Holy Mother of God" under his breath. "What do you want me to do?"

"I want you to take Jussy to Carl Sampson. Maybe he can figure out what killed her."

"You want a pathologist to autopsy your cat?"

"Can you think of another way?"

"Not off the top of my head. I'll see what my old buddy says." Rad scratched his chin. "If nothing else, I'll bet it's the strangest request he gets today."

"Your .38 is also in the bag. I thought you might want someone to dust it for prints. Yours and mine are all over it. This morning when I clicked the cylinder open, I probably smudged any decent ones the bastard left behind. It might be worth a shot."

"Maybe. But then you have no gun."

"Fat lot of good it did me. About as much protection as Fred and Ernie. I'm sure Fred will call you later today with some lame explanation."

Rad headed west on 496 toward Scoma's on Waverly. The drive gave me time to fill in the details. "I got a case on Dr. Cameron Day last week. Day's apparently a friend of Sawicki. Mark Rodgers from Executive wants to be kept in the loop. No pressure or anything, just kept in the loop." I abbreviated the story but covered the salient details.

"Polite way of telling you to back off?"

"You think? Pretty obvious, isn't it? Day's prescribing patterns landed him on my desk. I'm also working a case on Buy-Smart Pharmacy, which is three blocks from Day's office. A couple of days ago I took a field trip. Long story short, I picked up the pharmacy's scripts for the last nine months. Fascinating reading."

"Define fascinating." Rad rolled down his window and spit. I was tempted to do likewise.

"Same controlled substances to the same patients for months on end. Day writes scripts, and Buy-Smart dispenses them, like they were Good and Plenty."

He jockeyed for a parking spot, removed the key from the ignition, turned to me.

"Yesterday afternoon I got a call. Asshole wouldn't give me a name," I said. "Not even a fake one. Told me to back off Jim Allen, the Buy-Smart pharmacist. So far, I've been ordered to let Khoury off the hook, make the dirt about Wainwright disappear, proceed with caution on Dr. Day, and stay the hell away from Allen. I balked. Told the jerk that if I did all of those things red flags would fly. I assume Jussy was his way of convincing me I have no choice."

"My cop instinct says you have skated onto the tip of an iceberg."

"Yeah. And the guys running this rink make their own rules. I'm in over my head." I twisted the Kleenex in my hand until it shredded.

"You think our sleepy little Lansing has a major-league drug problem?"

"Until I hear a better explanation, that's my guess. I asked my neighbor, Jon Beckman, to stop by last night. He's a doctor. I hoped maybe he would have the skinny on any rumors floating around the medical community. He's pretty connected. Member of all kinds of medical groups or clubs, whatever they call 'em. Says he hasn't heard a thing. I don't know if I should go to the cops. With Jimmy Scroggins lurking in my past, that's potentially as unhealthy as cooperating with the bad guys. I'm scared shitless. They killed Jussy and threatened to hurt my daughter. Derek is missing, and I look good for his disappearance."

"You're lucky you got me."

Rad reached over me, opened the glove box, and took out another .38 Special, identical to the one that rested next to Jussy. "I happen to have a spare." He took a handful of hollow tips from a box under his seat and handed those to me as well. "Good thing you carry a big handbag."

"Good thing you carry a damn arsenal. Must be you live where these things grow on trees." I tossed the gun and bullets into my purse. They nestled next to my cell.

"I've collected a few extras, in case I find myself with a need. A gun doesn't eliminate your problem, but you never know when one might come in handy.

Until we get these motherfuckers, I want you to keep it loaded, lock your bedroom door at night, keep Natalee with you. Bring Fred and Ernie inside. Sit 'em at the foot of your stairs so no one can get anywhere near you without them seein'."

"Haven't I heard most of this speech before?"

His frown made it unnecessary to guess how serious he was. "Don't interrupt. Wedge a chair under the bedroom door knob. At least make the cocksuckers work to get in. The noise will wake you. Give you time to grab the piece." He was quiet for a few seconds before he said, "Maybe you should consider renting me your guestroom for a few weeks."

"I can ask Tom to stay."

"Suit yourself, but as nice as he is, I'm a whole shitload better protection."

❦

35

"Rad, you old son of a bitch." A wide-bodied hostess with sagging breasts and three chins greeted him as though he starred in her erotic fantasies. "Here, let me get you a good table." We bypassed a long line of customers. She grabbed two menus and maneuvered us to the far side of the dining room. "The steak sandwich is terrific today." She lifted a coffee pot from a nearby wait station, poured Rad a cup, and offered me one. I declined, and she disappeared.

"This was one of my favorite hangouts when it was Fino's on Larch, back when I worked for a living," he said. "I remember a night I got in a fight with one of the regulars. Being a cop, I had the advantage. I could beat the shit out of the hump, but he didn't dare beat back."

"Your friend was right. You were a real son of a bitch, weren't you?"

"Thanks for noticing. Still am. Sometimes you need a real son of a bitch in your corner. Don't forget that, Casey." He paused and scanned the menu for a second or two, and when our server came by, he ordered the meatball sandwich and a side of hash browns with gravy. I struggled to get the words "seafood ravioli" out of my mouth before tears trenched down my cheeks. Rad reached over and grasped my hands between his callused fists.

My runny nose kept pace with the tear flow. Neighboring tables showed the decency to look away. To my credit, it was a quiet display. Rad handed me a handful of extra napkins he yanked from the metal container.

Our lunches arrived, and we ate in silence until I composed myself enough to say, "That box in the back seat of your car. It's the scripts I picked up a couple of days ago at Buy-Smart Pharmacy. I made copies this morning and then stacked the originals as though they had never been touched. On the way back to the office, I hoped you would stop at Buy-Smart and let me deliver them to Jim Allen. Maybe if he thinks I'm playing the game, he'll call off the goon squad."

"My afternoon is yours for as long as you want me, CJ."

Even with my life in the crapper, I had to fight the urge to admonish him for a nickname I had detested from the first time he called me Casey the Just. It made me feel too squeaky clean for his taste. My current ethics might better suit him. Not quite a clone of crooked lawyer John Merritt who stole money from orphans, I was getting closer to letting the greater good theory get a grip on my life.

Rad continued. "Returning that shit sounds like a smart thing to do. But I'm going in with you."

"She started out as Skunk," I said.

"Who did?"

"Jussy. After a few days, Natalee decided her kitten deserved a more flattering name than Skunk so she became Justice, Jussy for short. Often, we called her the no-bones cat because she never gained enough weight to tip the scales at more than four pounds. If we held her under the front legs, she appeared to have no bones and drooped like a limp rag doll. We could feel her sharp ribs through the long fur."

Tears started again. I was about spent, and Rad had been indulgent enough for one sitting. He paid the bill. I wiped my eyes. Our next stop was Buy-Smart.

"Jim Allen here?" I asked. It was the same clerk I had charmed earlier in the week.

"What do you want this time?"

"I've got something to return to him."

She squinted at me, skepticism mixed with disdain. She seemed to recognize the Kotex box, and nobody argues with Rad who held it.

"Just a minute." She pressed a button on the phone. "That attorney person is here again." A second later she said, "You know the way."

When we got to the pharmacy area, Rad hoisted the scripts onto the counter. To my relief, Jim Allen checked out my burly companion and kept his mouth shut. I knew Rad itched for a reason to pummel him.

"I decided I didn't need these after all," I said. "Hope you find everything in order. Sorry to have bothered you."

The two men exchanged eye daggers, my friend's more piercing. "I don't know the bozos you work for," Rad said, "but give 'em a message. Tell 'em Mr. Radowski gets real pissed when someone messes with his friends. Anything happens to Ms. Lawrence, I've got as many buddies as your asshole pals ever thought of havin'. I'm better connected and to the right people. Are we clear? Hell, I'll give you my phone number and home address if you think the pricks might want to talk to me in person."

Allen didn't respond. His bulging eyes and tight mouth said it all.

Rad dropped me back at my office at three. "Are you sure I can't spend the night?" he asked.

"We'll be fine. I'll move Fred inside like you said, and I'll have Tom stay in the guestroom for a week or so. Let the neighbors gossip. I've already got a strange Camry parking overnight. They might as well think it's an orgy."

Rad reached under the driver's seat where he had retrieved the bullets earlier. This time he brought out another gun. Same make and model as the one in my purse. "Have Tom keep this one with him."

"Sweet Jesus in heaven, you get a deal on a dozen?"

"Just take it," he said. Then he answered my question. "Easy to pick 'em up when the department switched from .38 Specials to Glocks.

I dropped it in my purse next to its kin and hoped I didn't get stopped by a cop on the way home after work. I leaned over and gave Rad a peck on the cheek. "We'll be careful. And, Rad, thanks."

Walking back into my office I was still thinking about Jussy. Centuries of cat evolution endowed her with nine lives, and she had lost her last. On the other hand, I only had one, and it appeared to be in serious jeopardy.

The next day I got an email from Advice4U. It read: *Good Girl. Glad you came around and decided to make nice with Allen.*

The message required no response. The creep seemed mollified. I retrieved the Allen complaint from Shirley's desk where it awaited approval. "Got to incorporate new information in route from Gannon," I said.

Natalee came home from play rehearsal early Friday night. Her eyes grew wet when I told her Jussy was dead. Threads of truth ran through my account: "Jussy looked like she hadn't suffered. Her heart just stopped. Nothing the vet could do for her."

I skipped sugarcoating our further heightened security and opted for the truth. "I've gotten more threatening emails. We can't be too careful."

I expected questions, but Natalee held her thoughts close. After dinner, she agreed to watch *Exit through the Gift Shop* on the flat screen with Tom and me. He built a fire, and I popped some corn. To an untrained observer, the scene was a regular Norman Rockwell painting. All it needed was a cat curled up on one of our laps.

36

Saturday, October 8

The day started on a worrisome note. I sat at the kitchen table picking at a piece of cherry pie I found in the back of the refrigerator when my cell rang.

"Any objections to me taking another crack at our friend Allen?" Rad asked after he wished me a good morning.

"Hell, yes. We just calmed him down." I tried to remain logical but heard the shrill in my voice.

"I know—"

"He'll be on the phone with the hoodlums yanking his chains before you're out of the parking lot." I beat my fingernails against the hard surface of the kitchen table, an unsatisfying alternative to biting them to the quick.

"Look, there's no way to make this easy. You've bought yourself a few days, but time's short. It's been almost two weeks, and we're not much closer to the bad guys than the night they trashed your study. At this rate, you either cave or face the consequences."

"I understand, but—"

"No buts about it. They've handled you with kid gloves. It may not seem like it to you, but they've pussyfooted around without doing anything lethal, if you don't count Jussy. Whoever pulls Allen's strings wants you alive. You need him to want you alive. When he doesn't, you'll be expendable. Then you're a problem with only one solution."

I chewed the inside of my cheeks until the familiar sweet, metallic tang of blood jolted my taste buds.

He wasn't finished. "I've brainstormed the possibilities. I come up with two. We go to the cops with our information. Tell them about the emails, the threatening call, even the pictures dropped off in the middle of the night. Full disclosure except for the part about Mr. Scroggins. Lockhart thinks you smell guilty. I've got a few buddies with the State Police. We might get a shot of sympathy there. Still, chances are it'll cause you major grief. The alternative is to rattle a few cages and see what shakes loose."

"And you opt for the latter?"

"For now." His words stalled on a heavy sigh before he added, "Problem with cops is that once we share our information, reports get generated. We can't control who gets copies of those reports. And we can't prevent their nosing into your past. It's all about trust—or lack of it. They trust me, and I trust most of them, but I can't vouch for the whole kit and caboodle. And, though I would trust you with my Aunt Matilda's secret fruitcake recipe, that doesn't mean they would. You're their prime suspect and for some mighty respectable reasons."

"You'll provoke Allen." The vigor of my tapping intensified. The glossy red nail of my left middle finger broke off. "Could be dangerous."

"Aw, how touching. You're concerned for my welfare."

"Last thing I need is to feel guilty because you get your sorry ass killed."

"Let me worry about my sorry ass."

"It's too risky." I nibbled the ragged nail smooth.

"I'm asking if you got any objections because of where the info may lead us. Not if you have objections because you're a titmouse when it comes to my safety."

"Then how about my safety and that of my daughter?"

His voice dropped an octave. I struggled to hear. "You think I haven't considered that?"

I had struck his weak spot. "These people have a sadistic streak as mean as the one running through Hannibal Lecter."

"You're preaching to the choir."

I heard the blast of a car horn, followed by the screech of brakes. There was no jangle of metal hitting metal, so I assumed Rad avoided driving up the back end of another car. "You're on your way to Buy-Smart, aren't you?"

"In the general vicinity."

"So, you called to give me a heads-up, not to get my approval?"

"Not true. Say the word, and I'll abort."

I paused, tried to see it played some other way, and then said, "Do what you think is best."

"That's my CJ. After Allen, I may have a chat with Khoury. See how he squirms."

"Be careful. And Rad?

"Yes?"

"Could you please, please, please stop calling me CJ?"

"No to that last question. But you've got my promise that I'll watch my every step and let you know how it goes. By the way, Fred found no sign of forced entry. Your visitor was a pro. My guys figure he, or they, ditched their car a couple of blocks away and snuck in through the back."

I hung up. Butterflies the size of supersonic aircraft slammed against my stomach walls. Rad was right. Time was short. We needed answers before Khoury's next trial date. Before Wainwright recovered enough to return to practice. Before someone I loved got hurt. I repeated the mantra: *Rad can take care of himself.*

Natalee asked for permission to spend the afternoon helping her boyfriend, Ethan, rake his backyard and burn leaves. I acquiesced, so long as Ernie watched the blaze and their every movement. Fred had been duped once, and I believed Nat's bodyguards would die before letting someone get the best of them again.

At four, Nat tromped into the kitchen carrying the smell of smoke and the day's mail. She dropped the handful of flyers and bills on the snack bar where I nursed a Chivas, water, and Alka-Seltzer. She eyed my drink. I wished I had chosen a jar of Sander's hot fudge to calm my nerves instead of the scotch.

"I'm worried about Rad." I offered it as an excuse for drinking before five. She didn't ask for details. I added her silent treatment to my list of concerns.

I thumbed through the correspondence. A thick business-sized envelope with no postage and no address, just CASEY printed across it, grabbed my attention. I assumed it was from Ginny, who had promised to drop off the schedule from the Wharton Center for the Performing Arts. I had decided to spring for season tickets for Nat, Tom, and me. My daughter had bugged me to become a season ticket holder for two years. She could help me pick out choices for the Wild Card Series, and we would subscribe to the entire Broadway package. I smiled, happy for any pleasant distraction.

Nat opened the refrigerator and grabbed a gallon of chocolate milk.

My Alka-Seltzer cocktail was gone. "Pour me an iced tea, would you?" She didn't answer but set the pitcher of tea on the counter and reached for glasses. I ripped the envelope open. "You're gonna love this. It's a surprise."

She had a perfect view as a slew of greenbacks with Ben Franklin's face spilled across the granite.

"Holy crap, Mom. What's that?" It took her a full thirty seconds to take her eyes off the cash.

"More trouble." I knew a stunned expression underscored my sentiment. I recalled Advice4U's offer to drop off money. I had told him no. It appeared he hadn't listened.

Natalee fingered one bill, examining it as if it were a rare object of art. "I never knew whose picture was on a hundred. Can we keep them?"

"Of course not."

"Too bad." She flipped the envelope and then dropped it back onto the counter. "Who's it from?"

I preferred not to share more information with her, but I had run out of believable lies. "I'm guessing some bad guys who want me to fix cases." I picked up the bills and put them in a neat stack. I was pretty certain they added up to ten thousand. There was no note.

"What will you do with it?"

"Good question." I slid the money back in the envelope and parked it behind the flatware tray in the drawer next to the sink. "I'll come up with something."

After Nat went upstairs, I punched in Rad's number on my speed dial and left a message: "Call me."

It amazes me how the ordinary and extraordinary intersect seamlessly. I had received a small fortune and was mired in trouble, but when Tom got home, the big question was where to eat dinner. Nat opted for the Stillwater Grill. Over Tom's prime rib, Natalee's chicken cordon bleu, and my ahi tuna salad, I switched the conversation from the money back to the tickets I planned to buy for the Wharton. Both Tom and Nat gave it two thumbs up. "I hope they bring *Phantom* back," she said.

Nat talked about the school play. "Kyle's had laryngitis for a week. I've been practicing with the understudy. It's such a pain. I can't get the subtleties of Maria right unless I have the real Tony." When I asked how she did on her Latin test she said, "I don't want to talk about it. I'm sure I failed." I knew how she felt.

Tom beefed up the conversation with news that the Grove was going condo, and he could buy his unit. Minutia camouflaged our anxiety.

The answering machine blinked when we returned home. I pushed PLAY. "You have one new message." Rad's voice boomed, "Tomorrow, eight sharp. Meet me at Denny's on Grand River. We need to talk."

37

Sunday, October 9

The *Sentinel* hid his face, but massive biceps and the cinderblock fists that held the newspaper gave Rad away. I nudged my way through the crowded eatery to where he sat, scrunched at a table too puny for his legs to slide comfortably under it. He dropped his reading material. "Good morning, CJ." I plopped myself on a chair across from him.

Before I had a chance to respond, a server wearing a cheap blond wig refilled his cup with the dregs of coffee that wafted a slightly burnt odor my way.

"Coffee?" she asked as she flipped a thick overturned cup upright on its saucer in front of me. "I'll get another pot."

"I'll take tea," I said.

Rad's smile suggested he found either the black muck or the sight of me to his liking. "You look wide awake for this time of the morning," I said.

"The magic of caffeine."

"Bring me up to date." I unfolded a paper napkin wrapped around flimsy silverware and laid the skimpy square of white on my lap.

"Yesterday was an interesting day," he said.

"Interesting have more detail?"

"Allen was as tight-lipped as a virgin's—"

"Got the picture," I said.

"Little testy this morning, aren't we?"

"Spill it, Radowski. I was awake half the night worried about you. The other half, I worried about Natalee. Don't keep me waiting."

"Lighten up. The good news is obvious. I'm alive."

Before I bitched further, he leaned closer to me and lowered his voice. "Okay, okay. As we suspected, Allen's a voluntary partner."

"To whom?"

Blondie was back and handed us two menus. "I'll give you a minute to look this over." She set a saucer with a small metal teapot in front of me before walking away.

"You're getting ahead of me," Rad said. "Let's start with Allen and what I found out."

It was my turn to lean in closer. It was a crowded restaurant, and there was no hint anyone listened to our conversation, but prudence required we keep our voices down. "You said he didn't give you anything?"

"I said he wouldn't talk. I didn't say I didn't get anything. Big difference." Rad's eyes almost twinkled as he shook his head. "Don't ask—I got my sources, one with access to Allen's financials. Anyway, two years ago Allen was on the verge of bankruptcy. Filed a Chapter Thirteen. Before it went through, his attorneys withdrew it. Last year, our pharmacist bought a Mercedes. Him and the missus took a trip to Australia for three weeks."

"So, we assume he's dirty?" I asked.

"Dirtier than a pig in manure. But there's more."

"I would guess, or you wouldn't sit there like you have canary feathers stuck in your front teeth." Patience wasn't my strong suit this morning. I needed good news more than I needed either food or chitchat.

"Dr. Khoury wasn't as reluctant to talk," Rad said.

"I don't suppose you leaned on him?"

"Sure, I pushed, but I pressured Allen and got nowhere. Khoury's a different animal. He's scared. I figure he padded his bank account with bad scripts long before the crooks contacted him, but he never wanted partners. Especially not partners with gang or cartel connections. He's even worried about you."

"I'm touched." Raised eyebrows underscored my sarcasm. "And those wouldn't be my partners of choice either."

"Right, easy to understand why he's nervous." Rad paused when our Blondie returned for the order. I hadn't wasted time perusing the menu. The choice of artery-clogging special was less important than Rad's story, so when he said, "I'll have the American Slam," I said, "Make it two."

When our server was out of earshot, Rad continued. "Someone contacted Khoury by phone. Identified himself only as Dr. B. The major players in the operation are unknown to Khoury."

"How does he get them their cut?"

"Each month he's called and told to give the money to one of several different patients who apparently work for this Dr. B. The details and how it goes down after that, Khoury's not sure."

"How did Khoury get sucked in?"

Rad drained his coffee and motioned Blondie over before forging on. "He was told that some important people noticed he helped folks needing medication. He received a list of patients who would be coming through his clinic and was told to treat them right. If he didn't, his name would come to the attention of the authorities for irregularities in his practice. I had the chart you put together. I read off the names and the stuff the patients got. Khoury confirmed thirty-five of the thirty-nine were patients from B's list."

"He probably never would have come to Med Pro's attention if he hadn't gotten mixed up in whatever this drug scheme is."

"Right again. He wasn't greedy. A couple of thousand extra a month satisfied him. He would have avoided your radar. For the first few months after Dr. B contacted him, things worked pretty good. Khoury kept half the profit and kicked back the other half to his new partners."

"What caused it to head south?"

"B wanted to increase visits for select patients. Khoury balked. Complained he would lose his license. Explained he was already pushing it. Seems B didn't buy it . . . or give a rat's ass. A week after that conversation, Khoury's black lab became roadkill at the intersection of Waverly and Moores River Drive. Might have been an accident. But the phone call that told Khoury it could be his kid next time wasn't. He knew he was in trouble."

"Sounds familiar."

"Except he wasn't pure as water from a mountain stream when it started."

"I'm flattered. But a woman who murders a man doesn't deserve a sterling reputation."

He shoveled in a bite of hash browns, studied my face before he swallowed, and said, "Murder's a strong word. I can't hold a righteous kill against you. Favor to society. I figure other than that you're clean. Anything else, tell me now. I don't like surprises." His fork was poised for another scoop. "And you sure as hell don't want to piss me off. Not enough people in your corner as it is."

"A few bad judgment calls, but other than Scroggins, nothing that could land me in prison." I raised three fingers to my forehead. "Scout's honor."

Rad gave me a wink that suggested he was satisfied. "The first day of your trial against him, Khoury's daughter really was sick. I checked Lansing General records . . . yeah, yeah. I got sources there, too," he said when my eyes questioned how he received that information. "Report called it food toxins. I'm guessing tampering and intentional poison are more like it. She ate some granola that a nice man gave her as she walked to school."

"Jesus H. Christ. Could it be any more cliché?"

"Don't look at me. Kids aren't real savvy," Rad said. "This one was only seven years old. The school was less than two blocks away. The Khourys let her walk with an older neighbor kid. Anyway, this guy pulled up alongside the girls, rolled down the window, and told Khoury's daughter he was a friend of her daddy. He gave her some name she didn't remember. Said her Daddy was worried because she forgot half of her lunch. The guy handed her a paper bag with an apple, the granola, and a bag of chips. Pretty easy to lace granola with a small amount of rat poison. Make the kid sick and hard to trace unless you're really looking for it. So, that's my best guess of what happened."

"Did anyone question the kid who walked with Khoury's daughter? And did the hospital report the incident to the police?"

"No to both questions. Khoury nixed any follow-up. He told the ER doctor that his daughter was confused. That he did send her lunch over with a friend because she had left for school without it. He also claimed there was a bologna sandwich with mayonnaise in the bag. Khoury insisted the unfortunate incident was his wife's fault for putting mayo on a sandwich that wouldn't be eaten for several hours. The hospital thought it was suspicious but didn't push. The school didn't save the contents of the girl's lunch. The inquiry fizzled."

"Did Khoury ask his daughter about the man who gave her the lunch?"

"Of course," Rad said. "But she had been so thrilled with the treats that she didn't remember much about who handed them to her. She said he was white. He had pretty hair like Dr. Day. She knows Dr. Day because the Khourys and Days socialize. She said the guy drove a big dark car which fits Natalee's description of a black Lincoln. Not a lot to go on."

"So, Khoury is scared. Guess we have that in common. Why did he trust you?"

"He's worried that if he loses his license, he's a liability. He's rooting for us to figure out who the thugs are and put 'em away. Without involving him. It's his best chance to stay healthy. A little side benefit from our investigation." Rad flashed an after-sex smile of satisfaction. "At least we know more than the cops."

"We can't identify the guy calling the shots," I said.

"No. But I did a bit of recon with my buddy, Racer. He's in the Gangs Unit in Detroit Metro. He's heard rumors the 313 has set up shop in our hometown. They're trying to crawl in bed with a major drug cartel."

"Chace Gannon mentioned the 313. When I visited Khoury's office I saw their graffiti."

"Racer arrested a gang lieutenant in Lansing about six months ago. Goes by the name Scum Dawg. Fool sold Yellow Dids and Oxy to punks hanging out on MLK. It was enough for cops to bust him for distribution. Third-time offender. Judge threw the book at him. Scum Dawg don't like Jackson Prison. He talked to Racer in exchange for shavin' a dime off his time."

Rad took a couple of swigs of coffee, then hammered on. "According to Mr. Dawg, one of the Columbian cartels is exploring whether the money from controlled substances spends as good as that from cocaine. Bobby Kansas, known in the Detroit area as Dr. B, arranged a meeting with the Columbians."

I wasn't sure where the information got us, but it was a hell of a story. "Do you think this Dr. B or Kansas is Advice4U?"

"I would put money on it."

"What do we know about him?" I asked.

"I'm getting to it," Rad said. His voice remained so hushed that I strained to catch it. "Kansas was the son of a gangbanger shot in the mid-eighties. Little Bobby was three. The kid was holding his old man's hand as they walked home from the corner store. Dad had bought a pack of smokes for himself and an ice cream cone for young Bobby minutes before it happened. When the police arrived, the kid was sitting on the ground, sobbing, next to the body. Chocolate dripped into the puddling blood. Tyke had pissed himself and clung to both his ice cream cone and his daddy's shirt. Cops had to pry him loose. According to Dawg, it had a profound impact."

"Understandable." He might be a real bad-ass, but no one deserves to see that, I thought.

"Dr. B's mom came from an upstanding family. She took little Bobby and fled back to the safety of the suburbs after her husband was hit."

"What went wrong?"

"You ask me, I think Bobby—Dr. B—had gangster blood runnin' through his veins. Racer says he's one mean son of a bitch. Stays out of the limelight and sends underlings for routine business. But if there's a chance the job will draw blood, or if it poses a challenge, he wants to be there. Does those jobs himself. Sadistic appetites superimposed on criminal instincts, a dangerous combination. He's his father's son, destined to repeat the cycle."

"Maybe Racer is exaggerating?"

Rad shook his head and frowned. "Racer doesn't exaggerate. He described some crimes the cops like Dr. B for but can't prove. Enough to straighten your curly hair."

"Spare me. I've got it. He's cruel and cold-blooded."

"Way beyond that. He's downright savage. Ruthless. Merciless."

"Enough."

"On the plus side of his personality, he's a charmer. You'll never see it coming."

"Reassuring."

"He's different from the garden-variety hoodlum. Dr. B got a decent education at Cass Tech. Started college intending to be a doctor. Maybe was sidetracked when he discovered gangs offered more money for less work. He's smart enough to be a natural-born leader and smooth-talkin' enough to fit anywhere it serves his purpose."

"Advice4U comes across as bright and needing to flaunt it," I said.

"That's about right. Dr. B's clever. Unless it involves gore, reconnaissance to gore, or a game of wits that he can't resist, he puts six layers between his soldiers and himself. If he handles a job himself, it's guaranteed there will be no witnesses, or if there are, they'll be so traumatized . . . so terrified, you can bet your shapely little ass, they won't give him up." No one can or will point back directly to him. Lower-level hoodlums go to jail. He skates. He's come up in the world since his daddy was murdered. Lives in a mansion in Bloomfield Hills. Was a friend of the mayor and some city big shots in his early years. Most have cut ties with him because of his baggage."

"So, we have interesting information," I said. "What do we do with it?"

"I'm working that angle. I think at some point we have to bring the cops in, but I want to wait until the suspicion is off you, and I want to hand-select the guys who work it."

"Can you do that?"

"I'm not sure. I know some folks who might be able to finagle it."

Blondie delivered our order and left us to fill our faces as we each considered the options. I pushed the hash browns around on my plate and hadn't yet touched the eggs when Rad finished his breakfast. "You gonna eat those?" He pointed to the sausages.

What I had managed to eat lay like a rock in my stomach. "I've consumed enough grease to last me a month."

"Mind?"

I shook my head, and he forked both links and moved them to his plate. "What if I set up a meeting with Dr. B?" I asked.

He reached over and grabbed my hand, squeezed harder than was comfortable. "Not gonna happen. B is a dangerous bastard. Have you heard anything I said?"

I pulled my fingers from his grip and glared at him. "Like you're telling me something new."

"Leave the heroics to me." His voice rose louder. The couple at the table next to us glanced over. Rad shot them a sneer that turned their heads back to their own business.

I raised a finger to my lips to shush him. "Not even if you sat somewhere close, waiting to rush in and save me?" I hoped flattery might win him over.

"Not in this lifetime. Are we clear?" He lowered the volume, but the message remained unambiguous.

"Sure." I wasn't under oath.

If he noticed my hesitancy, he let it slide. "Okay, I've given you the lowdown according to Radowski. It's your turn. There was a message on my machine from you when I got home last night. I tried to return your call, but there was no answer, so I left the voicemail to meet me here this morning. What's going on?"

"Damn. I was so lost in your tale that I forgot. I got a present yesterday. Ten thousand in hundred-dollar bills. Left in an envelope in my mailbox with my name on it."

"I thought you told the punk-ass you didn't want his dough."

"I did. He offered to help me buy Nat's homecoming dress and make it a night for her to remember. I declined his generosity. Maybe he didn't hear. Scares me how much he knows about me."

"I've said this before, being scared is damned good." Rad pushed his black-framed glasses down his nose and looked over them as if assessing whether I was scared enough.

"I also told him I was glad he was going to make my cooperation worth the effort. I wanted him to think I was on board. I never planned to take anything."

"The bastard is trying to tighten a noose around your fine neck. Get you to spend some money. Clerks don't forget customers who pay with hundred-dollar bills. He's hoping you can't resist spending one little bill. Then another and another."

"I can't exactly return the money."

"Right," he said. "No return address."

"Something like that." I slumped toward my elbows resting on the table.

"What did you do with it?"

"It's in my kitchen drawer."

"Maybe you should give it to me."

"Love to—"

"Then if anyone ever suspects you of being bribed, you say you turned it over to me because I'm an ex-cop, and I offered to handle it."

"What will you do with it?" I asked.

"I'll give it to Racer and ask him to bury it in his property room until we figure out a better alternative."

Rad took the last couple swigs of his coffee and shook his head when the Blondie looked our way and held up the pot. Our dishes were cleared, and customers waiting for a table cast irked looks in our direction. I hated to leave. I felt safe with Rad, like he could prevent bad things from happening.

"Give me a minute to hit the head," he said. "Then I'll walk you to your car."

"If you've got time, you can follow me home. I would like to get the money out of my place."

Before he answered, the background chatter of diners was silenced by a deafening KABOOM.

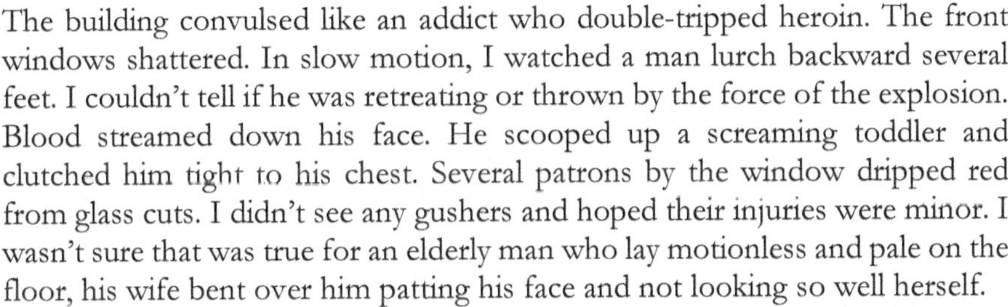

38

The building convulsed like an addict who double-tripped heroin. The front windows shattered. In slow motion, I watched a man lurch backward several feet. I couldn't tell if he was retreating or thrown by the force of the explosion. Blood streamed down his face. He scooped up a screaming toddler and clutched him tight to his chest. Several patrons by the window dripped red from glass cuts. I didn't see any gushers and hoped their injuries were minor. I wasn't sure that was true for an elderly man who lay motionless and pale on the floor, his wife bent over him patting his face and not looking so well herself.

"What the hell?" I stammered. Rad put one arm around my shoulders and maneuvered his body between me and the front of the building. With his other hand, he pulled a twenty out of his front pocket and dropped it on the table to cover our bill.

"Stay here," he ordered. "I'll check it out."

My ears rang. Rad's words sounded like they slogged through a bale of cotton. "No friggin' way," I said. He didn't have time to argue with me as I dashed to the front of the restaurant with him. We stared out the glassless window frames.

Rad's Merc was a flaming inferno. We rushed outside but couldn't get within thirty feet of the car. The smell of cordite filled the air, and the sedan's shrapnel still careened to the ground. A misshapen steering wheel hung from the branch of a nearby elm.

Twenty minutes later the bomb squad arrived and checked the car's remains, mostly unrecognizable debris. Several vehicles, parked close to Rad's, sustained serious damage and would require tow trucks to cart them away.

When the cops finished with us, Rad checked my car to make certain it wasn't booby-trapped, and then I drove him to pick up an Avis rental. I tried to convince him to go for a sporty Corvette and let me pay for it. "It'll make you feel twenty again."

He wouldn't go for it. "It would probably kill me if I tried to act twenty again." He insisted his insurance would cover the bill. He slipped behind the wheel of a red Cadillac CTS and followed me to my place. He proposed staying until Tom got home, but I declined his offer.

He checked every room of my empty house before he left with the dirty money. Even as the door closed behind him, I had a premonition that sending him away wasn't one of my wisest moves. Watching him back out of my driveway, I fought the temptation to race after him, beg him to come back.

Sundays are hard for me to be alone, even without exploding cars. As a kid, before Dad walked out on us, it was a family day. Mom, Dad, my sister Skylar, and I went to church along with everyone else in Bad Axe, Michigan. Afterwards, we stopped at Nana Rosebud's and Papa Bruce's for dinner. Often, Aunt Bea and Uncle Raymond joined us with their brood of five. Stuffed with roasted chicken and mashed potatoes, we whiled away evenings with decks of cards and bowls of potato chips. I learned pinochle when my hands could hold twelve cards. Euchre before that. Memories are a curse when they highlight failure. My current circumstances were nothing like I had imagined my life would turn out.

This Sunday, my daughter had dumped me in favor of a drive to Saugatuck with Ethan. I didn't like the idea, but Ernie followed their every move. Tom had driven to Flint to meet a client. Both left before the blast. Otherwise, even with a bodyguard, I would have forbidden Natalee to leave, and I knew Tom would have canceled his meeting to stay with me.

With Rad's departure, I had no company for my misery. It seemed pointless sitting around with a .38 clutched in my shaking hands, as isolated and emotionally destitute as a prisoner on death row. Listening to Kris Kristofferson's gravelly voice wail the old music my mother played when I was a kid wasn't going to solve this case, and I didn't need to be reminded that there's something about Sundays that makes a body feel alone. I opted for another oldie, but upped the tempo, and hoped Mom's "Good Vibrations" could temper the gloom.

I tried to imagine a better way to spend time than reviewing the stack of medical charts sitting on my kitchen table. I came up empty. Gannon had picked up records from Khoury's office for the thirty-nine patients listed on my chart. Most files were skinny, two or three pages each of notes to cover years of visits. They had all fit easily into my briefcase when I packed them Friday night before leaving work. Those stories volunteered to share the remainder of my day. I flipped through the medical histories and organized the names alphabetically.

Sherri Smith's file was bulkier than the others. I had forgotten the pregnant waif. I dug her phone number from behind Natalee's picture in my billfold and checked it against the intake sheet. It matched. A voyeur snooping through the secrets of her life, I began reading.

Sherri's first visit to Khoury's clinic was five years ago. The doctor performed a physical that suggested he was more thorough back then.

8/9. Patient presents as an emaciated 16 y/o white female. 5'5½". 98 lbs. BP 140/80. Temp 98.3. Lungs clear to A and P. Jagged, bumpy, keloid scar runs length of patient's left scapula. Domestic abuse. Nose broken twice. Breathes through her mouth. Correctible with surgery but no insurance. Suffers recurrent yeast infections. Admits to 2 abortions, 1 miscarriage. One live birth, a son, Samuel, born when patient was 15. Father's whereabouts unknown. Pt. underwent back surgery at age 14, related to near-fatal car accident. Dr. Calvin Streeter operated. Complains of pain since. Started on Tylenol 3 and Doriden. Been using her boyfriend's; says it helps.

There was a note that from the hillbilly heroin of her first visit, Sherri graduated to Dilaudid for several months. Then a notation: Dilaudid highly addictive, trying Empirim and Tylenol OTC to wean her off habit-forming substances. I wondered if Licensing Regulations had given the doctor a scare. If so, he had recovered by the next entry: Pt. reports Tylenol isn't working. Will try Vicodin.

Over the years Sherri consumed a steady pill diet, alternating Dilaudid and Percodan with OxyContin and Vicodin. Fastin and Ritalin added spice to the controlled substance smorgasbord. No tests, no lab work, no reports from referrals. No justification for prescribing a weight loss drug to a patient described as emaciated. And the only support for the Ritalin was "she can't concentrate," which was a normal side effect of the Fastin.

The most recent note in Sherri's file was from the day I stumbled on her a week and a half ago in Khoury's office. She was days past her twenty-first birthday and seven months pregnant:

9/27 Patient in last trimester of 5th pregnancy. One living child. Threatens to kill herself if she can't get relief from unrelenting pain. Discomfort worse as fetus grows. More pressure on her spine. Warned I am not her OB. Pt. claims not to remember his name. Likely no prenatal care. Discussed risks of pain meds on fetus. Referred her to a pain clinic. She promises to follow up. Gave her OxyContin because it isn't likely to cause birth defects. Better track record with pregnant patients than the Dilaudid she wants. Have explained OxyContin is a narcotic. May cause withdrawal in the infant after delivery.

The patient note sounded like Khoury had given the matter some thought; then I remembered he wrote it after our case against him was opened. Sherri's records documented a failed life. Her file provided most of what I would ever know about her. It was one sentence in her own handwriting on the intake questionnaire that intrigued me most. The question read, Are you ever depressed? She had scrawled, Sure, but suicide is always an option.

Sherri's finger was on the pulse of the drug scene. She had offered to sell anything I could get. With an afternoon stretching long in front of me and a serious lapse of good judgement, I packed the .38 in my purse and decided to pay her a visit. If she worked for Dr. B or one of his lackies, I might learn something. I considered calling Rad but figured he might not be keen on my idea. Better to beg forgiveness later than seek his prior approval. Sherri's medical records showed an address on Mifflin. I ran a reverse lookup of the phone number to confirm it was a legitimate address. Turned out she lived on West Oakland.

As I drove Grand River in East Lansing, I passed the People's Church and watched freshly forgiven congregants lolling amiably on the steps. Grand River split, and I followed it to the right and continued through Lansing, past downtown. It split again, and I stayed on Oakland until I reached the address. I pulled my Corolla in front of a neglected house that couldn't have been much even as the last nails used in building it were driven. Now, it looked a few days short of government-ordered demolition. Its postage-stamp lawn was a jungle of weeds destined to remain a tangle until recurrent frosts deadened their resolve.

With the back of my knuckles, I tapped on the door. As I waited, I contemplated the missing slats and chipped paint that gave two front shutters a mottled look. One had fallen and stood propped against the flaked paint of the wood siding. The other hung haphazardly by a whisper and a prayer.

No one answered. I knocked a second time. I turned to leave, but the door creaked open, and a little boy with skin the color of butterscotch looked up at me.

"Is your mommy home?" I asked.

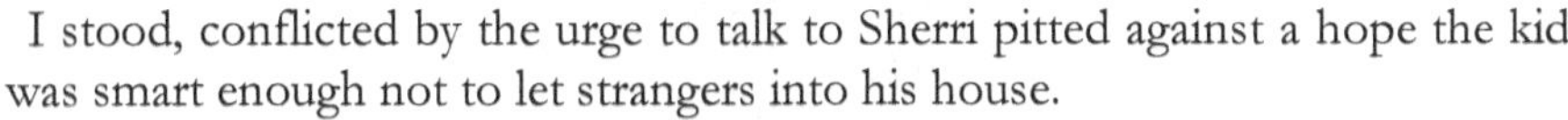

39

I stood, conflicted by the urge to talk to Sherri pitted against a hope the kid was smart enough not to let strangers into his house.

"She don't feel good," he said.

I looked him over. He wore Spiderman pajamas and was barefoot. His loose curls had been cut, a homemade job if the nicks and notches were any indication, but there was no mistaking he was the same boy I had bumped into at Buy-Smart.

I squatted to look him in the eye and resisted the urge to pat his head. "Does she need help?"

"Naw. She's just tired."

"That's what happens when you're going to have a baby." I smiled wide and hoped for the hint of a grin in return.

"She ain't gonna have no baby. It went away."

I abandoned trying to get a smile. "Are you Sammy?" I remembered his name from his mother's medical records.

"Yeah." He seemed more interested in the red, Hot Wheels sports car that he ran up the side of the doorframe than in the possibility he should not be talking to me.

"Sammy, do you think you could let me in to check on your mommy?"

"You kin come in, but Mommy will get angry if we wake her."

Even before stepping inside, I was assaulted by the stale smell of cooked cabbage mixed with less identifiable, but equally noxious, odors. "Astro Boy" blared from the TV.

I crossed the threshold and let the door close behind me. A green plastic garbage bag braced against the stove garnered my attention. Its cavernous open mouth had ingested the waste of Sherri's life. A cockroach scooted over the cardboard remains of a frozen dinner cresting the mound of trash. The bug's relatives feasted on a tub of potato salad, moldy bread, and the bones of Popeye's Fried Chicken.

I held my hand over my nose and mouth until I got used to the stench. The grimy, cracked linoleum had never had a helping hand from Mr. Clean. If the floor boasted a cheerful pattern when new, it had lost it to the dull gray wear of countless dirty shoeprints. Grease, combined with unidentified smudges, gave the cupboards their patina. I tried not to think about the vermin watching me from hidden crevices.

A voice from the next room called, "Sammy, who's out there?"

"A lady."

"What lady?"

I walked to the closed door and spoke through it. "It's me, Sherri. My name is Casey Lawrence. We met at Dr. Khoury's clinic."

"I don't remember no one named Casey Lawrence."

"Can I come into the bedroom?" I pulled my sweater tighter around me and hunched my shoulders, making myself as little a target as possible for germs that floated through the stagnant air.

"Nah, I'd rather not see anyone." She sounded small and tired.

"Are you okay? You need a doctor or anything?" I asked.

"I'm fine. How did you find me?"

"You gave me your number. I did a reverse lookup." The closed door wasn't conducive to conversation, but I wasn't sure I wanted to get closer to her.

"You that lady I told could bring me extra drugs? You must not be as dumb as you looked." I heard a giggle, and then she said, "C'mon in if you brought drugs."

I opened the door and considered how to answer her. "No, that's not it. I wasn't at Dr. Khoury's to get drugs. I'm an assistant attorney general. I take licenses away from bad doctors."

After several seconds, she said, "Fuck, just what I need. More trouble."

I stood, not wanting to lean against the wall, and stared at the sheet-swathed lump in the middle of a waterbed. As my eyes adjusted to the dim light, I saw blankets tossed in a heap on the floor. An empty pizza box and a fifth of something amber-colored sat on the nightstand.

"You aren't in trouble." At least not from me, I thought. I debated how much to tell her. "I'm the one who's got the problem."

"Right. Like some rich-bitch attorney needs my help. You gotta leave."

I pretended I didn't hear her last comment. "I think you might know a guy who goes by the name Dr. B."

"I know lots of people," she said, "and ain't none of 'em want to know you."

"The one I'm talking about . . . I think gets part of the drugs Khoury prescribes for you."

"Dr. Khoury gives me drugs because I'm in pain."

"I know. But I think you only use some of them. The rest you sell or give to the same people bothering me."

There was a ladder-back chair piled with clothes next to the bedroom door. This might take a while. I'd have to forget about the health risk and germs. "Do you mind?" I asked as I stepped farther inside the room, moved her garments to the dresser top, and sat down before she could answer.

The room reeked of unwashed bodies and cigarette smoke mingled with the musky smell of stale sex. "The people I'm talking about want me to fix Dr. Khoury's legal problem," I said. "He's going to lose his license. I don't know who these people are, but I'm scared. I'm hoping you'll tell me about them."

"Are you fuckin' crazy? It don't work like that."

"How does it work?"

"You're better off not knowin'."

It had been easier to talk to Sherri when she thought I carried drugs. I opted for a new tact. "Sherri, what happened to your baby?"

"I don't see that's any of your business."

"Maybe I can help you. I've got some contacts."

"Can't you see, it's too late?" She patted her flabby, deflated belly. "I don't need your help. You're gonna get me killed. If the wrong people see you pokin' around my place, they'll think I'm a snitch. You gotta get out of here. I got me a kid to raise. Just leave us the hell alone . . . please."

"I've got a kid, too. And I'm worried about her. She's sixteen years old, and these people have threatened to hurt her if I don't do what they want. I may not be the best mother, but I love her more than anything. You and I can help each other. And maybe keep both your Sammy and my daughter safe."

For the first time, I thought I saw sympathy or at least interest in her eyes. "There's an easier . . . better way," she said.

"And that is?"

"Do what they say."

"That won't work. Maybe once or twice I could help them keep a bad doctor licensed, but if I start losing cases, someone's going to figure it out."

"Damn. You're stupider than I thought. And that's when I didn't know you was a fuckin' attorney. These people get what they want."

One by one, Sherri opened three vials that stood on her nightstand, shook pills from each onto her open palm and tossed them in her mouth. I didn't ask if they were vitamins. She picked up a nearly empty Pabst 40-ouncer that appeared left over from the night before and washed them down.

With some effort, she swung her skinny ashen legs over the side of the waterbed and stood up. Disheveled and worn-looking, she matched the pile of clothes I had moved to the dresser. The ghostly pallor of her face backdropped a crooked nose that evidenced repeated breaks. Sherri finger-combed her matted hair. She shuffled naked to the foot of the bed and retrieved a pair of jeans and sweatshirt. She picked up a pack of Marlboros, jiggled one out, and lit it before she walked past me into the larger room, where Sammy watched TV from the pull-out couch that I presumed was both his bed and his playroom. Toys littered the rumpled, yellowed sheets.

"Can I git some ice cream from Bennie's?" Sammy asked.

"You got money?" Sherri asked.

"Enough."

"Then go ahead. And bring me a pack of my smokes." She pulled out a ten from her pocket. "And I want all of my change back."

"I know," he said. She tried to kiss his cheek, but he ducked away from her cigarette and stale-beer breath, and she missed. The door slammed behind him.

Sherri filled a kettle with water and set it on the stove. "You want a cup of tea?" she asked.

I nodded and assured myself that boiling water would kill whatever bacteria coated the cup. She seemed to have forgotten she had ordered me out, but even with the new hospitality, I couldn't come up with a convincing reason why it would be in her best interest to help me.

The fluorescent light above the sink showed her left eye was black and blue and half shut. I tried to remember the name of Sherri's boyfriend. She had told me when we were at Khoury's. Mickey? That was it. Mickey, like the big-eared rodent Nat and I met in Florida, but I guessed this one lacked the Disney character's good nature. I saw why Sherri kept suicide as an option.

"How did you hurt yourself?" I trekked dangerous territory but fumbled forward.

"You're damned nosy, ain't ya?" she asked. There was no anger, just a matter-of-factness to her question.

"I suppose I am. I shouldn't pry."

"You got that—"

"But it drives me crazy when a man takes out his anger on a woman. Is that how you lost the baby?"

"Nah. I went into labor the day after I met you. Guess I was farther along than I thought. James was stillborn. I'm not surprised. I didn't exactly take care of myself, ya know. That's what made Mickey so mad. He's been a crazy man since I lost the baby. He actually wanted it."

The teakettle whistled. Before she said anything else the phone rang. She answered it while dropping generic tea bags into two mugs that she had set on the counter between dirty plates and a Morton's salt box. She poured hot water over the bags. I heard her say, "Yeah, yeah, I'll be here, but you gotta pay me."

Sherri hung up and handed me one of the two mugs. "My sister-in-law. She wants me to babysit this afternoon for her two boys. Oldest is three, the baby eighteen months. Real pistols. Takes me two Valium and a shot of

Tussionex to get through a day with them. Tried givin' the older one a Ritalin once. It didn't do no good. But ain't like I can't use extra money. I ain't exactly flush."

"Things could be different," I said. "I've got friends who could help you."

"God, you're one dimwitted woman," she said. "Nice enough, but you ain't got a clue."

"Enlighten me."

Before she could do so, the phone rang again. She answered, then lowered her voice softer than a whisper. I sat only a few feet away, grateful for keen hearing. Even getting only one side of the conversation, I knew the call was bad news.

"I didn't invite her," Sherri said. "What kinda fool you think I am? Don't worry. Trust me. I'll take care of it."

When Sherri hung up, I hoped the question in my eyes would implore her to fill in the other half of the conversation. Instead, she said, "I'm gonna do us both a favor and decline your offer. I may not be much, but I'm all Sammy's has. I gotta stay alive. You have a kid and need to do the same. For both our sakes, forget you ever met me."

I took out a business card, printed my direct line and home phone numbers on it, and handed it to her. "Put this somewhere only you can find it."

She turned it around so she could read it, and then walked to the cabinets, opened a door that revealed a huge gun sitting next to pots and pans. For a split second, I thought this was how she would take care of it. I slipped my hand into my purse and clutched the .38, not sure I could use it, even if my life was at stake. Unlike Jimmy Scroggins, Sherri was a mother, and she didn't ask me to come here causing her trouble. Before I was forced to decide, Sherri slid my card under a roasting pan and shut the cupboard door.

I relaxed my grip on the weapon. "If you ever change your mind, give me a call. Not just if you want to help me. If you want to get clean, go back to school, or anything like that, call me. Like I said, I can hook you up with folks who can make those things happen."

"I 'preciate it." Her lack of eye contact told me she was just being polite.

"Thanks for the tea." I set my cup in the sink already full of dirty dishes. Other than with Natalee or Tom, I'm not a demonstrative person, so I don't know why I did it, but I gave her a hug before I walked out.

Two blocks down I saw Sammy shuffling along. I pulled over. "I don't see ice cream. Guess you haven't made it to Bennie's yet?" I wondered if I should report the store owner to our criminal division for selling cigarettes to a minor. I would have to witness the purchase, and getting some creep a slap on the wrist wasn't on today's agenda.

"I stopped at the park to see if I could hook up with some friends, but they weren't there." Sammy walked close to my open passenger-side window. How easy to grab him I thought.

"Do you think you could also carry milk and cereal and maybe some juice bars home?"

He gripped the window frame with chubby hands that reminded me how young he was. "Sure, but Mom would beat my butt if I spent her money."

"My treat."

"Why?" He leaned his head inside the car, closer to me.

"Because your mommy helped me out," I said. Sammy gave me an I-don't-quite-believe-you look, but didn't say anything before I added, "In fact, I'll take you to the store and then drive you home."

"Momma don't let me cop rides with strangers." He pinched the twenty from my outstretched fingers.

Sherri wasn't going to nab any mother-of-the-year award, but at least she had imparted one solid kernel of wisdom.

As I drove off, I noticed a black Lincoln Town Car follow me through several lights before it turned right on Washington. It might have escaped my attention if I hadn't seen it parked a half block down and across the street from Sherri's when I pulled away.

40

Monday, October 10

The press loved me so much these days I considered starting a scrapbook. The *Sentinel* carried a front-page photo of Rad's car glowing like the bonfire for a colossal weenie roast. The headline blazed, Car Bomb Linked to AAG Lawrence. The link was that I sat inside Denny's with the car's owner at the time of the explosion, not that I had anything to do with torching an automobile. The masses who limited their daily news intake to headlines and pictures would miss the distinction. I threw the paper on my kitchen counter and hoped it was the worst news of the day.

I arrived at the office early. I finished a re-draft of the Buy-Smart complaint, inserted the information from Gannon's new report, and attached the charts I had created from Allen's scripts. It was too soon to return it to Shirley for review. It might take my boss a week to get to it. A few more days would pass before Allen was served. Then he and his buddies would realize returning the scripts had been a mere pretense of good faith. I needed more time. I parked the complaint in my top desk drawer. I would sit on it until it was safe.

I quickly lost interest in playing the white knight. After a wasted hour, I told Louise, "I've got some research to do. I'll be at the Michigan Library and Historical Center, and if that doesn't pan out, I might stop by and see if Vital Records has any useful information. I'll be back by noon." I kept my explanation vague. I had no idea what I was looking for, but whatever it was, it wasn't case-related.

I had returned to my office and was contemplating the results of the morning's investigation when my phone rang. Sherri Smith topped my list of those I didn't expect it to be. "I need to see you," she said. "No cops. And hurry." Her raspy strangled words struggled through a thick soup I couldn't quite identify. Pain? Fear? Drugs?

"Sherri, what's going on? Sherri . . . Sherri?"

No dial tone interrupted the connection. I assumed she dropped the phone. Or it was taken from her. I hung up, grabbed my jacket, stuffed my feet into Nikes, and focused. It would be faster to run for the mud lot and call Rad to meet me at Sherri's, rather than have him pick me up. I prayed his cell was turned on.

Rad was the last person I had called. I hit redial as I tore down six flights of steps. I couldn't wait for an elevator that would stop on each floor. By the time I passed the second-floor landing, he answered. Breathless, I skipped the small talk. "I need backup." I gave him Sherri's address. "Can you meet me? I'll explain when I get there. It's okay to speed. And bring one or two of those guns."

Rad said, "I'm on my way," as I pushed through the front door.

I hadn't jogged in a couple of weeks, but adrenaline turned me into an Olympic class runner, though I doubted my sprint to the parking lot would garner a gold medal.

There was little traffic that early in the afternoon. When I slammed to a halt in front of Sherri's, a mere fifteen minutes had elapsed since her call. Rad stepped out of his car. A good thing because I would have thought twice about going in alone even with the .38 in my purse.

"What the fuck?" he asked.

"Not now." I pulled out my gun and held it at my side. Rad's eyes widened, but then he withdrew his weapon.

The front door was open about six inches. Before I could step in, Rad pushed me aside and entered ahead of me. The kitchen looked no different than it had the prior day.

I rushed into the bedroom. Sherri lay on the floor, a bloody cell phone and my business card next to her. The matted carpet around her was wet and dark. I placed my fingers on her wrist and got a weak pulse.

I screamed at Rad. "Call 911."

"No," Sherri moaned.

"We have to," I said.

"No. Please . . . better this way." Sherri's words came slow and soft. I knelt close to her mouth to hear them. I recalled her answer about suicide on the medical inventory. The optimism of lost hope. But this was no suicide. I had never watched someone die. I guessed this might be what it looked like.

"Dr. B?" I asked, certain I knew the answer.

"He came himself. No second-stringer like he sends to pick up the money." Her lips curled into a slight smirk. Maybe shock dulled the pain. Maybe she found something amusing at being worth B's personal attention. Or maybe she wasn't unhappy to be dying. She had embraced that as an option.

This was my fault, but Sherri didn't spit accusations. Pausing between words, she whispered, "He wanted you here. Said if I got you here before the police came, he wouldn't hurt Sammy. He's not someone to mess with. Please don't let Sammy see me like this." Her face was a swollen, dark mask imploring me to make sure her son didn't stumble in to find her half-naked and beaten and dead.

She could have added, "You owe me that," and I would have agreed.

It took explosive rage to refashion her features into such gore. Blood seeped from more gashes on her legs and arms than Rad could tie with strips of cloth he ripped from her grimy sheets. None of these lesser injuries appeared life-threatening. The small cuts were Dr. B's appetizer. The crimson that gushed from her chest was his entrée. Sherri kept her hands over the terminal wound to stanch the blood. When she finished delivering the message, she let her hands fall to the side.

"Hang on," I demanded, my hands replacing hers.

Rad abandoned his first-aid efforts. He dialed 911, but Sherri no longer protested. He took me by the shoulders and moved me toward the chair where I had sat talking to her less than twenty-four hours earlier. "Casey," he said gently, "she's gone."

Dead. I took the blanket from the end of the bed, wiped my hands on it and then covered Sherri's exposed breasts. I closed her eyes to avoid their empty stare.

"The police are on their way. You've got maybe three minutes to tell me what the fuck we're involved in here," Rad said.

"I got her killed."

"What the hell you talking about?"

"Sherri Smith. That's who she is. I got her killed." My voice quivered. I gnawed the inside of my cheeks and swallowed hard to keep from vomiting.

"How in God's name are you involved?"

"I told you about my visit to Khoury's clinic. I met her there." I fought to stop the sobs before the cavalry arrived.

"Okay, I'm with you so far. But, for Christ's sake, how did you kill her?"

"I came here yesterday afternoon."

"What, in the name of all that's sacred, induced you to think that was a good idea?"

"I hoped maybe she would give up her contact. We could follow a trail to the guy she gets the drugs for. Establish the link to Dr. B. You're the one who told me we don't have a lot of choices."

"Casey, I love you to pieces, but promise me you'll stop winging it. You're a damn fine attorney. I got nothing but respect for your talents. But you're not doin' so well on the investigating side."

"You can't make me feel any worse." I turned my lips inward and pressed them tight to keep from spouting something stupid since there was no reasonable answer.

"That's not my goal. But you don't seem to appreciate the danger. Didn't you consider you might be followed?"

"It was foolish. But—"

A siren drowned further talk and alerted us the cops had arrived.

"We'll finish this conversation later," Rad said. I dropped the revolver back into my purse. He slid his into the backside of his waistband, covered it with his corduroy jacket.

"Let me do the talking," I said.

His face broadcast doubts about the wisdom of letting me open my mouth, but he grumbled, "Okay," as two Lansing police officers burst into the room with their guns drawn. They quickly sized up the situation. They had evidence to bag and tag, and then a corpse for delivery to the morgue. Since Rad and I waited for their arrival, they took an educated guess we weren't the perps.

"What can you tell us?" The tougher-looking of the two asked, staring at Rad.

I answered. "I'm Casey Lawrence. I work for the attorney general. The deceased is Sherri Smith—or that's the name I know her by. She's a witness in one of my cases. I came by yesterday to talk to her about the trial. She told me she was afraid she would be killed if she cooperated with me. She called me about a half hour ago and asked me to rush over."

"And you came without notifying the police or considering whether it was safe?" He gave me a look I got a lot from cops these days: a grimace paired with a disbelieving shake of the head.

"I didn't expect this. But I had an uneasy feeling, so I called Will Radowski, my ex-cop friend here, to meet me. I would have waited in the car for him to arrive if he hadn't gotten here before me."

Rad interrupted. "We called you guys as soon as we realized what we had walked in on."

"She was still alive when we got here," I continued. "She identified her killer as a drug dealer who goes by the street name of Dr. B." Let the cops make a note of that. It was a dying declaration and would stand up in court against a hearsay objection.

"Okay, we'll secure the crime scene and call the detectives," the cop who did all the talking said. "If you got cards, leave 'em or write your phone numbers down so they can get in touch with you. We don't need you further contaminating the crime scene. You've probably done enough harm already."

"She's got a six-year-old son, Sammy. Someone needs to pick him up so he doesn't come home from school and find the police here and his mother dead. He's got an aunt who lives close by. The boy should be able to direct you to her house."

I searched the cop's face to make sure I considered him reliable. Hidden in a look that spelled business, I saw a trace of compassion. Maybe it was the way he glanced at Sherri, then closed his eyes before he turned away.

Rad had his arm around me and ushered me out as the officer said, "We'll take care of it. Kid must go to Riddle Elementary. We'll check to be sure. The school will have contacts. Either way, we'll pick him up and keep him away from this."

As we split for our cars, Rad said, "Follow me to De Luca's. I'm guessing you could use a drink. I sure as hell know I could. And you aren't done explaining."

41

"What do you figure happens to her kid?" I stared at the scotch and water Rad had ordered for me.

"Foster care. Unless Sherri has family that wants him. I doubt he'll be that lucky. Looking at that roach infested hell-hole and the drugs layin' around, I'm guessing anyone who wanted him would have expressed interest before now. Sherri wouldn't have hung on too tight. I'm assuming there's no father or grandparents in the picture."

"Probably not. That sister-in-law I mentioned lets Sherri babysit her toddlers. She can't be any great shakes. I doubt she wants another mouth to feed." I paused for a moment considering another option. "Think there's any chance I could take him?"

"Nice thought, CJ, but for God's sake, you can't get your own life together. You admit you got his mother killed. You want to put him at risk too?"

"Thanks."

"Sorry, but we've got a big enough job keeping you and Natalee alive. In case you haven't noticed, you aren't prime mother material at the moment." His words stung more because they were true. I dropped my head, wished I could disappear.

Rad ordered a meatloaf sandwich on whole wheat and when it came handed half to me. "You need to eat something."

"Thanks." I nibbled the edge. I squeezed on some ketchup and mustard but couldn't get excited about something that tasted like paste between two chunks of cardboard.

"It's probably not what you want to hear at this moment," he said, "but Jussy died from a quadruple-dose injection of Euthasol. There was enough in her system to kill a two-hundred-pound man."

My brain struggled under the glut of more bad news. "She would never let someone give her an injection without putting up a fuss."

"Remember, you were exhausted and groggy from the Ambien. The cat might have yelped, and you might have slept through it, or she could have been in a pretty deep sleep herself. Killer could have injected her right through the covers. However he did it, he managed to enter your bedroom and off your cat without waking you. I suppose it's possible he lured the animal downstairs, did her in the kitchen and brought her back to your bed."

"Not a chance. Jussy doesn't—didn't—like strangers."

"Right. But never underestimate the power of tuna."

Unsure I could handle the weight of my thoughts, I sat quietly for a minute before I asked, "Anything else?"

"Nothing but details of what we already knew. I did some checking. Talked to Max Schneider at Cardinal Insurance in Palo Alto just before you called me. They hold the life insurance policy. Your ex may have been every other kind of son of a bitch, but, as Lockhart told you, he intended to leave you something if he died."

"That makes no sense." I tried putting the pieces together, but they didn't line up, in part because I refused to entertain kind thoughts toward Derek right now. "He didn't give me a penny of child support, but I'm the beneficiary of his life insurance policy?"

"It didn't start as benevolence," Rad said. "Harbor Springs Investments, where he last worked, provided a great benefit package. Initially, the premiums were paid by the company. When Derek left six months ago, he had the option of continuing them. Embezzlement must pay. Your ex has made only one payment, and that was two weeks ago, the day before he disappeared. Could be that the timing of the premium payment coincided with a threat that worried him. He might have seen it as a way to provide Natalee a going away present if something happened to him."

I placed the palm and fingers of my right hand on my forehead and moved them in slow deliberate circles to ease the pressure. I finished my drink and turned down Rad's offer for a second. The afternoon had been long enough.

I drove home thinking how much better it would have been if I had sat around and ruminated yesterday afternoon. I would get no second chance. I stopped at Walgreen's and bought a card with a sad-looking beagle on the front. Inside were the words: Thinking of You. I wrote, "I am sorry about your mom. She was a courageous lady, and she loved you more than anything else in the world." I didn't know whether it was true, but it sounded good. I addressed it to Sammy

Smith and hoped someone would figure out where to forward it. I would have sent money, but there was little chance cash would find its way to Sammy.

A cheap card bought very little absolution.

42

Wednesday, October 12

Two days after the murder, I carried the *Sentinel* with me to the office and sat reading it before the troops arrived. I spotted a short piece about Sherri's death on the last page of the local news section. In the old days, I would have missed it, but since the paper ran frequent items about the assistant AG whose bloody study was ransacked and whose ex-husband had disappeared, I felt compelled to read every page to get a heads-up about what the police weren't sharing. Only fear of a libel suit prevented the newspaper from titillating their readers with a headline that blared, AAG PRIME SUSPECT IN HUSBAND'S DISAPPEARANCE.

Sherri's caption read: DRUG CLASH SUSPECTED IN WOMAN'S DEATH. Forty-three words were what her death was worth in print:

Sherri Smith, 21, of Lansing was found dead in her home on Oakland Avenue Monday morning, the victim of a homicide. Fentanyl and cocaine were found at the scene. The victim had a criminal record for selling drugs. The case remains under investigation.

I rated better coverage for standing in a restaurant and watching a car burn. A pared-down blurb in the obituaries noted: Ms. Smith leaves behind a six-year-old son, Samuel. There was no mention of funeral arrangements. I assumed there wouldn't be one. Sherri would be buried at state expense. Her story would have leapt to the front page if the police or reporters had connected it to my ongoing melodrama. There was an upside to the right hand not knowing what the left was doing.

So far it wasn't the worst day of my life. Not even close. A seventeen-year-old rape and Sherri's murder vied for that honor. But the day was young. By afternoon, it would rank right up there in the top three.

I lunched on Cheetos and Laughing Cow cheese, while I worked through piles of new correspondence attached to files littering my desk. Monotony beat bad memories. I embraced the lull.

At two-fifteen, I called it a day. I wasn't producing my finest work but couldn't motivate myself to leave. I was exhausted. Not the kind of tired that follows an honest day's labor, but the kind of tired that seeps into your bones and adds a hundred-pound weight to what you normally carry around.

I sat brain-dead at my desk at two-thirty when Lockhart called and kick-started my senses.

"Hello, Mrs. Lawrence." He immediately dispensed with small talk. "A fellow was out running his hunting beagles through the park on Okemos Road a few hours ago. He stumbled across a body."

43

My nerve receptors short-circuited under the enormity of the words. It was a moment like when I was seven years old and my mother picked me up at school and told me my father had left us. A moment like when I sat in my office at Employers Mutual on September 11, 2001, listening to Beethoven's Fifth, and my radio interrupted to report a jet had crashed into one of the New York Twin Towers. A moment that for the rest of my life would haunt me each time my cerebrum's recall spit it, uninvited, into my consciousness. That kind of a moment.

It hadn't been two weeks since I left the sergeant's office with the uneasy knowledge I was a person of interest in Derek's disappearance.

Lockhart curtailed my rampaging thoughts. "We have the body at the morgue. It might be your ex-husband. We've checked it against his DMV photo, but can't tell for sure. We need your confirmation."

It was an emotional one-two punch. First, it was likely Derek was dead. And second, I had to identify the body.

The body. I squeezed my eyes shut. My brain balked, trying to process the information. Unable to do so, it tiptoed around the gruesome news and concentrated on the mundane. "I don't know where the morgue is." I knew Lansing must have one, but for as long as I had lived in the area, I'd had no reason to ask where it was.

"It's in the lower level of Sparrow Hospital. I've been here with the State Police for the last couple hours. The body's processed and ready to be viewed. I'll meet you in the hospital lobby."

I looked down at a legal pad on my desk. Written across it in jagged schizophrenic script were Derek, dead, processed, and morgue. I scribbled furious circles around ominous words that had appeared as if by magic rather than by conscious effort on my part.

Lockhart cleared his throat. "Are you still there?"

"Yes."

"How soon can you be here?"

Get a grip, I ordered myself. I calculated time and distance. "Five minutes to walk to my car. Another ten to get to the hospital."

"I'll be waiting. You might want to bring someone along."

My first choice of escorts, Rad, was on his way to Detroit. I tried the cell I had bought him but got a message: "The person you are trying to reach is currently unavailable and has not set up a voicemail account." I considered other appropriate chaperones: Tom? He was in Kalamazoo today. Natalee? Easy decision. You don't take your sixteen-year-old daughter for moral support to identify her father's body. Ginny? My best friend was at work, and by the time I interrupted whatever she was doing, and she drove to Sparrow Hospital it would exceed the fifteen minutes that I had promised Lockhart. Gannon? I didn't need to fall apart in front of a cheating ex-lover.

Oh, God, I thought as I pictured a lifeless Derek. If it was my ex, how long had he been dead, and how had he died? Lockhart's suggestion to bring support implied this could be worse than brutal. I believed him but was flat out of choices. I wanted this over. I would go alone.

I parked in the ramp connected to the hospital. The complex groaned under the work tools of major renovations. Sick people and death are always a thriving business. I hurried through the connecting walkway into the reception area.

Lockhart slouched in a modern chocolate-colored leather chair, his eyes glued to the *USA Today*. He munched potato chips. Watching an autopsy hadn't killed his appetite. Neither had hospital ambiance nor the caustic odor of disinfectant. I was within whispering distance when he glanced up and spotted me. He stood, wiped greasy palms on his trousers, and stuck out his right hand. My autopilot shook it.

"Sorry about the circumstances," he said as he gathered the refuse from his lunch and deposited it in the trash.

I nodded but read are you responsible for this into his condolences. I followed him down a long hallway with brown and beige institutional marble floors and color-coordinated cream walls. Soothing, serious colors. The circumstances, and the way Lockhart studied me, suggested I wouldn't feel soothed any time soon.

We passed several free-standing partitions that hid hospital reality from curious eyes. We turned left at the Lobby Café and continued beyond a bank of elevators, then left again before he ushered me into the All Faiths Chapel. Under other circumstances, it would have been a pleasant room, a place of respite where I could collect my thoughts. But my thoughts resisted collection.

The cop picked up the phone hanging on the wall. "Ms. Lawrence is here." He took a chair next to me. We waited.

A few minutes passed before a woman who made a white lab jacket and green scrubs look stylish, joined us. "I'm Dr. Sharp," she said, "chief pathologist at Sparrow Health Systems." Her doe-like eyes offered unspoken sympathy. "You must be Casey Lawrence?" She didn't wait for an answer. "There is no way to make this easy, but I'll do my best not to make it harder." She reached out and took my right hand between both of hers. Hers were warmer than Lockhart's had been a few moments earlier. "I'll take you and the sergeant to the viewing room when you are ready."

I withdrew my hand from her grasp and clasped my fingers together to hide their trembles. "I'm ready."

She ignored my hasty response and sat on the other side of me. "I need to explain a few things first."

I wanted to avoid what she was about to share, but short of fainting, saw no way to accomplish that. I sank farther down in the chair.

"We try to spare loved ones this ordeal when we can," she said. "Usually we identify the body through dental records or fingerprints."

"So why am I here? Derek's prints are in the system." I sensed she was about to deliver a staggering punch line.

She lowered her voice, but soft words couldn't cushion the impact. "The fingertips have been burned off with acid, and we have no dental records. The cranium sustained a gunshot wound through the left occipital orbit. There's been considerable damage to the face and skull, so we made only a tentative ID from the DMV photo."

I swallowed bile that filled my mouth. It mingled with blood that seeped from open wounds where I gnawed the inside of my cheeks. I was grateful no one said anything for the next few seconds. The doctor and the cop had been through this drill before.

After the pause, Dr. Sharp said, "We'll enter a small viewing room with a glass partition separating it from a second room where the body is positioned. The curtain on the window between these cubicles will remain closed until you tell me to draw it. When I do, take your time. When you are certain, let us know if it is your husband."

I didn't bother to clarify, ex-husband. For the second time, I said, "I'm ready." My left eye twitched, and I tried to soothe it with sweaty fingers.

"Then follow me," she said.

Lockhart opened the door, stood back, and let the doctor and me enter the empty hallway. I was assailed by the cloying smell of Lysol ramped to industrial strength. There were no doctors, no nurses, no patients—not a living soul. We were alone in the stark hallway. I wondered if Dr. Sharp had ordered everyone out. We strode straight ahead to the bank of elevators that Lockhart and I had passed on our way to the chapel. Dr. Sharp pushed a button, and we went down one floor.

I grabbed the railing inside the elevator, fearful I might slump to the floor.

"Are you okay?" she asked.

Could I be okay with a brain as frenzied as a DVD on fast forward and a body that threatened to melt into a gelatinous blob before the elevator doors opened? The robot that was me nodded.

We stepped into the basement, where the hallways were narrower and the lights brighter, but, again, there wasn't another person in sight. We walked, chaperoned by the stillness of death. Dr. Sharp opened the door to the dimly lit viewing area. As she promised, the curtain was closed, so I saw neither the adjacent room nor the body that I had been warned lay there. She motioned toward an undersized loveseat, but I remained standing. If my knees buckled, I would reconsider. Lockhart dropped into the loveseat's matching chair next to a table with a phone. I'm not claustrophobic, but the walls closed in and threatened suffocation.

I wondered if I looked as pale as I felt.

"It might help to take several deep breaths," Dr. Sharp said. "Tell me when you want the curtain opened."

Since never wasn't an option, I took several deep breaths, and then said, "Let's do it."

I fought the urge to close my eyes. The curtain opened as if in slow motion. I saw a lumpy white sheet, more white sheet, and still more white sheet before I stared at what was left of a face. I sagged against Dr. Sharp for support, then jerked my head to one side and vomited. Lockhart covered his nose and mouth with a ruddy-looking hand. I think Dr. Sharp told me not to worry about it; the janitor would clean it up later.

The body, positioned with the less damaged side closer to the viewing window, lay on a slab that fit into the slots of a gurney. The sheet that had seemed to go on forever was pulled up to the neck. The cotton fabric didn't cling to the contours of a human shape. I assumed it was separated from the flesh by a stiff shapeless body bag that had been turned back far enough to leave the head visible. A fluorescent pink tag tied to an exposed zipper supported my conclusion.

"Is it him?" Lockhart asked.

It wasn't the Derek I knew. One eye socket was hollow and blackened with dried blood that hadn't washed off during the autopsy; the other eyelid was closed. What remained of Derek's face looked pasty. His bluish mouth appeared made of wax.

I wished for doubt. I begged for doubt. I prayed for doubt. But doubt was as absent as life in Derek's corpse. "That's him."

It was Derek. A cold, brutalized body with the spirit sucked out of it. What perverted son of a bitch crawled into our lives and killed Derek? Who left me this sick image?

"Are you absolutely sure?"

I wanted to scream, do you think for a minute that because we are divorced, I can't recognize the man I married, slept with, and had a child by? Instead, I mumbled, "See the mole at the side of his right eye? It's Derek."

44

Natalee burst through the front door minutes after I returned from the morgue. I had left a message on her voice mail telling her to head straight home after school. She threw her backpack and blue jean jacket to the foyer floor and kicked off her sneakers before she looked up and saw me watching her from the living room sofa. I had struggled with the corpulent weight of this impending disaster even before Derek's body was found. A wise person might confront calamities head on, but I wanted nothing more than to disappear. Cowardice doesn't permit a mother that luxury.

"Mom, why are you home so early? You look like shit . . . oops, sorry . . . are you sick?"

From the distance of the mirror on the other side of the room, my sallow face reflected a subdued matte of shock and told me it was a rational question. Nat's eyes caught the scotch and water in my hand and the foil from the Alka-Seltzer sitting on the coffee table. Before I answered she asked the more heartbreaking question. "It's Dad, isn't it?"

"Yes."

"He's dead." She said it as though she, too, had always known it would end like this.

"Yes," I said again.

She dropped on the sofa, leaving a gap between us. She folded her arms on her lap and leaned her face into them, eyes hidden. Her soft sobs communicated pain. At sixteen, death had been no more than malicious speculation. It had never meddled in her life. For several minutes, she said nothing. When she lifted her head and spoke, I strained to hear her tiny whisper. Her shoulders drooped like those of a puppet whose strings were loosened.

"He finally came back."

I hesitated, felt my way along, unsure of how to make this easier for her. I wanted to pull her close and promise her I could make it better, but this wasn't a scraped knee, and she wasn't a four-year-old. I couldn't kiss the hurt away any more than I could pretend her father wasn't dead because of me. I didn't know which I feared more, being rejected or worsening her despair. I stayed two feet from her and inched my left arm along the back of the sofa to within touching distance in case she was looking for a sign.

"He took me to the food court last week," she said. "We got Cinnabons with extra frosting. Trish and Kaitlin walked by and saw me, having coffee and sitting with my father. For once I wasn't the kid who didn't even know where her dad was." The words choked her, and she quieted again.

I knew my daughter needed to believe Derek loved her. He had reappeared in her life, and if they hadn't established a father-daughter bond, death now cheated her of that opportunity. A month ago, it might not have mattered. Now it did.

"Honey, grownups don't always do the right thing. It took your dad sixteen years, but he came back because he wanted to get to know you and make it right." It didn't matter if I believed my words, only that she did. Damn Derek for coming into her life and hurting her. Damn him for giving her false hope. And damn him for dying.

"He just got here, but now he's dead," she said.

I held no magic talisman to change the story's ending. I didn't even have words to soften her pain.

"How?" she asked. "How did he die?"

I wanted to twist the gruesome facts into a comforting fantasy where he died peacefully and was in a better place. The former I knew to be a bold-faced lie and the latter was questionable. With the delivery of tomorrow's *Sentinel,* she would have more detail than she could possibly want.

"He was shot." I kept it simple and didn't elaborate.

"By the bastards that messed up the study and are threatening you?" she asked.

"Probably."

"I hope they rot in hell." The muscles of her jaws clenched. She grabbed a pillow and pounded her fists against it. "It's because of your job he's dead."

Another sucker punch to my theory that guilt is a useless emotion. I foresaw therapy for both of us unless we buried this disaster so deep that we suffocated the life right out of it. I was willing to try that but dubious that it would succeed.

"I'm sorry." I inched my fingers closer until they rested on her arm. When she didn't flinch, I leaned over and hugged her to me. Her tears dampened the front of my blouse. I stroked her hair and kissed her wet cheeks, impotent to do more.

"I want to see him. Maybe it isn't him."

Telling her about Derek's murder was tough enough. There was no way my daughter would see her father's corpse with half its head blown off. "Sweetie, I've identified him. The police and coroner released the body to me when they finished the autopsy, and it's been cremated by Gorsline-Runciman."

"You had no right to do that without asking me." Her tone suggested I should add a second helping of blame for not letting her have a final goodbye.

"It was what he wanted," I said.

She pulled away. Her look called me a liar. "How would you know that?"

"Honey, your dad and I haven't always been divorced. There were years when we talked about everything. Married people tell each other what they want done in the case of their death." The subject of cremation had never come up, but I knew Derek would sanction the lie.

"Can we have a funeral?" she asked.

"It's so sudden. I haven't thought about it," I said.

"It's not right to throw his ashes in the ground like no one cares."

I spent the remainder of Wednesday making arrangements for a service and tormented with worry about who might be the next to die.

❦

45

I struggled to write a short obituary for the *Sentinel.* I noted the memorial would be held at 2:00 p.m., Friday, October 14, at Gorsline-Runciman in East Lansing. Beyond that, words to describe an ex-husband came hard.

In the final accounting, I wondered if Derek's life posted under the column for good or the one for evil. Maybe somewhere in between. I doubted anyone cheered, Thank God that son of a bitch is dead, but what he had done to make the world a better place seemed sparsely scrawled, providing few accolades for the obit. His greatest accomplishment was fathering my daughter, and that was pure accident.

Jon and Ginny offered their pastor to officiate since I wasn't on a close-enough basis with God to have my own minister. I accepted their kindness and told the funeral director his smallest room would suffice. Natalee, Tom, and I would pay our respects. Maybe Jon, Ginny, and Rad.

Derek was an only child, born to parents who wanted no children and had believed they were past the need for birth control. His mother was forty-four when she found herself pregnant, his father fifty-six. Natalee's paternal grandmother died of breast cancer before Natalee turned a year old, and her paternal grandfather was dead six months later.

As for my family attending, my mother subsisted in a nursing home suffering early-onset Alzheimer's complicated by years of binge drinking. I had no idea where my father was. Skylar, my free-spirited sister, lived somewhere in California, but we weren't close. She wouldn't fly in for the funeral of my ex-husband. Especially since I wouldn't call her with news of his death.

Natalee showed me a picture of her and Derek snapped by a server at the Cancun restaurant. Father and daughter beamed like they shared a special secret. For a microsecond, I was jealous. She wanted the picture at the funeral since there could be no viewing.

Thursday, I stopped at CVS and used the self-service machine to make an eight-by-ten copy of the photo. I inserted the enlargement into the polished teak frame that once held my wedding picture. I ordered a large spray of flowers from Natalee, beribboned with FOR MY FATHER.

The funeral director asked me to arrive an hour before the service to receive other mourners. It seemed easier to agree than argue. Somber organ music drifted from speakers to greet us as we entered. My left arm hugged Natalee's shoulders, and her right hand held my waist. I wasn't sure who supported whom. Tom followed behind us.

Natalee shuffled to the front of the room alone and set the picture on the heavy mahogany table where her father's ashes rested in a bronze urn next to the flower arrangement bearing her name. She ran her fingers along the sides of the vessel. Her hands fluttered, and she grasped the table's edge. I took a step toward her, but she seemed to regain her composure. I sensed she needed space to deal with her emotions.

I looked around and guessed there were enough folding chairs to accommodate fifty people. I wished the funeral director had been less generous. I was shocked by the profusion of baskets, plants, and floral arrangements adorning the front of the room on either side of the table. Dominating was a standing spray of roses, carnations, delphiniums, and asters in shades of pink, white, and purple. I read the card attached by a clear plastic-pronged stick: Our thoughts and prayers are with you at this difficult time. Condolences from Attorney General Sawicki and the Department of Attorney General. Jon and Ginny sent a circle of grapevine intertwined with tulips, iris, daffodils, lilies, and alstroemeria. Louise, Tom, and Rad each sent a colorful arrangement. Several friends at Employers Mutual expressed sympathy with an elegant mixture of fresh-cut flowers surrounding a living calla lily.

Ginny and Jon entered the room and offered quiet hugs. Rad came next. He plodded over, tugging the sleeves of his wool coat. He kissed my cheek and whispered, "You need to stand by the door to meet people as they arrive."

I expected only the half dozen mourners already present. I hadn't boned up on funeral etiquette.

"I like the picture," Rad said when Natalee joined us. "You look like your father." Natalee gave a tight smile and thanked him.

Over the next half hour, many of the employees of EM arrived. Ethan and several of Natalee's friends joined the crowd. A couple of dozen of my current co-employees, including Louise, showed up. Chace came without Katya. Ten minutes before the service, the funeral director opened the partition between the room I had reserved and adjacent spaces. By the time the minister began speaking, there were more than a hundred and fifty names in the guest book. I hadn't counted on the political ramifications that brought half of the legal community to show respect for the Department of Attorney General. Nor had I considered that curiosity seekers might join the crowd for the sport of deciding if I looked guilty.

"Dearly beloved." The minister held out his arms as though to embrace those gathered. "We are here to celebrate a life cut short. Depravity exists, but God has not abandoned us." That's the last thing I remembered other than the words, "O Lord my God, when I in awesome wonder" as they reverberated from the sound system and blended with live voices. The old hymn sent shivers rippling my spine. Religion wasn't the usual balm for my pain, but today I welcomed support from any source.

As we left the funeral home, I caught sight of a black Lincoln Town Car sitting at the back of the parking lot. I got the plate's first three numbers, BK3, before it pulled out the side driveway. I checked the driver's ruggedly sculptured facial structure, high cheekbones, wavy black hair, and complexion dark enough to suggest afternoons spent on a lounge chair by the swimming pool. He appeared about thirty-five. I wasn't close enough, and he wasn't there long enough after I spotted him, for me to see more. My first impression: he wasn't bad looking. If your tastes ran to sinister.

Later that night, Tom said, "I'm off to Meijer's. We're out of Diet Coke. You guys need anything?"

"I'd like a four-pack of Starbucks Cappuccino," Natalee said.

"You've got it. I won't be long." As he kissed me goodbye, he whispered, "I think you and Nat could use some alone time."

"I'm glad we had a funeral," Natalee said as we sat close on the couch, nursing cups of hot apple cider I'd nuked for us.

"Me too." I swirled the cinnamon stick in my drink and aspired to a moment of brilliance that never came.

"I think Dad would have liked it. Especially seeing the flowers and all the people who came."

"You made a wise decision." I ran the fingers of my left hand through her tousled hair and let them rest for a moment on her shoulder.

"Do you ever feel like you don't know how you are supposed to act?" she asked.

"All the time." For once the honest answer was easy.

"Is it okay to go to a movie with Ethan tomorrow night?"

I drew her to me. "Honey, that's up to you. You've done what you could to show respect. If you feel like going to a movie with Ethan, your father would approve."

"Do I go back to school on Monday?"

"Your choice. If you wish to stay home for a few days, I'll stay with you." My grieving for a lost marriage ended years ago. Shock at Derek's gruesome death was not something I wanted to wallow in, but if my daughter needed a few days, I would be there with her.

"And we'll do what? Mope and cry?" she asked.

"If that's what you need, then yes, mope and cry. I imagine the world looks pretty ugly right now."

"Mom, I don't know how I will get over it."

"Maybe you don't get over it, but you go on." My face felt brittle to the point of cracking, and tension throbbed in every muscle, but I was thankful to be sitting with my daughter. "How you feel is simply how you feel. Neither right nor wrong, it just is. Someday what you'll remember more than his death will be him standing on the front porch saying, 'Hi, baby,' with a huge grin plastered across his face. Or Cinnabons and coffee at the food court. Or your server taking a picture of the two of you while you shared burritos and stories."

She laid her head against my chest and cried. There was no quick recovery for the blow she had suffered.

"You will be grateful for those things," I said. Then I cried too.

❧

46

Monday, October 17

I smelled sweet onion, tomato, and garlic before I saw Rad. He breezed into my office Monday at noon with a Sir Pizza. I pushed aside an investigative report about the most recent piece of sleaze to become one of my files, and Rad dropped the box with thud.

"The four major food groups for your good health," he said. "Meat, dairy, grain, and fruits and veggies."

"How do you figure?" I knew I would enjoy the explanation.

"Are you disputing ham and sausage are meat? Because I know cheese is dairy and there must be grain in that crust. I asked them to throw on a few pieces of pineapple to cover the fruits, and mushrooms give it veggies."

"A regular nutritionist."

"Just eat." He handed me a napkin and opened the box. "I wasn't sure you'd be at work today, but when you weren't home, I figured it was a safe bet."

"You could have called."

"Sure, but I risked you being in a pissy mood. What if you didn't want to see my cheery face?"

"Would that have stopped you?" I was mouth deep to the center of my first piece of savory, lukewarm pizza. I retrieved the string of cheese hanging from my lips.

"Probably not." Rad swallowed the last bite of his first piece and reached for a second as he grabbed another handful of skimpy paper napkins.

"I'm glad you're here," I said. "I told Natalee we could stay home, but she decided brooding wouldn't be helpful. Said the longer she was away, the harder it would be to face her friends and deal with their pity."

"Smart girl, like her mother. Well, like her mother most of the time." He picked up a sliver of sausage that had fallen to the side in the box and dropped it on the piece he shoveled into his mouth. After a couple of strong chews, he said, "I got info on that Lincoln Town Car in the back of the Gorsline-Runciman lot at the service Friday."

"I didn't know you saw it." Before he could continue, I turned up the volume of my radio to blur our conversation, pointed toward the offices on either side of me, and half-whispered, "Pays to keep our voices low."

He nodded, then said, "Very little escapes these seasoned eyes. I even saw the bumper sticker. "LIFE'S ALL ABOUT ASS: COVERING IT, TRYING TO GET IT, KISSING IT, AND KICKING IT."

"I got the plate's first three letters, but he drove away too fast. I stared a second or two at the driver before I thought to look at the license."

"The difference between my years of investigative experience and you novices. That and I expect a woman to focus on a man's face and forget the important stuff."

I wadded up my napkin and threw a bull's eye, dead center of his forehead. "Feminists have a name for men like you."

"I think you've mentioned it before. You want to verbally flog an old man, or hear what I found out?"

"Your friends have already run the plate?" I asked.

"Of course. I'm just building a little suspense." He palmed a piece of pizza without the edges hanging over.

"No disrespect to a master's brilliance, but it's registered to Dr. B, isn't it?" I asked.

"Technically to Robert Kansas, Bloomfield."

"Filthy degenerate." I picked up the legal pad I had been writing on before Rad arrived and flung it across the room in anger. If Shirley was in her office, she had to wonder what was going on as it hit our shared wall.

"My sentiments exactly. But it supports what we suspected about the 313," Rad said. "Question is, what are we going to do?"

"While you ponder the ultimate question, let me add a shot of my own suspense. I had an email waiting for me this morning."

"Do tell."

I took a couple of swallows of my iced tea, helped myself to another piece of pizza. I picked off the pineapple. He collected the soggy discarded fruit, tossed it in his mouth, and waited.

"See for yourself." I shifted the laptop around so he could read what Advice4U had written.

Your ex-husband's death wasn't meant to hurt you or your daughter. Derek gave us no choice. We are sorry. You have our condolences, but it doesn't change anything. We appreciate your cooperation and, as promised, we will continue to make it worth your while.

"Have you responded?" Rad asked.

I jerked the computer back harder than I intended. "No, I spent the morning considering possibilities."

"Like what?" he asked.

"Like telling Advice4U to screw himself," I said.

"Bad choice."

"Or not responding at all."

"Not quite as bad, but it'll worry him."

I looked Rad straight in the eye. "Then there's that option you find objectionable."

He picked at the bits of remaining ham and mushroom, then gathered flaccid napkins and tossed them into the empty box before he scrutinized me. "Remind me how that one goes?"

"These guys know I have no love for Sawicki. I'm sure that, along with what they claim to know about my past, figured into singling me out for the job of inside man, or in this case woman. I've played with the wording of a response, even struggled to suggest to the sick twisted bastard that Derek's murder was no big deal. So, what if I sent something like this?" I brought up the draft document and turned it for him to see.

I understand loyalty. Until now, I haven't found anyone deserving of mine, not Sawicki and not Derek. I'm sorry about Derek, but I understand the predicament my ex put you in, and there wasn't a lot of love lost between us. I could be a big help to you. I suggest we meet to discuss a proposal.

"No. Double no. Double don't-even-think-it no." Rad's blood pressure must have spiked because a flush of red pulsed from the thick neck bulging above the open button at his collar to the top of his forehead. He coughed twice, but that may have been for effect.

"See, I knew you wouldn't be reasonable. You could put a wire on me, and I would get him talking. Might be entrapment, not admissible as evidence, but it would prove our theory and maybe convince the police I'm innocent. More important, it would help Lockhart follow the trail to Sherri's and Derek's murderer. Hopefully before anything happens to Nat or me."

"You're quite the detective these days. Put a wire on you? You think I keep that kind of equipment in my underwear drawer between rows of my socks?"

"I think you just might. Right there in the drawer next to where you stockpile your guns."

His tone changed from sarcastic to weary. "Look, CJ, have you forgotten he killed Sherri? No, that's not right. He didn't just kill her, he brutalized her. And he knows you know he killed her, and he doesn't trust you any more than you trust him. He shot Derek through the head and burned off his fingertips. Might have had his goons do it, but my money's on Dr. B himself. I told you before, word is he's got several screws loose and quite the taste for cruel pleasures. Enjoys the blood and gore. Even enjoys the stalking. That's why he was at the funeral—to mess with your head. He isn't a nice man, and the people who work for him aren't nice either. B favors keeping you alive because it suits his needs, but he won't flinch if it becomes expedient to waste you." He rested his hands on the closed empty pizza box and waited for his words to sink in.

I wasn't ready to give up. "You said it. He wants something from me. He won't hurt me if he believes I can deliver."

"Casey, dear Casey. Even Angelina Jolie isn't good enough to pull off the stunt you have in mind. You'll blanch or balk. You'll cower or cringe. You'll say something he thinks is odd. Or, accept it, he's a paranoid bastard who questions things when there's no reason. It won't work."

"First of all, I don't know if Dr. B would accept my invitation. Second, if he did, I would meet him in a public place, and you could park close by. I'm not exactly defenseless. I'm a brown belt with a gun for safe measure."

"Sweet Lord in heaven, you are obtuse. A skinny woman, brown belt and gun notwithstanding, and an old fart against a guy whose biceps pop the size of bowling balls when he flexes 'em." Rad shook his head, blinked a slow blink, and then shook his head again.

"You exaggerate."

"No. I don't. I can see it. You ask his permission to call me because you're in over your head. Dr. B says, 'Sure, why not?' rather than squeeze the old Glock and send a half dozen bullets into your head. And I run—no, make that pant—to your aid and order him to put down the semi-automatic?" Rad laughed to underscore the ridiculous image he painted.

"Do I hear a better plan?"

"My buddy, Racer, at the State Police. Made a visit to him last week. He's out of town now until Thursday. We'll have a sit-down, heart-to-heart with him when he gets back. Make yourself available."

"I'll think about it." I loosened my eyes from the grip of his hard glare and turned to the window. I wasn't ready to make him a promise.

"No thought needed," he said. "It's a done deal."

"Is this Racer guy a miracle maker?"

"He understands the Detroit gangs. He may have an idea or two."

"A vague idea or two doesn't reassure me," I said.

"Just be ready. I'll pick you up at four on Thursday. Until then, don't do anything stupid." Rad grabbed the pizza box and his empty Pepsi can. "Your response to B is fine except the last two sentences. Say, 'I plan to be a big help to you,' and then skip the sentence about meeting him." Rad blew me a kiss as he left.

With Rad gone, I scanned stations on my radio, searching for calming music to temper my wild fantasies. Rad had made a valid point. Meeting a lunatic whose body count stood at two in fewer than as many weeks—and those were the ones we knew about—could be stupid. On the other hand, Dr. B killed when he was crossed, and the last thing I'd do was give him reason to think I might cross him. He had demonstrated how dangerous he was when he killed Sherri and forced me to watch her die. That show of power had to convince him I would be afraid to sell him out. He had two powerful bargaining chips, my daughter and my past. If he agreed to a meeting, I would insist on a restaurant. Not likely he was going to torture or shoot me in front of a roomful of eyewitnesses.

I didn't plan to go without backup. My first choice had just refused. That left Tom, Jon, or Chace. Tom was easy to rule out. With his concern for my well-being, he'd try to dissuade me. Might even call the cops. I mulled the idea of Jon. Our bond didn't lend itself to intrigue. More important, Ginny was my best friend. I didn't want to risk making her a widow. That left Chace. My relationship with him was built on clandestine. It didn't hurt that he was a skilled investigator. I was annoyed that he might be having another affair, but I believed my welfare meant something to him. He was the best option.

I faced the chicken or egg situation: Send the email to Advice4U, who I was pretty certain was Dr. B, to see if he would go for a meeting, or confirm Chace was on board. Logic favored starting with Chace to book backup. Before I changed my mind, I dialed. When he answered, I gave it to him clear and simple. "I've got a harebrained scheme, and it takes an accomplice if I want to remain alive. You in?"

"Titillated, at the very least."

"Can you spare a few minutes?"

"I'll be there by the time you hang up."

I swore Chace to secrecy. If he disagreed with my plan or refused to be a part of it, it was imperative he not blow the whistle. Next, I explained how my situation had spiraled. I downplayed the danger but said, "I don't have much time. Lives are at stake. Mine and Nat's. I have reasons for not going to Lockhart. Please don't force me to share them. I'm a chicken-heart, but for Natalee's safety, I'll try anything." That was the other advantage to choosing Chace. He had daughters. He understood.

"I assume you've considered the alternatives?" he said.

"Of course. And I can't find a good one. The cops seriously believe I'm the perp here. With enough time, they may stumble on the truth, but time is something I don't have. Khoury's continued trial is two and a half weeks away. At that point, the bad guys will realize I have no intention of delivering on my promise."

"So, what exactly is the plan?" he asked.

I showed him my proposed email. "If Advice4U agrees to a meet, I would feel a whole lot safer with you close by, prepared to call 911 the minute anything turns shaky."

To my surprise, he said, "Well, I'm guessing you'll do this, with or without my help. I'd rather come to your funeral thinking I did what I could to save you. I'll be there."

"One last thing, any idea where I can get a wire?"

Sounding like a replay of Rad, he said, "This isn't a TV detective drama. All you need is a high-quality digital tape recorder, and I've got one of those. Put it in an open handbag, and it'll pick up every word clear as stars on a cloudless night. Standard state issue. I use it for taking statements, among other things. It's about fifty times better than the model attorneys use for dictation. I'll drop it off tomorrow morning."

I cut and pasted my original, unedited Word document into an email and hit SEND.

By late afternoon I got a response: *Sounds interesting. Where and when?*

I typed back:

Unless you have a better idea, how about Capital Prime in the Eastwood Towne Center, tomorrow night, 6:00 p.m.? It's a weeknight so it shouldn't be busy. We'll get a quiet booth. I'll leave the name Flowers with the hostess.

Before I left the office for another afternoon of researching old microfiche and checking vital statistics, I opened the reply.

It's a date. My treat. I know the place. You have good taste. They serve a killer filet mignon. I've only eaten there once, when I was meeting a business associate, but it was memorable. Looking forward to it.

47

Tuesday, October 18

I've made some mistakes in my life. And the rate of my judgment errors had escalated since my home was burglarized. It might have been unwise to keep the cops in the dark. It was a real boneheaded screw-up to go to Sherri's house for information. Her murder was on me. I hoped what I was about to do wasn't the gravest of my mistakes.

Natalee had play rehearsal, and Tom a late appointment with a client. Neither of them would be home before nine. They believed I would be safe, having dinner with friends.

Chace dropped off the recorder, and the plan was for him to sit at the bar and keep an eye on me. With his cell phone, he could snap a couple of photos of Dr. B and me. Even Lockhart should find it hard to believe I would implicate myself with damning photos. Add the incriminating admissions I planned to record, and the cop would be forced to rethink his primary suspect. I left work at five-fifteen, more jittery than a gambler betting a million on the twenty-to-one at Pimlico.

I had no trouble finding a parking spot. It was too early for most diners or theatre goers, and shoppers parked closer to the retail stores. A month earlier, Tom had taken me to the upscale restaurant for a romantic dinner. Now I tarnished that sweet memory by picking it as the place to meet a dangerous drug dealer.

I gave the name Flowers to the hostess and asked to be seated in a booth at the far side of the dining room where the man I was meeting and I could talk privately. At five-forty, Chace sauntered into the restaurant and took a stool at the bar. The plan was on target.

Still, this might be harder than I thought. My social repertoire didn't stretch to rendezvous between vicious Detroit gang lords and middle-aged Okemos mothers. I began to see Rad's point. I set my purse on the floor beside me. The recorder was inside the handbag, propped on the .38 I had brought along for company. The cigarette-pack-sized recorder had a nine-hour capacity. I pushed the ON button.

By six, I had finished off a full glass of water and my nervous bladder forced me to the ladies' room. I dreaded leaving the bathroom's security, figuring there might be company waiting at my table. There wasn't. By six-fifteen I needed a scotch and Alka-Seltzer. Maybe Dr. B wouldn't show. I began to relax.

When the hostess walked my way, I knew the meeting was on. She led a tall, athletic-looking man whose biceps were almost as big as Rad had described. I had trouble swallowing. I hoped Dr. B would start the conversation because I wasn't sure where I left my tongue.

I took in every inch of the man who was making my life hell. His tight, cable-knit sweater did nothing to hide the power of his muscled chest. His hazel eyes penetrated like infrared. They were framed by the longest, thickest eyelashes I had ever seen on a man. The irregular scar on his left cheek didn't diminish the good facial structure I had noticed in the funeral home parking lot, just made him appear more intimidating. Even after my trip to the restroom, it was a minor miracle I didn't wet myself.

"It's a pleasure to meet you, Miss Lawrence. I've looked forward to this."

"Likewise." My voice quivered as if I had been dosed with helium. The hostess handed us two menus. She flashed a conspiratorial smile as if to say I was one lucky woman.

"No need to be jumpy." He reached over and touched my cold shaking hands with his fingertips.

"Considering the circumstances, does that surprise you?" I asked.

"No, I guess blind dates are a bit awkward." His voice was as rhythmic as a jazz tenor's. He grinned, and I noted he had straight, bright teeth. Not what

I expected, but I reminded myself Dr. B's childhood move to the suburbs likely brought with it access to good medical and dental.

He studied the menu. "Any recommendations other than the filet?"

"I'm not hungry."

"Come now. Am I that big of a disappointment? I'm ravenous. Eating with a beautiful woman does that to me."

"A cup of decaf is all I want."

"Suit yourself. It's your loss. Remember, I'm buying." He closed the menu, and the server came over, pad and pencil ready.

"Looks like the lady isn't hungry. Bring her a cup of decaf. I'll have an espresso and a piece of double layer chocolate cake with two scoops of ice cream, one vanilla, one chocolate."

The server shot Dr. B a disappointed look. I supposed she worried about tying up a table for a small order and the promise of a meager tip.

After she walked away, Dr. B looked back at me. "Tell me a bit about yourself."

The odd statement confused me. "Like what?" I asked.

"You know, the standard first date stuff: Where you were born? Where do you work? Do you like long walks on the beach? Are you fond of babies or puppies? Do you like poetry? That kind of stuff."

My scowl must have trenched two deep ridges between my eyebrows. He had rattled me, and I couldn't frame my words.

"Okay, I'll go first," he said. "I was born in Detroit. Currently unmarried. I'm fairly well-off. Successful, I guess you'd say. I have a weakness for tall, foxy women. I still cheer for the Lions. I love dogs if they're well-trained. Kids even more if they're not."

I assumed I should play along, but his game flustered me. I wanted this over, so cut to the chase. "Do you want to hear my plan?"

The server dropped off our drinks and B' dessert. "You mean you have a plan for a relationship with a man you met five minutes ago? You're a fast woman. I like that. But let's enjoy our coffee for now."

What seemed like endless minutes passed. I didn't say a word. My companion broke the silence a few times. He mentioned he thought Detroit was recovering. Said he wished Michigan could get a decent governor. Asked me if I'd ever done any modeling. The first two comments I let pass without acknowledging. To answer the last, I shook my head.

Then Dr. B patted his napkin to his mouth, set aside the cake plate, and swallowed the last sip of his coffee. He laid a twenty and a ten on the table, leaned so close I thought he was going to kiss my cheek, and whispered, "You gave me too little credit. Don't make that mistake again," before he sauntered out.

I looked over to Chace, and neither of us moved for what seemed enough time to let Dr. B drive all the way back to Bloomfield Hills. I clicked off the recorder. When I was sure Dr. B was gone, I walked over to the bar.

"Don't ask. I have no idea what just happened," I said. "My ex-cop friend, Rad, warned me this couldn't work."

"Let's get out of here," Chace said. "I'm going to follow you home."

"Not necessary. It's over. I meet Rad on Thursday. Hopefully, he and his friend come up with something better than I did."

Chace walked me to my car. "You sure I can't come over?"

"Positive." I didn't need to make two huge mistakes the same night. "But you can check under the hood to make sure my car's not wired with dynamite."

I opened the overhead garage door, lowered it the second my car cleared the light sensor, and hurried inside. With one hand, I flipped on the kitchen light switch and with the other bolted the door to the garage. I dropped my jacket and purse on the coffee table as I beelined a path to the bar where I grabbed the bottle of scotch.

"Let me help you with that." The voice came from the unlit front entry hall.

I wheeled around and watched Dr. B walk from the shadows toward me.

I considered the gun. It was a thought born of desperation. A dive for my purse, and I was dead. I didn't kid myself. I was going to die. I had no desire to speed up the timetable.

"Didn't mean to scare you. I thought we needed more privacy for high-level negotiations. I'll fix the drinks. Your hands are shaking. You'll never get the Alka-Seltzer open. You sit down on the couch like a good girl." He wore surgical gloves like real doctors wore.

I was so screwed.

48

"How did you get in here?" I strained to sound outraged, but my squeaky voice carried no authority.

"Not important. Okay if I smoke?" he asked as though this was a social visit.

"I'd prefer you didn't. I'm not sure how I'd explain the smell to Natalee or Tom." I continued the illusion I had some say in what was about to happen.

"You'll think of a way." He lit up and, with the cigarette dangling from his mouth, draped his arm around my shoulder and guided me to the couch. He then stepped back to the bar, ripped open the Alka-Seltzer, and dropped it into my scotch. "I think I'll join you. I do appreciate good scotch although I can skip the Alka Seltzer."

I needed a clear head. I wanted liquor like I wanted Natalee to walk in but shuddered to think what happened if I declined. "Thanks," I said as I reached for the glass. It took both of my hands to steady the fizzing drink and keep it from spilling.

"I'm a damn fine bartender." His smug face was amiability set against the foreshadow of impending catastrophe. "I'm good at so many things. Drink up." He waited until I took a couple of swallows. "Now, ladies first. Tell me about this dynamite plan you have."

My voice quivered, but I managed to get out a few words. It wasn't the polished and persuasive argument I had rehearsed before meeting him at the restaurant, but at least I found my voice. "I've already told you it's risky for me to fix too many cases. I can't finagle keeping all of your docs out of trouble, keep them in practice. I'll do my best. But when they lose their licenses there'll always be others to take their place. I get the scoop on what's happening. I know who might be ready to listen to a good deal."

The prior look of self-satisfaction turned to a glower. He said nothing.

I rambled to fill in gaps in my proposal. "If I watch the ARCOS reports, I can identify doctors who might see the benefit of working with you. They won't keep their licenses long after Licensing Regulations gets interested in them, but it takes a while to prosecute. In the meantime, you make money, they make money, I make money. When that batch of docs is no longer of value, I give you new ones." It sounded stupid even as I said it. My delivery didn't improve its believability.

He smiled, but I saw no trace of affability in the chilling squint of those extravagantly lashed eyes. I hoped it was a bad read of body language. "What do you expect in return?" he asked.

"I want to be fair, but I figure I should get a cut of the action."

I leaned over and tabled the scotch that sloshed in my unsteady hands. I focused on an Ansel Adams photograph that graced the dining room wall, then glanced toward the fireplace. I kept my gaze moving, anywhere to avoid his menacing stare.

He jerked my head around, forced me to face him. "What do you think my action is?"

I steeled my courage, set my eyes wide and rock-steady. Then, without blinking, said, "You turn prescription drugs into street drugs and make a comfortable living at it."

"That's what you think? And I suppose you want me to tell you all about it?" He let the question hang between us.

I couldn't answer. There was no mistaking his challenge.

"I don't plan to do that, even though I assume you turned off the recorder after I left," he said.

"I . . . I . . ."

He put a finger to his lips to shush my stammer. "You don't offer me a real practical proposition. I get the ARCOS reports. If that was the way to go, I would be doing it. Sooner or later, one of those many doctors you suggest we speed through our pill-mill decides he doesn't like our enticing scheme. He'll go to the cops before we convince him it's healthier to keep quiet. It's better with fewer doctors and you keeping them licensed. They're happy. I'm happy."

"Okay." I blanched, my brain not outpacing my fear by much. "But when they seek reinstatement, three years at the most, I'll handle that proceeding and make them look good. After a cushy sabbatical that we make worth their while, they're back in the game."

"Spare me. You know it increases our risk." He cracked the knuckles on one hand and then the other, flexed his wrists, and shook his fingers like they were limp spaghetti. "So why did you want to meet?" He shrugged his shoulders as though limbering up. "You want a piece of the action? I'm going to give you a taste." With his arms close enough to grab me if I moved any direction, he spat the threat with such force that his spittle settled on my collar.

I cowered closer to the edge of the sofa. I wished that Rad was sitting outside and that screaming would do some good.

"I've survived in this game since before you drank lattes at some fancy rich-bitch college because I'm smarter than your average businessman." His words became chopped and indecipherable, as though filtered through a blender full of grated ice cubes. I felt woozy.

He stood, grabbed me by the arm, and shoved me to the floor before picking up my purse from the table and dumping it. The gun and recorder clunked when they hit the hardwood. He retrieved the revolver. I wondered if I would hear a boom before the bullet splattered my brain.

Feral rage flooded his dark eyes. Death closed in. I clung to a trace of optimism to prolong hope. I couldn't let Natalee be the one to find me.

"Please. Take me somewhere else," I begged. I had a flash of how desperate Sherri felt facing this monster.

He had no patience for my sluggish words. "You're one crazy bitch. I should shoot your sorry ass, but I'm a reasonable man."

His words were garbled, but I was pretty sure that was the gist of it. One thing was certain: there was more than Alka-Seltzer in my scotch. I had only taken a couple of sips. I wondered if I should have drunk more. Maybe comatose was better for what was about to happen.

"Now I want you to listen, and listen closely." He pulled me up by my hair and yanked my head backwards. "Am I clear?"

"Uh-huh," I whimpered.

He yanked again. "I'm not sure I understood that."

"Yes. Yes." Tears flowed more from fear and regret than pain.

With the index finger of one hand, he flicked the ashes from his cigarette. With his other hand, he ripped my blouse open. He fumbled as he tried to tear off my bra. The hooks defied him.

"Unsnap it," he ordered. Somehow my trembling fingers managed to unfasten it.

Rape is better than murder, I thought. I had survived it before.

He brought the cigarette's glowing tip so near my chest I felt the heat. He moved it in terrifying circles. I didn't dare shrink away and further fuel his anger. He clenched his other hand tightly over my mouth as he rammed the lit butt into my right nipple and held it there to extinguish the flame. I heard the skin sizzle and smelled the burnt flesh. The exquisite pain was worse than I had imagined it would be. I thought I might pass out but wasn't that lucky.

"Now, Miss Lawrence, I'm only going to say this once. Sherri is dead because she was a dimwit. Derek is dead because he disrespected me. I should kill you. You're crazier than both of them put together."

He jerked my head up and down in forced agreement.

"But you are worth more to me than either of them. So, because of my generous nature, you get one more pass. You ever try to find me again. You ever double cross me again. You ever do anything I tell you not to do, or fail to do something I tell you to do, and Natalee is dead. I'll slice her up. Butcher her in front of you."

His face grew animated and a perverse laugh accompanied his sick sport. He let go of me. I slumped to the floor.

"You ever heard a cat screech when you dump a gallon of gasoline over it and set a flaming match to its tail? You'll beg me to shoot your precious daughter to end the torture. But I'll drag it out nice and slow before I put a bullet in her brain. When I'm done, you'll beg me to shoot you too."

He stomped the heel of his boot on the tape recorder, smashing it into ragged plastic shards. He picked up the largest piece, and gently, almost like a lover, lifted me from the floor before he drove it into my bare back to underscore his point.

Excruciating pain jumped from one nerve ending to the next until my entire body suffered a vicious jolt. One of his hands prevented my initial shriek, and then both silenced the ongoing cascade of my screams. Sticky warmth trickled down my spine.

"It's been nice meeting you. Too bad we won't do it again."

He gave me a powerful shove to the floor. The back of my head hit the coffee table on the way down. No blood, but another sharp crack of pain. He snatched an apple from the fruit bowl on the dining room table, wiped it on his pant leg, started for the door.

Before he took the first crunch, I swallowed hard and whispered, "Bobby Mohn."

49

He pivoted a quick about-face. Dread masked my pain and dulled my senses. I detected a chink in his self-confidence. A bullet might come my way any second, but I banked on his curiosity. He didn't reach for my .38 stuck in his waistband, nor for his own weapon, which I believed was hidden somewhere on his body.

My audacity couldn't have shocked him more than it did me. I risked snatching death from an apparent reprieve. I didn't know where my sluggish words came from, yet I heard them, slow but understandable. "If you want to kill me, it's your choice. But I'm not the only one with secrets."

His unflinching eyes held a glint of interest. If I died for my impertinence, it appeared he was going to let me have my say first. Bleeding and frantic, I struggled to sit up.

He stood motionless. Waiting.

"My friend William Radowski has bigger balls than you could ever hope to have. Difference between you two? He's not a fucking psychopath. But don't underestimate him."

My vision, which had blurred when I struck my head, cleared, and Dr. B's impassive face came back into focus.

"Rad can be a calculating and dangerous bastard if you cross him," I said. "He'll do whatever it takes to get a job done. If that job is revenge, he'll see you are repaid in kind. Almost biblical in his approach."

I paused for a second to catch my breath. I patted my skull and felt a lump the size of a billiard ball. I expected Dr. B to stop my story, but he stood like he had been turned to a pillar of salt—except for eyes that twitched with outrage.

I continued. "Rad and I talked about your threats against Natalee. He's documented everything. Put it in a safe spot in case something happens to him or me. He's careful that way. And, like he warned Allen, your pharmacist puppet, Rad has friends with pull. Friends who, like him, believe in retribution."

B's eyes hadn't softened, and I knew he wondered where this was going. He didn't ask.

"I've got an interesting story about Bobby Mohn." I had thrown out the bait. I pushed my luck. "Before you hear it, I have questions about Jimmy Scroggins."

Instead of ending my bluff with a bullet, his sneer suggested he was relieved to share what he had on me. Scroggins was safer territory than little Bobby.

Dr. B's booming threats from moments earlier had quieted. Matter-of-factly he said, "Scroggins worked for me a long time ago. I bugged his phone. He skimmed money and was a snitch. I'm not sure what your beef with him was, but I can guess." He chuckled at what seemed a pleasant memory. "It wouldn't have been the first time he abused a woman."

He squatted, leaned against the wall, rested his forearms on his thighs. "You saved me the trouble of killing him. Your car pulled to a stop in front of his dump a couple of seconds ahead of me. I heard a shot. Waited for you to leave. When you came out, there was blood on your white blouse. Lots of it. You had a towel wrapped around your left forearm. I jotted down your license plate number. Found out later the car was registered to Derek Lawrence. Your ex was a Scroggins' customer."

He confirmed what I had long suspected, but knowing the truth stung almost as much as the gash in my back.

"Inside, the place looked like the St. Valentine's Day massacre. Even though you nicked the carotid, the poor bastard had a couple of breaths left in him. Pleaded for help as blood spewed between the fingers clutching his throat. I watched him die."

B's story added details I hadn't imagined. "And you never went to the police?"

"Why would I? I didn't need police investigating my connection to Scroggins. I let some big players in my business think I did it. Good street cred.

Police weren't going to bust their humps looking for Scroggins' killer. I figured if I ever got charged with it, there was plenty of time to bring up your name and lead the cops to the real doer. Evidence from the scene, added to my information, would point them down the right path."

"And my study?" I reached behind me and touched the wet spot on my lower back. When I glanced down at my hand, the blood covering my fingers made me queasy, and the pain was becoming a son of a bitch. "Why not just tell me what you knew?"

"I'm losing patience with these questions." In the dim light, I watched his eyes narrow and his hand move behind him. Before I got anything else out, he said, "I needed to confirm the evidence at the murder scene would tie you to it. Back when you did Scroggins, DNA wasn't too new to be very useful. I was pretty sure the reddish-blond hairs he clutched were collected, but nothing had been done with them.

"Messing up your study was for show. Get your attention. Scare you. Your intruder brought me your hairbrush. That and friends in the property room at the Ann Arbor Police Department cinched the deal. Don't worry, I didn't mention you. Just asked them to see if the hair samples found at the scene were still there and matched those in the brush. These are the kind of cops who for a price won't tell anyone about my snooping."

His left hand touched the butt of my revolver in his waistband. The gesture warned he was close to the end of his good nature. "You got something to tell me about your tough friend Radowski or someone named Mohn? Spit it out."

"It's not about Rad, other than he would do anything for me. The story is about a young boy who turns thirteen in a month. His name is Robert Mohn." B blinked, and I saw a faint tremble in the hand that still held the apple. I tried to gauge what was going through his mind and wondered how much time I had before he decided to shoot me.

"Not as colorful a name as Bobby Kansas, but that's okay with you. The boy lives in Royal Oak with his mother and the stepfather who adopted him. I'm pretty sure he's never heard about his real father, and you go along with that because you want better for him than to end up a gangster like his dad and granddad."

I heard Dr. B's teeth grind, but he said nothing. He gripped the apple so hard his knuckles turned white. I expected the fruit to squish into a pulpy mess and run through his fingers.

"This is between you and me," I said. "I'll work with you. You've tangled me between survival and conscience, and I prefer to live. But we keep our kids out of it. You ever threaten Natalee again, you ever show up in the same neighborhood she's in or, God forbid, you ever lay a finger on her precious skin and young Bobby's life becomes worthless. Rad will see to that. Now, am I clear?"

Maybe I was delirious from the pain and shock. All that mattered was that he believed me.

He remained quiet. I watched my words strip layers of tough veneer from his self-assurance. The exposed emotions hid from easy interpretation. I guessed he was a man with a huge tolerance for obstacles, but he now faced a hurdle he wasn't sure he could clear.

I knew Robert Kansas sent money, a good-sized chunk of it every week. No court order, all voluntary. Amazing what I had learned with a computer and access to government documents. I was convinced that abandoning his son was Dr. B's gesture of love, maybe the most decent and painful act of his adult life. My story about Rad might be exaggerated, but I prayed this lunatic believed that if he did anything to Natalee, Rad, or me, he would bring down on his organization the wrath of the entire Lansing Police Department and half the Detroit and Ann Arbor cops as well. And that, with those stakes, he wouldn't risk it.

I saw a slight nod. He might not have intended it, but I took it to mean we had reached an uneasy understanding. After a couple of seconds, he said, "Do as you're told, and we keep this between you and me."

As he turned to walk out there was less cockiness in his stride. My eyes followed him to the foyer where his fury exploded. With a swipe of his arm he sent my grandmother's crystal bowl, and the picture of Natalee standing beside it, crashing. Then the door slammed behind him.

I had survived.

I crumbled from sitting to face down, prostrate on the floor. I'm not sure how long I lay there before willing myself to get up. Dr. B had forced only a couple of swallows of the drug-laced drink down my throat, but my brain cells seemed shrouded in thick puffy cotton that prevented them from communicating with one another.

I rose, stumbled to the half bath and doused my face in cold water. I folded and pressed a towel against my back and secured it with my belt to stanch the continued slow seep of blood. From the utility room, I grabbed clean-up supplies: Mason jar, a plastic grocery bag, broom, dustpan, and a handful of rags. I had an hour before my daughter got home. She had been through enough. I wouldn't let her see this.

Rags soaked the blood from the floor. I swept up the glass fragments in my entry and moved a plant to the empty space on the table. Open windows and a few shots of Glade were the best I could do for the cigarette smoke.

I dumped the contents of the drink Dr. B had fixed me into the jar, tightly screwed on the lid and placed it, along with my bloody ripped blouse and the pieces of the recorder, in the plastic bag before I dragged myself upstairs and deposited the evidence in a box with out-of-season clothes at the back of my closet.

I closed the door to my bathroom and took two Vicodin left from when Natalee had her wisdom teeth removed three months earlier. I undid the blood-soaked towel, laid it in the sink, ran cold water over it, and then positioned a hand-held mirror to examine the gash on my back. The wound barely trickled blood. The cut could use stitching, but the flow was down to a slow drip, and this wasn't the time to call Jon for help. An emergency room was out of the question. A large adhesive pad applied tight over the gash might be enough to hold the edges together. I could live with an ugly scar. A huge gob of Neosporin for the burn on my breast and a covering of gauze would suffice to treat that injury.

I made one more trip downstairs, where I dumped the bloody towels in the washing machine and started a cold wash, shut and locked the windows, and checked to make sure nothing looked out of place. A note for Tom and Natalee posted to the refrigerator explained: *Had a ferocious headache. Sorry I didn't wait up. Nat, if you want to talk, give me a nudge. I love you both and will see you in the morning.*

As I wallowed in self-pity, a small voice reminded me it could have been worse. I wasn't dead.

$$\text{\it 50}$$

50

Thursday, October 20

I stumbled through the next two days, my equilibrium askew. Tom, rock-steady, tried to keep me on course, but he knew nothing about my encounter with Dr. B. I hoped he would credit my sudden loss of sexual appetite to preoccupation with my circumstances. I was thankful that our consideration for Natalee forced him to sleep in the guestroom instead of with me. One look at my injuries would spark questions.

My life fragmented as I parsed out information, sharing pieces with Tom, most with Rad, some with Lockhart, a few bits with Jon and Ginny, and as little as possible with Natalee. To Chace I offered, "The recorder's broken. I'll replace it, but please don't ask questions."

"Won't be necessary," he said. "I'll expense it. Tell the state of Michigan some hotheaded doc smashed it when he didn't like the tenor of my questions."

I made an appointment for Natalee with a grief counselor. My daughter surprised me and agreed without protest. Her resilience came through loud and clear when at dinner Wednesday night, just one week after Derek's death, she said, "Mom, I need a new suitcase for the Washington trip."

A grilled cheese sandwich stopped halfway to my mouth, and my blank expression told her I had forgotten.

"Earth to Mom. Earth to Mom. Come in, Mom. Remember my Economics and Advanced Placement Government trip?"

Natalee and five others from her AP class had been honored for participation and outstanding suggestions to Project Government Fix. They received glossy engraved invitations to a White House dinner. The trip would give the Okemos students a chance to observe government in action.

"Of course." I shoved my plate toward the center of the table and gave her my undivided attention. "I'm sorry I've been so distracted."

"You're forgiven. But I need the suitcase."

"I promise we'll go shopping." Since I forgot the school-sponsored trip, I owed her something besides my battered Louis Vuitton.

"Mrs. Hayworth has scheduled a visit to the Supreme Court while we're there, and we'll hear oral arguments. We may even have lunch with the justices afterward. Can you imagine sitting down with Justice Kagan like she's a regular, normal person?"

"It'll be her honor," I said. "Did I ever tell you I'm proud of you?"

"A few million times."

Late Thursday afternoon, Rad picked me up, and we drove to Art's Bar on Kalamazoo, where a couple of regulars nursed beers and made small talk with the bartender. They left the rest of the joint to us. We had no more than claimed a table in a dim far corner and ordered an iced tea and Pepsi when Rad jumped up to greet a giant of a man who sauntered over and stood eye to eye with him. I'd noticed a slight limp as the stranger ambled toward us. His head was as bare and smooth as a newborn's behind, and his smile showed an overbite yellowed by smoking or coffee. I expected someone in State Police blues, but he wore black slacks and a red cable-knit sweater.

"Racer, you old son of a bitch, thanks for coming," Rad said. The two embraced with man-hugs, slaps on the back, and fake punches before Rad looked toward me. "Casey, this is my ol' buddy Ed Tracer. Racer to those of us who know and love him. Racer and I go way back. Saved each other's lives a couple of times."

"If it weren't for him, I'd be dead instead of gimping around raising hell," Racer said. He turned a chair around with its back to the table and straddled it.

"So, you're the infamous Casey. Pleased to meet you." He stuck out his hand, and I shook it. "Your pal here has told me all about you."

"Not quite everything." It was time to come clean. It wasn't a hard choice. I had uncovered some interesting details, defied Rad's specific instructions, collided with Dr. B, nearly gotten myself killed, fabricated a whopper of a story, lost another gun, and run out of options. The decision was even easier because Racer's earnest eyes peered out of the face of a friend Rad trusted. "Something happened that I haven't shared."

"What are you talking about?" Rad asked. "You holdin' out on the Radman?" He tried for humor, but a stand-up comic he'd never be. When he squinted, his laugh lines paralleled his frown.

You've got no idea, I thought. "Let's just say I postponed telling you until I had protection." I would have paid handsomely to be a piece of dandelion fluff and disappear on the first air current. Fading to invisible would be my next choice.

"Am I going to need bourbon on the rocks for this one?" he asked.

"A double." I touched his folded hands to calm him, nodded as I looked down.

"Barkeep," he shouted across the room, "give us a couple of double bourbons on ice. She's paying. You want one?" he asked me.

"No, I'm good with iced tea." As the two men braced themselves with stiff swigs, I started with the easy stuff. "I thought I'd try a bit of investigative work. Gather some intel. I killed a couple of afternoons in the Library of Michigan. Glued my eyes to microfiche machines. Spent an equal amount of time at vital records. After that, I found someone to help me hack into bank records for a certain gangbanger. Don't ask. I, too, am owed favors."

Rad relaxed. I could almost hear his thoughts: *That's not so bad. Maybe she found something helpful.*

"Looking for anything in particular?"

"Just being thorough," I said. "I wanted to check out a few people. This damn shit at my house and the threats, well, it got me questioning everything, everybody. I looked for old newspaper articles where familiar names came up: Chace Gannon, Shirley Rathburn, Mark Rodgers, Joseph Sawicki, Ahmed Khoury, Jackson Wainwright, Jim Allen, and even Jon and Ginny Beckman, among others."

"Surprised you didn't run me."

I suspected Rad's laugh came more from relief than amusement. "Don't be so sure I didn't." I tried to enjoy the moment; it was going to spiral downward in a heartbeat.

"Anything vital pop?" Rad asked.

"A couple of things worth sharing. The *News* ran a feature about Caroline Kansas after her husband, Bobby's unfortunate father, was killed. After the murder, Mommy moved in with her sister, Emily Rodgers. The article also mentioned Caroline's maiden name, which made tracing the family through vital records easier."

"Get to the good stuff," Rad said.

"How about this? Mark Rodgers from the AG's Executive Division is the son of Emily Rodgers and a first cousin to Dr. B. They grew up practically brothers. Could be Rodgers is the mole in our office. He's shown an interest in my cases, and his name was mentioned in a couple of files Shirley closed without a full investigation."

"Go on." Rad sipped his drink. I preferred the contented smile he wore to the frown of moments earlier. Racer looked like he was trying to put things together. I wanted to tell him not to try so hard; there were a couple of pieces missing.

"I learned that Bobby Kansas's marriage was brief—six months beginning to end—but it made him a father. Boy's now a month shy of thirteen. Named Robert after his father, little Bobby's last name is Mohn. Stepfather's last name. I'm guessing Dr. B knocked up the kid's mother. That took college out of the equation. It might be why he turned to easy money."

"Interesting stuff," Rad said.

"Unfortunately, that's not all. Now the bad news." Acid curdled my stomach. It was a good thing I drank tea and not scotch. Before losing nerve, I launched into a detailed description of Tuesday night, skipping only the part about Jimmy Scroggins. I would let Rad decide if it was wise to share that with Racer.

When I finished, Rad's fixed glare felt as uncomfortable as trying to breath under water. Silence stretched the distance of a light year before he said, "Casey, I don't even know where to start." Anger and concern molded his face in a tight mask, but he moved his chair closer and reached out to put an arm around me. I folded against him and exhaled like the air had been squeezed out of me.

I could have used more comforting but instead, sat back up and moved away from Rad. "I know I should apologize. I'm sorry for not telling you ahead of time, and I'm even sorrier if I put you in danger. I threatened Dr. B that you'd take care of him if anything happened to me."

"I can take care of myself. We're talking about you here."

"Rad, you know you'd have foiled the plan. And dangerous as it was, I don't think Dr. B will bother Natalee again. To me, that made it worth it."

He ignored me and looked at Racer. "This changes the slant of things. I say we use a throwaway and rid the world of a major douche bag."

Racer fiddled with the swizzle stick before he removed it from his bourbon, laid it aside and chugged a couple of more gulps. "Enjoy that fantasy, partner, but it won't work."

"I'm tellin' you we can make it work," Rad insisted. "I can kill him and won't lose a minute's sleep."

I had no doubt he meant it.

"It's not your sleep that worries me. Kill Kansas and his first lieutenant takes over," Racer said, "and Casey's still in trouble. We need to put the operation out of business, and we need to nail Dr. B for something more than aggravated assault. That's the best we've got at the moment."

Rad looked like a five-year-old who didn't get his promised Skittles. He took the last swig of his bourbon and held up two fingers when the bartender glanced our way. "You got a more appealing strategy, let's hear it." He stopped, but I knew he wasn't finished.

Before Racer answered, I said, "It'd be hard to prove even an aggravated assault. I asked Dr. B to meet me. The emails clearly establish that. I'm sure he has copies. He wore gloves while in my house. I didn't report the assault, and I didn't get medical attention. Hell, I didn't even tell anyone until now. Any witnesses at Capital Prime saw a couple making small talk, and him smiling like a lovesick puppy."

"She's right," Racer said. "And there's the little matter of the ten-thousand she got in payment." He looked at me. "Rad told me about that. Wants me to bury it in my property room, but I'm not inclined to do a fool thing that jeopardizes my pension. Giving it to Rad hardly exonerates you. Just implicates him."

"That's not what I intended." I tucked my chin and stared down to deflect the anger aimed my way.

"Maybe not, but it seems a lot of shit that wasn't your intention makes for a reasonable conspiracy theory," Racer said.

I couldn't argue. "I know, and it looks like I wanted deeper into their operation. Lockhart already liked me for contracting Derek's murder. But I never meant to get Rad in trouble."

"So, where does that leave us?" Rad looked past me to Racer.

Racer said, "I think I can spare a couple of men to keep Dr. B and one or two of the other guys Scum Dawg mentioned under surveillance for a few days. We may have enough to get a warrant for a phone tap. That could break things open."

"He probably uses a cell. You can't bug that, can you?" I asked.

"Yeah. Cell phone providers ensure that base stations allow police to listen in without any appreciable drop in quality of the conversation. Still need a warrant to get anything that can be used—"

"Or it's fruit of the poisonous tree." I completed his sentence.

Rad harrumphed to get our attention. "If we get nothing?" He seemed less concerned with technicalities than either Racer or me.

"Guess you have to keep the faith," Racer said. "As soon as we have hard evidence, we'll bring in the Meridian Township Police and the state boys. And so you know, Casey, you seem like a nice woman and all, but I wouldn't be stickin' my neck out like this for anyone other than Rad."

I bit my lower lip and nodded.

"I still like my way better. More personal satisfaction," Rad grumbled. The bartender dropped off the two additional drinks and set a fresh iced tea in front of me. After he walked away, Rad looked at Racer and said, "I got a buddy I'll have watch Casey. The two private dicks that currently provide security take twelve-hour shifts, but when Natalee isn't home, they're glued to the kid. The current crew might be following the wrong Lawrence."

"I don't need protection."

"Oh, you do, foolish one. If only from yourself," Rad said. "I'm running out of guns."

51

Saturday, October 22

A Meridian Township police vehicle was parked a block away as I pulled out of my spot near the law library. I wouldn't have noticed it, if I hadn't dropped a page of notes that, caught by a wind gust, blew in the cruiser's direction. Lansing was outside Okemos jurisdiction, but cops kept tabs on my moves these days. Too bad their interest hadn't saved me from Dr. B. He had managed to enter my house without them noticing. I reconsidered that conclusion: maybe the cops had been watching, but couldn't connect the right dots. They didn't know what happened inside my house. If they were aware of Dr. B's visit, it might only have increased their suspicion I was involved.

Natalee and Ethan were hovered over a laptop at the kitchen table when I arrived home. The study was no longer off limits. I had scoured the last trace of the rampage from its shelves and surfaces. Except for the maimed desk, it looked pretty much as it had before the burglary, but it remained a less inviting spot from which to work.

"You guys hungry?" I asked. "It's not too early for dinner."

"I'm always ready to eat," Ethan said. In the evolving stages of handsome, he stood six feet, give or take an inch, and was lean to the point of gangly. His touch of shyness melded seamlessly with a dash of playfulness. I approved Natalee's taste in men.

"We have no plans for the night," Natalee said. "Any chance you and Tom are up for a couple of games of Risk?"

"Count me in," I said. "Tom's still smarting from the last time Ethan trounced him. He'd welcome the challenge. I'll have him pick up Chinese on his way." I savored a taste of ordinary slipped into the calamitous wreckage that had become my life.

My mood ratcheted up and stayed there until the games ended. "I'm exhausted," I announced. "Unless someone can think of a reason I need to stay up, I'm calling it a day."

"Can Ethan and I watch a movie?" Natalee asked.

"Sure. There's plenty of Coke in the fridge, plus chips and dip. Help yourself."

"Thanks, Mom." Nat gave me a kiss on the cheek before she and Ethan disappeared to the family room.

"If you don't mind, I'll use the kitchen table and hash out a proposal for one of my clients," Tom said. "Boring stuff, and I do boring well this time of night." He stepped close and kissed me goodnight. He still spent his nights in my guestroom, our extra layer of security.

I pressed hard against his body and whispered, "Don't sleep too sound. You may have company before the night is over." Even as I said it, a twinge of conscience clutched me. I had known I couldn't prevent Tom from eventually seeing my wounds, so concocted a story about my doctor removing two small cysts, one on my low back and one on my breast, to make sure they weren't malignant. For a woman who rarely lied, I'd become a master. Worse yet, I deceived the people I loved.

"How am I supposed to concentrate after a comment like that?" he asked.

"I don't know, but I felt obligated to warn you." He pulled me close, nuzzled my neck, and planted a real kiss on my eager mouth. I closed my eyes, in no hurry to pull away.

Upstairs I drew back the covers, propped several pillows against the headboard and leaned back. I hit the TV remote to catch the news before I wrestled sleep.

A camera zoomed in on Alex Pressman. With three major stations, I still chose to watch his newscast. He hid the instincts of a venomous snake beneath a pleasing exterior but was still the best local anchor in the area. If you avoided his fangs, his charm was undeniable. A voice as rich as Duke Ellington's music didn't hurt. And he got the scoop.

"Our top story tonight is a scandal swirling in the Attorney General's office." Pressman threw out the teaser. "We'll also bring you the latest on the new downtown development proposal. Reports on those and more after the break."

I waited, stunned, during the cut to commercials. A horrific scenario flashed through my mind, but I dismissed it. Not even Pressman could know about my meeting with Dr. B. Neither the thug nor I called the tip line. This must be something different. I had left the office early yesterday, but there was no gossip ruffling the air currents then. A minute stretched interminably. It allowed me to speculate and suffer as I waited through Preparation H, Viagra, and Lunesta commercials.

My mind turned to Joseph Sawicki and his heir apparent, Donald Sawicki. The story must be about the upcoming election and their political machinations to get Donald elected. I gave the Sawicki clan credit for moxie and perseverance. Even in his seventies, Joseph remained sharp as a Samurai sword. It was rumored he would carve to bits any outsider bold enough to fight his family for the office.

Pressman interrupted my mental leapfrogging.

"Tonight, Channel Six has learned that several of Donald Sawicki's major supporters are doctors who allegedly violated campaign contribution laws. Michigan allows an individual to contribute no more than five hundred dollars to any political candidate's war chest. Scrutiny of contribution records confirms that several well-known local doctors, plus their nurses and receptionists, made maximum contributions. More surprising, nearly a hundred patients, most of whom are unemployed and use Medicaid to pay for their treatment, also capped their contributions to Sawicki's campaign.

"Investigators say this begs the obvious question: where did those patients get the money they donated? Several told police that the doctors provided them money for their contributions to Sawicki's campaign. Some allege they got prescriptions for drugs to reward them for their trouble.

"Channel Six has also learned that misconduct charges are pending against several of the doctors involved. Dr. Ahmed Khoury has been charged with incompetence and dispensing controlled substances for other than legitimate medical purposes. Dr. Jackson Wainwright's license was recently suspended for drug-related offenses. Investigation continues into the conduct of several loyal Joseph Sawicki supporters who in this election have thrown their backing behind his son, Donald.

"In a strange twist to the story, Attorney General Joseph Sawicki was spotted last month lunching with Jackson Wainwright at upscale Shimmer Restaurant in Saugatuck."

Alex Pressman's voice spoke over an amateur film showing the two men with serious expressions as they talked around shrimp cocktails and martinis in a meeting that I believed had less chance of being innocent than I had of becoming Michigan's Attorney General.

"We will keep you informed as we follow the paper trail," Pressman promised before moving on to his next story.

Chace Gannon wasn't the only one who had his camera on Sawicki, I thought. The leak and the film must have come from challenger Marcus Springs' headquarters. With the election two weeks away, a scandal could torpedo Donald Sawicki's chances. I wondered who had tipped off Springs. I theorized a couple of good guesses.

I might have felt sorry for the Sawickis if I wasn't agonizing over more pressing concerns. My mouth was dry as I bit my lips. Would Dr. B presume I triggered the leak? I'd gotten no emails from Advice4U since his visit to my living room. The last thing I needed was for him to get suspicious. When that happened, people died.

This breaking news story moved me to the top of his list.

52

Monday, October 24

I took off my suit jacket and laid it on the bench beside me. The warm Indian summer sun grazed my forearms as I entertained an impulsive idea. I extracted my cell phone and hit three on my list of contacts.

"Beckman Interiors, Ginny speaking."

"Very professional," I said. "What have you done with my crazy friend?"

"Casey! I miss you."

"Got a minute, or am I getting you at a bad time?"

"Your timing's perfect. I just finished with a customer and poured myself a cup of espresso. I'm ready for a break. What's up, girlfriend?"

"I need a break too. I spent the last three hours in the law library splitting legal hairs about the proper standard of care for a nurse anesthetist."

"Sounds deathly tedious."

"My brain's turned to mush. I packed up my research and came outside to enjoy the warm and soak up a few rays. Best I could do on a Monday morning in Lansing. Then I thought of you."

"Because lunch with me would be a vast improvement to just another dull day in Lansing?" Her infectious laughter brightened my day more than the unseasonable weather.

"Lunch would be great, if you're available, but I have a different proposal." I paused, tallied where things stood, reconsidered the wisdom of my brainstorm.

"Casey. What's happening?" she asked. "Is this related to the burglary or what's going on in your office? We heard the news Saturday night and figured you're prosecuting the doctors they mentioned."

"In part." I looked down the Capital Mall and considered the big white-domed building a block away. Politics sucked. Getting away was a good idea.

"Spit it out." Her impatience came through as clearly as her words.

"I'm sorry. What's been happening the last few weeks seems to have finished off the carcass of any spontaneity that lived in this old body. I'm not sure I should—"

"Either you tell me what this is about within the next five seconds, or I'm jumping in my little MX-5 and heading down there to find—"

"When do you leave for Florida?" I blurted it out before rethinking it another time.

"In about six hours. Car's packed. Jon likes to start after work and drive through the night. I pick up in the morning near Atlanta, and then he sleeps. That guy catches a few winks scrunched in the passenger seat of a car and wakes feeling like a new man. Must be his clear conscience. We'll be basking in sunshine by late tomorrow night." She paused a few seconds and then added, "So, what about Florida?" When I didn't offer an immediate response, she said, "There must be more if you had to stammer and stumble for half your lunch hour to ask such a simple question. Come clean, what's up?"

"The invitation for me to tag along still good?"

"More than good. I'll put it in writing, have it engraved, and personally delivered, if that helps. What changed your mind?"

"My mind isn't convinced, but I'm trying to follow doctor's orders. Jon said I should get away."

"Sound advice from that brilliant husband of mine."

I brought up my calendar and looked at the rest of the week. Shivers of anticipation supported the wisdom of my decision. "I have a hearing tomorrow morning, and Nat leaves for Washington, D.C., on Wednesday afternoon. I could leave Wednesday night or Thursday morning."

"Did I tell you we catch the best lake bass you've ever tasted? Pan fry 'em every night."

"How can I turn down an offer like that?" It was the first time in days that a laugh almost broke through.

"I'll even throw in Disney World. At this time of year, you can get on the rides without long lines."

"You drive a hard bargain." I thought about my visit to the Magic Kingdom with Natalee a decade ago. I remembered those annoying signs: 40 MINUTES FROM THIS POINT and APPROXIMATELY A ONE HOUR WAIT. After eight hours we'd gone on three rides and through five exhibits. My daughter was cranky, and if I asked her today, I wasn't sure she'd remember much about our big adventure.

"If that's not enough, I promise outlet malls," Ginny said.

The laugh that simmered a moment earlier finally boiled over. The sound had a tinkle akin to hope. "You're a top-notch salesperson, Ginny Beckman. Let me talk to my boss. See if there's any problem. But with Natalee in D.C., it might work. I'd fly back Sunday."

"We'll take whatever we can get," she said.

"I'd fly into Orlando, rent a car, and need directions. At least an address. The GPS can do the rest."

"Rent a car? Are you crazy? Orlando's an hour away. If you arrive early enough, we can head straight to Disney World before driving back to Crooked Lake. If you come later in the day, there's a great rib joint I'd love to take you to."

"I'll see what I can do."

"Let me know when to pick you up. Seriously, Casey, this makes my day. Even the local cows don't consider Babson Park a swinging hot spot, and Jon spends most of his time in a damn motorboat. I'll look forward to this trip a lot more with my best friend for company."

The hardest call to make before I booked a flight was to Sergeant Lockhart. I wasn't under arrest so he couldn't nix the trip. I toyed with the idea of leaving and not telling him, but if he tried to contact me, it would add another tier of suspicion to strike his antennae. Racer had suggested we get more evidence before we laid our story out for the sergeant. Until then, although he couldn't prove it, Lockhart remained convinced I had hatched the plot for Derek's murder.

I made the call and didn't waste time on preliminaries. "I wanted to let you know I'm taking a few days off work and flying to Florida for a short vacation with friends." It was good that Lockhart couldn't see me squirm. There was nothing unreasonable about my decision, it shouldn't sound irrational, but saying it to him, it did.

"I guess we can't stop you."

The slow way he said it made it sound like he'd developed a Texas drawl in the last few days. I heard the gears of his mind shift, and I didn't like the conclusions they clicked.

"I'd think you'd want to stay and see this thing through," he said. "Your husband's body is barely cold. You just buried him."

His comment was chillier than Derek's corpse, but I swallowed my distaste and counted to ten. "No way to avoid seeing this through," I said, "but maybe you'll catch his killer while I'm gone."

After Lockhart, everyone else was easy. Rad thought it made sense for me to blow town for a few days. "It'll give Racer and me a chance to get some answers," he said. "Maybe without worrying ourselves sick about what Dr. B's gonna do if he figures you're responsible for the leak and all that trouble at the AG's."

Nat was happy I wouldn't be home while she was in D.C. Fred agreed to fly to Washington, rent a car, and keep an eye on her from a discreet distance. I believed Dr. B and I had an understanding, and he would not come after her, but it paid to be careful. Shirley was thrilled to sign my leave slip. I coaxed Tom to come with me, but he begged off citing "too much work, too few bodies to do it." For my mental health, he urged me to go.

I persuaded Natalee to scout the Meridian Mall with me Monday night with an offer to shop and dinner at Yum! Japan. We'd find her a suitcase. And I couldn't leave for Florida without a one-piece swimsuit so I could avoid answering Jon and Ginny's questions about the gash healing along my spine. Tom might have bought my lame explanation, but it wouldn't hold up to a doctor's scrutiny.

Beachwear was out of season. Wool sweaters and leggings had arrived. Ghouls and Goblins filled display windows as though I needed to be reminded that evil lurked everywhere.

Macy's had a sale rack of swimsuits, slim pickings, fantastic prices. Nat assured me that for frumpy, the one-piece boy-leg-cut suit I modeled for her wasn't bad. "I guess if you're going for the middle-aged mom look, it's okay," was how she put it.

"I am a middle-aged mom," I said.

"You don't have to flaunt it. I don't understand. You got that snazzy little two-piece tropical number last year." She rummaged through the rack but found nothing to her liking. "Not many of my friends' moms could get away with it, but you looked terrific, even without a tan. What's wrong with that suit?"

"We're going to a little fishing village in central Florida, not a beach in Rio. I'll be with married friends. I want to feel comfortable, not naked."

"Frumpy?"

"Frumpy's a nice look. And it's eighty-five percent off. I'll have more to shell out for your suitcase."

On Wednesday a freezing wind blew in, and we awoke to frost on the ground. Michigan's like that. If you hate the weather, be patient, it'll change in a few hours. The balmy weather couldn't last forever.

Natalee's group departed Detroit at four-thirty p.m. Tom and I drove her and two other students to the airport. I had a six forty-five a.m. flight out of DTW the next morning, so we booked ourselves into an ultramodern room at the Airport Marriott and indulged in the amenities: in-room movies, king bed with pillow-top mattress, crisp white linens, bolster pillows, and someone else to wash the sheets and towels after we left. We ordered room service, chilled a bottle of Veuve Clicquot, made love with no fear of anyone hearing or walking in, and lay in each other's arms until five a.m. When the wake-up call came, Tom kissed me and said, "Why so early? We're already at the airport."

"Right. That was the plan. Make it easy on ourselves. They recommend I be at the gate an hour before take-off." I threw the sheets off. Neither of us made a move to get out of bed.

"It won't take more than fifteen minutes to get through security at this time of day," he said.

"Uh-hum."

"It takes you fifteen minutes to shower and pull on clean clothes."

"Right, again." I pulled him close, knowing where this was headed.

"That leaves fifteen minutes to spare." In the dark my imagination filled in his delicious grin.

"You got any ideas—"

He stopped my question with another kiss, and then said, "Just one."

53

Thursday, October 27 and Friday, October 28

For two hours and forty-six minutes, I sat in a cramped seat on Spirit Airline and thought about four days of sunshine a thousand miles away from Dr. B.

I spotted Ginny wearing a smile and a spaghetti-strapped sundress as she waved for my attention from the other side of security at Orlando International.

"Okay, old friend," she said after she hugged the air out of me. "What'll it be, Disney World or the outlet mall?"

"Do they allow unaccompanied adults in Mickey's place?" I asked.

"Hell, yes. Best trip ever was when Jon and I were married only a couple of years, and we scraped together the dough for tickets. We made out in every dimly lit inch of Space Mountain. Rode it six times. Very romantic."

"So, it's great for kids and lovers. How about for mature women seeking an escape?"

"Trust me." She winked and then pointed. "Car's this way."

"Promise I don't have to kiss you in dark places, and that you won't make me ride It's a Small World? The melody could make someone with a cast iron stomach puke, and I'm not much into boats of any size."

"I can't promise the latter." She clutched my hand and pulled me through the line of cabs, cars, buses, and limos. "What I can promise is that Jon got two free passes, so if we're bored, we leave."

Gentle eighty-degree breezes blew the intoxicating fragrance of jasmine and honeysuckle my way as I flirted with the notion that Lockhart had cause to worry that I'd escape to a tropical island with no extradition treaty. It was a gratifying fantasy.

Five hours into our Magic Kingdom adventure we laughed and giggled like schoolgirls who had played hooky. As we rode the tram back to the car, I teased Ginny about the promising boy-man who made eyes at her all through the Oasis Exhibit. "His acne is almost cleared up. Another year of Clearasil, and you'll pay more attention to his butt than his zits."

"When it comes to butts, I've got a picture on my camera that's good for major blackmail. I'm sure you'd prefer Tom never saw this." She hit the back arrow on her Nikon until she found the shot and shoved it in my face. She had snapped an octogenarian whose nurse pushed his wheelchair close enough that he could fondle my ass. I had to give Ginny credit for being quick on the click. She caught the glorious grope, as she called it, at the perfect millisecond.

"Enough. Enough," I said. "I'm taking you to dinner. First installment of the hush money. You choose the place."

"Smokey Bones it is. And I get a margarita too."

It was nearing ten when we drove through Babson Park and turned right on Ohlinger Road. There was an advantage to first seeing the fishing cottage at night, but I wouldn't appreciate the blessing until the next morning. Even without bright sunshine, it was obvious Jon hadn't exaggerated when he described the place as "a nothing-fancy little shack." Still, it wasn't Michigan, and that was worth more than trappings.

Friday morning, I was up by seven, tempted awake by the aroma of fresh-brewed coffee. A three-inch-long cockroach skittered across the counter as Ginny handed me a mug. From a streaked kitchen window, I caught sight of Jon as he stashed his gear in a rust-trimmed boat and pushed off from shore.

Ginny and I carried our cups outside and sipped a strong shot of caffeine tempered with heavy cream and sugar. It made me rethink my preference for tea. We hunkered down in webbed aluminum chaise loungers and watched the lake. A blue heron glanced up at us as it stalked fish and frogs.

"That's Charlie. He provides us with hours of entertainment," Ginny said. "Cheaper than movies and less effort than fishing." The ungainly bird tossed a water snake in the air, caught it as it plummeted, and then swallowed it whole.

A few minutes before nine we went inside, and I cracked the half-dozen eggs that Ginny handed me. She pulled apart thick, lardy slabs of bacon and tossed them into the frying pan, where they sizzled, sending savory maple-hickory smells throughout the kitchen. Our work was overseen by a spider peeking from a corner where the peeling brown vinyl baseboards met the bottom of the cabinets. I would have missed the oversized arachnid if I hadn't reached for the ancient two-drawer toaster on the bottom shelf. I stifled a scream, grabbed a paper towel, pinched it tight around his hairy body, and dumped him into the trashcan under the sink.

"Here comes Jon," Ginny said as I plunked dishes and silverware on the table.

We watched him drag his little tub ashore. He carried a string of largemouth lake bass in front of him like a proud offering. He stashed the fish in a bucket of water as Ginny opened the back door to greet him.

"Dinner," he said, pointing to his catch.

"Breakfast," Ginny shot back and nodded toward the table. She put her hands on his shoulders and gave him a kiss. "Sit down, it's ready."

"What do you think of our humble little fishing cabin?" Jon asked as he spooned strawberry jam on toast. He had a two-day beard growth and smelled somewhere between due and past-due for a shower.

"You didn't tell me about the cockroaches," I said. "Okemos zoning wouldn't permit them."

"You're such a wuss. They don't hurt anything." He scooped a pile of scrambled eggs to his mouth and reached for the crisp bacon.

"They're big as goddamned mice," I complained.

"At that size, we don't accidentally pack 'em up and take 'em home," Ginny said.

"You sure they don't carry typhoid or something?" I heard another boat motor grow louder as it approached shore. A few seconds later it quieted.

"They're harmless and safe," Jon said. "You guys are welcome to take the boat out for an hour or two. I'll clean up the kitchen, maybe sneak a little nap. Fishing's tough work."

"Is that your way of getting rid of us?" Ginny asked.

"You might say that." He let his hand linger on hers when she passed the eggs for a second time, and I caught his wink. Their easy way made me miss Tom.

When we finished eating, Jon carried our plates to the sink. There weren't enough crumbs left to provide a decent meal for one of their gargantuan bugs.

I watched him knock an ant to the floor and stomp it under his boot. One less mouth to feed.

"I think we should take him up on it," Ginny said as she handed empty cups to her husband. Her jet-black curls bobbed, trying to free themselves from the lavender ribbon that constrained them. Everything about her looked effortless. She was only a couple of years younger than me, but I imagined she still got carded.

"I guess I could give it a try if you want." That was as close to enthusiasm as I could muster. I hate boats, I hate water. I especially hate floating in a boat on water deeper than I am tall. But at a fishing village in Florida, I would seem like an ingrate if I bitched. "If you can handle the boat, I can handle a lifejacket."

"Boat's a piece of cake. It's a little 10-horse."

I felt nervous even with a life jacket squeezing me to within an inch of asphyxiation, but I wore a game face. "Are there alligators in this water?" I asked as I stepped into the boat.

"I've seen one or two little ones on the banks. They lie around sunning themselves during the day. Once in a while, you hear they grabbed a dog or something at night."

Ginny used one paddle to push us a few feet out from the shore and started the motor. Already I longed for dry land. I couldn't see more than an inch or two below the surface. "It's hard to believe anything lives in this sludge," I said.

"And we're eating them for dinner. Jon says it's the natural growth in the lake. He swears it isn't polluted. He knows I won't eat fish that can shorten my life."

"I'm trying to remember how long you guys have vacationed on Crooked Lake," I said.

"About seven years. Jon's an outdoorsy type. He loves to get away and fish all day. He'd live here, if I'd agree. Probably give up being a doctor. We compromise and come two weeks a year. For those weeks I don't complain that there's no dishwasher, or that the shower's so weak you can't rinse off the soap scum. Not to mention it stinks of mildew."

"I think I prefer my water chlorinated and clear. And only then from the safety of a poolside chair." I dragged my fingers along the water's murky surface. "Don't think I'm ungrateful, it's super to be here, but you wouldn't get me to take a dip in this for a million dollars."

"Me either. What say tomorrow we head over to Vero Beach, do some shopping, watch waves roll in as we sit under a beach umbrella?"

"A woman after my own heart."

When we got to the middle of the lake, Ginny cut the motor and we drifted. I got used to the water, and my knuckles regained their natural color.

After a while, she asked, "Do you think you and Tom will get married?"

"It could happen. He's self-supporting, laid back, easy on the eyes, puts up with my foolishness." I raised my eyebrows and hummed. "Sounds like a relationship washed in Ivory soap, doesn't it?"

"I'm glad I didn't say it, or I might be dog-paddling for shore," she said.

"I could dirty up the ninety-nine percent pure image and tell you he's terrific in the sack. There's something to that old saying about still waters."

She grimaced at whatever image shot through her mind. "I'll never look him in the eye again and not imagine him lying in bed with the family jewels exposed."

"He'd be mortified to hear that." Our comfortable laughter echoed across the water.

For several minutes we floated without additional conversation. Then I added, "Marriage is a scary thing when you've messed it up before. Very few of my friends seem ecstatic about theirs. In fact, I can count on the fingers of one hand the couples I know who seem to even like each other."

"Do you think Jon and I are happy?"

"Is that a trick question?" When she didn't answer I said, "Sure, you're the ring finger of that one hand."

"Yeah, we're happy. Endured a rough patch when he gambled. He joined Gamblers Anonymous, and we got through it. Lost a house and an earlier practice before it was over though."

"I'm sorry. You've never mentioned it."

"And I shouldn't have now. But I think it made our relationship stronger. He'd never put me through that again. Besides his practice, we lost the decorating business I'd built."

I turned away, uncomfortable with one friend betraying the confidence of the other. "I'm glad you're okay now." To lighten the mood, I added, "Since I didn't meet you until you were perfect, I'll always see you as the golden couple. Give Shakespeare his due, all's well that ends well."

"My sentiments exactly. This is the best of times for us."

She started the motor again and navigated around the edge of the lake while pointing and telling me who lived in homes we passed. Some dwellings boasted colonnades, manicured grounds and geometric-shaped windows peering out of elegant, architecturally interesting frames. Others, like the cabin she and Jon rented, needed repair and were a mild category-one hurricane away from tinder.

"I haven't thought about work or what's going on in Okemos since I got here yesterday," I said.

"I'd think that's a good thing."

"A very good thing."

54

Jon greeted our return with two plastic glasses of fresh-squeezed orange juice.

"This boating stuff isn't half bad. I could get used to it," I said. "Ginny's a good captain."

"Ginny's good at everything." He hugged his wife and then turned her to face him. "Are you okay?" he asked.

"I'm fine. Casey and I have places to go, things to do." She focused on me and asked, "What strikes your fancy? We have outlet malls, thrift stores in Lake Wales. Or we could stop and smell the flowers at Bok Tower Gardens. On the way, I'll show you Spook Hill."

"How about we kill a half-hour and watch heron entertainment while we think about it," I said.

"Right," she said. "No need to rush, we're on vacation."

"I could lace those drinks with a couple of shots of vodka. It's well into the happy hour in Mumbai," Jon called after us as we headed outside.

"I'm good," I said. "Don't want to ruin the natural orange taste."

As Ginny and I relaxed, idly watching Charlie stalk lunch, her eyes grew puffy. She closed them and was quiet for several minutes before she mumbled, "I'm sorry, Casey, but I've got a doozy of a headache. You may have to amuse yourself or depend on my husband this afternoon." She held her head in her hands and rubbed her temples.

Her grimace made me wince. "A migraine?"

She nodded no more than a half inch and didn't say a word.

I draped my arm around her, and we shuffled inside. "Don't worry about me," I said. "A lawn chair, a box of bonbons, and rereading East of Eden.

Ingredients for a perfect afternoon. Only thing missing will be my best friend sitting in the chair next to me."

"Serious headache?" Jon asked as he studied Ginny's ashen pallor, now replacing the glow I'd envied earlier. He took a plastic case from the refrigerator, removed two capsules, and handed them to her. She swallowed the pills without speaking and disappeared into the bedroom.

After she was gone, he said, "I could take you to the mall or something."

I shook my head. "Sweet, but not necessary. I prefer my book." Him lumbering along behind me as I tried on clothes wouldn't make for a memorable afternoon.

"You sure?"

"Positive. I don't need a social director. Seriously. Free time to read with no one pestering me is a pleasure I've almost forgotten." My life was complicated. Sitting by a small lake with no agenda wasn't.

"Then you don't mind if I head out to take care of a bit of business?"

"Not at all."

He planted a brotherly kiss on my cheek and stuck on a fisherman's cap that fought to contain his disheveled hair. The hat had two lines of print, the first, in inch-high letters, read TGIF; the second, smaller, explained, THANK GOD I'M FISHING. A well-off doctor and he preferred a fishing shack in Central Florida to a luxury condo on the ocean. That's what comes from having your priorities straight, I thought.

"I'm cooking dinner," he said. The words trailed after him as he headed for the Bronco. "We'll eat about six. Don't fill up on junk. I've got a treat in store for you."

"I'll give you ten-to-one odds you never got anything like that in a restaurant," Jon said.

"I just wish Ginny could join us."

He nodded. He had cleaned and pan-fried the fish. He steamed brown rice. I combined olive oil, lemon, garlic, and a short squirt of mustard and poured it over mixed lettuce.

For the next half hour, we ate with little conversation. When we couldn't stuff down another bite, we nursed white Chai tea with honey and cream.

"That's the best fish I've ever tasted."

"The secret's in the timing. I leave the whole string in a bucket of water 'til we're ready to eat 'em. They're still flopping when I whack off the heads and tails and scrape out the guts. I plop 'em in a hot sizzling pan before their hearts stop beating in the slop pail."

"Very graphic," I said. "I prefer to think they magically appeared on my plate, a delight for my taste buds. Skip the rest of it."

"I'm glad I didn't offend your delicate gastronomic senses until you finished eating."

"Me too." I had polished off seven or eight pieces. My stomach was so full I wasn't sure I'd be able to move from the chair.

"Ginny would make you look like a wimp. If she feels better tomorrow night, we'll have a contest. My money is on her."

I laid my paper napkin over my plate and slid it to the side of the table. As my brain caught up with my eating frenzy, I preferred not to be reminded of what a glutton I'd been. "I'm sorry about Ginny. We had tickets for Les Miz at the Fisher last time I saw her sidelined by a splitting headache."

Jon nodded. "A splitting headache would be a godsend compared to what she endures. She doesn't get migraines often, but when she does, they put her out of commission for at least a day. She holes up in a dark room when she's not vomiting. The miracles of modern medicine and we can't eliminate migraines or cure the common cold."

After a second cup of tea, I said, "You cooked, I'll do the dishes."

"I've got a better idea. Have you ever been fishing?"

"It's a pleasure I've avoided."

"I'll help you clean the kitchen, and then we're going to fix that."

"It's getting dark. Aren't they forecasting showers?" I tried for an excuse other than my aquaphobia.

"I have a light on the boat, and showers aren't expected much before morning. C'mon, it'll be fun. Some of the biggest fish are caught at night."

"Is that true, or one of your fish tales?"

"Give it a try," he said. "Then answer for yourself."

Maybe it was good to face my fear of water and remaining in a musty cabin that smelled of stale cooking wasn't my idea of how to spend a night. "Okay, sure. I'm in." My halting answer did little to mask my ambivalence.

I cleared the table, Jon washed dishes, and we stacked them to air dry before we let the screen door slam behind us. We descended the small slope that led to the lake. I climbed in the boat before Jon pushed it into the water.

"Where are the life jackets?" I asked.

"You won't need one," he said. "I'm a good boater and a better swimmer."

"Not funny."

"Jake, next door, borrowed the ones you and Ginny used earlier. He was taking his boys and two friends out and needed the extras. He'll bring them back tomorrow. I'll be extra careful tonight. I promise." Before I could protest, he yanked the rope on the little motor and steered toward the middle of the lake.

He cut the power and our conversation drifted like the boat. I told him about yesterday's Disney World adventure, about Tom's booming business, about Natalee's trip. He told me he thought he'd buy Ginny a Jack Russell terrier for Christmas.

I was happy to steer clear of unpleasant topics, but then he asked, "What's going on with this thing at work?"

His question brought back all the ugly baggage I preferred to leave in Michigan. "I wish I knew," I said.

"The news mentioned a campaign scandal. Some of the same doctors you talked to me about earlier. Do you think it's related to your break-in and the drug problem you suspect?"

"I'm not sure."

"Casey, maybe you should quit that damned job and get out before you or someone you love gets hurt."

I let his advice go without comment; this wasn't the time to fill him in.

He was less willing than I was to let it drop. "It doesn't sound like these people appreciate you nosing around. With your medical background, can't you get another job? You'd be a natural for med-mal. It pays better and seems a lot safer than your current employment."

"On the flight down, that's exactly what I thought, but I've decided I can't do it."

He scowled. In all the years I'd known Jon and Ginny, I didn't remember ever seeing him scowl. "Why not? It makes perfect sense to me?"

"It's complicated. But I promised myself I was here to forget for a few days. Maybe when we get home, I'll break out the good whiskey and pour out the sordid details."

"Fair enough. But I worry you're involved in something bigger than you understand. I've been caught between two evils a time or two in my life. Sometimes you need to cut your losses."

Darkness consumed the night. I grew quiet again, hoping he'd let it slide. I made out vague traces of trees and buildings around the perimeter of the lake, but everything blurred. I watched the moon, a sliver short of full, peek between clouds and offer a tiny streak of illumination around the edges of blackness. Heat lightning zigzagged across the sky, piercing the gloom. The temperature had cooled a degree or two since the sun disappeared, but without a breeze, the air felt oppressive. A sweaty sheen covered my arms, and my back felt damp.

"This is where the big ones bite." Jon took a rod and cast out. "You want to give it a try?"

"No, I'll watch the expert."

After ten minutes, I was bored. Jon reached in his pocket, took out a tiny clear plastic case and shook something into his hand before he guided it to his mouth. "Want one?" he asked.

"What is it?"

"A Tic Tac. Fish taste great going down. Not so great burped up."

"Sure." I held out my hand, and he shook two more from the rattling container. I sucked the artificial sweet taste of citrus. "I didn't think anyone bought the orange ones. What's wrong with spearmint or wintermint?"

"There's no accounting for taste." Jon picked up the paddles and paddled a few feet. "We've got to find the right spot. Sure you don't want to give it a try? I brought an extra rod."

"I suppose it would be more fun if I had a stake."

"There are a couple of tricks," he said. "I rowed these last few feet because, as fish go, bass are pretty smart fellas. They hear a motor and head for quiet. We sit without saying a word. Can you do that?"

"Try me," I said.

A half hour later my type-A personality strained under the yoke of silence. "Can we pack it in? I'm a mosquito feast. Little bastards love my rare Rh-negative blood. I'm scratching like I got a bad case of chicken pox."

"I'll call you a quitter," he said.

"I'll live with that." I dug at the welts rising on my arms, and the itch worsened.

"All right. I suppose we can try again tomorrow." He reeled in his line and stowed his rod along the side of the boat. I cranked mine in. He reached for the paddles.

"Hand it over here, so you don't accidentally step on the hooks," he said when I rested my rod next to me.

I half-knelt, half-stood in a crouch as I passed it to him. I straightened a few degrees to slump back toward my seat. Jon let go of the paddle that was in his left hand to reach for my rod. I saw a vague movement and twisted away from it as the paddle clutched in his right fist whooshed toward me.

I heard a crack like a tree split from lightning. I felt a thwack and instant pain as the makeshift weapon hit my lower back, knocking me off balance.

I struggled to grab the side of the boat. I wasn't quick enough.

"Fuck!" I screamed as I sailed overboard.

Death, disguised as an inky lake, swallowed me. I floated toward the surface and heard the motor start. I saw the boat's light reflect on the water as it took off. Away from me.

55

For the second time in less than two weeks, I believed a solitary minute separated me from the end of my life. Unable to swim, my options were limited. Panic and the brackish water conspired to bring about my demise.

I choked. Swallowed. Convulsed. Pain surged up my nose. Excruciating pain. Pain like I'd been struck by a two-by-four between the eyes. Thrashing pulled me under. I stretched my toes and hoped to touch bottom. God, let there be muck so I can stand and breathe.

The water was too deep. Nothing under me but more water. Despite the burning in my lungs, I fought the breathing reflex. I kicked off my sandals and paddled with my feet. Natural buoyancy took me up.

Before I broke the surface, I choked another gulp of nasty scum and spewed it out my nose. It stung like a swarm of bees had buried their stingers in my nostrils. Somehow, I again propelled my mouth above water and gasped fresh air to mix with the flood that gagged me. Coughing took me back under. My head threatened to burst. Right after my lungs exploded.

My contacts washed out. I couldn't see a foot in front of my face. In the darkness, it made little difference. The cold water numbed me. It would not be a soft, easy death.

My life didn't pass before my eyes. Maybe I hadn't reached that moment. Maybe I had a couple of breaths left. Maybe I hadn't suffered enough. If I fought this enemy, it would kill me. That goddamned son of a bitch. Why did he do this?

Hope vanished. I couldn't make it to shore. I would be grateful just to get another clean breath of air before I died.

In a flash of clarity, I remembered the old promise made by my YMCA swim instructor: Everyone can float. He shared that revelation during my

Chicken of the Sea class when, unable to convince me to put my face under water, he conceded I'd never be a swimmer. While others had practiced their breast stroke, I had worked on staying afloat. Right now, my life depended on being able to lie on my back and relax. The second part was tricky, but I needed to believe that my swimming coach was right, and I could do it.

Every muscle in my body was rigid as ten-gauge steel. Calm wouldn't come easy. I stopped flailing. I visualized my body as a log. A log that, stiff and unyielding, floated. I could do this.

My hips and legs hung below the water, but my face rose to the fresh night air. I sucked another breath. I took too much, and the movement submerged my head again. I was a hair's-breadth away from giving up. Then the thought of Jon came back. Damn him. He can't have my life.

I forced myself motionless again and held my breath until my body floated to the surface. My chest gurgled. I sucked in oxygen. It was agony to breathe. More agonizing to not.

A few seconds passed. I didn't go under. I took only tiny short gasps that didn't sink me. They caused less pain.

Something hard touched my arm. It could have been a twig, an oar. I doubted it was an alligator, or there'd be empty space where my limb had been. This was worse than my worst drowning nightmares. At least in them, it was a sunny day, and when I rose to the surface I could see.

I experimented. Wiggled my feet, almost imperceptibly. I moved, not with any speed, but it was motion. I had no idea which way to shore. I supposed it was any way I paddled. If the moon came out again, it might help. Then again, without contacts, my vision was quadruple the standard for legally blind.

Something brushed against my buttocks. I prayed it was a largemouth bass. I shivered and tried to think of something besides water. A twitch and my head bobbed under. I didn't inhale until my nose and mouth emerged.

How was Jon involved in this? He didn't have a drug habit. I'd bet my life on it. Maybe I had. I couldn't have misjudged him for all those years. You bastard, I'll survive just to make you look me in the eyes and explain.

A dog howled on the beach. Dogs came third on my list of phobias, right after drowning and heights. With minuscule twists, I moved away from the yelps.

I thought about Natalee. I had to live. I had to see her as Maria in West Side Story. I had to help her pick out her homecoming dress. I had to watch her leave for college and get married and give me grandchildren. My life didn't pass before my eyes, but I regretted all of the petty nagging about dishes left in the family room and dirty socks thrown on the bathroom floor.

I'd mailed a postcard to my daughter this morning and told her how much I loved her. At least she'd get that. I hadn't worked out my relationship with God, but this appeared a good time to ask for a little help.

Time didn't whiz by, and I couldn't judge if I was getting anywhere. I didn't know how long I could stay afloat, but I believed morning was beyond my endurance. Fishermen headed out at six or seven, at least that's when Jon left. What if he were the one to find me? That was crazy thinking. When he arrived back without me, he'd have to call the police.

What will you do, Jon? Figure how much time I have before I drown? Then report my accident so the coroner's time of death will match your story? Did you capsize the boat and swim the last few feet to shore? Did you look devastated as you described risking your life to save me? I'm sure you explained my fear of water. Did you tell them I struggled, and there was nothing you could do? Did you manage to shed a few tears? I'll bet you spun a convincing tale. Lots of ways to finesse it.

I deserve to hear your version.

I thought about all of the people in my life. There's so much territory in a lifetime that a dying person can't cover it in a split second. As close as I could guess, I'd been floating for an hour, and I'd gotten almost back to the part where my sister was born. Her birth caused me to scribble with crayons on my mother's new couch and take scissors to the living room drapes. As I analyzed my childish jealousy, I felt sticks. Lots of them. They were thin. They stuck out in the air. I stood up.

Thank you, God. I love reeds.

56

I thanked whatever god or gods exist for that blessed muck. I stood, floundered for several seconds, and then dragged myself ashore. I fell to my knees and puked up slime that tasted worse than fish smell. Doubling as an apparition from *Night of the Living Dead*, I trudged, shoeless and soaked, across the lawn ahead of me to the first house pressing the lake's shore. Without contact lenses, only generous squares of illumination guided me through the darkness to a door. I tripped on a step, regained my balance, and peered through long, skinny windows on either side of the entry. I made out two fuzzy shapes sitting in what might be matching Barca-loungers, one on each side of the Technicolor blur of a TV. I knocked.

A man's voice called from inside. "Who's there?" He sounded timeworn, but with little hint of the frailty that can wrap itself around the words of the elderly. I hoped he wouldn't be afraid to open the door.

"My name is Casey Lawrence." I raised my voice so he would hear me. My throat felt raw. The words sounded raspy. "I was pushed overboard. Please help me. Or call the police."

"For God's sake, Melvin," a woman said. She sounded like the other half of this matched set. "Open that door. It's the Christian thing to do." It wasn't a voice to argue with.

I heard footsteps coming toward me. The door creaked open. "Well, ain't you a sight," the man said.

He was shorter than me, carried little weight on his slight frame, and wore a bright-colored shirt. His features remained bleary. "I'm not exactly at my best," I answered.

"I don't know. You're alive. If you've been through anything near bad as you look, that's gotta be saying something."

"Melvin, stop waggin' your tongue. Do like the lady said—call the police."

The woman introduced herself as Ethel, and she hovered over me like a mother bird. She guided me to a kitchen chair and wrapped an afghan around my shoulders. The house smelled of pot roast and menthol.

When her husband got off the phone, Ethel said, "Set the teakettle on the stove. This poor child needs a cup of something hot, and bring over that plate of oatmeal cookies." She vanished down the hall and returned a minute or two later with an armful of clothes. "Here, you go. Not high fashion, but at least they're dry. I've set out a towel so you can take a quick shower. I also left a plastic bag for your wet clothes."

She pointed toward brightness shining through a doorway several feet away. I chomped the last bite of the cookie to help kill the fetid taste in my mouth and headed in the direction of the light.

I peeled off my clothes, stepped under the hot shower spray, soaped and rinsed. Flashbacks of the evening's horror didn't wash down the drain as easily as the lake's sludge.

Ethel's long, billowy skirt and Dolphins sweatshirt were meant for a shorter, wider woman, but they felt like cashmere against my clammy skin. I helped myself to a safety pin from a clear Lucite container sitting on the vanity and used it to take up the slack so the skirt didn't slide down my hips. I returned to the kitchen, sat down, and clasped my palms around a cup of steaming tea. The shivers had lessened by the time I accepted a refill. The caffeine didn't concern me. I wasn't going to get a good night's sleep no matter how this played out.

By the time my cup was empty, an officer arrived. Ethel let him in and I said, "I'm Casey Lawrence. I'm the one who got pushed overboard."

He looked me up and down as he introduced himself. "I'm Officer Posey."

I wouldn't be able to pick the officer out of a lineup, but his shape was portly, and he stood close enough to me that I noticed wattles of excess skin moving under his chin as he spoke. His voice sounded soft for a man who seemed to cast a big shadow.

"It looks like you need a doctor," he said. "You want me to call an ambulance, or are you okay in a squad car?"

"I don't need a hospital. I'm okay, thanks to Melvin and Ethel."

"Lift up your sweatshirt in the back," he said.

I shot him a confused look.

"There's blood seeping through."

I stood, and Posey assessed the damage before he said, "Guess you'll live. Looks like you reopened a recent wound."

I waited for him to ask about that recent wound, but, to my relief, he went on without questioning it. "Might not hurt to put some pressure on it," he said.

Ethel handed me a kitchen towel. Every inch of my body ached from the ordeal I had endured, but I managed to hold the cloth against the gash.

"We'll get you to Lake Wales Medical Center, and they can check you out," Posey said. "You can tell me what happened on the way."

My story, including Jon's betrayal, ended as we pulled into the emergency entrance. Posey stopped his squad car, hustled around, opened my door and, with one hand on my shoulder, guided me inside. He left me in the care of an ER attendant and disappeared to "verify some things."

An ER doctor stitched and bandaged Dr. B's slash wound where the oar had struck and reopened it. To my surprise, he, like Posey, didn't seem interested in how I got the original injury. My back throbbed like it was on the wrong end of a good beating. A stern-looking nurse offered me a Percocet along with a paper cup of water. Posey returned in time to hear me pronounced "in surprisingly good shape, considering." If emotional trauma were visible, I might not have been released.

Posey drove me to the fishing cabin to pick up my belongings. As we turned onto Ohlinger Road, dread choked me. The cabin was dark when we pulled onto a patch of weedy yard that served as a parking spot.

There was no way I could avoid it; I needed my driver's license and extra set of contacts. And, as grateful as I was to Ethel, I preferred not to fly home without underwear and looking like a bag lady. Still, I made no move to get out of the patrol car.

Posey must have sensed my reluctance and said, "The Beckmans have been hauled to the police station."

I imagined questions lobbed at my best friend as she endured a killer migraine and learned her husband faced charges of attempted murder. The police would question her as though she'd been complicit, but I needed to believe Ginny was a second victim.

"I want to have a look around before we call the forensic guys," Posey said. "I doubt they'll find anything. This wasn't the crime scene. But get your things and sit down. Don't touch anything that doesn't belong to you."

A cloud of betrayal stunk up the deserted shack. I stuck in my spare pair of contacts, grateful to have the world back in focus. I dressed, packed my belongings, then rolled my suitcase from the bedroom, and stood it by the front door. My cell phone lay on the kitchen table. It showed six missed calls from Rad. I took enough leeway with Posey's order to drop onto the couch and pull a blanket over my legs. As sticky warm as the night was, I couldn't rid myself of the chill. I dialed Rad.

"It's Casey."

"Get out of there. You aren't safe." His words were double-timed and frantic. I was certain Posey heard them two rooms away.

"I'm safe. I'm here with a cop in the other room."

"Shit, Casey, you worry me even when you aren't doing something stupid. Sure you're okay?" His volume dropped from a hundred-fifteen to sixty decibels, but he was still talking with the speed of a Cessna Citation Ten jet.

"Positive. I can put the officer on if you want confirmation." My fingers trembled, a reminder that although my voice was steady, my mind needed time to restore calm. "I take it you found out about Jon?"

"Right. While you sunned your sexy little ass, my man Racer and I learned Jon's on the verge of bankruptcy. I guess the ARCOS reports haven't caught up with the spike in his controlled substance prescriptions. Gannon may have your neighbor on the radar, but he might not know there's a connection between you two."

"You called to tell me Jon was overprescribing?" I asked.

"I don't give a rat's ass about his drugs. I needed to tell you to get the fuck out of there. Racer got the authorization for a tap of Dr. B's phones. My buddy didn't get a chance to listen to the recordings until you were in Florida. We figured you were safe, so no harm—until we overheard Dr. B explaining Jon's choices. Get you to cooperate or back-off. If he couldn't guarantee one or the other, he had a choice: you or Ginny." Rad paused before adding, "So you already know about Jon?"

"I didn't put the pieces together until he tried to drown me about five hours ago." I looked up and saw Posey coming out of the bedroom. "When I get back to Lansing, I'll buy you a drink or two. We'll compare notes."

"Not so fast. Racer called me about an hour ago. The Drug Task Force just arrested Robert Kansas. Dr. B is sitting in a Detroit jail without bond."

With Posey shuffling his feet waiting for me, I said, "Rad, I have to go."

"Don't be in such a hurry. I've got a couple more things to tell you."

"Make it quick."

"Tom is squeaky clean."

"You checked out my boyfriend?" I was surprised to gather the energy for indignation.

"We had to cross him off the list of suspects, no matter how unlikely." I heard the ding of a microwave and the clatter of dishes in the background. "And don't get high and mighty with me, CJ. It wouldn't be the first time you misjudged someone. Or lied to me. Anyway, as I was sayin', Tom's clean."

"You said a couple of things. What else?"

"While crossing the Gannons off our list, I learned he isn't having another affair, in case it matters."

"It doesn't." I stopped twisting my unity ring, stood, folded the blanket, and laid it back on the couch. I walked toward my suitcase and the door.

"Jesus, Rad, is there anything you don't know?"

"You asked for my help. I'm a former detective. I've got sources everywhere."

"Is that all?

Posey had opened the door and was carrying my suitcase to the squad car. I followed far enough behind that he couldn't hear Rad.

"No, there's one last thing. If anyone wants to discuss ancient history, decline the offer until we've talked."

Rad might not spit out the name for fear my phone was tapped, but he didn't need to worry. My lips were sealed on the matter of Jimmy Scroggins.

57

Saturday, October 29 and Sunday, October 30

It was after midnight when Officer Posey drove me to the Orlando airport and explained to Spirit Airlines why they should re-issue my ticket and put me on the next flight to Michigan. They rebooked me on Delta to depart at 6:00 a.m. with changes of planes in Atlanta and Detroit.

I faced a long night on hard airport chairs with nothing but unnerving thoughts for company. I called Natalee. It was worth waking her to tell her we were safe. She had questions, and I had five hours to explain. Some details I skipped. I told her Jon had been involved in the drug scheme. She didn't need to know he'd tried to kill her mother.

"I suppose you need to get some sleep," I finally said.

"Probably. We're going to the Smithsonian when it opens tomorrow."

"I love you. I want you home with me."

"Mom, I'll be there Sunday afternoon at two."

I raised the plastic shade of the tiny porthole by my window seat as the plane dropped to the landing strip at Capital City Airport. The sun sparkled off the hoar-frosted ground of an early season cold front.

"The temperature in Lansing Michigan is thirty degrees Fahrenheit and the local time is one p.m.," the pilot announced.

It had been sixteen hours since I cheated death and more than twenty-four since I'd slept. Tom was waiting for me, slouched against the wall on the other side of security. His expression wore questions that I was too exhausted to answer.

When we got to my house, he suggested I take a nap. I took a remaining Ambien to hush emotions that might keep me awake and slept until Tom woke me with a kiss at eleven on Sunday morning.

"Time to get moving if you any hope of making it to the airport before Natalie's plane touches down. I'll fix breakfast while you shower."

Fifteen minutes later, I joined him at the kitchen table and devoured scrambled eggs and toast.

"Want to come along?" I asked as I savored the last sips of strong coffee.

"Wish I could, but it won't work."

"Then how about I take you and Nat out for a proper Sunday dinner after we get home? To make up for being such poor company last night."

"I didn't mind. I picked up a Tom Clancy from a shelf in your bedroom, helped myself to a great bottle of your wine . . ." His eyes had the look of a puppy when it pees on the kitchen floor. ". . . and finished both. But I can't do dinner either. My mother called yesterday. Today's the anniversary of my brother's death. She asked me to drive to Albion and have dinner with her. I want you and Natalee to meet Mom. You're welcome to come along if you get back early enough."

"Probably not the best circumstances, either for meeting your mom or dragging Natalee out of here. I could use some alone time with my daughter. Tell your mother she is in our thoughts." I reached out and took his hand. "I wish I had been able to meet your brother."

"Me too." He lifted my hand to his mouth and kissed it. "Maybe we can plan a special date for the weekend? We could both use it. And I'll tell you all about him."

"It'll give me something to look forward to while I struggle to get my head straight."

Later Sunday afternoon, as I pulled into our garage, Natalee looked at her father's car. "What do we do with that?" she asked.

Without adding detail, I said, "The Porsche is legally yours." Her eyes widened at my extraordinary revelation, then returned to normal when I added, "Sort of."

"What does sort of mean?"

The conversation continued as we exited the car and went inside. She dropped her suitcase on the kitchen floor, opened the refrigerator door, and took a gulp of orange juice straight from the plastic container.

"You're a minor. I make decisions on your behalf until you turn eighteen. There's no way you're driving a Porsche while you are still in high school. You can have the car when you turn eighteen, or—"

"Or what?" She asked it like an attorney cross-examining a hostile witness.

"You sign over the Porsche to me, and I'll give you the Toyota. I've got the papers inside on the kitchen table."

Her jaw dropped. A frown replaced her prior look of astonishment. "You want me to trade a Porsche for a beat-up Toyota?"

"Not exactly. The Toyota is what you'll have for transportation after I buy myself a new car. What I'm offering in place of the Porsche is two hundred thousand dollars—more if it takes it—to put you through the best university you can get into. Plus, reasonable spending money. You've been considering West Coast schools, and I'll foot the bill for Stanford or Berkeley, or even the University of Michigan, if you decide to stay local. We'll take a trip to visit any campuses you want."

She didn't move a muscle. Maybe she was waiting for me to sweeten the deal. The strategy worked.

"I'll also pay for the study-abroad program you wanted the summer between high school graduation and college, and when you graduate from college, I'll spring for a brand-new car. A Honda Accord or something reliable for transportation to and from your first job."

"You're bribing me?"

"You could call it that."

"Did you win the lottery?"

"Not exactly, but I can afford it for my favorite daughter."

According to insurance guidelines, Derek's death was neither suicide nor natural causes, so by a stranger-than-fiction definition, it qualified as accidental.

The logic escaped me. But when Cardinal paid off the policy limits for double indemnity, I'd have three million dollars. Plenty for Natalee's education, plus an indulgence or two for each of us. "Do we have a deal?"

"You're sure I can't have the Porsche?"

"Absolutely."

"We have a deal," she said. "By the way, I was testing you. I don't want the Porsche. Too many memories."

"You were negotiating?"

"You could call it that."

Her giggle at besting me rang in my ears as she bent over and picked up her suitcase again. I couldn't miss the tattoo I'd relegated to the back burner. It would simmer a while longer. It could have been worse. As rebellion went, Nat's was pretty tame. It wasn't cartoon characters engaged in coitus. It wasn't obscene words. It wasn't even Ethan's name. Just a tiny, elegant calla lily. Maybe in a month or two, I'd take my daughter to lunch and warn her that if she ever did anything like that again, while living under my roof and without discussing it with me first, there would be hell to pay. I might even ask her where she had it done and invite her to come with me when I got a very small, very discreet lotus flower tattooed on my back between my scar and my bikini line, a permanent reminder that I was a survivor.

"Mom." She interrupted my thoughts. "Would you mind if I went out with Ethan tonight? I haven't seen him in a week."

"I guess that's okay." Part of me was sorry my daughter didn't want to spend the night at home with me. The other part of me embraced her resiliency. "I need to talk to Rad anyway. Be home by eleven. It's a school night."

Rad was an easy sell. "How about meeting me at Dusty's Cellars at six?" I asked. "I'll spring for dinner and all you can drink. Call it a debriefing." I could have stopped halfway through my spiel and still gotten a "yes."

I bribed the hostess with a twenty and requested seating that ensured privacy. She gave me the Napa Room. Its deep red walls and dimly lit chandelier were warm and welcoming. The table and chairs reminded me of my Grandma Rosebud's dining room, though the shelves of wine outside the door would never have found their way into her house. The room accommodated up to ten people, but it was a slow night, and we'd be alone. I nursed my scotch and had a bourbon and water waiting for Rad when he walked in.

He gave me a peck on the cheek before he sat down. "CJ, you look better than I've seen you look in weeks," he said.

"Might as well tell me I've looked like shit."

"Isn't that what I said?"

I gave him a playful punch. "At least I'm alive."

"Thanks, in no small part, to me."

"It feels good not to be scared. To breathe normally and not look over my shoulder to see if Dr. B is there." Part of me preferred to blur out the last six weeks and never speak of them again. The braver part of me said, "Quit stalling. I'm here for details."

"And I'm here to accommodate, so let's see if I can answer some of your questions without taking the joy out of you being home and safe." He took a long sip of his drink and started. "I've followed up with Racer and the boys. Lockhart flew to Orlando yesterday. Paid Jon Beckman a personal visit in the county jail. Then accompanied your neighbor's sorry ass back to Lansing. Jon didn't fight extradition. Fact is, he was quite the talker during the trip home. Didn't care about a lawyer or anything."

Rad reached over, picked up my drink, and handed it to me. He then took my other hand between his two. The implication was as clear as a poker tell. The information he was about to deliver would not make me feel warm and fuzzy.

"Jon's the one who messed up your study." That was hardly news. I'd guessed that much. "He's also the one who broke in during the night and did in your cat."

Jon killed Jussy. Another layer of betrayal roiled my stomach. After long seconds, I found my voice. "Killing a cat that never hurt a soul? That's sick."

"He claims he tried to talk Dr. B out of it, but B had his mind set. Your doctor friend figured there was less chance of Natalee or you being injured or killed if he did the dirty work rather than stand by while Dr. B or one of his henchmen carried out the plan."

I stopped, swallowed hard. So far, my scotch was unadulterated. I pulled out a blue foil package and ripped it open. "I know Jon was involved. Makes sense in a perverted way. He's a doctor and could get the drugs that were planted in my desk. But Jussy." I dropped the two tablets into my glass. "I'd never have thought he could do that."

"It sucks, CJ, I can't change that. But in exchange for a lighter sentence, Jon coughed up enough information about Dr. B to ensure the thug never breathes fresh air again. Along with the top honcho, the upper tier of underlings is crumbling. A couple of Dr. B's goons had paid Jon personal visits, and he identified them. Every crook involved seems anxious to save his own skin. Looks like Robert Kansas—Dr. B—will have plenty of company in the joint. The cops haven't figured out a way to stretch the conspiracy charge to the cartel, and it isn't likely they will."

I watched the Alka Seltzer fizz in my glass. "Where does all of this leave me?"

"Lockhart will probably call you tomorrow. You'll have to give a statement. You're an attorney. You know to keep it short, simple, and as truthful as possible. Give them the bag of evidence you saved. Your bloody clothes and the jar with the drink in it. No sense mentioning the naked pictures of Derek. The prosecutor has enough evidence without complicatin' your life adding piddly details. And you've never heard the name Jimmy Scroggins. I doubt it'll come up."

We ordered another round and looked at the menus. Suddenly, I was ravenous.

"What happens to Allen, Day, Khoury, and Wainwright?" he asked.

"They'll lose their licenses and face criminal charges, but they'll get a break if they cooperate."

"Allen should rot in prison," he said. "Khoury isn't such a bad sort."

"He'll get a chance for reinstatement in three years, if he's free by then. For now, I won't lose any sleep over him. Have your sources spilled anything about the Sawickis?"

"No evidence of criminal activity by either Joseph or Donald unless the prosecuting attorney makes a case out of the campaign contributions."

"The appearance of impropriety will destroy their political careers," I said. "It's time for an infusion of fresh blood. That can't happen if the baton passes to an heir apparent."

I laid the menu down. My next comment surprised me. "Much as I dislike Joseph Sawicki, I'm glad he wasn't involved in the racket." Sometimes two fiery objects with random momentum simply collide. That would be my final take of the relationship between the attorney general and me.

"Any mention of either Shirley Rathburn or Mark Rodgers?" I asked.

"Nobody's looking at Shirley. Doesn't appear she was ordered to do anything illegal. The police are trying to build a case against Mark Rodgers. Dr. B isn't giving him up, so it will be hard to prove Rodgers has done anything criminal. He might avoid prosecution."

"I'd guess his legal career is in jeopardy. The bar ethics committee is big on good moral character."

Our server came over. We ordered the eight-course dinner and a bottle of Dusty's recommended cabernet sauvignon.

Rad scrutinized me. His expression defied a clear read. "The cops are also looking at Robert Kansas as a person of interest in several unsolved homicides over the past couple of decades."

My heart lurched. I waited for the bad news.

A wide grin broke out across Rad's face. It spread until it stretched his lips tight. He then opened his mouth to accommodate a full smile. Even his smoke-stained teeth looked happy. "By some screw-up, the blood and hair samples in an old murder case have disappeared from the Ann Arbor Police Department evidence room." He arched a bushy brow in what I assumed was a gesture of feigned innocence. "If anyone ever opens that case again, Dr. B's fingerprints might be on a couple of shards of glass. Don't ask questions."

The implication made me return Rad's chuckle.

"There's as much chance of Dr. B goin' to heaven as anyone believing him if he tells some horrific tale of anyone else committing that crime. Consider it my gift to you."

I leaned over and kissed Rad on his whisker-stubbled cheek. If they charged Robert Kansas with the death of Jimmy Scroggins, I wouldn't even blink. With two brutal slayings, extortion, conspiracy, and a shitload of drug trafficking charges, I'd figure the police were just closing a cold case, one I damned well wanted closed. He was going away for the rest of his life. One more charge wouldn't add to the time Dr. B served. I thought back to that day in my office when Rad explained his first rule of engagement: *Sometimes you gotta do what you gotta do. It's all about the greater good.* Maybe he was right.

"What are you going to do now?" Rad asked.

"For tonight, I'm going to enjoy being alive, knowing Natalee's okay, and sitting here with a friend. I'll worry later about how awkward it will be to live next door to Ginny. I don't like my job, and Natalee's talking about school on the West Coast. You ever considered moving west?" While I talked, I reached into my purse, extracted a small package wrapped in Spartan green and white, and set it on the table. "You and I made a pretty good team."

He hoisted his drink to mine. "I'm too old to compete with that young stud of yours, so it probably can't happen, not even for the sexiest, smartest attorney God ever put on this earth."

"Ahh, you old charmer. Trying to let me down easy."

"No. And let me go on record: all the other attorneys I know should be fed through an industrial-sized, government-subsidized meat grinder and used for alternative fuel."

The server had delivered two small plates, each with a single coconut shrimp. Before we took a bite, I pointed to the package. "It's for you."

Rad picked up the tiny box. "Couldn't you have wrapped it in blue and gold?"

"Just open it."

He ripped off the paper, removed the box top, and lifted a Michigan State University key chain with a single key from a bed of cotton. "What's this?"

"Exactly what it looks like. You lost a car because of me. Remember? And I don't need a sixteen-year-old driver hitting the highways in a fast car. Besides, you're never too old for a babe magnet."

His jaw dropped a foot and froze in that position.

For the first time in too long, all my ghosts were quiet.

The End

Acknowledgements

As I close the pages on this project, I am reminded of something A.A. Milne said of Piglet: "Piglet noticed that even though he had a very small heart, it could hold a rather large amount of gratitude."

In expressing my appreciation, I know that I will miss many, so to each of you, who provided a suggestion or an encouraging word, I am indebted.

Thanks Susan and Joe Jurkiewicz, Maureen Scully, Barb Hill, Linda Cutler, Bev Bremer, Jes Phillips, Courtney Phillips, Bonnie Albrecht, Peter Dudley, Sheila Bali, Anne Koch, Carl Gamaz, Julaina Kleist-Corwin, Vee Byram, Paula Chinick, Neva Hodges, Lani Longshore, Vi Moore, Elaine Schmitz, Gary Lea, Sharon Svitak, Eloise Hamman, Bonnie Degan, and Sally Kimball.

A special thanks to George Cramer, for not only reading the novel, but for helping me make police procedure more believable. There would have been glaring errors without him.

I am indebted to Dr. Joyce deJong for her valuable time describing the autopsy process and showing me the facility at Sparrow Hospital, and to Chief Dave Hall of the Meridian Township Police Department for providing answers to questions that arose during the writing of this novel.

My editors, Peggy Lucke and Violet Moore, came later in the process with their suggestions.

My artist friend, Julie Rosas, deserves special recognition for the cover. Her help came near the end of the journey. I knew what I wanted, but she improved on my idea and turned it into a reality.

And, of course, I will always be thankful for Bob Royce, my patient, ever-enduring husband who helped in more ways than I can possibly catalogue.

About the Author

Julie Katherine Albrecht Royce grew up in Michigan's Thumb. She received a B.A. from Michigan State University and an M.Ed. and J.D. from the University of Cincinnati. After completing her education, she returned to her home state and practiced law for twenty-five years.

Working in the Health Professionals Division of the Michigan Attorney General she saw the seedy side of the medical profession. She drew on her experiences to shape *PILZ*, a fictional novel of doctors peddling prescriptions for profit.

Ms. Royce has written magazine articles, has been included in several anthologies, has had stories accepted in the California Writers Club Literary Review, has published two travel books, and a historical novel about the French/Native American fur trader, Magdelaine LaFramboise.

She is working on a second novel of crime fiction set in the Mission District of San Francisco. She is also tackling a third travel guide, *A Traveler's Companion to Exploring the Cities Along Michigan's Great Lakes*. In her spare time, she is helping her nine-year-old grandson, Noah, publish his second book.

Julie and her husband, Bob, split their time between Michigan and California.

www.ingramcontent.com/pod-product-compliance
Lightning Source LLC
Chambersburg PA
CBHW021811110726
47902CB00006B/1735